Andrei Tarantsev: The moody, introspective Spetznaz officer had fought his way up through the ranks. Now he was deep in American waters, with sonar pinging off the shell of his mini sub, and only death ahead. He was being sacrificed . . . but for what reason?

Tim Sullivan: When his dolphin made contact with something on the bottom, Navy SEAL Sullivan knew what it might mean. And when the animal didn't come back, he knew that his enemy was incredibly talented—and dangerous . . .

Praise for Charles D. Taylor's

Silent Hunter

"A STERLING SILVER UNDERWATER THRILLER, LOADED WITH INTRIGUE, SUSPENSE, AND PLENTY OF ADVENTURE."
—Clive Cussler

Books by Charles D. Taylor

Show of Force
The Sunset Patriots
First Salvo
Choke Point
Silent Hunter
Shadows of Vengeance
  (pen name—David Charles)
Counterstrike
Warship
Boomer
Deep Sting

CHARLES D. TAYLOR

DEEP STING

POCKET STAR BOOKS

New York   London   Toronto   Sydney   Tokyo   Singapore

A Pocket Star Book published by
POCKET BOOKS, a division of Simon & Schuster Inc.
1230 Avenue of the Americas, New York, NY 10020

ISBN: 0-671-67631-8

First Pocket Books printing June 1991

10 9 8 7 6 5 4 3 2 1

POCKET STAR BOOKS and colophon are trademarks of
Simon & Schuster Inc.

Map designed by Jeff Ward

Printed in the U.S.A.

This book is for my sons,
Jack and Ben.

Captain Larry Bailey, Commander...ren...Simmons, and...

Bernie Ryng has become the quintessential fictional SEAL, along with his peers, David Chance, and Henry Cobb, who appear in other novels. This is not "by chance"—they roam through the pages of fiction but their personal accomplishments and enduring character are based on men who roam our real world as US Navy SEALs. I have been privileged to spend time at the Center for Naval Special Warfare on two separate occasions, once as the guest of the late Captain Dave Schaible, a SEAL of mythic proportions, who insisted on separating the everyday world of the SEAL from the fictional one. Captain Larry Bailey commanded the Center on my initial visit and Captain Tom Lawson the second time and they were most cooperative hosts. My purpose was to learn how SEALs are molded at the BUD/S (Basic Underwater Demolition/SEAL) School. I understood and I came away impressed. I wish I could remember and list the names of all the dedicated instructors who took extra time to teach me what it took to produce a SEAL; to overlook one would diminish all of them, both past and present, for their graduates are without equal.

I would like to thank the following individuals for reading the manuscript and providing comments: Dan Mundy and

ACKNOWLEDGMENTS

Ted Magnuson, shipmates from long ago, and the SEALs, Captain Larry Bailey, Commander Larry Simmons, and Lt. Commander Jake Jaquith, each of whom helped to ensure Bernie Ryng remained within the SEAL tradition. Ted Magnuson also personally guided me through the waters of the northwest and shared a toddy or two in the process. As always, I would like to thank Captain and Mrs. Bill McDonald, my commanding officers for almost thirty years now; Dominick Abel, my rational agent; and Paul McCarthy, who has become the SEAL of editors. The best book I encountered to learn about those amazing mammals was *A Dolphin Summer* by Gerald Gormley, published by Taplinger in 1985. I would also like to extend a special thanks to Navy EOD (Explosive Ordnance Demolition), who unknowingly lent their dolphins to Bernie Ryng for this special operation; they maintain the same affection for their animals that the SEALs have shown in this story. I would also like to make it clear that no SEAL worth his "budweiser" operates alone in the water; "swim buddies" entrust their lives to each other.

And thanks and love as always to my wife, Georgie, who is understanding of my whims and crash programs.

"The only easy day was yesterday."

(This short statement appears beside the grinder at the Captain Phil H. Bucklew Center for Naval Special Warfare in Coronado, California. Every prospective SEAL reads these words each day of his six months of the most demanding physical and mental training in the world.)

"Honi soit qui mal y pense."
("Evil to him who evil thinks.")

—Edward III
(Motto of the Order of
the Garter, circa 1349)

"Anything, any time, any place, anyhow . . ."

(SEAL motto attributable to
Jake Jaquith, SEAL)

Prologue

WHISKEY ON THE ROCKS." THE INCIDENT HAD TAKEN PLACE so long ago—a decade? More than that? Was she still living in England then? Were Ken and Cory still alive?

"Whiskey on the rocks," Corinne murmured to herself, leafing through the pages of the article written so many years before.

Those words, as simple as they seemed, brought a knowing smile to Corinne's face. An Americanism, of course. US journalists couldn't write more than one good article without coining a term to attract attention to themselves.

We Brits turned up our noses at that one. "Rocks" was an Americanism for ice, and only savages put ice into a good single malt, much less a second-rate whiskey.

The Russians, with no sense of humor, failed to understand it initially but they knew the term was meant to embarrass them. The Americans would say perversely that it added insult to injury.

The rest of the world, if they cared at all that a Soviet Whiskey-class submarine was hard aground off the Swedish naval base at Karlskrona, had read dry, straightforward, unimaginative reports in their own papers. No cutesy words to attract their eyes to any story. Just boring news.

Corinne sipped her scotch, a decent single malt, as she read about how the Russians made one mistake after another at Karlskrona. The gods were looking kindly on man when they allowed him to create that liquid gold. She swirled the ice cubes absentmindedly with a finger—*you've gotten just like the savages you used to abhor, lady*. Not so savage a habit now that she was a Canadian, ice cubes and all, just like a damn Yank. When a fine scotch was iced, one sipped, enjoyed the flavor longer. Straight, it was too tempting to put it down in a swallow or two. If there was one thing she now knew they ought to be easier on the Yanks for, it was iced drinks. *How the hell did that asshole know I liked single malts? Dumb question, Corinne. The KGB knows everything*. They were the ones who'd stocked her cottage on the little island, including single malt scotch. It was no more than a hundred kilometers south of her cozy apartment in Vancouver but this was an American island and she was acting like a damn Yank.

She placed the finished pages on the side table, careful to keep them from the little circle of dampness that had dripped from the side of the cold glass. That was decidedly a problem with iced drinks—the glasses sweated, especially in this damp weather. *Easy there, Corinne, you're a lady and ladies perspire. They don't sweat. Same with their drinks, lady*. The air was decidedly more humid on the island than up north in Vancouver.

She'd looked up the "Whiskey on the Rocks" story with the help of the librarian in Vancouver—told him she was doing some research for a prof at the university—and dutifully inserted her coins in the machine to make copies of the available articles covering the Russian foolishness off Sweden. Then, back at the apartment, she packed only a few personal items that her handlers would have forgotten to stock on the island—no reason giving nosy neighbors the idea that she might be spending some time away from there. She took the ferry from Vancouver across to Departure Bay, then rode the bus south to Victoria where she spent the night. The next day she took another ferry and entered the

US through Seattle. From there she took a bus ninety minutes north to Anacortes where she slept the second night before taking the ferry out to the San Juan Islands. It was roundabout, but there would be no trail.

Reading those articles brought essentially nothing new. Beyond that incident with the Whiskey-class submarine, they used mostly miniature subs to accomplish their goals. The Soviet Union had been making preparations to neutralize Scandanavian naval units years before, even employing mini subs to lay mines to be activated in the event of hostilities. They'd also used swimmers to chart the Baltic's western shoreline to determine amphibious landing points, sometimes moving ashore to gather intelligence on military sites, civilian transport, communications facilities and key government buildings, all with the intent of neutralizing the populace if necessary. They never gave up preparing for war. *Is this what you're getting yourself into, Corinne? Are they going to do it again . . . right here?*

She understood it all. Years before, it had been preached so often by the leftist societies from the universities back home, especially back at her precious Oxford. There was a natural order of selection in the world of power politics, a survival of the fittest, just as there always had been in the animal kingdom. Brute force was not always the final solution. No other nation had a better understanding of that than the Russians.

But now these were the days of *glasnost* and *perestroika!* Now that military arsenals were being reduced with a great flourish, the USSR was once again expanding its intelligence collecting abilities considerably. They understood how critical their needs would be at the cutting edge of advanced technology. When you reduce your military capacity, you increase your intelligence capabilities. The objective—always—is to weaken the other side's offensive power.

So, she noted, the Kremlin's latest effort was apparently with midget submarines once again and this time it was drawing her into a game she'd never played before. Appar-

3

ently it would take place on American turf this time. That was why she had been sent out to this island in the middle of the San Juans north of Seattle to man a radio that might, or might not, be critical. She knew there was no point in asking questions. They would tell her what they considered necessary.

As sort of an aside, perhaps to make conversation, her contact had said that the man she must be prepared to help had taken over the submarine intelligence program after that incident on the Swedish coast. It hadn't taken much effort on Corinne's part to figure out that the incident had not only revealed the operations of the Soviet miniature subs to the Swedes, but it had shown the Kremlin how weak their own program really was. Her contact noted that this man she might aid had a reputation as a seer, apparently capable of both understanding future strategic situations and communicating their import to the right people.

It was obvious her contact didn't think she was very bright. He'd only made those statements in an effort to impress her with the importance of the individual who might one day depend on her. They all acknowledged the life of a spy was pretty dull in Vancouver, but maybe that was about to change. She knew it wasn't intended that she understand this unnamed individual was also involved in spying with these miniature submarines, but it was obvious after reading the articles. Maybe her contact was too obtuse to realize that she would learn for herself what he was hinting at. The Russians would never allow themselves to be embarrassed twice. Perhaps this individual her contact mentioned was their renaissance man, the one who would rejuvenate a failed program.

Time to pay the piper, Corinne. That was another Americanism. Clever devils, a cutesy term for everything, even when the devil had called in your soul for payment. Well, she'd allowed the KGB to do it. She was the one who accepted the deal. England, the university, her husband's and daughter's deaths—all of that was behind her now.

4

They paid for everything when she emigrated to Canada, arranged all the paperwork, the new identity, even a very comfortable existence.

She'd been given a new life and now . . . now . . . she was being asked to pay for it.

Time to pay the piper, Corinne. Your turn in the barrel. That's how the Americans would say it.

One

Good-bye to Leningrad

HOW LONG WILL YOU BE GONE?"

"Perhaps forever." The tone of his voice indicated that he really didn't care.

"Please, I'm serious." Each time Nicholas prepared to leave over the past few years, his answers grew more cutting. "It means a lot to me, and to the children, if we can look forward to when you're coming back."

Nicholas Koniev studied his wife curiously, wondering if she were about to cry. Their offspring were becoming young adults. They were no longer children. Soon they'd be off to schools, or on their own if they failed to pass their exams. Whatever, they weren't children, not like Galya was trying to make him believe. That's what happened when women got to be that age, tried to make believe nothing was ever going to change.

"I don't know," he said irritably. "There is no schedule. We'll be north, at Severodvinsk, to complete fitting out, then who knows."

"You're not coming back here?"

"No." Then, after a moment's pause, "What does it matter?"

"I'm your wife, Nicholas," she shot back. "This is your

home. We've been here for years. You have two children who live here who will ask for you every day you're gone and all I'll be able to say to them is that I don't know when their father is coming home. Don't you think that after a while they're going to begin wondering about us?"

"That's our business. I'm a sailor," he added.

She moved over to the window and stared out at the canal where apple blossom petals had drifted softly on the water earlier that year. Then she looked back over her shoulder, staring ruefully out of the corner of her eye. "And I'm Catherine the Great." If there was one thing Nicholas Koniev wasn't, it was a simple sailor. In years past, when they were closer, he'd told her most everything about what he was doing.

Submariner. That's how he started out in the navy. *Genius*—she knew that even before she married him. He'd even read some of his original papers to her before they'd been passed on to the admirals and she knew his work was beyond most of the officers his age. It was the "Koniev Abstract"—that's what he said they called it—that had really done it. It was Nicholas's theory for limiting the potential for a missile exchange with the US, negate their access to oceans, or something like that. There was more but he'd never discussed that with her. But she knew it was the one thing that was now controlling him. *Intelligence.* That's how he'd gotten into the miniature submarine program. That's when they'd been transferred to Leningrad.

And he'd trained with the Spetznaz, the underwater branch. That was his own idea. He'd never been required to do that but he insisted on it anyway. Maybe that was when the new Nicholas first appeared, the cruel Nicholas who became more secretive, more cutting in his remarks, harder on the children.

Koniev shrugged. "I'm not supposed to tell you such details anyway."

"What do you think I'm going to do? Call the American Embassy and tell them the great Nicholas Koniev's latest assignment?"

"Don't talk like that." Why had she become such an

irritant? Did all women get like that when they aged poorly?
She had put on weight, and her hair was graying at the edges.
She could see that as well as he. "If the Americans wanted to
know, they'd have ways of making you tell them. So it's
better if you don't know."

"What would they do—torture me?"

Well they certainly wouldn't do anything sexual to Galya,
he thought. She was right. It would have to be torture. "They
might. That is, if you didn't tell them what they wanted to
know."

She turned to face him, her arms folded. "This isn't what
I'd call a loving departure." She remembered years ago
when they'd spend all of the day before in bed, and then
sometimes he'd come back an hour before his ship got
underway for one more romp. Last night, he'd just gotten
drunk and ended up snoring in his armchair. No, definitely
not your average sailor, and not your average husband off to
sea either.

He rose from the chair and went over to the table to pick
up his hat, settling it squarely on his head, looking in the
mirror to make sure it was perfect. He picked up his coat
and folded it over his arm. What was it she'd said—not a
loving departure? "I suppose it might look that way, but
that's not how I wanted it." If she'd acted differently, maybe
he would have been more responsive. She really wasn't that
bad in bed, still at the point after a couple of drinks where
she was willing to do anything to get his attention. But
somehow . . . "It will be different if I get back . . . when I
get back," he added as an afterthought.

That was it. The tears came. "Please, Nicholas, please
don't talk that way. Of course you'll be back. We wouldn't be
able to get along without you." Then she ran the few short
steps and her arms were around his neck, pulling his head
down. "Please come back. I love you . . . so, so much." She
kissed him hard, pushing her tongue against his clenched
teeth.

His free arm went around her back briefly, but he didn't
open his mouth. And he hated the tears. She should know
that always bothered him. He pulled away, reaching into his

back pocket for a handkerchief, and dabbed at the dampness on his cheeks and rubbed the lipstick off. "Well, good-bye then. And say good-bye to the children for me." He opened the door, picked up his attaché case, and nodded without smiling as he pulled it closed behind him.

The son of a bitch! Galya wiped her own mouth, disgusted that she'd tried to use her tongue. He didn't deserve it.

Good-bye, Galya!

Good-bye to Severodvinsk

Koniev rolled over gingerly. The last thing he wanted to do was wake Anna, who snored softly beside him. His dreams the last few hours had been too good, much better than anything Anna could possibly do for him. She provided a release and any man in as vital a position as his needed such an outlet.

The unique thing though was that he was also capable of controlling the dreams as long as he wasn't disturbed . . . although perhaps they weren't really dreams in the true sense of the word. He was too aware of them, capable of repeating the parts he wanted to go over again. At the same time, he could sense what was taking place around him. They usually came early in the morning in that delicious borderline between sleep and wakefulness, that mystery moment when you feared neither world.

He had been back in the Baltic in those dreams, flying his miniature submarines. Yes, it was flying—no doubt about that. The medium may have been water but these new ones performed unlike any undersea vehicle man had yet conceived of. And they were the fruit of his mind, his invention, wholly unique, tiny submarines able to sustain themselves submerged for up to a week away from the mother ship, and capable of replenishing in just twelve hours. Never again would they suffer the embarrassment of Karlskrona. With a crew of only three men, they could penetrate foreign harbors for intelligence gathering, deposit time-delayed mines and torpedos, and deliver underwater demolition experts—all of it soundlessly. *And they were all his.*

Years ago, when Nicholas Koniev was still a promising young submarine officer and Sergei Gorshkov was Commander in Chief of the Soviet Navy, the old admiral had reached down to select him as the one who would reorganize a failed program. When that Russian Whiskey-class submarine ended up on the rocks off Karlskrona, naked for all the world to point at, Gorshkov knew instinctively he needed a man like Koniev to rebuild confidence in the system. The old bottom crawling subs had done their job planting mines and listening devices but they were too slow. The larger diesel submarines used for intelligence gathering were too old and their captains were deep water sailors.

The young officer had forseen a new generation of mini subs, sophisticated, self-sustaining for long periods of time, and aggressive with newly designed weapons. He also established a vital point that, although so obvious, seemed to have escaped his superiors. When you design a craft as effective as his unique little fleet, you also train a new generation of men to handle them and mother submarines to nurture them.

Koniev's dreams never bothered with the early years of development, the pain of experimenting with flawed designs, the loss of dedicated men, but he allowed little flashes of those times to interfere. They passed in seconds when the brain was in that state. He still allowed them to intrude momentarily because *none of it would have happened without Nicholas Koniev.* He was absolutely sure of that.

Oh, how he would fly those little devils in his dreams, just as he had when he was their test pilot. They were his and he insisted on taking them down as soon as the builders were satisfied. It took absolutely everything he had to pilot the final models—they were that good!—but then he knew there was nothing like them in the world.

He remembered how the divers who flew with him were in awe of his tiny craft. Those naval Spetznaz, the best of the lot selected for the underwater service, were considered perfect fighting machines. But they were wary of his mini subs when they saw how beautifully they flew. So Koniev underwent naval Spetznaz training to learn how to understand these undersea warriors better. That was how he learned that they would be much more accepting if they, too, were allowed to fly the tiny craft under certain conditions. With understanding came cooperation.

Anna snorted and moaned, turning her head toward him without opening her eyes. Still asleep. Maybe he could get out without awakening her. Better yet, maybe he should just stop her breathing. She'd kept him comfortable for the past week and served her purpose, but she was so stupid. Better looking, though, than Galya was these days, at least by Severodvinsk standards. On the other hand, he hadn't seen a woman in this arctic town who could come close to those who strolled beside the canals back home in Leningrad on late summer evenings.

This Severodvinsk, once an Arctic railhead, was the end of the world. Spring was simply a change from snow and ice to a sea of mud. Autumn was a change back to darkness and ice. But it was also out of the mainstream, away from the prying eyes of the Americans and their satellites, a perfect place to finish *Gorki's* shakedown. Intelligence suspected that one of the US satellites had been maneuvered to take photos of the port and the ships that visited. Good luck to them. How many days had it been since he'd seen the sun? Let the Americans try to penetrate the cloud cover long enough to photograph *Gorki,* his electronic marvel of a submarine. What they needed was intelligence on the hoof, good, old-fashioned eyes to tell them what she was doing.

Then he remembered the face he'd seen once too often the past few days. The man was dressed like a shipyard employee and he carried tools, so he must work there because Koniev had seen him comfortable with others near the submarines.

Koniev first noticed the man when he'd taken Anna out to the movies one night—anything to shut her up. Then last night, he was sure they'd been followed by the same individual. What the hell did he want? Only one thing. It had to be *Gorki*. That's why they'd left Leningrad sailing ahead of schedule, and that meant the man probably knew too much already . . . and then he glanced briefly at Anna.

That was it! Anna . . . the bitch! He sat upright. The dreams were gone.

He got out of bed as quietly as he could, briefly proud that he could do it without waking Anna. He pulled back the shade over the window ever so slightly and peered down on the street. And there he was again—the same one. No mistaking it. Walking purposefully by on the opposite side of the street without looking up, but Koniev knew how the window was being watched.

He continued to hold the shade exactly the same way, barely away from the window, and waited, naked, never moving a muscle. Fifteen minutes later, the same one passed again, never looking directly up, same objective stride . . . but there was no doubt. The stupid son of a bitch! Somehow he must have learned of *Gorki*'s imminent departure. Now he'd blown his cover . . . and Anna's!

The man was not around the submarines that morning and toward noontime Koniev decided it was worth checking back at Anna's. Just as he suspected. When he tiptoed up to the door, he could hear a man's voice inside. Not once did he question who it might be. It never crossed his mind to knock on the door or use the key she gave him. That would just give the other a chance. The Spetznaz had taught him how to wait.

Koniev heard the footsteps coming toward the door, overheard a male voice say, "I will repeat once more that you will be a very comfortable woman if you can find out where he is going after Severodvinsk. If not, you will probably want to move away for your own safety." There was no doubting the tone of voice for the last statement, threatening.

"I'll try. But I have nowhere else to go, and I have a child staying with my mother."

Imagine that. She'd never said anything about a child but,

13

then, that would explain the sag of the belly. *Were there any women you could trust these days?*

"You know how to get hold of me."

"I will, if I learn anything."

Not a chance, dear Anna, not a chance. Just no one you could trust!

The door opened and he—the man whose face had become so familiar—stepped into the hallway. There was no opportunity to call out, no chance to defend himself, not even the liberty to rage at his attacker before he was dead. Koniev caught the body and dragged it back into Anna's apartment, hissing, "Close the door, quickly. Don't give anyone the opportunity to stick their nose into the hallway."

"Why did you . . . ?"

"Just do as I say. Quickly now. I'll explain."

Anna peered into the hall, saw no one, and shut the door softly. She had no idea what Koniev intended as she turned toward the room. The stranger was propped in a chair as though he'd selected the spot for himself. And Koniev was at her side, looming over her.

She had no more chance to call out than the stranger. She saw a flurry of movement, much too fast to understand. Then Anna, too, was dead, slumping into his arms. He placed her in the other chair, pleased with himself, sure that someone at first might have thought them in conversation . . . until they noticed the curious angle of their heads.

So much for my last evening ashore. I don't think I could have stomached one more night of Anna anyway.

Gorki departed early the next morning, almost a week before her schedule, diving as soon as the admiral's guide boat sounded her horn three times in salute.

Whoever the man had been, no one was any the wiser about *Gorki* or her captain. Koniev had no idea how much intelligence the dead man might have passed on, but one thing he would never have the chance to report was *Gorki*'s departure. Better to leave Severodvinsk early than to risk an American submarine waiting to trail them a week from now.

Good-bye, Anna.

Good-bye to Petropavlovsk

No matter how many times Nicholas Koniev surveyed the exquisite body that lay beside him, his glance would return to her face. Those penetrating gray eyes were what he would remember most. The first time they had made love, he opened his eyes to find her looking at him with a bemused expression. And each time afterward, no matter what their position, he found her eyes looking dreamily into his own, her lips parted in a curious grin. She explained calmly once in a deep, soft voice that those were the moments she was able to see the real Nicholas Koniev, the man-child she called him, the real person who lived under that stern exterior.

Never before . . . even more importantly, perhaps never again . . . would he meet a woman like Alix.

"Please . . . stay this time . . . even just a few hours." Was that his voice? Was that Nicholas Koniev asking, almost begging, it seemed to him, a woman to allow him the pleasure of her company for the remainder of the night?

Alix was not a citizen of Petropavlovsk, nor would anyone ever have mistaken her for that. She was a sometime Moscow model and actress who had attracted Admiral Alexandrov's attention at one of those parties attended only by senior level politicians and military officers. They were a tight coterie with two distinct levels of social functions—*wives and no wives*. Many of the older men preferred the latter but age also entitled them to a wisdom which counseled common sense. They would not allow overindulgence to destroy a good thing. Women like Alix were guests at the no-wives functions.

She would have been called a mistress if Alexandrov had remained in Moscow, but his assignment as commander of the Pacific submarine base in Petropavlovsk, *Gorki*'s last Soviet port after transiting the Arctic Ocean submerged, changed that. Alix was in the city as his guest, "to chase away the early autumn chill" as the admiral put it, but they both knew she would soon return to the sophistication of Moscow. What the admiral did not know was that she had agreed to remain an extra few weeks because she knew Koniev would be there. She occupied an elegant apartment off the base, distant enough to avoid rumor, close enough for the admiral to slip away from the quarters he and his wife occupied on the base.

On this particular evening, the admiral had enjoyed enough vodka at the reception for Koniev and the officers of *Gorki* that his wife had been forced to take him home earlier than usual. This was disappointing to Alexandrov's wife for she had been placed next to Captain First Rank Koniev at dinner and found him absolutely charming.

There were other officers of Captain Koniev's rank who were certainly pleasant enough, but the admiral's wife had never met a man who made her feel so feminine. Of course, she was older than he but that never seemed evident in their conversation. He treated her as if she were the only person at the table that evening, as if they were enjoying a candlelit dinner alone in an apartment far from the navy where all that mattered was the two of them. It was too bad that her husband had monopolized the captain after that, and amusing that her husband had been unable to keep up with Koniev and his officers after dinner. There was one benefit, a personal one of sorts. The admiral was too drunk to leave her for that slut he kept in town.

As the admiral's wife drifted off to sleep, she allowed her imagination to run loose for a moment. It was a brief reverie, one that would never come true at her age— especially apparent as the admiral snored drunkenly in the bed next to her—but she imagined Captain Koniev spending the night with her, so enchanted with her lovemaking that he implored her to stay with him for the entire night. She'd seen other women staring at him. No doubt he was a lady's man. How, she mused, did he treat the ladies?

Koniev reveled in the sight of Alix's long, brunette hair falling over her breasts. She hadn't answered him. Her tongue ran over her lips as if she were about to speak but she simply smiled back at him. He didn't realize that Alix was so taken aback by his question that she had no idea whether or not he was serious.

Once again, he asked, "Please, will you stay?" They were in a hotel room he had taken, off the base. Even the famous Nicholas Koniev wasn't so arrogant that he would seduce the admiral's mistress in the admiral's apartment.

Alix looked at him strangely this time, knowing he had always preferred to be by himself afterward. She'd first learned of the famous Nicholas Koniev by reputation alone. Since they'd met at a party in Leningrad two years before, she knew very little more. There was no one more charming, no one more close-mouthed. She said, "I'll stay if you tell me why," sure that he wouldn't, not really caring if he didn't.

"This is our last time." His eyes held hers and she knew he was serious.

"Why?"

"I'll probably be dead in a few weeks," he answered matter-of-factly, struggling to maintain a sense of detachment from the reality of death.

"I'll stay," Alix whispered, knowing he'd ask her to leave if she cried.

Alix watched from her window early the next morning as *Gorki,* the mother submarine for Nicholas's mini subs, departed the harbor of Petropavlovsk. Not until the black sail blended with gathering dark clouds on the horizon did she cry for that strange, beautiful man.

Good-bye, Nicholas.

TWO

BEFORE HARRY COFFIN MADE A DECISION, HE LIKED TO CONSIDER every possible aspect whenever time permitted. He was sure he never went into a situation with his mind already made up, or at least that's how he pictured himself—systematic, fair. He even told himself his approach to the dolphins would be no different. But he knew there was a little white lie hidden way down deep waiting to be discovered. He was believing what he didn't want to believe.

There were always warnings concerning possible Soviet intelligence penetration of the base. Bangor, Washington was the Pacific home of the Trident missile submarine. There was never any specific method mentioned. No names. But, this time, there was a heavy hint from a CIA connection of Coffin's back in Langley that it might be more than rumor. A very deep plant had been found dead, murdered, in the arctic city of Severodvinsk, a major submarine base suspected of being a training center for the miniature submarine program. Coffin's connection couldn't go into detail but a couple of reliable people had suggested that Trident security ought to be beefed up since satellite recon could no longer locate what they thought was the mother sub for the new program.

When the official CIA intelligence report was an admission they couldn't justify their suspicions, Coffin listened more than if some tight collar type had offered detailed research. The concern about how to increase security beyond what he already considered superb was self-generated. The solution had come from some intelligence admiral in D. C. who'd gained Coffin's respect years before.

Harry Coffin commanded the Trident submarine squadron in Bangor and he looked every inch an admiral even though he was sure he didn't always think like one. He was short and slender and Coffin was sure that in his summer white uniform, and with the lack of gray in his hair, he must look like the youngest flag officer in the navy. He was also convinced he was an independent thinker.

Well, did he already have his mind made up? How could he be so matter-of-fact about using dolphins when he took his kids to Sea World and watched those handsome creatures perform? There wasn't a youngster who'd been there who went home with anything but love for them.

So Coffin had begun the experiment with a slight prejudice. *Go ahead, convince me. But you better be damn good so I don't chew you up and spit you out and send you packing.* That's how he'd approach them even though he wasn't about to admit that he was less than open-minded.

When the security team arrived in Bangor, Washington, they gave no indication they were even in the navy. Their leader presented himself at the main gate in civilian clothes. The marine guards had to call Admiral Coffin in his office to make sure he was expecting this individual. And when the other three made their appearance, they announced their arrival on the port frequency by requesting a pilot and a yard tug three miles north near Vinland. They'd come in what looked like a local fishing boat. Base security responded automatically to the call and reported the boat innocent enough. There was, however, a large tank instead of the normal holds for the catch and this apparently doubled the boat's normal draft. The tank was empty.

What the hell, Admiral Coffin thought to himself, the navy allowed SEALs to march to their own drummer and he wasn't about to argue with them. The officer in charge, the one in civilian clothes, identified himself as the Commander Ryng who was indeed the team leader noted in the orders Coffin had received. The balance of the team members had been released at the head of the Hood Canal and would report for duty after chasing down a fresh meal. Ryng then suggested that the rest of his team also functioned much better with a full stomach.

The admiral joined Ryng and his men for lunch. By the end of the meal, he'd concluded that they really didn't fit the mold that the hosts on those TV shows hinted at. These guys were quite personable, they loved their work, and they gave every indication of being as attached to their animals as any other trainers—except their animals lived in the sea. Yet they really weren't fish. Dolphins were mammals. They breathed air through their lungs and they panted like a dog if they held their breath for too long. The men treated them like pets, speaking affectionately about each individual by name.

This wasn't what the investigative reporters claimed when they stared from the TV screen and stated with a mournful expression that the dolphins were trained to kill and were treated like so much cannon fodder.

Harry Coffin could understand why the commentators probably reacted to Ryng like that. It had to be his blue eyes, so clear and so expressionless. More than likely, he must have looked right through those reporters when he was trying to be polite to them. Like any other man his age, his hair was thinning, or perhaps he could be called partially bald, but his white hair was so short it was hard to tell. Coffin was sure that ruddy complexion was permanent after so many years in the sun. But what he knew innately with more than a little personal envy was that even though Ryng was about his own age, he had this broad, compact build that so often identified a navy SEAL. They were tough, hardened, and it showed in their faces. By the time lunch was over and Ryng and one of his men arrived at a float next to the pier, Admiral Coffin had concluded he liked each of these guys—*screw the reporters.*

Bernie Ryng turned his face away from the sun and opened his eyes in a squint against the water's reflection. He nodded in Tim Sullivan's direction. "Ring the dinner bell for the admiral, Tim."

Sullivan dropped to one knee at the edge of the float and stuck his hand in the water. Almost instantly, there was a swirl that Ryng pointed out about a hundred yards straight out. A dark fin, easily mistakable for a shark, appeared just in front of the roiled water and headed directly toward the three men. Then, a shiny, torpedo-shaped body rose above the surface in an easy, graceful movement before the dolphin disappeared beneath the surface.

When it surfaced with a soft snort just in front of the three men, the animal seemed to be standing on a pedestal, motionless. The nose had a distinct bottle shape, made more pronounced by an open mouth and assertive lower jaw. Although the mouth was lined with sharp teeth, it still seemed as if the animal might be smiling at them. A high forehead sloped gracefully back into the solid body. The head, or forward part of the dolphin, was turned slightly to one side so that an eye, well back of the mouth, could peer back at them curiously.

"Seems like it's looking at me."

"It's a he, and he is looking at you, Admiral," Sullivan answered.

"Dolphins have eyelids, sir. That's why you know they're looking at you," Ryng said. "His name is Bull, after Bull Halsey. Say hello to him if you want to make friends."

Rear Admiral Harry Coffin had spent twenty-five years in submarines and he'd heard every sound that sea life could possibly make—but he'd never said hello to a fish before. He'd heard enough that day though that he finally said, "Hello . . . Bull . . ." in an uncertain voice.

The dolphin's mouth opened as if it were smiling at him and it inched toward the float and waved a flipper in their direction.

"Bull's sorry he can't talk, but if you were underwater you could probably communicate pretty well with him." Ryng looked sideways at the admiral and grinned at his discomfort. "I know, it's a dirty trick." He pointed at Sullivan's hand, which was still underwater. "Show him."

There was a tiny object in Tim Sullivan's hand that shone brightly in the afternoon sun. "Not much different than a toy you probably had when you were a kid, sir. We called it a cricket. Remember when you used to play with those things during the summer? Press down the rigid strip of metal and it would make a clicking sound, supposedly like a cricket."

"When I was a kid," Ryng said, "we used to use them at night to play spy games. So many clicks identified you as being from one team instead of one of the kids on the other team. We used to try to figure out signals with them, just like the spies in the Saturday morning serials. By the time school started in the fall, we'd put them away and forget them until the next summer, if we could find them again." He nodded toward Bull. "Dolphins communicate in the same way, only they have different speeds and tones to their clicks, and they whistle, too. Go ahead and call the others, Tim."

There was nothing audible above the surface, but in less than a minute Ryng pointed out two more dorsal fins in the distance. "Ernie and Chester. Bull's buddies. Named after King and Nimitz, of course."

Tim Sullivan patted Bull before standing up. The man was built much like Ryng, a little taller but just as stocky, his neck thick over wide shoulders. Tanned, well-muscled arms stood out against short sleeves. Unlike Ryng, he had a thick shock of reddish brown hair that hung over his forehead. He was applying a sun block as they waited for the other two dolphins.

Admiral Coffin hadn't heard the other two SEALs appear behind him when he said cordially, "They don't look like hired killers to me," as Chester and Ernie poked their faces up for Sullivan.

"I've been called worse," Danny West said with a grunt and then a smile when Coffin whirled around. He and Len Todd were in their wet suits and only nodded as they eased into the water with the dolphins.

"Inspection time, troopers," Todd shouted as he threw an arm around one of them.

Harry Coffin was comfortable with these men.

Corinne Foxe stepped backward a few feet to appraise her reflection. The mirror was square and perched on top of the wooden bureau, and small enough that she had to recede into the background for a full-length profile. At least they'd had the good sense to provide her with a mirror. Actually, she thought as she turned for a side view, they might not have such good taste—not with a cheap blond bedroom set—but someone had remembered the amenities a woman preferred.

The image of the woman who looked back at her wasn't unattractive, even in the poor light from the single window. *Still pretty damn tough for anyone to peg you in your late thirties, lady.* She had shoulder-length brown hair, wideset green eyes over high cheekbones, and a smooth complexion, not even crow's feet around the eyes. There was a slight bulge to the belly just below her navel, nothing to be ashamed of. Tensile strength couldn't last forever, and perhaps the cheeks weren't as tight as they used to be. But overall it wasn't too upsetting. Legs still long, still smooth on the backs of the thighs. Reasonably flat midriff. Gravity was a fact of life for the breasts, but maybe they were a bit larger, too. If you took care, Mother Nature had a way of making up for her faults. *Everything would be perfect, Corinne, if there was a man to appreciate it all.*

There wasn't much else to do at this point but take advantage of the chance for a tan. Washington state wasn't known for warmth or sun, at least not the coast, and the San Juan Islands were no match for Hawaii, so this pleasant interlude was welcome, a rare, early autumn gift from Mother Nature. Sunbathe during the day, listen at night.

The island was one of the smaller of the San Juans with less than a thousand yard channel separating it from the one to the north. On clear days from her location on the north side, it often looked as if a solid drive with a one wood might make it across. But there were lots of roads and people on that one while only two hard-surfaced roads crisscrossed hers, with mostly paths connecting everything else. With the exception of some seasonal fishermen who sometimes occupied cabins on the eastern end, Corinne Foxe was one of the few inhabitants this time of year.

The KGB did their homework effectively when they set up something like this. There were any number of islands in the San Juans, but this one had been selected for a reason she might never know—was it isolation specifically, or were there other purposes she was unaware of?

How did they supply it so well? She had no electricity, but there was gas that operated a refrigerator with a small freezer, a stove, a water pump, reasonably effective lights, and a muffled generator which ran the radio equipment.

And no outhouse for Corinne Foxe. They'd been kind enough to remember that women had a preference for flush toilets. Admittedly, it was crude. The pump was hooked up to the generator, which was noisy when it was functioning, but it worked. She could take a spartan shower if she added some heated water on her own. There were three rooms—a small kitchen, a living/dining area, and a comfortable bedroom—plus a screened-in front porch where she could watch both sunrises and sunsets through the trees. The food they'd stocked, from a list she provided, was more than she could possibly use. There was no television but there was a good portable radio and, again, they'd been sure to provide an excess of batteries.

Corinne walked through the living room and out onto the porch where she'd dropped a beach towel. The cabin was set far enough back from the water to be protected from passing boats by a grove of trees, thick enough at night that even the gas lamps wouldn't penetrate it. There was a large clearing in front with a picnic table and lawn furniture, even a chaise longue where she'd thrown a soft mattress earlier in the day.

Stretching out on her back, she closed her eyes and revelled in the heat soaking into her body from the mattress. It wasn't that hot, maybe seventy in the clearing because there was no breeze, but it seemed hot for early fall, accentuating the heavy damp aroma of fir that hung over the island. The only sounds that came to her were the gong on a nearby channel buoy rolling lazily in the outgoing tide and the gulls who floated overhead in the air currents screeching irritably at the world. People would pay extravagant sums for such solitude, asking only for the chance to lie in the sun like this. There wasn't a soul nearby and it was highly unlikely there would be.

Corinne rolled over and pushed up on an elbow. She hooked a thumb under the waist of her bathing suit and pulled it down. Sure enough, there was a line from yesterday's sun. *Lady, what are you developing those lines for? Here's the opportunity of your life for a complete tan and no chance of anyone peeking through the bushes to make you paranoid . . . as if you gave a shit.*

With a few deft movements, the top and bottom of her bathing suit lay on the grass. She stretched out on her stomach this time, once again luxuriating in the warmth. *This is what life is all about, lady, if . . . if you had a man who loved you.*

There once was a man, Ken, and he loved her, *loved her like no man had ever loved a woman.* She remained sure of that to this moment. In those days—was it thirteen years now?—she had loved him, too . . . so very much, *like no woman ever loved a man.*

And there was a baby, a very perfect baby. Cory, she was called. When she was born, Ken had insisted they call her Corinne because that name made the most beautiful sound in the world. But soon after, he decided she would have to be Cory because two Corinnes were more than any man could handle, and her mother had the name first.

Ken Foxe was tall and ruggedly good-looking behind his beard, threatening to some because his flowing black hair and beard magnified flashing dark eyes that seemed to hypnotize those he spoke to. Their group used to tease him that he looked like an American mountain man from the movies. Ken was anything but a mountain man. He'd always been a city boy, wretchedly poor, roaming the ancient, narrow East London streets. Raised in a socialist family, he was a professed communist by the time he passed the exams for Oxford, doomed before he understood why.

Corinne was from the Midlands, outside of Coventry, a child of a mining family. *Coventry*—the very nature of the name forced a bilious gall, *ostracism . . . exclusion.* To be from any other place would have been a personal victory.

The brightest child in her school throughout her teen years, she studied toward one objective, social change. She was determined to alter a world her family was unable to escape, sure such change came as the result of government mandate. Hopelessly idealistic in her youth, she was convinced the path to influencing that change was to gain the best education available. She made it to Oxford by challenging the odds that said a poor miner's daughter would never achieve her goal.

Oxford was the opposite of a Coventry. It was a place where brilliant men and women gathered, many of them the cream of British society. It also drew an equally brilliant radical left, who dedicated themselves to bringing down that same British society.

Ken Foxe believed much the same as Corinne about changing society but he lacked patience. He was sure that violence was the only way to bring about social change. Ken arrived at Oxford because there were a number of others who thought exactly as he did and they came to Oxford for the same purpose, to meet the Ken Foxes of the world. Their group was vocal, cerebral, and appealing to romantic young reformers from the Midlands like Corinne.

She lost her idealism and her heart at roughly the same time. No one back home, not even her mother, had ever had the time to acknowledge how pretty Corinne really was. Ken Foxe discovered her, then he modeled her after what he considered a perfect partner, and finally he fell in love with his creation.

Corinne rolled over on her back and squinted up at the clouds drifting over the island. The plastic cover on the mattress was making her perspire and now the combination of hot sun and a soft breeze drying the sweat on her naked body made her tingle all over—*just like Ken used to. . . .*

There was no longer any need for tears. The years hadn't so much mellowed her as toughened her. *You've given up one Coventry for another.* Corinne accepted what life brought, like it or not. There was no desire to meet another Ken, no wish for another Cory—she would only hurt again if she were so lucky. But someone to love . . . in a different way . . . yes, she could accept that. But she would have control.

The years at Oxford were both wonderful and ignorant at the same time. To draw attention to one's intent to foment violence was utter stupidity. It seemed pure and brave at the time, utterly foolish in retrospect. They accomplished little except to create a notoriety for themselves. Arrests, finger-printing, newspaper photos, each of those results would have been anathema if there had been any logic to their actions. The romance of rebellion kept their spirits alive. But it was love that sustained them through the un-heated flats, dirty mattresses on the floor, faucets that dribbled rusty cold water, and candles that illuminated cold meals with perpetual rotgut wine when there was no electricity. *But while we lived in ignorance, we also lived in bliss.*

Corinne continued to attend classes while she was pregnant. Somewhere deep inside a faint voice told her that she was doing the right thing, even when Ken argued that she should quit and work fulltime for their group until the baby was born. But she couldn't do that, not when there was a distant voice in the back of her head that kept pushing.

It would have meant so much to her to have a mother to talk to, a woman who was just like what Corinne wanted to be to her unborn child. She wasn't ashamed of being pregnant. It was a lovechild she was carrying and there was no fear or shame in that. But there was no one back home, not even her stooped, overworked mother, who would understand why she wanted so much to be pregnant. Thank God for love, thank God for Ken who taught her what love really meant. She could face anything armed with his love.

Cory was beautiful, more lovely than any child she had ever seen. Corinne was sure that it wasn't just because Cory was her own. The child was beautiful, special, unlike any other in the world. Ken had promised her their child would be special. Now he challenged anyone who even teasingly might disagree. Good fortune had indeed settled with them. Material goods meant nothing, Ken said, because they had what no one else could possess—Cory.

Cory was a day shy of her first birthday—the date Corinne had chosen as the time she would take her back to the Midlands, back to Coventry, in an effort to show her family what she had accomplished, their granddaughter— when Ken insisted that they take her to London for a rally. Ken Foxe had spoken there. He'd helped to incite the crowd that was suddenly out of hand, literally encouraged them to violence. And when the police reinforcements arrived to disperse the gathering, it was Ken who exhorted them to hold their ground. He couldn't resist, even as he balanced Cory on his shoulder, urging them forward.

The men in the fire brigade had no intention of harming the man carrying a baby on his shoulder. He had been caught in the flow of the throng. And the men operating the second fire engine that crushed the life from both the man and the baby had no chance to stop their vehicle as the two were knocked backward by the force of the water and fell under their wheels.

Corinne had watched, horrified, unable to break through the crowd to their side as Ken and Cory were swept along with the mob. She remembered nothing after the screech of brakes and shouts of horror. She had no idea why the surging crowd stopped in their tracks, then drew back aghast as the firemen leaped down to pull the limp bodies from under their vehicle, no memory of the stream from the firehoses suddenly halted, nor of the absolute silence that fell over the street. She was told afterward of the desperate firemen who attempted to breath life back into the crumpled bodies, of how she sank to her knees in the street beside them to watch, of how they brought her along in the back of the ambulance.

The one memory that persisted through those hideous days was that her own family refused to attend the funeral for Ken and Cory because they had never been married and the baby was a bastard. Corinne adopted the Foxe name from that day on, and she never returned to her home, nor did she ever contact her parents again. It was part of the continuing process of forming her own Coventry, her way of excluding the reality of the past.

That was the last time she ever cried. In a silent promise made only to herself, she decided there would never be another human entanglement again in her life. There would never be a reason to be so deeply hurt, so savaged, that she could not control her emotions.

The breeze had died to a whisper on her island and the sun actually felt hot. Corinne moved her hands across her breasts, then down to her belly. The heat felt wonderful, erotic. It reminded her of Ken. His hands were like a surgeon's as they moved across her body in those days so long ago. Yes, she'd like another man to love again—but that would be on her terms alone.

If she lay in the sun like this much longer, drifting through those distant memories, she would begin burning seriously. It was delicious to be nude in the sun, especially when nature had gifted her with this strange, warm autumn spell, but she reluctantly put her bathing suit back on and went into the cabin for something cold to drink and some suntan lotion. More than likely, this mystery man that she might meet wouldn't have the slightest interest in an overall tan. There was no need to burn herself like that for a man who didn't exist. A regular tan would be satisfactory.

No, on second thought, she didn't need a man who loved her. That would be inconvenient, unnecessary. She needed a man who would serve her needs. *Easier said than done, Corinne. But not out here. Not likely.*

Once back in the sun, lotion slathered on her body, dozing yet vaguely aware of hot sun, pleasant breeze, and calling gulls, her imagination began to play tricks. Was it like this the day of "Whiskey on the Rocks?" Did the Swedes flock to the shore on such a lovely day as this to get a glimpse of the Soviet humiliation?

She imagined miniature submarines, some in schools with menacing teeth painted on their snouts, others crawling along the ocean floor like so many spiders, all heading toward an ill-defined something she couldn't identify. If intelligence was their primary mission, why did they appear so aggressive? She assumed this mystery man would come in a new, modern one. Were they completely different, more peaceful in appearance? The idea was so new to her and so foreign in nature, their form remained unclear.

Then there was this individual she was waiting for, the one her contact hinted at, a seer who was perhaps years ahead of his fellow man. Her imagination had run away with her this time. She could see his form, vague, distant, but it was him because he was in a naval uniform of some kind. Did he have a full black beard? And was he tall and handsome? No . . . no, he was in a mist, a sea mist perhaps, and she couldn't tell. No matter how she tried, she was unable to bring his face into focus. *Is this what they call a sexual fantasy, Corinne?*

It was a strange sensation, almost controlling—but not quite—a series of dreams. If only she could block out this island and the sensations around her, she might ascend above the real world and learn who he really was and—

A gull swooped low over the clearing, landing just feet away with a great flapping of wings and a provocative screech to investigate the nearby container of lotion. Corinne lurched up to a sitting position, frightening herself and the gull. The bird danced backward with its wings spread defensively, challenging her sudden move with a blank, yellow-eyed stare.

Corinne picked up the lotion and hurled it at the bird. "Go away," she shouted, waving her arms. "Go on."

The gull turned away, running foolishly on its spindly legs and flapping its wings until it was airborne.

Quite suddenly, it was very quiet and Corinne experienced an empty sensation that went beyond the loneliness she had come to accept.

After years of dreaming what his first sight of America might resemble, Nicholas Koniev was forced to stew in his own frustration. The name of that tiny island on the northwest tip of Washington—Tatoosh—fascinated him. But to raise a periscope at this point simply to satisfy an ambition, after an undetected crossing, would be foolhardy. Visual approaches were a thing of the past.

The mother sub, *Gorki,* had been at sea for two weeks, a leisurely passage across the Pacific. She had left Petropavlovsk on a cloudy day to avoid detection by US satellite surveillance, diving before she was out of sight of land. There had been two American tracker submarines, the first one perpetually on station off the Soviet port, the second unexpectedly waiting near the end of the Aleutian chain. A screen of Russian submarines successfully confused then drew the first away from its quarry. *Gorki* detected the second one herself on the fourth day out and slipped silently off to the south.

It was certainly unusual, and had come as somewhat of a surprise to the submarine community, when Nicholas Koniev was appointed *Gorki'*s first commanding officer. While such unique commands were normally reserved for a Captain First Class, it had been years since he'd served at sea. The fact that he was now considered a strategist and spent much of his time with senior staff was of even more concern to line officers awaiting their first afloat command.

Senior officers in Moscow had never discussed other men for *Gorki.* They were fascinated with Nicholas Koniev. In effect, they were allowing him the chance to personally confirm his thesis of denying the missile submarines' access to the ocean. He was the one who would turn his volunteers into a cohesive support crew for the miniature submarines' penetration of the American Tridents' lair. Koniev had originated the strategy and he understood more about his ultimate goal than any other man in the Soviet Union. And only three other men were aware of his actual mission originally proposed in the Koniev Abstract which was now locked deep inside the Kremlin.

The uneventful crossing allowed two final weeks of vital at-sea training for the crew but, while they blossomed as a unit, it was all wearing on Koniev. Details irritated him. Impatience had consistently been a weakness of his, and fourteen days beneath the sea conducting the same exercises again and again lowered his tolerance level considerably.

Now, when his navigator innocently announced that Tatoosh Island could probably be seen from the surface, none of the crew could imagine how badly Koniev wanted to bring *Gorki* to the surface and be the first man through the hatch to the sail.

Instead, he followed the doctrine ingrained in every submariner and asked his executive officer to order a complete passive listening search. Once he was satisfied that no danger existed, he then gave permission to deploy the first of their hydrophone detectors. Powered by a silent electric motor, the expendable detectors were programmed by *Gorki*'s oceanographer to follow a preplanned search to seek out possible listening devices planted on the ocean bottom. As Soviet intelligence had indicated, the Strait of Juan de Fuca, the exit point to the Pacific for America's Trident submarines, was well-protected. Each detector was programmed to sense the magnetic properties within these hydrophone devices. A signal would be sent to the mother submarine if nothing was located at the end of its sixty-minute life span. But the lack of a response after that hour indicated that the tiny swimmer had located a listening device and was reporting its success by its silence.

Two days beforehand, assuming that American listening devices did extend well out from the coastline, *Gorki* had gone as silent as possible, cutting her speed and limiting normal shipboard work. Nuclear submarines making an approach on any shoreline crept in on cat's feet. Twelve hours before Tatoosh Island, Koniev had shifted the engineering plant to electric power. *Gorki*'s approach was but a whisper in the vast ocean. Now she would enter the strait like a ghost, avoiding any possible contact and constantly charting the invisible ocean bottom listening devices intended to protect Puget Sound which was about a hundred fifty kilometers to the east.

As she proceeded into the Strait of Juan de Fuca, *Gorki* also seeded a string of self-propelled acoustic mines behind her. They would rest on the bottom and, if they were ever activated by Koniev, would serve as a defense behind Gorki if she was forced to depart the area under pursuit. But, if all went as planned, the mines' future target might be any Trident submarine passing through the Strait of Juan de Fuca. If the United States refused to discuss a mutual neutralization of seaborne ballistic missiles, the mines could be activated by a distant sonar signal—they would close the strait to submarine traffic, seal the Tridents in their lair. If the Americans wouldn't listen to Soviet reason, then the reason would be delivered to them.

Almost every individual in the Soviet Union involved in planning truly believed this was the major purpose of *Gorki*'s mission. Only Nicholas Koniev and three other men in the Kremlin knew it was so much more. There was too much danger in relying on weapons, whether active or passive, to achieve the objective of denying ocean access to lessen the awesome threat of the Trident missile. The Koniev Abstract insisted that the only solution was to neutralize the heart of the system itself.

In a way, though none of them would ever admit it to the other—whether because of pride, or arrogance, or simply fear of being labeled a traitor by the others—this was an act of desperation. Trident could never be neutralized by peace talks. The US would never agree. Though the actual act, if it ever took place, might be called imprudent, wanton, impulsive, even *desperate,* not a soul would ever admit to such a thought.

Nicholas Koniev trusted only one man to accomplish that goal—himself.

Three

Danny West experienced a strange, inner comfort whenever he swam with the dolphins. He wasn't sure when that sensation first occurred although he decided in conversations with the others that it definitely should be considered a rite of passage. There seemed no set time when a SEAL achieved it but each man seemed to know when it was silently passed on by these sensitive creatures.

Perhaps it was because the ocean was the dolphins' element, not his, not any other human being's, but these animals seemed to treat Danny as one of their own once they knew they could trust him. That was another aspect of these unique animals. They accepted these strange two-legged creatures only after they'd passed whatever a dolphin's concept of qualification might be. Did they consider West a poor version of dolphin, mentally able to cope with their environment but physically limited? Did they comprehend that it was he who was able to adjust for limited periods to their world while they were incapable of joining his? In all probability, they couldn't have cared less. They were creatures of the interface where air and water came together.

Of course, he reflected, a SEAL was really at home only on land regardless of his talents. With the aid of parachutes and air tanks they had conquered the sky and the sea, but they remained limited by time. All in all, West decided, as Bull raced happily ahead then shot by him in the other direction, man would never come close to adapting to the dolphin's natural environment.

Bull rushed by again and turning, came to a dead stop no more than a dozen feet ahead. He seemed to stare back, no different than a dog running back to make sure his master was still following, though it was his sense of hearing that he relied on. Then with a swirl of water that pressed Danny's diving mask tight around his face, Bull flashed gracefully ahead.

Patience with man marked a dolphin's personality. Most of them were friendly enough, many so naive that their friendly nature became a danger in itself. It was more than the frozen fish proffered as a Pavlovian reward that kept a dolphin's attention during training. Dolphins actually seemed to enjoy the process of learning. They possessed a natural ability to adapt themselves to man's weaknesses in the water while at the same time they were learning how they might help this awkward creature.

Danny West squinted at his watch through the murk and moved his wrist closer. There was less than a minute to go on this course. It probably made little difference to Bull what courses they'd followed or how much time had to be spent on each one but that's the way the book said it had to be done. Challenging exercise procedures wasn't in Bull's job description. So, no matter what these men did, Bull always went to the heart of the matter as soon as he was allowed.

But this exercise required the SEAL to navigate on a series of courses toward the objective so that he could be sure of the exact location of the target when the dolphin was sent on his way. That was a critical part if Admiral Coffin was to accept the team as added security for the Trident base. The animal was expected to stick with the trainer as a part of the exercise—all navy, no matter what, no matter that the expert in question was proficient in the water.

When he stopped, West made sure his body was turned away from the direction of the target. He knew its bearing from his position, but had no idea how far away it was.

Bull instinctively recognized that the casual swim was over. He swam in smaller circles around West until the swirl from his tail rocked the man in the water. For the SEAL, the sensation was like an invisible hand shaking him.

West extracted the cricket from his belt and signaled that the fun was over.

Bull hovered about ten feet in front of him, seemingly motionless, excited that the game was about to begin.

The SEAL pulled a barbell-shaped object from his belt and held it out. The center of the device was firmly wrapped with canvas since dolphins possessed an aversion to anything metallic in their mouths. With an imperceptible flick of his tail, the dolphin was in front of him and had grasped the object in his jaws. West gave another signal and Bull instantly disappeared. The man turned quickly but there was no sign of the animal. The dolphin's inherent sonar, consisting of a combination of clicks and whistles, had been adapted by man to locate man-made objects. For man, another asset had been harnessed for his benefit. To the dolphin, this less-than-perfect creature of the surface had provided yet another game.

West swam slowly in the direction of the target, anticipating that Bull would be back beside him at any moment. And sure enough, he felt the swirl of water wash over his body before Bull appeared to his left. There was nothing in his mouth now.

Danny pulled the direction finder from his waist and switched on the activator. This would provide a bearing to the electronic device in Bull's barbell that was now magnetically attached to the target. An interior glow illuminated the compass heading—exactly where it should be! He wondered if these tests had become too easy. Even though the dolphins were required to search a wide area, they knew innately what they were looking for. It must even have been obvious to them that the test area was not extensive, that they could win this game without exerting themselves.

The dolphin darted back and forth with exaggerated rolls and swoops that carried him in circles while the man followed, too slowly to satisfy Bull. West increased his depth as they approached the target. With his vision limited to about ten feet as they neared the bottom, the SEAL continued to rely on the locator to tell him when he'd navigated within range. Now, Bull was diving toward the bottom, then circling, then returning to the SEAL to show that they were approaching the metal object. *These men were all right but their sonar was definitely inadequate. Perhaps that was why they swam so slowly.*

And there it was, the carcass of an old torpedo, now partially filled with cement. The homing device planted by Bull was magnetically attached to the side. Once again, the animal had performed perfectly, searching for a familiarly shaped metal device on the bottom and attaching the homer to it. The dolphin, utilizing his sonar, had scanned the area in a fraction of the time it would have taken a man. There were other metal objects, a generation of discarded junk, but he'd located the torpedo by its shape. Then, very gently, in case the object was overly sensitive to physical contact, the dolphin placed the barbell against the outer casing.

West indicated his pleasure to Bull, a silent hand signal that said there would be a reward back at the pier. Then he released a green smoke flare that rose quickly to the surface.

The sound of the props on the launch came to him as he headed slowly up. It was bright on the surface and West bobbed in a slight chop as the boat eased up to him.

Admiral Coffin was leaning on the gunnels as the coxswain cut the engine. "Less than half the allotted time, Lieutenant. Not bad at all," he added over his shoulder to Ryng.

"If Bull could answer, he'd explain how easy that was, sir." West had pushed his diving mask up on his forehead. Heavy dark eyebrows glistened damply in the sunlight over black eyes that seemed to sparkle with delight. A white-toothed smile spread across his swarthy face as he recognized Len Todd balanced on the edge of the launch, pulling his own mask down over his face. "Straight down, Lenny, just off the bow," he said as he pulled himself up the ladder.

Todd eased over the side with a small splash and disappeared beneath the surface. He would attach the line from an identification buoy to the dummy torpedo for later recovery.

The dolphin surfaced a few feet behind West and studied the launch curiously.

Once again, the admiral was sure he saw the animal smile. "Does he sleep?" Coffin asked over his shoulder.

"Sure," Bernie Ryng responded. "He needs rest just like we do. It's just that dolphins have more stamina. They move faster, no air tanks to refill, perfect underwater navigation with their built-in sonar system. That's why your security increases so much with them. Swimmers can penetrate almost any subsurface area defense if they have enough patience. But the dolphins are a roving security system. No perimeters. No depth problems. No time limitations. A swimmer doesn't know they're there until Bull or one of his buddies is right on top of them. And a dolphin can kill a man with a head butt at full speed."

"So what do they need SEALs for?" Coffin asked Ryng with a slight grin. "Why don't we just send them off on their own?"

"Like all kids, they need direction," Ryng answered. He indicated Tim Sullivan, who was helping West with his gear. "Tim's written the book on dolphins and security. It took years to get them to this point. Now you have three of the best here. Let them understand something's on the bottom and they'll lead you to it. You want to find something that moves underwater like a man or a submarine? Get the message across and they're relentless."

There were more tests that afternoon that would be performed by Ernie and Chester, too, but the admiral was already sure of the results. If a combination of man and dolphin couldn't do the job, then . . . "Commander, do you know what I want you all to protect us against?"

"Vaguely," Ryng answered. Then, "Not really, I guess.

I've heard rumors about miniature submarines, swimmers, things like that, nothing specific."

"Good. Then you have about as much information as I do."

Harry Coffin was pleased that Bernie Ryng wasn't especially bothered by the ambiguity of their objective. His few times working with SEALs had always been a confidence builder. It seemed that once a man completed BUD/S (Basic Underwater Demolition/SEAL) school he was convinced that he could accomplish anything. And if it had never been done before, it was worth a shot. For such men there was more satisfaction in conquering the unknown.

Men like Ryng, men his age who had survived life-threatening situations around the globe, found no reason for concern until they found themselves actually facing death. Training had reinforced their confidence, and a dedication to maintaining that fine edge was what kept them alive.

Harry Coffin had been briefed on Bernie Ryng before he ever agreed to go along with SEALs providing security for the Trident base. The name was familiar. He'd heard about the man in the past. Anyone in submarines who'd transported SEALs to an inshore mission, and Coffin remembered those experiences well, had heard tales of Ryng.

Too often, those few men who become legends in their own time are not around to hear the stories of their adventures. So, the tales become exaggerated over the years. Bernie Ryng was not only alive to correct some of those stories, he made sure that there was always a postscript that included the men he worked with. After all the stories were told about a sixth sense for survival or superhuman efforts, Ryng explained the real basis of his success—training, planning, execution . . . *training, planning, execution* . . . training . . . planning . . . execution.

Training was not something a SEAL ever completed. It was something he learned on an ongoing basis. Once it was ingrained in his very soul, he never let up. It simply became a personal accomplishment rather than a group objective. A SEAL trained himself continuously and assumed the responsibility for his own conditioning, expecting no less from any other SEAL. He remained an expert with all weapons, a master of all tactics. It was a matter of self-discipline. If you couldn't keep it up, it was better to resign.

Survivors understood *planning* inherently. It was the single most important reason they continued to live. SEALs planned every aspect of each mission, *including their return.* If their planning was accurate and comprehensive, they expected to return with every man who started out. Losses were unacceptable. They happened, but afterward the mission was analyzed thoroughly to find out how and why they'd failed. No man would ever die again for the same reason.

Execution always justified the other two absolutes. It was physical and mental at the same time—physical because theirs was a sacrosanct (I'm alive and the other guy's dead) pleasure in the performance, mental because that part of the experience could be relived. The learning never stopped. A SEAL's education would continue as long as he continued to execute his mission and his individual responsibility perfectly.

Bernie Ryng was the father, the son, and the holy ghost when it came to *training, planning and execution,* a living example of why a man should expect to survive in this business . . . *living proof.*

"Once you're happy with these final tests, Admiral, I'd like to establish my initial procedures." Ryng was bored by the type of exercises they were performing. The fact that he was there was proof that his methods worked. They would establish security procedures that should be impossible to penetrate without some detection. Once they were aware of an enemy probe, if it ever occurred, then the fun would begin.

"Go ahead," Harry Coffin answered. "I just want to see for myself what the rest of your team can do." There were now three dolphins gamboling near the launch, and each one seemed to be smiling at him.

There is a point near the eastern end of the Strait of Juan de Fuca, about five miles north northeast of New Dungeness Light and a couple of miles beyond the Puget Sound traffic lanes, that is close to six hundred feet deep. It is a few miles west of Admiralty Inlet which is the entrance to Puget Sound; it is also convenient to the Hood Canal, which branches off the entrance to the Sound, where the Trident base is located. Nicholas Koniev had selected this as *Gorki*'s destination. Once he was satisfied with the navigator's assurances, he ordered his two miniature submarine captains to run their predeployment tests and had his weapons officer prepare to offload a stockpile of time delay mines and torpedos. If *Gorki* was forced to run, both mini subs would still have a source of ammunition replenishment.

Leon Donskoi and Andrei Tarantsev commanded his mini subs. Each man was trained in submarines in the same manner as their captain, each one a naval Spetznaz also. Koniev studied the two men now sipping tea across the wardroom table. Perhaps they were wondering what their chances were for survival? Minimal? Nonexistent? Of course, if he had misgivings about his own return, why should they possibly think their odds were better? Donskoi and Tarantsev knew they were wholly dependent on him for their survival. *If only they could somehow know . . .* Koniev, his features expressionless, gave no hint of his expectations, nor was he especially concerned that Tarantsev would eventually be sacrificed for the sake of a mission he knew nothing about. Donskoi?—even his chances of survival were minimal. It was unfortunate they could not be made aware of their contributions to the ultimate mission.

"You understand that direct communications with *Gorki* or with our land contact should be effected only at the proper times and only in the gravest emergency."

They nodded and mumbled their "yes, sirs" to him politely. Why was he going through that again? He'd written the operation plan with their assistance.

"What I mean is that the Americans aren't easy. They're not to be underestimated. There is a distinct possibility that their intelligence has some idea of *Gorki* and your submarines . . ." Koniev, having said nothing about the man he killed in Severodvinsk, was grasping for something that even he was unsure how to express, ". . . though I can't imagine how they could possibly assume this is where we'd turn up." He was never certain how to be sure that men under him were willing to sacrifice themselves if necessary. To Koniev, such dedication seemed as natural as getting out of bed in the morning—at least it should be if one had undergone Spetznaz training, and Donksoi and Tarantsev had no equals in that regard.

They had been selected before they were ever called for active duty. The Spetznaz skimmed the cream of the athletes and prospective army recruits before they were due for service. It was a simple habit of Spetznaz wanting to know about their people before any time was wasted on training a man who would later have to be dropped. Dedication to the party, superior physical and mental abilities, and the cleanliness of their personal and family record were reviewed in detail. Even out of this preliminary group, only the best were selected and then they were sworn to secrecy for they were often sent back to regular units until their special abilities were required.

Spetznaz training was harsh, brutal. Those who endured it would never forget the experience. They were capable of surviving the very worst the Soviet military could hand out. Since many in each group survived injuries to complete their training, Spetznaz graduates insisted on nothing less for those who came after them. There were always some talented but unfortunate individuals who died in every class.

Tradition was also a great motivator for the survivors. They took pride in accepting the fact that Spetznaz were either healthy survivors or dead heros. A custom of leaving no wounded developed during the Great Patriotic War and achieved mythic proportions in Afghanistan. Wounded rapidly became excess baggage and any attempt to help them could endanger an entire unit. A commander who failed to eliminate his wounded honorably and as quickly as possible was considered a failure. Those leaders who took pity on their wounded were more often than not killed by their own second in command, who would then take charge of the unit. It was a tradition that endured. Success on a mission was achieved only by healthy people. Those who were injured understood and accepted their fate.

Donskoi and Tarantsev were perfect examples of their training. Beyond the fact that they survived the brutality that few men could endure, they possessed remarkable technical capabilities. The modern mini subs developed under the leadership of Nicholas Koniev bore no comparison to the old, slower ones that crawled the bottom of the Baltic in the 1980s. These new craft were sleek, electronic wonders. Their most valuable asset was an ability to survive as long as a week away from the mother sub because of their unique engineering plant and, even when they were low, *Gorki* could replenish them in twelve hours. The mini subs were capable of silent high speed travel, yet they could still bottom crawl, depending on the nature of their mission.

The miniature submarines carried a crew of three men. In addition to the officer in charge, they were crewed by an engineer and a weapons expert. Each of them was a qualified diver and each was capable of assuming the responsibilities of the others. They knew their mission was intelligence and therefore detection would likely hazard, possibly destroy, their mission. At this stage they were to remain defensive rather than go on the offensive, at least until they were forced.

No, neither Donskoi nor Tarantsev needed a pep talk from Koniev, nor was one more review of their responsibilities necessary. They were chosen to command the mini subs because they were the two best men in their profession. Their talent and dedication were unquestionable and they fully understood how the fates would treat them. Koniev had no doubt that the best men he could select were facing him.

"I guess what I mean," Koniev finally said, "is that I am aware of the danger you face and I know you will perform . . ." Again he paused, knowing that he was no more capable of this kind of conversation than he ever had been. Sympathy, understanding, good fellowship—such feelings were foreign to him. He understood missions. It would have been preferable if his missions could avoid human involvement, if hardware and weaponry, futuristic delivery vehicles, could deliver for him. Unfortunately, the human being was still a necessity.

Koniev liked these two men. They were like him in many ways. Generally, he cared little about human suffering and death. But their loss would be a tragedy for the entire force. "I look forward to your return," he concluded quickly, ashamed that he might have shown any emotion. There was no room here for personal relationships.

While Nicholas Koniev's mini subs were technologically superior to their predecessors, "space age" as the navy's senior admiral had said, their creature comforts were minimal compared to the mother ship.

Modern nuclear submarines like *Gorki* placed a reasonable emphasis on habitability. Their messing and living spaces, though still cramped compared to surface ships, were unusually comfortable in relation to their sister ships of the diesel era. Officers shared tight but efficient quarters and their wardroom provided adequate space for both dining and socializing. Enlisted spaces lacked such niceties but there was no need for the bunk sharing of the past and there was room for the men to eat comfortably. Sanitary facilities actually allowed some privacy. Air conditioning had solved the problem of human, galley and engineering odors. Time at sea was limited only by the amount of food they could carry. While increased periods away from port could soon became nerve-wracking, operating spaces had become modularized, comfortable, and oriented to making a man's job more pleasant.

It would have been convenient if each of these goals had been obtained in the new mini subs. But their mission guided their design. The size limitations for *Gorki* were the basis for the size of the smaller craft. While *Gorki* was four hundred fifty feet in length, she still required reasonable space for weapons systems, operations, engineering, crew habitability, plus excess support and storage space for the miniature submarines.

The mini subs were nestled in a garagelike structure, which Koniev called "the hangar" because of its similarity in design to that of an aircraft carrier. The hangar had been designed behind the sail, similar to the launch section on guided missile subs, and was recessed into the hull to avoid excessive drag. When *Gorki* was underway, this area was as accessible as any other compartment in the submarine. It was only sealed off from the pressure hull when it was flooded for launch operations.

The two smaller craft had no names. They were referred to by the names of their commanders—*Donskoi* and *Tarantsev*. When preparations were made to launch them, Nicholas Koniev was able to oversee the entire procedure from a viewing port at the rear of *Gorki's* sail above the hangar after it had been flooded. There he also enjoyed listening to the banter between the mini subs and the operations officer that was piped in as he sat perched in his tiny space, as excited as any child. This was payment in kind for his effort, and it meant far more to him than anything else his nation could offer. The fruits of his labor lay before him.

Flooding the cavernous hangar area was a tedious process. Water was pumped in slowly to maintain essential silence as the pressure was equalized with the outside. As this process was taking place, the team in the control room would be struggling to maintain the submarine's depth and stability as this additional weight was added. It was time-consuming and nerve-wracking and *Gorki's* captain knew enough to stay out of their way.

Koniev had a habit of crossing and uncrossing his legs whenever he wasn't directly involved in a shipboard evolution. It was a controlled luxury allowed only when he was alone. As far as he was aware, this was his only outward sign of nervousness, one he was forced to live with. But he'd trained himself to limit the physical reaction to private moments like this one because vanity was paramount in his makeup. His wife, Galya, often claimed in exasperation that such displays of vanity were an unavoidable sin common to brilliant men. They were driven by an ego that demanded perfection of themselves, physical as well as mental, and appeal to the opposite sex was as vital to them as it was to their peers.

Nicholas Koniev was reasonably handsome, about six feet tall, slender even as he approached middle age, and his black hair, turning gray at the temples, remained thick. Green eyes from an Estonian mother seemed vacant unless someone interested him, usually women more than men. They were set wide over the high Georgian cheekbones of his father. He'd once tried a mustache but that simply made him appear sinister and it took only one admiral's remark for him to shave it off. Koniev was also vain about his dress, insisting on tailored uniforms as soon as he could afford them. Because he was Spetznaz, he kept himself in remarkable physical condition which enhanced the close-fitting clothes.

Now, as *Donskoi* and *Tarantsev* were preparing for their first mission in American waters, Koniev's legs began their controlled dance. The water level increased at a painfully slow rate in the floodlit hangar. He listened to the conversations between the hangar and the operations crew but it was frustrating not to actually see what was happening. He scratched. He even eased out through the hatch once and dropped to the control room, but the watch there was completely engrossed in their part of the operation.

He was unable to relax until the giant hangar cover began to move, spreading slowly open like a giant chrysalis. While there were floodlights within the hangar itself, and one recessed in the sail just underneath Koniev's position, it was so dark at five hundred feet that the giant shadows within the hangar presented a surreal scene.

The mini subs were pointing aft, one behind the other. To Koniev, they appeared poised like fighter planes on a carrier's flight deck in that moment before they are hurled into the air. Yet the process aboard *Gorki* was exactly the opposite. No catapult. No screaming engine. No craft straining against its bonds. After the complexities of maintaining the mother ship's buoyancy as the hangar was flooded, the launch process was a simple one.

The arms holding *Donskoi* were released electronically from the inside of the craft by the pilot and withdrawn hydraulically into the mother ship. The umbilical insert, the final contact, was the last to be removed. Slightly more buoyant than *Gorki,* the first mini sub rose slowly from inside the hangar, matching the submarine's course and speed until she was totally clear of the after hull. Only then did Donskoi maneuver his small craft a hundred yards abeam to starboard once again matching course and speed. *Tarantsev* did exactly the same, taking station on the opposite beam.

Koniev strained to catch sight of his small craft but vision was too restricted at that depth. He uncrossed his legs and sat for a moment staring at his hands. There was nothing more to see on this historic venture. Now everything was in the hands of the men he had trained—and Tarantsev's fate was already sealed.

Corinne observed the dancing shadows with the fascination of a little girl, her green eyes darting from one that seemed to vanish into thin air to another appearing to rise like a genie. A soft breeze announced by autumn leaves rustling like dried corn stalks had come up after sunset. It drifted now through the open windows to caper playfully with the flame of the single candle on the dining table. Shadows flickered across the far wall, etching a series of figures, diving, leaping, dancing. They became whatever her imagination decided they should be.

As she stared, hypnotized by their motion, she remembered that many years ago shadow figures were one of the few things her father was able to do well. Winter nights at the dining room table, if he hadn't spent too much time at the pub on the way home, he used to switch off the dull overhead bulbs and light a candle, sometimes two or three. Then he would escape to another world, fashioning his hands and fingers into shadow animals—dogs, cats, rabbits, whatever she and her sisters asked for. After a time, everything seemed to look the same. But she remembered her mother saying before she tucked Corinne into bed that you could see whatever you wanted to see and it never had to be perfect as long as you knew in your own mind what it was.

What did she see now? She tried in vain to identify the long ears of the rabbit but they became the periscope of a submarine. The dog turned into a wolf with jaws opened wide. The duck stretched its neck until it became a rifle. The little girl inside Corinne Foxe was gone forever. She'd taken her shadow animals with her. There was a woman in her place, one who'd seen much too much of the world, a woman who could no longer delight at the shadow animals and the dreams they inhabited after her mother turned out the light.

Now, she could turn on the gas lights if she wanted . . . but that would defeat her purpose. The KGB, predictable in their twisted wisdom, had made sure everything for gracious living had been provided. Corinne had insisted on it even though she'd been unsure if they thought she was worth the trouble. There was even a nice tablecloth, plastic rather than linen, because whoever stocked the cottage probably had no concept of civility. But it made her feel more comfortable. The dishes were cheap but they boasted a pleasant design, as did the flatware. *Maybe not so much comfortable, Corinne . . . human . . .*

She'd asked for wine, and some tasteless soul, probably one who tossed back vodka by the quart, had purchased two gallons of each color and plastic wineglasses to go along with it. If nothing else, that had confirmed what she'd expected —this stay could be more than a couple of days. The food in the small freezer substantiated that.

Years ago, once they'd provided her with a new identity and moved her to Vancouver, she began to develop a taste for good food. The new Corinne was damn well going to be a joint venture and the KGB was going to pay whether they liked it or not. There'd been no time to pay attention to such luxuries during the days of rebellion at Oxford. In those days, they ate primarily to sustain their hatreds. She had no memory of the food, only that she didn't starve to death.

Vancouver was cosmopolitan and Corinne now had money, compliments of her benefactors, not wealth but enough for comfort. They explained that they didn't want her to draw attention—neither rich nor poor, well-dressed but not too elegant, capable of handling herself among the right people yet not too memorable.

Corinne made the decision herself to learn how to cook once she discovered the exquisite pleasures of good food. At the same time, she also found that wines were a pleasant complement to a meal. She eventually came to realize that she was becoming a lady and that she liked herself better as a result. After all, if you were going to become a spy and still make your way in the world—even better, if you had no choice—treasure life while the opportunity exists.

While life in this new world was comfortable, it could also be lonely. The men she met on her own were initially more appealing than those selected for her by her handlers, but the latter were important to those who paid her bills, enough so that she soon dropped the others—*bad business to mix pleasure with business.* The men she entertained were mostly married and preferred her company on evenings away from Vancouver or weekends in the country. It was difficult to believe at times that these dalliances were contributing anything but she was assured that the most valuable intelligence was often unrecognizable and came unexpectedly. It was impossible to quantify because the true benefits might come years later. One benefit to such an existence, a very simple one, was that the men she entertained were gentlemen and treated her like the lady she intended to become. *Not a woman of the night, Corinne, not a call girl by any means—you're, I'd say, a spy, if that's the word, utilizing natural talents.*

She studied the flickering shadows on the wall and saw nothing. The little girl who delighted at her father's shadow animals and dreamed grand adventures for them was now unable to hold them long enough in her mind to give them a life of their own. The breeze drifting through the cottage that evening enhanced her fantasies as much as the shadows from the candle's flame, but the direction of her dreams had changed forever.

Corinne had no fear of being alone. Isolation such as this was completely different from loneliness. She enjoyed companionship, more often on her own terms, but she also yearned for privacy. Perhaps that's why the KGB considered her so valuable. The men whom they wanted her to encourage were thankful that she had no interest in forming a permanent liaison. Was that why her *handlers*—oh, how that term used to infuriate the KGB contact who used the name Roberts—were so pleased with her manner of work? It was only logical that no sane man wanted a woman like Corinne demanding more time from him than he could safely offer. And she could enjoy those moments of solitude afterward.

The ones who entertained her so elegantly, taking her to the finest restaurants and hotels, were also the ones who were willing to accept an invitation to dinner at her apartment. Even the handlers hadn't appreciated their own genius at setting her up so well. No man could resist the idea of a liaison in a private place complete with candlelight, exquisite food, and fine wines, all provided by a woman who truly fascinated him. She enjoyed the preparation and presentation of such a meal as much as actually sitting down to dine. And it was equally satisfying when they had to leave, whether it was late in the evening or the next morning.

Companionship, physical pleasure, then privacy—the best of all possible worlds to the Corinne Foxe who now contemplated the shadows on the wall of the tiny cottage on the remote island. This evening she had prepared herself a decent meal which had pleased her a great deal. The bulk wine didn't add to the occasion but the clown who stocked it on the island probably would have turned up his nose at the escargots. Bulk wine would never enhance any dijon sauce she'd tasted before, but the fool wouldn't have known the difference. As much as she would have enjoyed companionship this evening, she thanked her lucky stars that the clown wasn't a guest. One's companion must be discerning, capable of understanding when a lady wanted him to stay and when she required privacy.

She bent forward, cupping her palm behind the candle, and blew softly until the flame died. When she looked up, the shadows had disappeared from the wall, extinguished as easily as the candle. But the fantasies remained, as clear as the stars in the sky. She could shut her eyes and still see that rabbit with the long ears turn into the periscope of a submarine. And when she opened her eyes, it remained, even in that dark room.

It didn't frighten her. There was little she feared, even alone like this. But it was a new experience.

Corinne . . . Corinne, she murmured to herself, *if you're there, somewhere deep inside this brave body, you've got to be very careful this time. Someone . . . or something . . . is telling you . . . be careful.*

She glanced briefly at the luminous face of her watch. Then, in the dark, already able to navigate through the cottage sightless, she switched on the radio receiver to listen . . . for what?

Four

Launch!

Not Koniev's, not *Gorki's*.

His launch! Donskoi's. It was an intensely personal, solitary experience.

There were no flames, no searing heat, no ear-splitting blast bursting from engines with immense horsepower. This launch was cautious, achingly slow, precise, and absolutely silent.

Yet it was a physical and mental, almost spiritual, sensation. A tremendous *rush,* a term Donskoi had read somewhere. That was the word used by people who put drugs into their bodies—that's what they said they experienced in those initial moments. A rush of pure pleasure that was impossible to put into words. He'd told no one about his feeling because he felt that might be unprofessional.

But that's how he'd assessed the experience in training.

This one began just as all the others during training, just as it should have. *Yet it was so different*. This was enemy territory. He was out of his trench and crossing the lines onto their side, *yet he was invisible*. No, he wasn't totally invisible. They could locate him if he gave them the slightest indication of his existence.

Koniev had pounded that one aspect into their heads—they weren't dealing with fools. It was vital to acknowledge from the start that the Americans were close to their equals. Give them the opportunity, just one stupid mistake, and they would hound Donskoi, Tarantsev and Koniev to their deaths.

Now—with this launch, this penetration into enemy territory—he was on his own, making decisions that would mean life or death for him and his crew. No one, not Koniev, not the admiral in Petropavlovsk, not a soul in the Kremlin could control him at this point. They'd delegated the responsibility, and the sensation surged through his veins and gave him a strength he had never before realized.

Viktor Donskoi was admittedly a complex individual. That he understood the oddities of his psychological profile better than any of the military doctors who were confused by him had been a decided plus as far as Nicholas Koniev was concerned.

Donskoi had been selected for Spetznaz training before even he knew his military duty would commence. At the age of eighteen, he was naive enough that he assumed all military training must have been as rugged and brutal as his own and that all recruits took the same oath of secrecy. He was physically powerful for his age and had no trouble absorbing the beatings that seemed to be a part of surviving instructors who delighted in savagery.

The accomplishment that attracted the most attention from his superiors occurred when his senior sergeant ended up in the hospital. The man, who barely survived the ordeal, had been known particularly for his brutality and for the fact that a number of his recruits had been released from military service because of their injuries. The one who'd put the sergeant in the hospital, Viktor Donskoi, was immediately promoted even though a month of training remained. He was also given his choice of duty.

Donskoi was a young man who intended to expand his horizons. Naval Spetznaz accomplished much the same tasks as their army brethren, but they also worked underwater. They specialized in underwater demolition but were equally adept at removing explosives directed toward their own forces. They also functioned as intelligence operatives, sneaking ashore to reconnoiter both civilian and military objectives, and they could assume the role of a vicious commando force. Each of these challenges appealed to the multitalented Donskoi.

Work with explosives revealed another of the young man's skills, a latent technical capacity well beyond that of his peers. When he eventually applied for the miniature submarine program, his technical abilities as well as his Spetznaz training attracted Koniev's eye. He needed two men capable of taking charge of his two tiny craft, individuals with the capacity to enjoy overwhelming challenges and accept miserable odds.

Donskoi fit the specifications for one of them perfectly. He was compact enough, two inches under six feet although he weighed two hundred pounds, which he could accommodate to the limited space in the mini subs. His reaction time and understanding of relative motion made him a perfect pilot. Technically, he was able to learn the propulsion, weapons, electronics and survival systems of the mini submarines, and could function in any of the three positions. So the blond, handsome young man with pale blue eyes and a smile that remained even when he was physically beating another became the captain of Koniev's first tiny craft.

The passage from *Gorki*'s staging area to the Hood Canal was relatively simple. Commercial shipping crowded the sea lanes entering and leaving Puget Sound. There was so much noise around them that Donskoi was convinced he could have entered the area pounding his hull with a hammer and no one would have been the wiser. The sub moved out of the Strait of Juan de Fuca into the narrower confines of Admiralty Inlet within hours. Turning almost due south, it was another eleven miles to the entrance to the Hood Canal. Five hours after her launching, Donskoi's mini sub lay off Tala Point at the mouth of the canal, unnoticed, quiet, exquisitely dangerous.

Technical support equipment in the subs, while inconsequential compared to their full-sized brethren, was well beyond anything found aboard their predecessors. Navigation was supported by a system of mini computers that captured the position of the mother ship at the moment of launch. Position data was compiled from both the actual movement of the craft and the external forces of tide and current that affected their motion. It was as accurate as modern science could make it without using the periscope and exposing the submarine. Their location was automatically transcribed on an overlay chart of the entire Puget Sound area.

Even with such a system, Donskoi still navigated with caution. He used a bottom reading device to balance his depth between the constantly changing harbor floor and an upward looking one to avoid the deep drafts of tankers that might pass overhead. There were more ships operating above than any of them had ever experienced in training. Even Donskoi became irritated by the deluge of sound that would have been nerve-wracking to the average submariner in the open ocean. And while Koniev likened their travel to flying, it was anything but, in these waters. It was more like driving an eighteen-wheel truck in heavy traffic.

There was a single view port directly in front of the maneuvering station. Its purpose, with the aid of an external spotlight, was purely to identify objects they encountered. They were forced to stop completely for such purposes.

Because they were designed to operate just like any other submarine, maneuvering by sight was restricted and in these waters, almost impossible. The combination of junk from heavy surface traffic, effluents pumped from coastal plants, and the mud and sand suspended by tide and current changes reduced vision to that of a heavy fog. Donskoi was flying blind. Yet his confidence in the mini sub never wavered. His craft's sensors, combined with his sense of relative motion and the display before him, brought him exactly where he'd planned, five hundred yards in front of the movable bridge at the head of the canal connecting the eastern shore to Termination Point on the west.

Donskoi maneuvered across the channel to the eastern

shore where the water was deeper and the bottom was pure sand. He had no intention of moving farther ahead without a visual investigation of the area. The bridge's pilings were not marked on his chart, and there was a note to mariners indicating submerged mooring cables. It also seemed a likely place for submarine nets. He pushed the button to deploy the hydraulic landing skids and let the craft settle to the bottom.

Kolarov, who acted as a copilot during operations, was already suiting up for the excursion. He listened quietly as Donskoi explained exactly what information he needed before they could proceed. Like his captain, Kolarov was calm. Although this would be his first deployment in foreign waters, his training over the past few years had been for missions of this nature. He possessed a confidence similar to Donskoi's, an inner strength that seemed to instill in him a sense of invincibility. That was why Koniev had insisted on all-Spetznaz crews.

The pressure chamber above the maneuvering room could handle two men. Koniev had intended that one man would always remain on board as a safety measure in case men returned injured and unable to re-enter. And if they failed to reappear, the submarine could still return to the mother. It was easier to train new men than it was to replace a submarine.

Kolarov was back within two hours and, along with the engineer, Tikhvin, they plotted their course into the canal which cut into the Olympic Peninsula at a southwest angle. Each of them was capable of assuming the other's responsibilities and Koniev's standing orders insisted that all three involve themselves in decisions once the mini subs were on their own.

Donskoi, her propulsion system no more than a whisper, passed quietly beneath the bridge and began the process of reconnoitering both sides of the Hood Canal. Their initial objective was total familiarization with their operating area. They would memorize the environment outside their submarine before they selected the sites for their mines. The special mission that Koniev had hinted at just before their launch from *Gorki* disappeared from Donskoi's thoughts as they began their initial scouting run.

It would be a long time before the first mine was planted.

A SEAL's swimmer propulsion unit (SPU) offers a high mix of advantages from the moment of activation. Compact and efficient, it is best explained as an outboard motor designed for a human. But the comparison ends there. The small unit pulls, rather than pushes, a single SEAL through the water at a reasonable speed allowing him to reach his goal more quickly and with a minimum of exertion. It is quiet, easy to operate, and above all saves a great deal of time and swimmer's energy. The SPU achieves the objective of placing a dangerous, well-trained individual near his target without being seen. The fact that there is no warning to an enemy of his arrival is the SPU's greatest benefit. In a security sweep, the unit greatly expands the area to be covered.

Tim Sullivan had bummed a ride halfway up the Hood Canal on a security patrol boat from the Trident base. The dolphin working as usual with Tim was Ernie, who traveled the distance in his preferred method, dining on schools of bait fish on the way. Occasionally, Ernie came back near the boat and circled a couple of times as if wanting to insure that he was still needed. What he was actually doing was responding to Tim's sound signals that were intended to keep him nearby. Even a dolphin with Ernie's training tended to wander when the fishing was good.

The Hood Canal is a natural inlet that meanders for almost eighty miles from Puget Sound into the eastern shore of Washington's Olympia Peninsula. Bangor, the town that is home to the navy's Trident submarines, is situated on the Seattle side of the canal about ten miles south of the Hood Canal bridge. Except near its entrance, the canal is never more than three or four thousand yards across. Its wide channel is convenient to the deep-draft Tridents which could even operate at periscope depth in these restricted waters if necessary.

While the canal is an excellent home for the immense

Tridents, it is so spacious that it also could harbor undesirable elements, such as miniature submarines or unfriendly swimmers. As a result, security efforts beneath the water's surface become complex, more so when the CIA issues a warning like the one directed to Bangor a few weeks before.

That was the reason Harry Coffin had agreed to bring in Bernie Ryng's SEALs. They and their dolphins possessed the ability to adapt effectively to this foreign element. Coffin's CIA contact had made it quite clear to the admiral that, with as little intelligence as they had gained on *Gorki* and her miniature submarines, there was no more likely place to experiment with these new craft than near the Trident base. Nothing was of greater concern to the Soviets than the capabilities of these SSBNs and the range and accuracy of their D-5 missiles.

Sullivan left the boat near the breakwaters at South Point, about three miles below the bridge. Ernie's superb hearing detected the SPU's silent motor seconds after Tim entered the water. Whatever the day's game might be, he was ready to play. He swam a series of perfect circles descending to Tim's level, then leapt out of the water for a breath before diving back with a tremendous splash. That was one of Ernie's ways of demonstrating his pleasure.

Security for the Trident base was state of the art. In addition to the standard methods which would normally have made it impregnable, there was a constant patrol on both land and water. Satellite coverage provided a visual picture of any changes in the surrounding area. Beneath the water's surface, hydrophones on the bottom of the canal overheard literally everything, alive or manmade. The computers linked to them for analysis were able to identify every standard sound that occurred there. Any foreign noise could be electronically filtered out and analyzed. In most cases, this passive listening system would be adequate protection. Its one weakness was an inability to detect exceptionally silent propulsion units like Donskoi's when other sounds were present.

Harry Coffin's initial determination upon taking command at Bangor was that the security methods appeared so excellent to the uninitiated that penetration of that security envelope by experts would be a definite possibility. That wasn't an unusual analysis given the admiral's thought processes. Placing himself in the other guy's position, Coffin would have found one of those genius-types who could come up with something totally unique to penetrate the ultimate security system. Sea bed hydrophones had been in business for a long time; nothing secret about them. Submarine nets had been great ideas the first half of the century; they were so much gauze now. Magnetic detectors were great at sea, but with all the junk dumped in the inland waters, they were more a tease. Innovation on the other guy's side was the answer and had to be met with similar imagination. Bernie Ryng's team was Coffin's answer.

Ryng and the three other men in his unit all took turns working with Bull, Chester and Ernie. From the early days of the team, Ryng's doctrine insisted that each of the dolphins must respond to each of the men. Man and animal had grown together in the process of learning to understand the other. But each man eventually became attached to one of the animals, and it seemed to work the same way for the dolphins. Once a trainer and a dolphin learned to work together in the advanced training stages, they became inseparable. The human qualities of dolphins astonished even the SEALs.

Ernie was the first of the dolphins to join the team, not quite full grown when Ryng decided to recruit him. Fishermen in San Diego reported how a particular dolphin often followed certain boats whose owners brought their children to sea with them. He would cavort around the boats like a circus animal entertaining both kids and crew alike, and always seemed to reappear each morning when the children were looking for him. There were times when some of the superstitious old-timers even felt the animal was herding schools toward their nets.

The dolphin attained permanent respect among the fishing fleet very early one morning when a younger child, a girl no more than five years old, fell over the side of her father's boat in rough weather. Life preservers instantly surrounded her. She could swim, but surprise and the shock of the cold water overwhelmed her. The friendly dolphin hadn't been seen that morning but was beside the child instantly, pushing her above the surface whenever breaking water engulfed her. While a boat was put over the side to retrieve her, the animal grabbed the rope on a life preserver in his mouth and brought it to the little girl.

Once she was pulled from the water, the dolphin remained beside the rubber boat as it headed back to the fisherman. Alongside the larger craft, in the lee of the waves, the animal rose and rested his beak momentarily on the side of the little boat. When the terrified youngster saw the dolphin eyeing her, she reached out tentatively. The dolphin remained alongside and opened his mouth as if he were smiling. Her first touch was tentative and she withdrew her hand quickly. But the dolphin seemed pleased and slid his head closer, allowing her to pat his silky-textured skin before he dove beneath the boat.

That day, when the boat returned to the harbor, the same dolphin escorted them to the pier. His picture was on the front pages across the country the next morning, with the little girl patting him.

When Bernie Ryng and the red-haired Tim Sullivan appeared at the fish piers a few days later in their wetsuits, the dolphin instantly decided they could be enjoyable playmates. Man and animal appeared to have recruited each other. On the third day, the dolphin followed them.

Over the next couple of weeks, two more of the animals attached themselves to Ryng's unit. It was never a matter of capturing the dolphins. Rather, the animals seemed to adopt them. A level of understanding between the mammals who lived in the water and those who tried to adapt themselves to that element gradually evolved.

Men cannot live with animals without naming them. Nor is the navy able to design a shore base without naming its streets after heros or famous battles. With King, Nimitz and Halsey streets nearby, named after three great admirals of World War Two, the dolphins subsequently became Ernie,

Chester and Bull. They even seemed to acquire the personality traits of their namesakes.

Ernie was at home with his trainers, the men he trusted implicitly. He was diffident toward others, imperious in nature, even displaying an evil temper when he experienced trouble learning something new. Eventually, he selected Tim Sullivan as his favorite and Tim became the only one he would play with.

Chester was the calmest of the three, hesitant to learn a new trick until he was perfectly sure of himself. He was the only one who never made a mistake, nor did he challenge the system by chasing off after bait fish when he was working.

Bull was the flamboyant one, playful, frequently tearing off after bait in the middle of an evolution, yet often the first one to perfect a new lesson if he wasn't distracted.

Tim Sullivan's relationship with Ernie was as close as a man and an animal could be. They protected each other. When Ernie was tangled in the lost trawl of a dragger, he became trapped completely as he fought to free himself. The struggle exhausted him quickly as the need for fresh air increased. Tim swam directly up to the terrified animal, using his cricket to attract Ernie's attention long enough to calm him down. Then he put an arm around the dolphin so it could feel his heart beating normally. The sense of another creature reacting that way calmed Ernie long enough to allow Tim to cut away the net. When the SEAL reached the surface, Ernie was floating, barely moving while he panted like a dog. The dolphin had been close to drowning.

It was just weeks later that another detachment of SEALs worked with Ryng's small unit in refresher survival training. The dolphins had been left to fish for themselves. The SEALs worked through one drill after another with their swim buddies. They went through loss of tank pressure, equipment casualties, life saving.

During the self-defense exercise, Ernie decided to return the favor of a few weeks before. As Tim Sullivan practiced his skills in fending off the attack of his buddy, Ernie appeared from nowhere, darting through the others involved in the same drill and slammed into the one engaged with Tim. A butt from a couple of hundred pounds of dolphin moving at full speed can be deadly. Tim escorted Ernie away from the group while the others helped the injured SEAL to the surface. Ernie's human qualities of loyalty remained unquestioned.

The two worked well as they began their first underwater patrol in the Hood Canal.

Donskoi, over the objections of Kolarov and Tikhvin, selected himself to activate the third mine. Duty on a mini sub was the ultimate challenge. He was sure of that. But he had come to the silent realization that even he possessed some limitations. One of them was idleness, especially when others were actively involved in what he wanted to do himself. He knew innately that it was time for extra vehicular activity.

Their tiny craft had grown smaller, or it seemed that way as each hour passed. Hardly noticeable that first day, the size had decreased significantly as the hours passed. It was as if some unknown physical law was operating. The entire craft, not just the tiny control area Donskoi occupied, was reduced in size. A giant hand seemed to be compressing the hull, but it was applying equal pressure throughout. The propulsion space seemed to be contracting at approximately the same rate as control, lock out, and tech/ops. Then there was the smell that was increasing even though the computers indicated the air scrubbers were working properly. While the designers had indicated that noticeable aromas would likely be human, Donskoi had mentioned two or three times to the others that he was sure there must be electrical wiring smoldering or mechanical equipment overheating.

Kolarov and Tikhvin checked and rechecked their spaces and came back with negative reports.

But the submarine was growing too small.

That was when Donskoi acknowledged, but only to himself, that he must have been suffering from a form of claustrophobia. It wasn't serious. Full-sized submarines actually did compress as they went to greater depths. You could even hear them creak and crack as the hull was compressed by the tremendous water pressure outside. But you couldn't see the spaces getting smaller!

They had actually been at their deepest when launched from *Gorki*. Since then, even when their skids were resting on the bottom, they were never more than half that deep.

So Donskoi had appointed himself as the next swimmer because it wouldn't do to have a captain who was developing a phobia, even if he did recognize it. He actually enjoyed the preparations in lock out, the feeling of the wetsuit, the weight of the tanks, going back over the checklist with Kolarov. And when pressure was equalized with the outside and the space began to fill with water, he felt a release that seemed to return the submarine to its original size.

Three mines, the extent of *Donskoi*'s initial payload, had been deposited in strategic locations: the base of the narrower channel near the bridge, off the breakwaters at South Point because they were sure the Tridents would stay away from the shallower east side of the channel, and near Vinland where the canal contracted considerably. The mines off the bridge and Vinland had been prepared for activation by Kolarov and Tikhvin. Donskoi had volunteered himself to prepare the one near the South Point breakwaters.

He had been in much colder water before. He remembered missions off the North Cape of Norway when they operated from submarines. It was winter and the water temperature had been bitter beyond belief. Back aboard the submarine he'd been absolutely sure he would succumb to his shivering before the water was evacuated from the pressure chamber. Those operating the safety valves for him seemed to take forever before he was finally released to the warmth of the ship.

This water was cool, nothing like Norway, but he would probably look forward to his return to the boat's warmth.

Right now the feel of the wetsuit against his skin and the temperature change was a welcome reward from the confinement.

There was little Donskoi needed for his mission. These mines had been designed for ease of preparation. He carried a detonator that would be screwed into the top of the mine and a timer that attached to the detonator. The timers had been sealed well before they left Petropavlovsk.

They were told that the politicians would worry about how to deal with the United States once the mines were in place. But Donskoi and his men would have to worry about deactivation if that became necessary. It all sounded absolutely plausible to the mini sub crews. There had never been any intention of being honest with them, to tell them that the mines were no better than decoys, that they were actually ineffective, or that such loyal men were but a ruse. That would have invited too many questions. Koniev had commented with a sardonic laugh that there would be no need for deactivation if the Tridents never again transited the Hood Canal, but that would be the closest they would ever come to understanding their role in the Koniev Abstract.

The mine was in about 180 feet of water. The bottom was primarily mud and the tide had left a light film over the dull, metal surface. Donskoi cleared it with a blast of compressed air from a tiny tank in his belt. When his light showed some mud still on the contact, he blew that out also. Bubbles and mud flowed back in his face, clouding his vision. The sound seemed loud and would have unnerved less skilled swimmers. Donskoi drifted backward and waited until the water cleared before continuing his work, slowly and precisely. He enjoyed the physical labor, luxuriating in the mental release experienced outside of the confines of the submarine.

Ernie raced through the dark water and into Tim Sullivan's vision like a torpedo, gliding so closely that the force of his passage rocked Tim like a boat on the surface. Then, the animal swam in circles before coming close enough to nudge the man. It was Ernie's way of saying he'd found something. For Tim, it was no different than the sign language employed by the SEALs on patrol. Ernie's action said all that was necessary.

Tim extracted one of the barbell-shaped locators from his belt and held it out. Ernie took it in his mouth and was gone in a flash. The SEAL swam in the direction the dolphin had taken, knowing there was no sense in trying to follow. That would be like trying to outrun a horse.

Moments later, Ernie returned without the locating device, apparently still agitated by his find. He knew that was only half the mission.

Sullivan switched on the activator—weak signal. *Maybe . . .* he thought *. . . just maybe Harry Coffin was right.* He considered providing another of the devices to the dolphin, then held it out to the animal. Always employ two of them in case one fails. Ernie was gone just as quickly as he'd appeared.

Donskoi was returning to the mini sub, swimming casually and enjoying his last moments of freedom, when he noticed a flash of something close by. Instinctively, unsure of what he'd seen, he grasped his knees against his chest, barely pulling himself into a ball before the animal hit him. *Dolphin* crossed his mind. He'd seen a dolphin butt a man and knew how seriously a swimmer could be injured. Men had been hit full force, their internal organs burst by the impact. Donskoi, anticipating danger, hadn't taken the hit full on. The animal grazed him, hitting the lower part of his body. Even so, it was akin to being thrown to the ground.

Sensing instinctively that it was a trained dolphin and would make another run at him, Donskoi tore the knife from his belt, again drawing his knees up. But this time his knife was in front of him.

When the animal came, it was from the side. Donskoi turned. He had to take the animal full on. No time to think, no chance for anything more than an instinctive reaction. He thrust the point of his knife in the dolphin's direction in both hands as the animal's form seemed to fill his faceplate. Donskoi's arms were rigid.

The impact hurled him backward, twisting his mask sideways, blinding him. Rubber ripped into his eye. He tasted the cold and salt as the water rushed down his throat. There was nothing he'd ever experienced, nothing he'd ever been told, that could be compared to this. His right arm felt as if it had been torn away at the shoulder. And there was fear, fear of the known—the dolphin, the water choking him—fear of the unknown . . . death.

Somehow, the dolphin was still there, thrashing wildly. But it wasn't making another run to butt him. They were both attached to the knife. And as long as Donskoi held on to the handle, he knew he would continue to be tossed about by this wildly flailing animal. If he let it off the knife, he surely would be a dead man.

Donskoi ripped blindly at his face mask with his left hand in an effort to see the animal that was thrashing at the end of his other arm. The first thing he was able to see was an object in the dolphin's mouth that fell free as it fought against the pain. Then he saw that his hand—the knife had disappeared inside the animal—was literally buried inside a gaping hole in its belly.

Donskoi grasped the weapon with both hands and fought back, twisting and ripping. The animal's weight aided him. Both hands, then his forearms, disappeared inside the cavity. He could feel the knife moving back toward the flippers, tearing at the viscera. Then he was blinded by the animal's blood. The water around them was a scarlet fluid.

He had no idea how long he was locked in battle with the dolphin, but when he felt its struggles gradually subside and he relaxed, he could sense that he had not taken a second breath of salt water.

Donskoi let his hands fall from the cavity. He felt for his mask and pushed it firmly over his face, almost choking as the water rushed back out of his air passages. He knew he could still be in trouble if he didn't get back to the sub. There had to be more damage to his equipment. As he struck out for the mini sub, he caught a glimpse of the dolphin's body drifting with the tidal current toward the bottom beneath a stream of blood.

Donskoi was pleased with himself. A potentially damaging problem had been taken care of. This incident once again justified years of training. His mission could continue.

Tim Sullivan knew instinctively there was a problem when Ernie didn't return as quickly as before. If any animal was habitual, it was Ernie. There was no chance he'd been sidetracked by a school of bait fish, not when he was working. Ernie'd been much too animated to be distracted when he'd returned the first time. Sullivan knew Ernie like he knew his own family. He trusted the animal with his life.

Tim swam ahead for a while through the dark, muddy water, using his cricket to call Ernie. That always worked. It was a given. But there was no response. He continued slowly, alert now for whatever Ernie had found. Tim was sure he would find the dolphin near whatever it was, sure he could help. But how long would it take? He switched on the homing device and followed the signal to the bottom where one of the locators lay in the mud. No response from the other. No Ernie. Tim continued his search although he sensed it was futile in the opaque water. No sign of the dolphin.

When he checked his pressure gauge, he saw the air would be running low soon. There was no choice but to head back to the boat. It was the first time since they'd been together that Tim ever returned without Ernie.

The dolphin's corpse was found at sunrise the next morning at Termination Point by a fisherman. When Tim came ashore from the boat as the sun was attempting to cut through the fog, he studied the bloated body closely. Then he gently rolled it to one side and studied the severed belly. The insides had already been torn away by other fish.

He imagined the struggle that Ernie must have put up before the knife ripped apart his insides. He understood the pain his friend must have experienced before the cold water flooded his lungs and choked away his life.

Tim turned away and stared over the Hood Canal and hoped that perhaps the shock had killed Ernie before the pain became too severe.

On the following day, Bull and Chester went out with the SEALs. Man and animal worked hard until the humans were exhausted, but they found no clue, no reason for Ernie's brutal death.

Harry Coffin's sixth sense told him to take additional precautions. No Tridents were to leave the piers at Bangor. No Tridents were to enter the Hood Canal.

Five

CORINNE AWOKE WITH A START.

The light!

Although there were low-hanging clouds in the early morning sky, it was already light outside. The birds had failed to do their job properly. She'd been depending on them to make sure she was awake. But, now that she thought about it, they had made some effort at first light. It must have been the clouds that discouraged them.

Lazy birds.

It was ten minutes after six. Corinne was supposed to establish contact ten minutes earlier. But it didn't matter, at least not enough to get excited about. They knew as well as she that she'd have contacted them on the dot if there was a reason.

Considering how tired she was when she went to bed and how pleasant the evening breeze felt flowing through her room all night, it had been a lousy sleep. The shadow animals that danced on the cottage walls just hours before, as her father's had done when she was a little girl, followed into her dreams. The rabbit ears that became periscopes had turned into strange animals that grew to enormous sizes as she slept. They'd been in the woods. She knew that because she could hear them rustling. Then they crept from the trees behind the cottage, paced about nervously outside, rose snorting on their haunches to peer through the screens, suffused the air with their hideous breath, and eventually materialized inside to pad sullenly about the rooms. They did not attack—but they would occasionally pause to stare at her through blank eyes.

It was not a continuous sequence. There is never anything logical in a dream world. Corinne awoke any number of times. On occasion, she rose from bed and moved from room to room to clear her mind. Once, she poured herself a glass of wine but that only seemed to magnify the beasts when she fell asleep again. Another time, she fixed a cup of coffee. That was after she was sure she could smell their breath pervading the cottage.

Corinne wasn't afraid. Rather, she was angry with herself.

It seemed now as if she'd been alone all her life. She was comfortable with that. Fear was a sensation experienced by those who had no confidence in themselves. Such people were open to subterfuge, to an inner coercion. They deserved that wall of fear surrounding them.

What was there about her—or was it that *mystic* Russian, the submariner, whom they spoke of in such roundabout ways—that generated this anxiety? Now this was a man she knew she would give a great deal to meet. She considered her handlers for a moment, all male, self-important, normally evasive in their comments, unnecessarily furtive considering how little danger they faced in peaceful Vancouver. How much would it take to make them run for cover? They really weren't sure how to treat her. Perhaps they were even a bit intimidated by her because she had no fear. More likely they were cautious only because she was a woman.

Men were afraid of women who used their femininity for personal gain. Yet her handlers had used her for such mundane purposes up to now—entertaining men mostly. There had been no effort on her part to inquire what benefit these men might offer to her handlers and they hadn't taken the trouble to tell her. In a way, it was comfortable work, if one could call it work. Corinne enjoyed it most of the time because many of the men were in powerful positions. That made them appealing, not so much physically as intellectually, although she did rather enjoy the sexual aspects with the right ones. She never once considered what she was doing could be thought of as immoral. No money ever exchanged hands. She was in an unusual branch of intelligence that demanded talents well beyond the physical abilities of her peers. Her handlers compensated her well for her efforts and she was comfortable in knowing that she was making a contribution to the international effort. Often, the job was fun and she thoroughly enjoyed herself.

Her island was a new experience, certainly welcome as a change of pace. It meant they trusted her now more than ever. No one was there to check on her activities. They acknowledged her intelligence, spending just a short time explaining how to operate the radio. The only requirement was to check in at six each morning, most likely to prove she was still alive. *And if she didn't do so right now, they'd certainly wonder.*

The radio check-in was simple. A few code words. No questions why she was late. They trusted her. *They ought to.*

Breakfast was what she needed. When a body felt like hers, the muscles tight and achy after a night of tossing and turning, it had to be fed. Start on the inside and work out—that's what Ken had always said. But he never cared much about what he ate. Just fueled the engine, kept it running. He was a believer in sustenance, quantity rather than quality . . .

Ken . . .

Had she been thinking about him when she fell asleep? Whenever that happened, less now than in the past, she could almost always depend on a rough night.

Corinne sipped a glass of orange juice while she scrambled some eggs. No, it wasn't Ken, at least she had no memory of him in her dreams. It seemed to be this someone who might—and they only said *might*—contact her on the radio. And if he did, he would be in trouble. He remained as shadowy as Ken had become. But Ken was of the past. He would never return. This submariner represented the future —perhaps her destiny?

After thirteen years, she could still remember Ken up to the day he died. But his face wasn't as clear as it used to be. Sometimes she had to get out his picture to remember exactly, to fill in the shadowy areas.

This other man—she didn't even have a name—had no features to speak of. Maybe she'd unconsciously filled them in with Ken's likeness. If she had, she didn't remember but that would have contributed to making sleep difficult.

The eggs and the English muffins tasted wonderful. The handlers had found the New Orleans coffee she loved, the kind with chicory. They even provided real cream to sweeten it. Yes, they had been good about providing everything she asked for.

The food did the trick, or most of it. Ken had been right about that, *start on the inside*. Corinne pushed back from the table and stretched, pointing her toes straight out. Her muscles loved it. She forced her arms as far behind her back as possible and arched her shoulders like a cat.

Exercise. That's what she needed. The hell with the dishes. A splash in that icy water would make everything right with the world again. Corinne strolled outside in her bare feet enjoying the sensation of the chill morning dew awakening her toes. She followed the path down to the shore, peering down cautiously to avoid the thorns she was sure must be there.

A low fog hung over the water but it was low enough directly in front of her so she was still able to see the higher parts of the bigger island across the way. The invisible thrum of distant boat engines echoed through the heavy air but it would have been impossible to see them even if they were as close as twenty yards.

Corinne was wearing a pullover bathrobe which she hung on the nearby branch of a gnarled madrona tree. The water was even colder than she'd expected as she eased in over her ankles, and the smooth, slippery stones on the bottom made movement difficult. But this was exactly what she'd been looking for. That masochistic numbness would wake up her body, soften the last of the tight muscles, put everything in the proper perspective. The shoreline dropped off quickly and she dove straight out. Fifty yards out and back would have been perfect, but the water was too bitter. She could feel her limbs ache from the cold and her breathing was constricted.

Corinne turned quickly in the water and stumbled back ashore over the loose stones. She grabbed the bathrobe as she ran by and flipped it over her shoulder. No need to cover up. Just heat some water and get into that spartan shower in the cottage. That would complete the circle—taking care of the outside after she'd satisfied the inside . . . just like Ken said . . .

And she did feel like a new person when she began to towel off. It was much like recovering from a hangover.

When was the last time she had been so cold? It had been so . . . so long ago that she squeezed her eyes shut, as tight as she could to erase it from her mind. It was an unconscious reaction at first, then she was aware of why she had done it. That had been the low point of her relationship with Ken. It was so cold that single winter they had with Cory, colder than anyone around Oxford could remember, and the snow was the worst in memory.

Cory was just a few months old. Friends had loaned blankets to wrap her in, but no one they knew had money. There was supposedly steam heat in their old building but none of the flats were ever really warm. When the wind howled down across the Midlands, the building shook and a careless piece of paper on the floor would actually flutter. The radiators would rattle and wheeze and bang but there was never enough steam pressure to take off coats when they weren't in bed.

"Ken, I want to get out of here." She might have taken it if just the two of them were there, but not with Cory. "I want all three of us to get out while we're still healthy."

"Where would we go? There's nothing better for what we're paying."

"Anywhere there's heat." Corinne remembered her words as if she were reading them out of a book. And she was. The pages were turning in her mind and they contained pictures and words that mirrored a pain she knew would never vanish.

"For God's sakes, Corinne, do you want to become a Tory? Open a checking account? Hire a maid? What do you think our relatives did before anyone ever thought about central heating?"

"I don't give a shit about our relatives," she answered vehemently. "I only care about here and now, you son of a bitch." She could still see his head jerk back as if he'd been slapped. "Don't you care about Cory? What if she gets pneumonia and dies?"

"Children have done that through the ages," he answered derisively. "They call it the survival of the fittest. She's tough," he concluded more quietly, unable to look her in the eye.

"She's got diarrhea. Every time I change her, she starts to shiver and get goose bumps. I don't give a shit about your relatives, your revolutionaries, your terrorists or any of the assholes who love to suffer for their goddamn causes." Her voice had grown shrill, so close to the edge. "I just care about Cory getting enough decent food to eat so she can learn how to shit again, and I just care about living somewhere she has a chance to be warm."

The anger and the shouting had gone on until Ken stomped out of the flat. When he came back, he said, "Cory'll have enough to eat and she'll be warm. Let's forget it." Then he smiled and gave her that little boy look she'd fallen in love with.

Within an hour, a friend arrived with a bag filled with baby formula and the strained foods she'd been told Cory would need at her age. It was less than another hour later that the radiators began to bang louder than ever before. By the time the building was warm, even with the wind still fluttering the paper on the floor, she knew that the food was stolen and that the landlord and his family were in fear for their lives. But it was what Cory needed and it didn't matter to Corinne that to get it they'd abused a tiny part of the system they were fighting.

After dressing, Corinne walked out the front door of her island cottage into a sun that was burning hazily through the fog. The air was still damp in the refracted sunlight and the sharp smell of spruce needles tickled her nose. A sunbeam accentuated the deep green of a clump of holly that grew wild on the island. Corinne hugged herself tightly, still feeling the cold of that long-ago flat.

There was no way you could fall out of love with Ken, not if he remained a symbol of the coming revolution, whatever that meant . . . not if he could charm your pants off no matter how mad you got with him. That was their last winter together—Cory's only winter—but Corinne was never that cold again.

She continued to hug herself tightly against that distant British winter as she sat down on the front steps of the cottage, squeezing so hard her knuckles grew white and she could see the marks forming on the bare skin of her upper arms. *You can't let go! Can you?* The accusation came from deep within and echoed again and again through her head. It was so hard to let go, even after you managed to tear your eyes away from the pages of that book in your mind and slam the covers shut . . . so hard.

"You made a new world for yourself!" she shouted out loud at the same time she released the grip on her arms. Her skin was a deathly pale where her fingers had cut off the blood. "Remember what you did," she added more softly. "Remember. That's when you learned just how tough you were, lady."

Corinne had gotten herself a clerk's position in a bookstore, and settled in a tiny, single room with a toilet down the hall. She also finished the requirements for her degree. None of those decisions were hard ones—you can maintain your beliefs and take advantage of the system at the same time. There was plenty more of her life left to be a rebel, and Corinne Foxe had made a solemn promise to herself that she would never be cold again, not like that winter with Ken and Cory.

Over a period of time, friends, even good ones, gradually distance themselves from people in Corinne's situation, and their group was no different. After all, they were more Ken's friends than her own. Some tired of the privations that were the privilege of the rebel. A few drifted to other universities. Others seemed to disappear entirely from the face of the earth. It could have been that they were fated to do so like Ken and Cory, or it could have been the result of their own crimes, or drugs, or perhaps just an inability to sustain themselves.

That was how she learned the pleasures of independence. She thoroughly enjoyed the Corinne who had enough money to buy decent clothes, enough food to waste, and enough time to read the books she'd only learned about at the university. She even dabbled briefly with some Communist Party meetings because she thought Ken might have been pleased with that. But those meetings were boring in comparison to the old days. While their goals were similar, Party methods as practiced in England would take forever.

She had, however, been recognized—and appreciated.

"We have our ways," she murmured gruffly with a slight smile, finding the expression just as amusing on this island as it had been years before. That wasn't exactly what the one called Roberts had said to her in Vancouver, but it was something like that. She enjoyed rolling those words over in her mind—*we have our ways*—with a twisted Peter Lorre accent. Yes, they had their ways, but the ones whom she knew in England were so serious . . . so passive. They never would have hinted at that. Even as communists, they remained too British to deviate far from accepted political decorum.

They, the few who'd been trained overseas, knew she wasn't happy with the meetings because her attendance declined until she rarely put in an appearance. Much later they would explain, not caring that it was just an excuse, that those gatherings were a sort of melting pot of possibilities. That was where they found people like her who possessed genuine abilities to contribute.

She enjoyed their methods, more for the humor she saw in their seriousness about everything they did. Later she would learn that these self-important individuals were nothing but minor players who by some sort of dumb luck sorted out people like Corinne who would eventually be taken away from them. They never realized that they accomplished little, that they were only a source for the talented few like her.

It must have been her determination to remain politely aloof to the men's advances that appealed most to the senior people. They must have been testing her in their awkward way. She couldn't remember how many different ones made fumbling attempts to seduce her, but there was a point early on that she knew that such ineptness had to be a way of testing her though she had no idea why.

How many years was it before she was fully trusted? Five? Six? More? The years seemed to run together as she progressed through a series of better paying jobs. They had long ago moved her out of those local meetings.

But she remembered distinctly that blustery, rainy day in Brighton and she was thankful that the gentleman who met her at the train from London wanted to enjoy a casual lunch. There had been no way of knowing that he was the KGB's senior man in England. That was one thing they did efficiently, cover themselves and their contacts well. You never knew what was happening, or with whom, until you put in your appearance. Neat. Secure. So efficient at the upper level.

She never knew his full name—David was what he called himself—but he seemed more American than Russian. He ordered a dry gin martini for himself, then sent it back for more ice, just like an American. He also returned a steak to the kitchen because it wasn't red enough for his tastes. Did he really enjoy these things that way or was it just another backhanded way of making the British think less of the Americans? That was the way the good ones operated, never an indication that they might be Russian.

David was so smooth. Cocktails before lunch. Small talk. Wine with their meal and more small talk. Before dessert, he knew everything he could have possibly wanted to know about her and she was aware that the only thing she knew about him was that his name wasn't David. She commented on that over coffee and he smiled and said that if she was so good at recognizing his cover then she ought to be able to create the same thing for herself. He ordered some cognac before suggesting that they go to bed together, and he was thoroughly delighted with the charm she employed to turn him down as they cradled their snifters.

It was only later in London, and on her own terms, that she slept with this man called David, and then she insisted on a hotel rather than either of their places. That was how it was supposed to be done if one intended to maintain privacy. It also raised her confidence when she realized that it was he, not her, who had given in.

Corinne knew more about David in six weeks than anyone he had ever come in contact with before. He had no idea that he ever revealed so much of himself but he was delighted when she explained how she had gathered her data patiently over numerous evenings—in bed. The idea that she could by sheer cunning derive information from another person without their ever realizing it wasn't apparent to Corinne until David. At that point, she decided that her native intelligence would be forever wasted in the dull jobs that were available to her even with a degree. And when she realized she possessed enough information on David to "hang him out to dry" as he later put it, Corinne was determined to start a new life similar to David's. She was a confirmed loner now and she wanted to do something to upset the staid, materialistic world she and Ken had hated so much.

David's greatest concern was that she possessed so much talent that he and Corinne wouldn't be able to maintain this relationship forever. And when she rolled over on top of him and explained that that was exactly what he should have known when he allowed himself to be trapped like this, David knew he had created a superior agent—*his loss, the KGB's gain!*

There had never been any doubt about selecting Tarantsev as the other officer-in-charge of the mini subs. He had been the brightest of those few who eventually were selected for the miniature submarine program. Like Donskoi, he was also physically tough and hardened to the realities of Spetznaz training though he never possessed the tendency toward cruelty the other man took for granted.

Once the students reached the stage where they could work with the automated trainers, they were transferred to the secret installation on Kotlin Island near Leningrad. Koniev had supervised the design of the trainers, insisting on the most complex programs for simulated missions.

The Baltic became the computer's playground. Problems encountered by the earlier mini subs were included along with ideas generated by existing submarine captains. Trainees were expected to be overwhelmed. Tarantsev, however, displayed an uncanny ability to pilot the imaginary craft through a series of realistically simulated missions. He was a natural at navigation, displaying an uncanny ability to solve the problems that increased in difficulty during each session.

That was the reason he had been chosen as the alternate mini-sub commander, and was ordered to gather additional intelligence in Puget Sound, possibly even serve as a decoy if Donskoi ran into trouble. Koniev, though readily acknowledging to both men that trapping the Tridents in Bangor was more critical, still emphasized the importance of Tarantsev's operation. It would prove the efficacy of the miniature submarine program. And it was equally meaningful to show that one of these tiny craft could navigate through one of the busiest waterways in the world—Puget Sound. *Tarantsev would be a pioneer!* It was such a convincing argument that no one would have believed that Koniev was creating a brilliant ruse with both Donskoi and Tarantsev to cover his ultimate objective.

The mini subs could have launched together. They'd practiced the maneuver off Petropavlovsk successfully. But Koniev decided against such a tactic unless there was an emergency. They were not offensive weapons as such. They were designed for covert operations. In his opinion, two of them operating together doubled the possibility of detection. There were two missions, he announced, that would establish the quality of their system. Therefore, they would operate separately. His reasoning sounded so logical that the morale aboard *Gorki,* and among the two mini-sub crews, had never been higher.

One hour after Donskoi piloted his craft away from *Gorki,* Andrei Tarantsev departed the area. He was the opposite of the other man—dark hair and eyes, slender, nondescript features. Tarantsev had survived the same training as Donskoi and he was equally deadly, but he didn't enjoy the killing as the other man did. He was a thinker who rarely spoke and then only when he required a specific answer he was unable to obtain on his own.

Tarantsev was bubbling with pride as he set course for Admiralty Head on Whidby Island. Everything he'd encountered in the trainers now became a reality and he met each situation head on—the heavy merchant traffic on the surface, the noise and confusion of operating in a congested environment, even the fear of claustrophobia that comes with the darkness of the mini sub's operating envelope.

As he turned southeast down Admiralty Inlet, following much the same track as Donskoi, Tarantsev quite suddenly realized how pleased he was with himself. His ability to absorb the lessons of his training so well were now justified. Captain Koniev had insisted that he possessed the talent from the very beginning—*and he'd been correct.*

Tarantsev knew he really was flying as he maneuvered down Admiralty Inlet. His speed may have been slow but the sensation was no different. He experimented with minor course and speed changes and gloried in the sensation. He may not have been "pulling G's" but he was operating his own craft in a three dimensional environment and, at the same time, experiencing the added thrill of invisibility. While his computer was able to classify and display his enemy, *none of them had any idea that he was even there.* He was like a shadowy matador for his quarry had no idea of his existence, yet his sword could plunge whenever he chose.

As Tarantsev passed Point No Point to starboard, a few miles beyond the Hood Canal entrance, he turned almost due south and hugged the western coastline of Puget Sound as he approached Seattle. There was no possible way either he or Koniev could have anticipated what he would encounter.

USS *Kinkaid* slipped out of the narrow channel off Orchard Point and eased around to an easterly heading, pointing her sleek bow in the direction of Seattle, whose tall downtown buildings stood out through a light morning haze across Puget Sound. This was her initial shakedown after six months in the naval shipyard in Bremerton, and her captain, Hal Davis, felt exactly like a kid with his first bicycle. He'd assumed command while *Kinkaid* was on the blocks in the yard so now the least motion of the deck under his feet was a thrill. She was *his ship*.

With her bow in line with the Alki Point standpipe on the opposite shoreline, *Kinkaid* slid into the northbound traffic lane before turning almost directly north. The early morning sun had now burned most of the haze off the Sound and the whistles and horns of the merchant ships and scurrying ferries had died away to be replaced by screaming gulls searching for their morning breakfast.

Passing ships saw a handsome destroyer, freshly painted and riding higher in the water than usual without her full load of ammunition and fuel. Inside, a combination of sailors and shipyard workers prepared for a variety of tests on engineering and electronic equipment that was either new or just overhauled.

This was only a day trip but Davis knew he would never leave the bridge. They would proceed up Puget Sound experimenting with their new equipment, then run the necessary tests in the open spaces of the Strait of Juan de Fuca before returning to Bremerton at the end of the day. They would spend no more than twelve hours away from the pier but that was enough for their first time. His ship would show her stuff under his command and that knowledge created a heady sensation.

After passing Seattle to starboard and watching the buildings decrease in size until only the suburbs were clearly visible, Davis increased his speed. A steady stream of reports came to him on the bridge as each piece of equipment tested out until he gave up keeping a mental list. It was much more fun getting the feel of how his ship maneuvered.

He had no memory of when the request to light off the sonar came up, but he did hear the initial report when the huge system housed in the bow was reported functioning normally. Everything seemed to be operating exactly as advertised—a nice way to start out.

"Bridge, this is sonar. We have a contact . . . bearing three three zero . . . range about five five hundred yards, closing."

Ridiculous.

Yet all eyes on the bridge stared off the port bow in the general direction sonar indicated.

"Sonar," the Officer of the Deck (OOD), Jack Kirby, responded, "you've probably got an inbound fishing boat around that bearing."

"Negative, bridge. This isn't the fishing boat. We've got that separated from this contact."

Hal Davis reached forward from his captain's chair and pushed the button for sonar. "Chief, you've probably got some bottom return there. We hold Apple Cove Point on that general bearing and the chart does show tidal rips there."

"We're aware of that, Captain. Believe me, this is a contact. Bearing now is about three one five, about four thousand yards, and it's showing me every indication that it's a submarine, although it's not like anything I've run into in my career."

"Chief," Davis answered with good humor, "submarines are required to run on the surface in this area. Maybe the shipyard's given you a glitch in the equipment to play with."

"Captain, you've got to believe me. I've got a target I'd classify as a submarine and it's inbound on almost a reciprocal course to our own. It's going to be running down our port side shortly."

"Give me another range and bearing, chief," the captain called down a minute later. Davis turned to the quartermaster. "Plot this one on the chart," he said as he climbed out of his chair and moved over to the chart table.

"Two niner zero, two thousand," came the voice from sonar.

Davis looked at the spot on the chart. It was directly off the flashing light on Apple Cove Point, but it was also well within the southbound traffic lane. The fishing boat had already passed down *Kinkaid's* beam. "Clear bearing, sonar."

"It's going to pass our beam at about fifteen hundred yards, Captain. Recommend we come about to prosecute."

Davis looked up in puzzlement. *Prosecute!* In the Puget Sound traffic lanes? With no weapons?

There was nothing in the southbound lane other than the fishing boat that had just passed by. Two merchants and some random fishermen were a good distance away and presented no problem. He stepped out on the bridge wing and looked astern. A couple of freighters were far enough back that he wouldn't disturb them.

What the hell.

"Left full rudder," Davis called out to Jack Kirby. "Let's see what we come up with."

It was eerie. Tarantsev had no idea why any sonar, particularly one so powerful, would be operating in the Puget Sound shipping lanes. There was no reason for it. At first, he was frightened by the sound. The incessant, perfectly measured pinging echoing through the tiny submarine was a complete shock. It was as if someone suddenly appeared behind you in an empty, closed room and tapped you on the shoulder. The first tap was a shock; you finally got used to the ensuing ones. The reactions from Tupolev, his copilot and weapons specialist, and Osipenko, the engineer, were no different.

"What the hell . . . ?"

"Andrei, what's wrong?"

Both comments came as high-pitched shouts. Like Tarantsev, they were also in that empty room and felt that pressure on their shoulders. They, too, were frightened by the unexpected. Yet none of the three was a coward. Each had already proven that he could survive more than most men. But it was a powerful sonar and the intense sound seemed to go right through the tiny craft.

PING.

The powerful sound struck their hull then reverberated through the submarine like a BB in a tin can. But it was no longer unexpected. There was no doubt it was a ship's sonar. They'd experienced plenty of those before. But why was it operating in the confines of Puget Sound? Could someone know . . . ?

"Pay no attention . . ." Tarantsev began. No, that was stupid. "No need to be concerned yet. They don't . . . they can't have us. More likely, someone is testing their equipment." He automatically punched the proper buttons for the computer to locate the source.

"You don't want to stop?" Tupolev ventured.

PING.

"Not yet. They must think they have a wreck, or maybe something else on the bottom. No reason for them to decide otherwise." Tarantsev's voice was firm and positive but he wasn't so sure he believed what he was telling them.

PING.

It was a powerful, high frequency sonar. Odd that it would be used in an area like this, Tarantsev thought, frowning to himself. There was no problem isolating the source. His computer was tracking it for course and speed.

Each succeeding sound transmission was as nerve-wracking as the last but there was no indication that the source was turning in their direction. More than likely, this was a chance encounter.

"What's the makeup of the bottom in this area?" Tarantsev asked his copilot.

"Mud everywhere," Tupolev answered. "There's fast shoaling water off to starboard according to the chart, along with tidal rips. Probably heavy current there."

"We'll stay on course unless he . . ." A red light blinked over the dials that displayed the track of the surface ship pinging on them. The computer instantly reported the change.

"Contact's changing course," Tupolev barked. "He's closing."

Tarantsev already was turning the wheel. The mini sub banked slightly as she headed toward land. "He'll lose us in the bottom return from the shallower water."

The hydraulic skids were deployed in twenty fathoms of water and they settled gently onto a combination of hard sand and mud shoal packed by the tidal currents. Osipenko secured any equipment that might radiate enough sound to give away their position. Then they waited, conversing softly among themselves as the pinging ship came in their direction.

They felt secure once again. The surface ship could not take the chance of entering the shallower water nor would her sonar be effective there. Obviously, the captain would halt the active sonar and attempt to listen for whatever their target might be. Tarantsev knew there was no way they could be detected.

Hal Davis studied the coastline around Apple Cove Point. *The first day at sea aboard his new command and the land was rushing toward him at an alarming rate.* "What have you got, chief?"

"Bottom return, Captain. Mush all over the screen. We're zapping lots of oysters and that's about all."

"Go silent," Davis ordered. "And whatever you're looking for, you better find it super quick. I'm not about to take us ashore to pick apples, chief, and from up here that's what it looks like we're going to be doing in the next few minutes."

"Quiet as a mouse down there," was the only response.

Davis turned *Kinkaid* down the landward side of the southbound traffic lane, skirting the shoal water by no more than a few hundred yards. He reduced speed, then he waited. Nothing from sonar. Then he stopped his engines altogether.

"What gives, chief?" Davis asked impatiently, when he could wait no longer. "Everybody ashore is going to think I'm crazy. Help me."

"Both of us are crazy then, Captain. I got nothing anymore. Whatever we had has disappeared. Nothing. Zip. Squat. Zero. Gonzo," he concluded. "But I also have it all on tape. So if they decide you're crazy, there's going to be two of us in the same boat."

"Come on up to the bridge, chief, and help me prepare this message. I think the admiral's going to want to send a helo to pick up that tape." Davis was absolutely sure now he hadn't wasted his time with a ghost.

When his computer indicated that the contact was moving off to the north, Tarantsev ordered Osipenko to bring all his equipment back on line. In a matter of minutes, the skids were retracted and they were underway.

Nothing was said for the next few minutes. The ship's sonar was once again pinging but it was also drawing away to the north. Then Tupolev ventured, "Do you think they'll forget us?"

"Impossible. If they came after us, someone on that ship must have developed a plot. I think we'll find a secure location to hide. After dark, we'll establish contact with Captain Koniev. He may want to alter our orders."

Tarantsev decided on a spot north of Bainbridge Island where there was sharply shoaling water, a place where few boats would venture. His Exxon roadmap showed no paved road in the area and an Indian reservation on the mainland to the west. There shouldn't be anyone there to notice them when they poked their antenna above the surface to contact Koniev.

Six

Ryng's eyes swept the room quickly. So early in the morning and look at them. *Horsepower!* Too damn much of it. They must have stayed awake all night just to get their butts to Bangor so early. There was enough gold on all those shoulder boards to screw up everything. He looked at the lieutenant with the gold braided loop attached to his shoulder. *A goddamn admiral's aide.* You wouldn't find someone like that hanging around with the SEALs. *I wonder if the lieutenant carries toilet paper in that briefcase to wipe the admiral's ass with.*

Harry Coffin was just fine for an admiral. He was the type who could handle any problem that came near him. Why the hell did they have to screw up a good thing and send all these admirals and captains and commanders in? The best way—the only way—to counter whatever was happening around Puget Sound was to act like you weren't paying any attention to it. If the bad guys were led to believe they were going to be able to operate without anyone's noticing, they'd keep right on at whatever they were after. That was how you nailed them—sometimes it took longer than you anticipated, or you just got one at a time—when they weren't looking over their shoulders. But bring in all these bodies, *then watch everything turn to shit.*

Quietly—that was the way Bernie Ryng preferred to operate. Don't let anyone know the SEALs were involved. Play everything by ear, go with the wind. The minute Ryng noted a change of any kind during a mission, he altered his plans. That's why he was a survivor. Never give the other guy a second chance. And, if you did something dumb like that, don't bitch about the consequences.

In a way, he felt odd about this mission. Here he was in Bangor, assigned to sniff out another guy's covert operation and he definitely had a strange feeling about it. It had always been Bernie Ryng who planned and led covert ops in the past and he'd been comfortable being the aggressor. Counteracting his specialty was something new, but Harry Coffin had decided that in this case the best defense against the unknown was a SEAL.

Ryng looked up as one voice rose over the others. A vice admiral from Washington held the attention of the rear admirals from the west coast. He'd been sent to react to *Kinkaid*'s submarine contact. His idea was saturation. Fill the waters of the Strait and Puget Sound with destroyers and frigates and submarines. Toss in a helicopter squadron to work with them. Outside of three days, he claimed, anything larger than a razor clam would be identified and tracked and nothing could move without his knowing about it.

The only trouble, Admiral, Ryng said to nobody but himself, *is that if the bad guys are half as good as I think they are, they'd make themselves scarce half an hour after your task force started operating. And they'd wait you out.*

There was only one mistake that they'd made—killing Ernie—and it was likely in self-defense. Give that one the benefit of the doubt. But it meant there were swimmers and that convinced Ryng that this admiral was pissing up a rope. The only thing Ryng would have done differently was make sure the dolphin's body never turned up like it had this morning. But that could happen to anyone. He could conceive of any number of situations where the same thing might have happened to him. He wasn't about to let on to any of the brass about Ernie. Then they'd come up with a hundred and one ideas why the SEALs' security was inadequate and then his job would be almost impossible.

And that submarine yesterday, that was just pure, dumb luck on that destroyer captain's part. No submarine would ever expect a destroyer pinging in those waters. *If that was in fact a submarine.* Ryng wondered about that. Yet it appeared to be a sub to the sonar chief on *Kinkaid.* It sounded like one to those experts they'd brought in to analyze the tapes. And it acted like one when it disappeared so quickly. But what the hell would an unidentified submarine be doing in Puget Sound only ten miles from Seattle? It certainly wasn't a full-size one . . . couldn't have been . . .

Couldn't have been!

No, it couldn't have been a full-size submarine with all the trimmings. And it couldn't have gotten here under its own power either. He thought back to Harry Coffin's mention yesterday of an intelligence briefing. The CIA knew about a new Soviet submarine class designed around their miniature submarine program. At least one of them had apparently been built at Admiralty Shipyard under superb security. No one had gotten wind of it until it was already a done deal. When the Russians were really motivated, they could make something disappear behind a curtain of silence. Its existence was at first a rumor, then an actuality after confirmation by informants, finally an object in a high resolution photograph after arriving in Murmansk. And that was the last clear evidence of its existence.

That's what *Kinkaid*'s contact had to be, one of the little fellas. Somehow, they'd reappeared right where Coffin's CIA contact thought they might. And that mother ship had to be nearby, and she had to have carried in one or more mini subs. She had to be around to provide services—food, weapons, crew recharging for that matter. No one could continue in one of those tiny things forever. Crew efficiency would drop radically if they couldn't be properly rested.

But what the hell was a mini sub doing heading toward Seattle, or Bremerton for that matter? There wasn't anything to get the Russians terribly excited around Puget

Sound . . . at least not like the Trident submarine base at Bangor.

The vice admiral, who still held the floor by virtue of seniority and voice, was anticipating the damages that could be inflicted on the yard at Bremerton, even to the Boeing plant. Torpedos, short range missiles, whatever possibility came to the speaker's mind compounded the threat. *I'll bet he's doing exactly what he's expected to be doing,* Ryng thought, *worrying about the rabbit.*

Harry Coffin lurked in the back of the crowd, glancing around the room as if he needed an excuse to disappear. Ryng eased over and put a hand on his shoulder. "Admiral, before things get too well organized around here, I think you and I have to get back to worrying about your submarines. I don't like the idea of getting drawn away from the target."

Coffin was the one who'd initiated the security expansion in the first place but he'd done it his way, quietly, no muss or fuss. He was aware of *Gorki's* potential, he understood from his contact that she'd left Petropavlovsk undetected, and he'd been reminded time and again by the Pentagon that the Soviets' overwhelming concern was the Trident missile threat. Once that Trident was at sea, the Russians were at its mercy because they didn't have the vaguest idea where it would turn up. The navy had taught Harry Coffin that a wise commander is one who anticipates a problem and takes the necessary precautions. The admiral had taken that to heart. His answer had been Bernie Ryng.

"They're smarter than we ever give them credit for, Admiral, and I'm not just imagining that. If they hadn't been forced to kill that dolphin, the two of us would probably be just as worried about that submarine contact in Puget Sound as all the brass are. But I don't think you can give me one good reason why they'd be risking everything to mess around with a few surface ships and some old submarines over in Bremerton, not when they're spending all their time at the conference tables worrying about our Tridents."

"That's what's been in the back of my mind, too, especially after listening to all that noise in there." Coffin jerked his head in the direction of the conference room. "But you got to remember that a lot of those people haven't had any potential for some real activity like this for a long time, so they want to justify their budgets."

"That Russian submarine, whatever its name was—the new one you told me about—has to be out there." Ryng waved toward the north. "For Christ's sake, that swimmer who nailed Ernie didn't come from the shore and he didn't paddle a kayak in from the Pacific Ocean either. I'm willing to bet my nuts that he came from one of those mini subs we've been told about."

"The one *Kinkaid* picked up?"

"Could be, I suppose, though I wouldn't put money on it. But we should be spending a lot less time worrying about the smoke and concentrate on the fire. Why the hell waste time over in the Sound when our main concern should be the Tridents?"

Coffin shrugged. "Beats me. Unless, of course, the idea is to create all the noise that's coming out of that room."

"I realize that guy in there's a vice admiral and he wants us all to recognize his stars, but he's creating confusion. Do you have a line to his boss so we can calm him down or have those stars been on his uniform too long?"

"Better than that, Bernie. But leave senior admirals alone. I'll tell you what we're going to do." Harry Coffin was going to protect his Tridents and he was going to use Ryng exactly as he'd originally intended.

The night before Admiral Coffin's Trident base had been overrun with brass, Nicholas Koniev had listened intently to the voice transmission from Tarantsev. It was perfectly disciplined, as it should be. He gave his coordinates first— near the northwest corner of Bainbridge Island. The quartermaster plotted the position on the chart. Shoal water. Few navigational aides. No commercial traffic. Koniev studied the road map next to the chart. The only town of any size was a village on the Port Madison Indian Reservation, Suquamish, and there were less than fifteen hundred residents. Shouldn't be any problems there as far as security was concerned.

Koniev waited patiently for the details on the condition of the submarine and the crew to be concluded. That was the way they had all been trained to report unless there was a dire emergency. It was essential to discipline, perhaps even survival.

But why was Tarantsev there?

Their communications were considered as secure as could be. They employed short range voice, although there was always the possibility that someone could stop on that frequency by mistake. But it was also electronically garbled on transmission and reconstructed only by the receiver on board *Gorki*.

Finally Tarantsev explained his pursuit by the American destroyer. The surface ship had broken off the search because the mini sub knew enough to disappear. But Tarantsev concluded he'd obviously been tracked and held long enough to be classified as suspicious and that required this report. Such an occurrence also required a decision from Koniev concerning any alterations to the mission.

Koniev considered Tarantsev's situation. His objective was to draw American attention away from the Hood Canal, perhaps even toward Bremerton, but not this soon. He wasn't quite ready. But would there be an advantage to moving ahead now, or should Tarantsev be cautioned to remain hidden? Certainly everyone involved in the mission understood the stated objective was paramount, and Koniev didn't want anyone thinking differently. Beyond a few senior officers in the Kremlin, not a soul realized that the actual purpose was completely different, that Tarantsev was expendable.

There wasn't enough information to make a decision. Although he wanted to limit use of the radio, it was necessary to establish contact with his shore base intelligence system. Tarantsev was ordered to remain on the bottom and reestablish contact the next evening.

Koniev passed the remaining moments before establishing contact with his land base wondering if Donksoi might contact him. There was no need if his mission had been accomplished. Koniev had explained he wanted to limit radio contact to absolute emergencies. Donskoi and Tarantsev were expected to think for themselves. If they could complete their mission, then they could save reports on their problems until they returned to the mother ship. Koniev was relieved that Donskoi remained silent.

At exactly midnight, Koniev shifted to the designated short range frequency. "Vancouver station," he called, "this is dragger number nine. Over."

He waited three minutes, then repeated the same call. Two minutes later, he did the same thing.

One minute afterward, a female voice responded, "Dragger nine, this is your Vancouver station. I hope your hold is nearly full and you are preparing to come home. Ready to copy your message. Over."

A female voice! It was decidedly pleasant to hear a woman responding. How many weeks had it been since he'd had the company of a woman?

The response had been correct. Koniev was not concerned about eavesdroppers since their conversation would sound garbled to anyone who chanced upon it, but it had been necessary to ensure he was in contact with the proper station. "My number two fish has experienced some unfriendly company and I need to know during our next contact what the reaction ashore will be. I don't think I need to proceed too rapidly."

The voice that came back to him was soft and even. "You do realize there will be a delay. I'm unable to establish contact with them until six in the morning, and I have no idea how long it will take them to respond. I'm sorry it's such an inefficient system. I'd like to be able to help you immediately."

Why was this voice so worried about him? He tried to imagine the features that might accompany the softness and concern he was sure he detected. But all that would come to him were the faces he remembered from his brief stays in Petropavlovsk and Murmansk. His wife's face was already too far back in his memory to project at this moment.

"Time is something we can spare," Koniev responded. "I intend to make my decision only after I have the proper response from you. Out." And that was the end of their communication. Short and to the point as they had all been trained. But Nicholas Koniev allowed himself to wonder what this woman might look like. He closed his eyes for an instant. Even though her voice was electronically altered, he was sure from its sound that she must be young and attractive. She was the only woman he had talked with in weeks. And for a man with Koniev's imagination, coupled with his compulsion to attract women to himself, she became more appealing with each passing moment. He was absolutely convinced she must be attractive. She had to be. He was also positive she would find him appealing. She had to.

Gorki had come close enough to the surface at the assigned midnight communication period to poke her antenna out of the water. Now, Koniev gave the orders to bring her back to depth. She would remain at the eastern end of the Strait of Juan de Fuca north of Dungeness Spit, the same position from which she had launched her mini subs. The remainder of the night she would maneuver in a tight box at minimum speed. It was a triangular area on the chart surrounded by the major shipping lanes. Koniev had chosen the area because he felt it would be most difficult to locate *Gorki* amidst the heavy merchant traffic all around him. It was a perfect place to waste twenty-four hours.

Nicholas Koniev had always been an ambitious man. He was also brilliant and well-aware of the fact. The combination of those particular traits often produced individuals who were extremely overbearing and difficult to get along with. Koniev consciously established a goal of appearing exactly the opposite. He was open and pleasant, certainly not aloof, and almost painfully polite to his peers. He was also capable of flattery, especially when he was younger and eager to get his way—some called it "kissing ass" but he was confident enough to let them think whatever they wanted.

He also maintained perfect control of himself around his peers. No one ever saw him lose his temper and some even called him an iceman behind his back. It seemed unnatural to them to exercise such control in a military organization where anger often seemed the only way of exercising authority or attracting attention.

His ability to express himself in writing probably attracted more attention among senior officers than anything else he could have done. Professional articles, especially if they are either unique or controversial, are the best method of attaining recognition. When a younger officer produces ideas that are so attractive that his superiors suppress their publication, his reputation has been established. The so-called Koniev Abstract originally intended for the well-read *Morskoy Sbornik,* though removed and classified before editors, peers, or even other senior officers were aware of its existence, was his career maker.

Koniev was a natural submariner, pegged for early command even before he was attracted to miniature submarines. The naval Spetznaz, in charge of that program, indicated there would be a morale problem if he were not required to complete their training. The navy was hesitant. He was already too old to be admitted under normal standards and training was rigorous, even dangerous. It was Koniev who insisted on undergoing their program.

Within weeks, it became obvious that he was capable of handling even the most physically demanding aspects of it as he ruthlessly established his leadership. Another personality trait rose to the surface when his superiors learned that he actually enjoyed the brutality that was a major part of rising to a senior level. Upon completion of that program, he insisted on immediately entering the underwater swimmer school. He finished at the top of his class.

Everything about Nicholas Koniev indicated that there were no limits to his career. His reputation as strategist and writer were established by the Koniev Abstract. His military capabilities were without question. Surely he was destined to be an admiral.

Yet the private, inner man was anything but perfect, as a throng of women who had spent time with him might testify. He possessed what they would consider a personality aberration, one that Koniev himself was aware of but never considered a problem. While he found the company of some women appealing, his primary interest in them was sexual. He was most comfortable utilizing them as a commodity. What could possibly be wrong with a man whose desire for women was insatiable?

He did marry but that was more for convenience since officers at his level were expected to display such stability. But from the day he exchanged vows, he had no intention of being faithful to Galya. As she later came to realize, he probably had no understanding of the meaning of love. He was dominated by the need to possess as many women as physically possible. As long as they cooperated, he was easy to get along with. Those who tired of his demands or saw through his facade found that he could be both mentally and physically abusive.

Koniev maintained a fine line between his physical desires and his professional life. His only concern was the times when he found himself hurting a woman and actually enjoying it. It was a new source of pleasure which he knew would displease his superiors, perhaps even threaten his career if it was revealed, and he struggled within himself to keep it in bounds. After his Spetznaz training, he was better able to understand why he enjoyed inflicting pain. There was also a distinct advantage in rubbing elbows with other men who actually boasted of such experiences with women.

Now it was a woman's voice he was fascinated with, a voice altered by complex electronics, but still a female voice even if it was from a world that seemed beyond reach at this stage. Try as he could as he lay in his bunk on *Gorki,* Koniev was unable to create an image of what the woman on the radio might look like. The saddest part, he admitted as he fell asleep, was that it was unlikely that he would ever have the pleasure of meeting her.

A pity.

Decisive . . . very decisive—that had been Corinne's first thought after "dragger number nine" had broken radio contact. But he was also cautious enough to ask for an intelligence report before committing himself to a course of action. It was certain that this particular submariner would not be rash in his actions.

His voice. How had his voice sounded? It was so hard to determine a personality when a voice was converted to an electronic signal. Yet had there been an element of concern for his "number two fish"? *Oh, forget it, Corinne, because there's no way you can tell anything about a man in a few short sentences over the radio.* She'd only been on the island a few days and she surprised herself over how lonely she felt already. It was a strange feeling, especially since she considered herself a loner.

Say, lady, what's with you that a voice has you turned on? Come on now, grow up.

Her sleep had been fitful at best after that very brief conversation, if that's what their initial contact could be called. And it wasn't shadow figures that occupied her dreams that night. Rather, it was a Russian officer, or officers—she couldn't be sure—who may have appeared in the form of her submariner. They were variously tall or mid-size, none short; some were slender while others became increasingly thick or stocky in the western image of Russians; blond or dark; high or flat, squared cheekbones; aquiline or pug noses; broad or pointed jaws; and all had either blue or green piercing eyes. It seemed impossible to sustain any of these images for long and her dream turned into one of those child's games of piecing together funny faces with cutouts. It was the mental effort of straining to wake up, to rid herself of these troubling visions, that left her feeling exhausted when she forced herself to sit on the edge of the bed at five-thirty in the morning.

The floor was cold. It forced a wakefulness that rose from the soles of her feet. It had to be foggy again for the room was a vague gray and the outside air echoed the mournful cry of gulls and foghorns. She slipped her feet into the woolly slippers and flannel bathrobe she'd put out even before the midnight radio call and shuffled into the kitchen. A swallow of grapefruit juice direct from the container provided the first early jolt. The next step was preparing the coffee. That rich mix of coffee and chicory would melt away the cobwebs.

She contemplated her situation as the first aroma of fresh coffee reached her nostrils. This was so much bigger than she'd anticipated. Or was it just that it seemed to be? *Unfriendly contact . . . number two fish.* What did he mean by that? It was unusual terminology but if these were miniature submarines it meant one of them had somehow been located.

Where? It must be nearby.

How? Mistake . . . accident . . .

Who . . . ? The latter question had to have an obvious answer—the Americans. She had no idea where this Russian was calling from but there was little doubt that he was speaking about the United States. There was nothing in Canadian territory that would justify something like this. It had to be the Americans . . . and it had to mean that somehow they had located a miniature submarine!

She stepped outside the front door and looked toward the sky for the morning weather report. Once again there was only a ground fog because it was growing brighter to the east, an indication that the rising sun would burn it off quickly. Gulls, still invisible, screamed overhead with increasing impatience. There would be no easy breakfast until they could see the water's surface to commence their day's hunt.

A cool breeze rattled the yellowing alder leaves behind the cottage, carrying the smell of fresh coffee out to Corinne. She turned abruptly, almost slipping on the dew-slick front step, and went back inside, knowing the thick brew would refresh but no longer needing it to wake her.

Everything seemed so different when her submariner finally had become a reality on the radio. This was nothing like those exquisite evenings with influential men that seemed to mean so much to her handlers. No, this was something vital—perhaps a man, men, in trouble—and she had just become a critical part of their lives. This meant something . . . something real.

The Russian had been cautious about saying anything

extensive over the air. That was natural, good discipline, of course. He was operating in a foreign country, behind the lines so to speak, and it was unnatural to trust the security of any system when he was using an unfamiliar language. She could hardly blame him for that.

When her watch read exactly six o'clock, she punched in the frequency for her morning report. After the details of the code words that confirmed each station, she repeated the exact words she'd heard after midnight, just as she'd been trained.

"We're well aware of his problem."

Whose voice was that—Roberts'?

"It was purely chance. Tell him that. An American destroyer was experimenting with its sonar. It had been on blocks in the shipyard for six months. Yesterday was its first day at sea. You can assure him—repeat, assure—it was entirely by accident."

There was a pause. Was he repeating what someone in the background was dictating?

"However, the Americans are taking it very seriously. They've brought in people from all over the country. We're not sure why. Our analysis indicates they know nothing about this operation." Another pause. The button on the other end was released for a moment, then the voice resumed. "We anticipate they will conduct a detailed search. That submarine must not—repeat, must not—be located. His orders are to avoid Bremerton—repeat, avoid Bremerton. If necessary, he must scuttle it to evade—repeat, scuttle. Capture is out of the question. Request you repeat these orders. Over."

She could tell from the pauses that Roberts, if it was him, was repeating whatever someone was telling him or else he was reading it off a piece of paper. His words were too clipped. She repeated the orders exactly as she'd copied them.

"Captain Kon . . ." the other voice corrected himself, ". . . the commander who is calling you must now contact you every midnight regardless, and he must remain available for one hour. The situation has changed too radically.

These orders are direct from his superiors. We will guard this frequency at that time to eliminate further delay."

She was tempted to ask why they didn't get on the same frequency with the submarine but that was a foolish question. They'd taken the time to explain that to her. If there was the slightest chance that someone might break into her conversation with the Russian, they did not want to be traced themselves. *She would be the goat if there was to be one.*

"Is there anything else you must relay to us? Over."

No, she'd told them exactly what the Russian had said. "Negative. Over." She was only a relay station. There would be no decisions made here.

"You will contact us tonight after you have relayed our orders. Out."

So that was it. There were certainly things about her career in the city as a hostess that were more exciting than this. No, that wasn't quite right. There were some pleasures, mostly physical. She really did enjoy her work. And there was a distinct feeling of—what was the word one of them had suggested with a touch of good humor?— "omnipotence" when she knew these men were under her control as long as they remained with her.

But there was a sense of danger here that was delicious. Even if that danger would not encompass this island, the man she was responsible for—*yes, responsible, Corinne*— might be in danger and he would depend on her. That did mean something. Could she convey that in her voice at midnight? Could she reinforce the fears he might have in a foreign country with the Americans trying to hunt him down?

Midnight. Why did they tell him he could use his radio only once every twenty-four hours? That was foolish because problems could come at any time. Was he so perfect they assumed he would avoid trouble? It was going to be so long before she could speak with him, warn him. Would the other one, his "number two fish," be able to avoid the Americans wherever he was hiding? She tried to imagine the fear that came with exposure in an unfriendly place. Would these men be afraid for themselves or were they the type she'd read about who reveled in fear and challenge?

When the sun was high enough to warm the air sufficiently, Corinne took a book outside when she went to sunbathe. Once again, the weather wasn't hot but the sun and the protection from the wind were sufficient. As she had the day before, she removed all her clothes. There was a delectable sensuousness to moving about completely naked. This time, she slathered her entire body with lotion that would enhance her fledgling tan.

She'd decided after breakfast while cleaning up the cottage that her next man would experience a woman with a complete tan, or as close to one as possible. It could never be absolutely complete, but it would be captivating. *Basically, lady, it would be overpowering and that's what you want— complete control.*

An hour after opening the book, she realized that she had only turned four pages and hadn't the vaguest idea what the words had said. There were only luscious fantasies lurking in the recesses of her mind, reminders that her thoughts had been concentrated on this man who had spoken to her only once. And that conversation had been basically one-sided and over the radio.

Easy, Corinne, this one isn't like the others . . . he may be dangerous . . . and you'll probably never see him. Then she realized she was still squeezing her legs together.

Seven

DURING HER MORE THAN TWENTY YEARS OF SERVICE, USS *Seahorse* had performed a variety of difficult assignments around the world. Now she was involved in her most unusual one. The nuclear attack submarine had received orders before dawn to establish a boundary patrol between Port Angeles on Washington's Olympic Peninsula and Victoria, the Canadian city of flowers twenty miles north across the Strait of Juan de Fuca. *Seahorse* was there because she was one of the few submarines homeported in Bremerton. Another would be joining her in less than twenty-four hours and the two of them could establish a more effective search. Then a king salmon would have trouble getting past them. But it became obvious to *Seahorse*'s captain shortly after they moved into the strait and dove that the cacophony of sound in the traffic lanes was going to make their job difficult.

After reaching their depth, they set a course almost due west while the executive officer set up a search pattern. Earlier that morning, a patrol aircraft had established a weak magnetic contact in the deep water of the restricted area north of New Dungeness Light. Since there were no known wrecks in that location, *Seahorse* was ordered to sweep that area first. If they established contact, and that contact could readily be classified as a Soviet submarine, they were to engage immediately.

There was no secret about *Kinkaid*'s sonar contact on the previous day. *Seahorse*'s captain was aware that an intruding submarine could be in his vicinity. Not only had the destroyer processed a subsurface object that was definitely moving, but it had then escaped her. His briefing indicated a possible encounter with either a miniature submarine or the mother craft. Either one could be dangerous.

Another boundary patrol covered the outer end of the Strait just before it broadened into the Pacific. That involved a narrower stretch of water and the two nuclear submarines already patrolling there were intended to cut off any escape for the intruders. The concept was simple: deny an escape route, then pressure the intruders into a corner. A combined air and sea sweep north from Tacoma was intended to force anything in Puget Sound out into the Strait. Wherever contact was reestablished, the other units would close in a pincer movement.

It was a logical strategy, one that certainly appeared proper to the various admirals involved, but there was a distinct difference when you were alone in a submarine at two hundred feet attempting to sort the signature of an enemy submarine out of the melange of sound that emanated from one of the busiest stretches of water in the world.

Seahorse's captain studied the search pattern his XO had devised, and nodded. He could imagine no reason in the world why an enemy submarine would station itself in this area. More likely than not the aircraft had detected a spot where a barge master had been well paid to dump barrels of toxic waste or something else illegal—and now it had become a contact. There was nothing more he could do or say. Here's the haystack. Now find the needle.

The submarine proceeded on the designated course and sped into an area of deeper water. The tracking team was set in the likelihood that something might be detected.

Seahorse was a quiet submarine. There was little self-generated noise to disturb the sonarmen as they listened for the faintest unidentifiable sound with their passive sonar and hydrophones. But their search area was filled with merchant traffic, ferries, tugs, and private craft, each one with a different sound signature to sort out and identify.

It was complex work even for *Seahorse's* best sonarmen. The open ocean was a submarine's natural environment. There it could operate alone, so silent and so very deadly, sneaking stealthily through the depths like a scorpion ready to sting any unsuspecting victim unlucky enough to cross its path. And when submarines went about seeking each other out in their winner-take-all game, they made every effort to avoid restricted waters where other ships operated. They were more like two lone gunfighters attempting to get close enough to kill the other with the first shot. For *Seahorse* to be operating in a heavy traffic environment where the surrounding waters sounded more like an echo chamber was a challenge.

Seahorse tiptoed into her designated area while everything around her appeared to be charging like reckless, uncaring bulls. Her commanding officer was not really confident that another submarine would have the courtesy to reveal itself to them.

"Captain."

Koniev recognized the voice of his senior sonarman, always even, never excitable. He rose expectantly on his tiptoes and turned, looking tentatively at the man.

"We have a contact, sir, another submarine, I think."

"You think." Koniev's green eyes narrowed slightly.

"We have many contacts . . . contacts everywhere . . . like a symphony." The sonarman spread his arms out to the captain as if he was about to conduct an orchestra. "But we detected sounds of diving. At first, it disappeared. Now I believe we've been able to isolate the contact. It's still very difficult out there but I think it's a submarine, and in these waters it has to be an American." Long ago, back before he was a petty officer, the man had learned of Koniev's reputation for perfection. "If I had to stake my life on a sound, I'd do it on this one." In submarines, it was better to be wrong than to be surprised by the enemy.

Koniev paused momentarily. His orders were explicit— *avoid contact if at all possible . . . do not engage unless your primary mission is endangered . . .* his primary mission had yet to commence! *. . . if forced to engage, it is your responsibility to ensure your target is destroyed . . . you will leave the scene of engagement immediately to avoid further contact . . . you will then disregard alternate objectives and proceed immediately to complete your primary mission.*

"Your ears are sharp," Koniev complimented the young man. Then he nodded to his executive officer who was hovering expectantly at his elbow. "Set battle stations, very quietly," he added, making a hushing motion with his hands. "I expect the torpedo room to be prepared to fire on my command, muzzle doors open now." He wanted any sound preparatory to shooting out of the way, muffled by the sounds flowing around them. One could never tell. "We may have no time for the luxury of a perfect solution on our target."

As far as Koniev was concerned, there was no time for a cat and mouse game if the other submarine appeared likely to come too close, not in this situation, not in the other man's waters. He knew where his mini subs were. This definitely wasn't either of them. Nor were there any other Soviet submarines nearby. If this was a legitimate submarine, it also must be a target. It was therefore his enemy. He remembered his orders—if it came within his security envelope, if he was forced to engage, then . . .

Gorki's crew had been exercised at action stations—in the Baltic, daily out of Murmansk and Petropavlovsk, and as they crossed the Pacific—so often that they were ready in an instant. Their captain had conditioned them well for a wartime situation. That was the manner in which the Spetznaz responded and that was the only way he knew how to train them. What this crew lacked in actual time at sea together or in realistic training encounters they made up for in enthusiasm. Nicholas Koniev had established an enviable reputation for himself, and his crew expected him to bring them back home alive.

There was but a single aspect he was unable to control directly. His crew sensed the tension—hell, they could taste it and smell it, too—yet they knew so little about their mission. But that was also the Soviet way. It was assumed that the less men understood of a mission, the less there was to concern them. That worked with the average Soviet recruit whose singular goal was to serve his time as a conscript as uneventfully as possible and then distance himself from the military. The theory had little success with more intelligent men, especially those who were capable of operating a specialized submarine like *Gorki*. Koniev understood that and attempted to achieve a delicate balance between doctrine and his own concepts of leading men. Yet he sympathized with many of them who sensed they remained uninformed of their true mission. There were times when he even felt badly about it.

They maneuvered cautiously. *Gorki* possessed the advantage because she was able to remain at depth and continually maneuver in an oblong track at minimum speed. That also allowed her to operate at maximum silence as if she were tiptoeing on a field of silk. The other craft had just transited to a nearby point and dived, creating a sound that had been different from everything the Soviet sonarmen had been hearing. That was akin to waving a red flag. Additionally, the American submarine also had the unenviable task of identifying a profusion of sounds as it searched for a possible enemy submarine.

Koniev's men were cautious, attempting to maintain their tenuous contact among a diversity of sounds assaulting their senses. Even with their advantage, it remained a difficult task.

"Contact seems to be tracking northwest at about ten knots."

That was almost directly at them. Was it purely by

chance? "I want an accurate course," Koniev responded sharply. He turned to the Officer of the Deck. "Maneuver according to sonar's needs until they have a specific answer for me."

Moments later, "We have contact moving along a course of two nine zero at thirteen knots."

"Is that steady?" It appeared to be reciprocal to his current track, almost a collision course.

"As of now. They aren't maneuvering, Captain."

Koniev created a mental image of their relative positions. If the other craft actually heard him at this extended range, even sporadic traces of a foreign sound, it would maneuver to improve the contact and obtain its own solution. If he tried to escape, that would be a dead giveaway. *Gorki* was so silent, or that's what every sound analysis had indicated. Was he fooling himself? They might hear a new and unusual sound signature but there was nothing existing that would identify *Gorki*. If they were hunting, it made sense to close and analyze a strange sound. As long as he acted normally, they might lose him, or decide there was no purpose in further investigation.

But as long as that contact remained on course, it must be considered a target. "No further maneuvering. Hold your course and speed," he murmured to the OOD. He might just as well treat this as a classic approach because there was no other choice, no rationale in attempting to disappear and giving himself away. He gave orders to the tracking team to stand by their torpedoes. If anyone was going to shoot first, it would be *Gorki*. *If you are forced to engage* . . .

Seahorse's captain was the picture of frustration. They were surrounded by sound, none of it suspicious, all of it intrusive. The quartermaster had reported their passage through the center of their designated search area. It was nothing but a point on the chart where a few hours before an aircraft had recorded a magnetic indication of something large beneath the surface. No physical law required the producer of that anomaly to remain in that exact location.

But up to this moment there was no hint of a foreign sound. If it was out there, it was hidden.

"Circle." His next logical tactic was to circle to cover any blind spots and expand their area search.

It was a boring, time-consuming effort. The captain stepped into the sonar room. The screens in front of the operators were a cascade of sound images. The men worked patiently at isolating and identifying their contacts, searching for that one tiny indication of something unfamiliar that shouldn't be there.

After the circle was completed, the captain stepped back into the control room. His interest was waning rapidly. Chasing after apparitions was one thing. Identifying them in a crowded room was quite another.

The executive officer was given free rein to concoct whatever search pattern was appealing to him. He decided to maintain his base course until he was beyond the twenty-mile circle the quartermaster had placed around the aircraft's contact.

"They appear to be back on track again, Captain."

Koniev nodded to himself. His quarry must have completed a circle. That was certainly normal if the other submarine was looking for something. But it was right back on a course that would literally run over his position. It was obvious. They must have had a definite reason to dive in this area to be conducting a search in this manner. Would the American also be ready to shoot instantly?

Ranges to the target were reported every two hundred yards. *Gorki* was approaching to a position off the target's port bow, silent, undetected. Her torpedo solution was perfect. They were in a superb position, the kind that was taught in classrooms and practiced in trainers, but never expected by any submariner. It was a dream.

Koniev's torpedos were high speed and designed to home on the churning propellor of his prey. If he was forced to shoot, it would be convenient if the other happened to turn to starboard just before his shot, presenting the sound of his props to the torpedo's homing device and decreasing the torpedo's time on target by just that much more. Even if the enemy attempted to outrun it, he would still have little chance. The actions of this American submarine cried out that it had them and was closing.

Seahorse's sonar chief heard the sound first. It was faint, so indistinct the others couldn't have noticed it, but he called out, "Captain—something close aboard, a manmade sound." The tenor of his voice was urgent. "Permission to activate . . ."

"Go active," the captain interrupted, anticipating the need.

The ping from *Seahorse's* active sonar burst across the water reaching out for the sound the chief had heard.

PING!

"He knows we're here, but he doesn't know what we are yet," Koniev called out. Now he had all the reason he needed for that first shot.

A couple of men turned slightly and indicated their silent agreement but no one dared to break the inescapable, systematic chain of events leading to launching their torpedo.

". . . if forced to engage . . ." They had been lashed . . . found out . . . Their range already entered into the other's fire control solution.

When Koniev gave the order to shoot, the torpedo ran perfectly.

That was also pleasing.

"Torpedo in the water, close aboard!" The sonarman's cry shattered the boredom of *Seahorse's* fruitless search even before he could report the contact's range. There was no chance one could mistake the sound of the water slug hurling the weapon out of the tube—or the high speed scream of its propellors. "Port bow."

"Emergency ahead full," *Seahorse's* captain shouted.

"Right full rudder." She heeled at a sharp angle. Then he gave orders for the ship to dive. Almost instantly the deck inclined sharply down. "How much water beneath us?"

"Almost two hundred fifty feet."

Not enough, not enough for what he wanted to do. They should be in the open ocean where they could plummet away from the high explosive that was racing behind them. It had to be a Soviet torpedo and he knew it was faster than *Seahorse*. They had to maneuver to confuse the weapon, to keep it from that final homing run.

"Eject decoys." Give it a false target. Draw it away from *Seahorse*. Give them time to turn and get off a snapshot, anything that would prevent the other from shooting at them again.

Seahorse reversed course at the same time she was forced to break off her too short dive just fifty feet above the bottom. More decoys went into the water.

But it was indeed a homing torpedo closing the American submarine and it functioned exactly as intended. The thrashing propellors of the target acted like a magnet. The decoys simply weren't effective enough to deter it from the much more intense sound of *Seahorse*'s high speed dash. Nor was the target able to dive deep enough to confuse it.

The torpedo was relentless in its pursuit, adjusting to the movements of its target until it impacted fifteen feet ahead of the propellor. The explosion shattered the hull, disabling the shaft at the same time water burst into the engineering space.

Seahorse lost her forward motion as she was hurled sideways by the blast. Tons of water poured into the stern dragging her toward the bottom.

The orders were given for emergency blow to counteract the weight of the water surging into the hull, but *Seahorse* was already too heavy. When water reached the electrical boards seconds later, power winked out throughout the ship.

Those still alive in the forward section of the ship experienced a final sense of terror and helplessness as the emergency lights came on to pierce the pervasive white smoke. Then she collided awkwardly with the mud and sand floor where she tumbled over on her side. *Seahorse* became a steel coffin where she lay dark and cold four hundred eighty feet below the surface.

Nicholas Koniev experienced much the same fear as he gave orders to turn *Gorki* due south. He'd listened to the sound of bulkheads shattering, imagined the final thoughts of the men who understood how they had lost their part of the game. The sound of his target crunching into the bottom had been followed by silence.

It was quite possible a nearby ship might have heard the powerful blast, even more likely that lubricating oil or flotsam from the dead submarine would soon float to the surface offering grim evidence of the grave beneath. It may have been noted by hydrophones on the floor of the strait. He had his orders. Remaining in this locale would be senseless, suicidal. His target was finished. There was no further danger. He also had no doubt that searchers would soon saturate the area.

Gorki's navigator, prodded by an unusually tense Koniev, eventually settled on an area to the south near Dungeness Spit where the bottom dropped off steeply. The depth was a fairly constant three hundred feet and they could remain close enough to shore to hopefully avoid detection. The nearby land also appeared remote enough that poking an antenna above the surface that night would be fairly secure.

Koniev retired to his stateroom again to rest, but sleep was impossible. Had his main objective been compromised by a chance contact, or was there a breakdown in Kremlin security? Or could *Gorki* have been a victim of a series of unavoidable but costly errors? No, he decided, they weren't even errors if that was the reason. What had taken place was purely by chance. It had to be. He was quite sure the Americans weren't completely aware of what was happening yet. They couldn't be if *Gorki* and her mission had remained as secure as intended.

But it wouldn't take long for the US to learn about their lost submarine. He had no more than a few hours grace at the most. The evidence would come to the surface. Security would automatically be increased around the Trident base, dramatically so. It was common sense to protect your most sensitive areas whenever the potential threat was increased. Logic dictated to Koniev that he must diminish that potential by drawing the Americans in another direction. He had a mission of his own to accomplish, one that was more vital than any individual under his command. He'd promised to wait for instructions during the next radio contact, but that seemed a luxury at this point. Sinking the American submarine changed everything . . . it was time to get on with his own mission.

How unfortunate it was that Tarantsev was in such an unenviable position. But it had to be done. And Donskoi— tough, faithful Donskoi—mustn't know about it at all.

Admiral Harry Coffin hunched his shoulders, appearing to stretch from the inside out. It was the third time he'd done that in the last half hour and Ryng knew it was a combination of mental and physical exhaustion. Men could age in minutes when a tragedy like *Seahorse*'s occurred. If it had been an accident, it might have been easier. But the last communication before she dove, just hours before, was still fresh in his mind. There was no doubt how she'd met her fate. A patrol aircraft had spotted the small telltale slick and the first bits of wreckage floating to the surface. What had appeared was sufficient indication. Helicopters were already depositing the grim evidence on the pad outside. Submarines simply weren't ripped apart in that manner in five hundred feet of water, not by any accident he was aware of. And men's bodies could only be torn like that from an explosion.

If their assumptions were correct, it had to be a torpedo or a mine of some kind, more likely the former because the bodies were all engineers from the after compartment. The Soviets used torpedos that homed on the prop and that would explain it. On the other hand, nothing was explainable. What reason could justify sinking another submarine in peacetime?

The phone buzzed on Coffin's desk and he lifted it tiredly to his ear. After a few seconds hesitation, he said calmly, "No. I don't want to speak to him now. Say that I'm off on another part of the base." He replaced the phone and looked at Ryng. "When someone calls who really is more important than he thinks, then I'll speak to him."

Bernie Ryng was as baffled as Coffin. Why would the Soviets sink an American submarine in American waters? Their existence was obvious. That contact of *Kinkaid's* in Puget Sound had confirmed a foreign presence. It was inconceivable that any other nation could be as brash. Who else would be snooping there? But it would have made more sense to avoid *Seahorse* to keep from revealing themselves. Had *Seahorse* forced her own destruction? What mission could be so important that a Russian submarine captain would sink an American in his own territorial waters?

Was this attacker the same one *Kinkaid* had chanced upon? Or was there more than one of them? And wasn't it obvious that sinking *Seahorse* magnified the international situation considerably? Before, it was a simple matter of diplomatic concern. Now, the diplomats would be shunted aside by the politicians and the military.

Or was someone leading them in the wrong direction?

"I think this place is still what they want, Admiral. They may be going about whatever they're after in a halfass manner, but they wouldn't waste their time around this neck of the woods unless Tridents were somehow their target."

"I think you're absolutely right, Bernie, but there's a lot of brass out there, along with their civilian buddies, who aren't going to look at things the way you and I do."

Ryng glanced quickly in Coffin's direction but remained silent. Who would coordinate an operation like this? Someone who could care less for body counts. *Spetznaz*. That's who he always blamed whenever he failed to come up with an answer, and generally he'd been correct. Spetznaz wouldn't hesitate to sink *Seahorse* if she appeared to be in their way. And what were they specialists in? *Deception*.

"Spetznaz," Ryng murmured.

"What'd you say?"

"Spetznaz, Admiral. I can smell it. None of us can figure out exactly what's going on. That's their trademark. Except there's a couple of things they didn't anticipate—*Seahorse*. They could probably accept luck on our end—like our dolphin, even the chance sonar contact by *Kinkaid*—but I think someone thought there was no other choice but to sink *Seahorse*."

"She screwed up their plan?"

"Perhaps. It depends on what happens next. If they disappear from sight—no sonar contacts, nothing but safe waters and fresh air—then maybe I'm wrong. But if they turn up somewhere else, then you got to figure someone's playing with us. I'll bet my last dollar this base is still their target." He shrugged. "Hell, what else is there around here to make them sink one of our submarines?"

Coffin nodded. "It wasn't a rational response," he said with a grimace. "What I'm hearing, whenever someone bothers to include me, is that the few civilians close to the White House who have access to this sort of thing are pushing for the UN even though this thing's only a couple of hours old and we have no proof of what happened. Some of the military types who've been in the Pentagon too long are arguing for retribution. It's going to be a son of a bitch keeping this sinking under wraps if any civilian craft pick up some of the junk coming to the surface."

"I wouldn't worry about that right away. They'll bring it in and they'll do all sorts of speculating and the navy will hopefully keep its mouth shut until we come up with something feasible. But we have enough time before someone decides it's from a submarine, more or less one of our own. Whatever this mission is, they intend for it to be over before anyone figures out what went wrong. That's the way the Spetznaz do things."

"But *Seahorse* . . ."

"That was probably unavoidable. Whoever's commanding will adjust."

Coffin nodded grimly. "I asked for you to beef up security because I anticipated something . . . but not like this," he added. "So I'll ask the expert what's going to happen now. Tell me about it, Bernie."

"Who can say? The one thing I'm positive of," he reminded Coffin, "remains right here."

"You can have whatever you need."

"Let's not make a show out of it. That's what they'll be looking for. Maintain normal patrols on the canal. You can vary the times. Nothing ostentatious. If they're waving their arms somewhere else, we'll wave back and scream and shout. But we're going to do a lot more swimming. We'll operate from your boats. But we'll do it on a twenty-four-hour basis. I've got a few more of my people coming in any minute now to back us up. Whatever's going to happen ought to come off in the next day or so."

The admiral looked across at Ryng and pursed his lips skeptically.

Ryng nodded knowingly at him, as if that was absolute confirmation.

Coffin raised his eyebrows. "You seem awfully goddamn sure of yourself for someone who doesn't know what the bad guys are after any more than I do."

"They operate just like we do."

Andrei Tarantsev rarely smiled. Normally, his expression remained blank, impossible to read. But now he was frowning. The orders that had just come over the speaker in the tiny control room of the miniature submarine were so contrary to what he'd anticipated that surprise, even a tinge of shock, animated his features. Tupolev and Osipenko recognized that this unusual change in his expression matched their own. Since their commander rarely displayed any emotion, they were relieved that he was apparently as concerned as they were.

So, while all three men heard Koniev's words that evening, Tupolev and Osipenko remained disciplined as they, too, considered Koniev's orders. Their exchange of glances was the only indication that they were as surprised as their commander. They knew without saying it that Tarantsev would do everything possible to protect each of them.

Tarantsev was so deep in thought that he failed to acknowledge Koniev's message while he considered his alternatives. There was no thought of disputing the orders. He was more occupied with determining how he might accomplish them and still save their necks.

"Did you receive my last transmission? Over." Each of them could sense Koniev's irritation, even with the metallic echo of the radio.

"I believe so," Tarantsev responded mechanically without paying attention to the formalities Koniev enjoyed so much. "Please repeat to avoid misinterpretation. Over."

"Immediately after conclusion of this message, you will proceed south down Puget Sound to a point off the entrance to Rich's Passage, the channel to Bremerton. Stay as close to the western shore as possible during your transit to avoid detection. Since the distance is no more than ten miles, you should arrive there well before first light. Providing there are no military ships guarding the entrance, you are to proceed to a position east of the shipyard where their ships maneuver to get underway. There you will deposit the two mines you now have on board. Upon completion of your mission, you will return to your current location to establish contact and arrange for replenishment. Over."

That was exactly what Koniev had ordered in his previous transmission. Perhaps a few of the words had changed, but there was no doubt about his intent. Their return was based on the completion of this mission, and he did not expect them to return unless they succeeded. But he had altered the original plan.

"Is that understood? Over."

"My suggestion would be to deposit mines in the narrowest part of the channel, off Point Glover. The water is still deep enough there for me to maneuver. There is no, repeat no, water deep enough for a submarine to operate near the shipyard. Over." He turned to see if Tupolev and Osipenko were as involved in the discussion as he assumed and found both of them staring back at him.

"Negative. Proceed as ordered. Use swimmers if it becomes necessary. Do you copy? Over."

Tarantsev inclined his head knowingly. He understood there were others in *Gorki's* control room who were also listening for his assent. It would be logged. Once again, his eyes moved to those of the other two. Each one nodded their understanding.

"Our orders are understood. Out."

So there it was. *Use swimmers if necessary.* That was not the way it should have been planned. What was it that they were being sacrificed for? That was it—*sacrificed.* Tarantsev knew it. He could see in their eyes that Tupolev and Osipenko also understood it was impossible to carry out these orders and return safely. They were being sent to their deaths . . . knowingly. The Americans knew they were in the vicinity. Security precautions would be overwhelming. The benefits of a midget submarine had been cut away from them. They were being sent where they couldn't operate, didn't belong.

The original concept of their mission was to be a backup to Donskoi's craft if he encountered difficulties. That was the purpose of two equally well-trained crews. To move into the shallow waters off the shipyard was nothing more than suicide.

What was the purpose? There had to be one, that was for sure. There always was when you were ordered to die. Tarantsev just wished for a reason to justify their deaths. Then again, Spetznaz training prepared you for the moment.

But not to pull the trigger on yourself, Tarantsev snarled inwardly.

"Prepare to get underway," he said to Tupolev and Osipenko without looking in their direction.

Leon Donskoi was equally surprised when he established communications with *Gorki* for the first time to report that he would have to depart the Hood Canal to pick up more weapons. There was no reason given to return to the mother ship. Their engineering plant and human services were operating exactly as designed. The orders were clipped and to the point—"Return to mother immediately taking all necessary precautions for safety. Out."

There had been no opportunity to question.

Eight

DANNY WEST NEVER CEASED TO MARVEL AT THE EXCITEMENT of swimming with a dolphin. Each time was as thrilling as his first experience, and that had been a simple training run in shallow waters during the day.

Now it was nighttime and completely black beneath the surface. There was nothing to orient himself with in such a void, no way to place himself within this liquid environment where gravity's influence became a plaything. He was forced to rely totally on his judgment when vision no longer responded to the dimensions. When he was alone, only his acute senses coupled with his compass and chronometer offered reassurance that he was proceeding exactly as planned. Even so, he would snap the cricket to reaffirm his confidence.

Then Bull would appear beside him. There was no warning, just the sudden pressure caused by the motion of water against his body to tell him that the dolphin was at his side. Then he would flash his light and find the perpetually smiling creature swimming beside him. Bull would appear as normal as always, a convincing sight for a blind man. And Bull had no need for sight. This liquid element was his home and his refined sonar system was all that was necessary.

But there was one ability the dolphin could not master. He was unable to speak and therefore unable to report what he found in his travels. That was why they were a team, why it was necessary for the man to tag along. With his superb echo-ranging abilities, Bull could locate any unusual mass on the bottom, but he couldn't identify it and return with the information. So the man and the animal were forever dependent on each other.

The mission that brought Bull and Danny into the Hood Canal in the middle of the night was a critical one because Harry Coffin had been successful in conveying his feelings to those admirals whose opinions were respected in Washington. Bernie Ryng and his team had convinced him that the Hood Canal was the obvious target. The odds were that someone wanted to bottle up the Tridents at their own base. Pentagon decision makers agreed and had allowed him to restrict the Tridents. White House power brokers agreed that was possible and they accepted the Pentagon decision, even to the point of remaining absolutely silent, but they also included a time limit. Then they told Harry Coffin to back up his assertions. *You said it—now prove it.*

Bull was Danny's eyes and ears that dark night as they conducted a sector sweep in the Hood Canal just north of the submarine piers near Vinland. The man marked their coverage on his waterproof chart each time he turned on the light. His job was to coach the dolphin throughout the area, investigating whenever the mammal returned with an indication that he'd found something else of interest. On almost every occasion, it was trash dumped thoughtlessly from a passing boat. There were times that Bull found old outboards that had fallen into water too deep for recovery, and there was one old sealed barrel that West decided had been in that location for years. It offered no threat.

It was near the end of their sweep that Bull went through another of his usual displays of success to show that there was still more to locate in this game. He was waiting to be handed the magnetic locator and Danny almost decided to dismiss Bull's latest prize. It seemed they were operating too close to shallow water. Ryng had assumed even sound-activated mines would more likely be planted near the channel.

West was gradually nearing the limits of his reserve energy. The cold northwest waters were beginning to have an effect through his wetsuit and his air supply was close to thirty percent. That was when you thought about heading back, giving yourself enough time in case your pickup was late. But Danny gave Bull the magnetic device and turned on his locator to follow. When the man finally caught up to the dolphin, Bull was sweeping around the object in large circles stirring the mud into smoky swirls. It appeared to be the edge of a barrel sticking out of the dark shadows, or that was Danny's first impression.

He swept away some more of the mud. It was actually a soft layer of silt that had formed over a much larger object than was first evident, almost as if it had been buried by hand. And then he noticed that the metal was much shinier than anything they'd located that night. A few more seconds work revealed the casing of a long, thick tube that he knew instantly was a mine activated by sounds specifically programmed into its memory.

This was it. This was what Admiral Coffin had been looking for.

He had no doubt that when activated the mine's memory core would have recognized the distinctive signature of a Trident submarine passing down the channel. That sound would have energized the weapon, starting the engine that would drive it directly into the screws of the passing submarine. There was likely more than enough high explosive in the warhead to drop the Trident right there.

Good old Bull. West said a silent thank you for dolphins who could survive this environment indefinitely and had the intelligence and persistence to drag their human wards along with them. He scratched the rough location on his chart before firing the green flare that would also mark the spot for the men on the surface. The explosive ordnance people would be called to take care of the device immediately.

But that green flare was also noted by Viktor Donskoi

prior to departing for his rendezvous with Koniev. It was purely by chance that he made one last periscope sweep of the Hood Canal before departing. The green arc in the sky to the south appeared so close that it momentarily frightened him. But he marked the estimated position of the flare on his chart, then studied with concern the mark he had just made. It was too close to Vinland, the location of one of his mines, to be a coincidence, particularly at that time of night. Something was wrong. He remembered the dolphin that attacked him, an oddity in these waters. At the time, he'd dismissed it as a fluke of nature because there was no indication of any human involvement but . . . was it possible . . . ? part of a security effort . . . ? Perhaps he should have reported it the previous night, perhaps even when he established that initial contact an hour before. Had his reticence to use the radio possibly created a larger problem?

It shouldn't take more than a couple of hours to rendezvous with *Gorki* in her new location after they cleared the Hood Canal Bridge. Donskoi concluded that, since it was nighttime and water traffic was minimal, he would be able to make the transit quickly and report both the dolphin and that green flare.

There were no dancing shadows for Corinne to ponder this night, no need to read herself to sleep by the light of the gas lamp. She knew the radio would be in use that night. Her situation was no longer a backup in case of emergency. Whatever the nature of this operation, one planned by people she couldn't imagine, it wasn't following their script. Something had gone awry, badly. The people she was in contact with, her *handlers,* had reacted overanxiously.

The original rules for radio communication had already been broken by the operatives back in Vancouver, if that was where their radio was located. And why had they chosen her and this island rather than establishing a central command post? The purpose escaped her. Once during the day, about noontime, while she was sunning in the front yard, she was jolted by the radio speaker unexpectedly coming to life. It was as eerie as it was frightening to hear a voice behind her on this otherwise deserted section of island. There were some reef-net fishermen who occupied rough cabins at the other end, but she thought that season was over. That left only the nuns who were also on that end. They ran the combination general store, post office, marina, and ferry terminal whenever there was some demand. But she'd yet to see or hear a soul since her arrival. She actually heard herself gasp and felt the adrenaline surge through her body before she realized the voice had come from the radio.

What she received was a complete report on the expanded activities of the US Navy in the region, one that should have been relayed that evening. Why did they choose the middle of the day? Why break communications security? There was no need for it. That, in itself, was disconcerting for a woman alone on a small island. Break the rules once, just once, and that was the beginning. Someone was panicking.

She couldn't help imagining that if this break of security allowed a foot in the door, if somehow the Americans might be able to trace her . . . but then she realized that was foolishness. The events were taking place in Puget Sound and that was more than thirty miles south. It was next to impossible for anyone to trace her radio signal to this island, much less decide to come after Corinne Foxe. Or was it? The Americans had more important things to be concerned with. No one would come here. But then she remembered her encounter earlier that day with the fisherman.

After her first full day on the island, Corinne had found that the immediate surroundings of the cabin could become a prison of sorts and decided that exploring the island would alleviate the boredom. Sunning in the unusual weather was a special treat, but she wasn't cut out for total inactivity.

There was a chart of the San Juans inside the cabin and she used that to cut her little island into pie-shaped segments. If she explored only one section each day, there would be something new to look forward to every morning. The island was no more than four miles across at its widest and maybe three miles long between the northernmost and southernmost points.

She decided to start from the small beach near the cabin

and move in a counterclockwise direction because the area to the east was where the nuns lived and the fishermen stored their boats.

Earlier that day, while she was working her way along the shoreline toward the point on the western tip of the island, a fishing boat had appeared from around an outcropping of tangled spruce and madrona trees hanging over the water. It was so close to shore there was no time to slip away.

There appeared to be only one man on the boat and he saw her instantly. "Toot . . . toot . . ." went the whistle. She supposed that was the way these island fishermen attracted someone's attention. Now if she faded into the undergrowth, it would certainly appear suspicious.

She stopped at the water's edge and shaded her eyes with a hand, watching as the boat maneuvered closer to shore. It came within twenty yards before backing down to go dead in the water.

"Are you alright?" the man at the wheel called out.

"Yes, thank you, I'm fine," Corinne answered.

"How about being lost?" He finished what he was doing in the pilot house and moved quickly forward on the bow to drop the anchor.

"Not at all."

He squatted on the flat bow, pulling on the chain until he was satisfied the anchor was secure. "There," he called over his shoulder, "she's not going anywhere by herself."

As the boat swung gradually into the wind, the man came back toward the stern which now faced Corinne no more than thirty feet away. There was a name across the back—*Dream Girl*.

He dangled a leg over the stern and sat with one foot just above the water while he lit a cigarette. "So you're OK and you're not lost. Then I guess there's no chance of saving you." He was tall and broad-shouldered and the wine-colored chamois shirt he wore made him look bigger. The combination of sun and wind had turned his hair to a blondish brown and his face was weathered a copper color. He stared back at her with friendly gray eyes waiting for a response.

Corinne thought her long experience qualified her as an expert on men, if nothing else, and everything she noted about him before he spoke again seemed to indicate this was a chance meeting. He wasn't dangerous.

When she didn't respond, he said, "I've been anchoring here for years and you're the first person I've ever run into on this end of the island this time of year. You scared me for a moment." There was a trace of humor in his expression.

"How do you think I felt when I saw your boat come around that bend? For someone who was looking forward to absolute peace and quiet, a big boat like yours isn't exactly what I was hoping for."

"The *Dream?*" He bent over and patted the stern. "You don't like my *Girl?*" There was a curious expression on his face as he talked between puffs on the cigarette. "This is my pride and joy. Everything I've got has been put into the *Dream*. You're not going to break my heart and insult her, are you?" Again, there was humor, this time in his eyes.

"What brought you here?" she asked defensively. "Are you looking for something?"

"Nope. How about you?"

"Well . . . not really. I was just taking a walk."

"Never heard of anyone taking a walk around here. This end of the island isn't exactly everyone's idea of paradise."

Corinne smiled. The situation was absurd, making small talk with someone sitting offshore on a boat when you'd been absolutely sure there wasn't another person to talk with in your entire universe. "I didn't expect to see anyone here."

"That's my line. I'm sure I've been coming to Cook's Bay a lot longer than you have."

"Is that what this is called—Cook's Bay?"

"That's what I call it, mostly because I'm the only one to ever come here, except for you, of course." He rose to his feet and offered a sloppy salute. "And I'm Cook, Jimmy Cook. Since I haven't found a name on any chart, I decided to name it after myself." He smiled pleasantly. "I'll bet you have a name, too."

"Corinne," she said hesitantly.

He sat back down again. "That's a pretty name, Corinne. And what are you doing wandering about my own special bay?" He raised a hand. "You don't have to tell me, if you don't want to. I'm not nosy, just curious. Besides, after all the times I've anchored here and never seen another soul, I'm wondering if you plan to build condos on the island and force me to find another bit of paradise somewhere else."

Their conversation struck her as nonsensical, something you might encounter on a TV situation comedy, but nothing one might personally experience in real life. This Jimmy Cook had appeared from nowhere and begun talking with her as if they were at a cocktail party. That had happened to her before but always at real, fancy-dress cocktail parties, more often in some fancy place like Grouse Mountain that looked across the inlet to the lights of Vancouver—*but not on this remote island.*

"No, I don't intend to build any condos. I'm doing research . . . on the birds out here."

"Ah, hah, a scientist." He clapped his hands. "I've seen some out in the San Juans before, but none here, of course. What kind of birds? Maybe I'm conversing with the world's foremost expert on seagulls? That's what I notice most around here."

He was amusing. At first, she'd suspected he might be taunting her. Too many men approached strange women that way, especially if they thought she might be too bright. They found it necessary to display some sort of strength. It was a defense mechanism. But his conversation really was quite pleasant and unassuming, and there was a touch of good-natured humor in everything he said. "Sea birds in general—herons especially, and I'm interested in nesting eagles. But there's always room for one more study, Mr. Cook, if you have a new species of gull out here," she answered with a grin. It was refreshing to talk in this manner after the forced isolation of her tiny cottage. Corinne had always found it much easier to talk with men than women.

"Mr. Cook, you say. Please don't disappoint me. I'm not that old. That's what people used to call my father—Mr.

Cook. I'm Jimmy. And I know you can say it. Everybody tells me it's a relatively easy name to pronounce."

"I'm certain it is." She smiled back when she saw how much fun he was having with his gentle teasing. "And I guess I can assume you're a fisherman," she added, waving a hand at the boat.

"Most of the time, at least until I get bored. That's when I come here and drop anchor and read a book. Up until today I used to read, that is, until I found civilization had crept out to this island."

"How do you think I feel, when I thought it was just going to be me and the birds? For all I know, you may be disturbing nesting locations and invalidating my study."

"Be honest now, have you even seen a fishing boat that the birds didn't like?" He swept his arm about for emphasis. "Look at that bow. Look at the raft on top of my little pilot house. Why even the stern I'm sitting on. Guano! Everywhere! Can't you see that the gulls perch right here where I'm sitting more than I do?"

Corinne shook her head with a smile. He was funny.

"Now that's something for scientific study. Why don't you learn why the seagulls prefer fishing boats over sailboats ten to one?"

She folded her arms self-consciously. "Alright, Jimmy, you win. You're not disturbing nesting birds."

He talked about other birds inhabiting the San Juans, mergansers, scaup, kingfishers, stopping occasionally to ask if she happened to be interested in them, then continuing without apparently paying attention to the answers she gave. She'd found a flat rock to perch on and she drew her knees up and wrapped her arms around them as he talked. Jimmy was fun and he was amusing, a refreshing addition to a day that had been growing heavy with tension.

Then he stopped in the middle of a sentence and winked at her with a knowing grin. "I suppose there's nothing I've said about birds that you don't already know. Do I sound dumb?"

"On the contrary. I think you've contributed to at least one research paper, maybe two or three."

"Thank you. I tend to talk a lot when I find someone who listens and I'm told that comes from living alone. Now we have to decide if you're disturbing tired fishermen who are just looking for a quiet harbor to drop the hook in and relax for an hour or so."

"Well, I would have kept moving if you hadn't come around the corner and surprised me like you did. And you can have Cook's Bay back again. As a matter of fact, I'll be on my way if you prefer."

"Actually, Corinne, I'm enjoying talking to you. Seriously now. I'm not kidding. Really I'm not." He made a little cross over his heart. "Fishing gets dull very, very fast some days and this is one of them. You see I'm not really a full-time fisherman. I go to school, too. After a couple of years of fishing convinced me I wasn't going to get rich quick, I decided to go back to school and learn something that will make me rich, or at least smarter if I'm never going to get rich. I already have an associates degree from a community college," he added proudly. "Halfway there, you see."

He was a strange and interesting man. Corinne thought about how difficult it must be to be at ease with a complete stranger until she realized that she was no different. She came in contact with strange men all the time and she enjoyed the challenge immensely. She was good at engaging them in conversation and making them comfortable even though they knew they were about to engage in an affair with a woman other than their wives. As a matter of fact, she was so good that they never realized how much of themselves they were compromising.

Jimmy Cook was certainly one of the most open men she'd ever met, totally uninhibited about himself. How long had they been talking?—less than an hour and they seemed old friends. So many of those others she'd spent time with spoke mostly of money and power. Jimmy talked about life. He was running on about his education when she interrupted. "Does that mean the *Dream Girl* will have a new owner someday soon?" Corinne asked. "When you get your degree, I mean."

"Never. Without the *Girl,* I'd never get away to Cook's Bay, and I'd never meet someone like you."

No, he never would have. It was a fluke, an oddity that they both should have ended up here at the same time in need of another human being to talk with. Corinne was overwhelmingly aware as he spoke that not only did someone now know this end of the island was inhabited, but he also had a name to go with a face. That's not the way her handlers expected her to react in such a situation. Everyone remained nameless if at all possible. It was little security breaches like this that could bring castles tumbling down. But, then, neither of them had anticipated human contact out on the island . . . had they? And where were the castles?

Jimmy saw a shadow of concern cross her face. "I can tell by the expression on your face that you're worried about me," Jimmy said. He held up both hands in mock surrender. "Believe me, I'm harmless today. But I won't forget that this had to be my day, what with meeting a lovely girl in Cook's Bay when I thought the place was deserted."

"It will be again in a few days. There's only so much time I can spend on research and then the papers have to get written."

"I'll tell you what. Just so you don't think bad things about a nice guy like me, how about some fresh crab legs for your dinner? You do eat, don't you?"

The provisions they had stocked for her were excellent, but his offer was too good to turn down. "Sounds good. Sounds great as a matter of fact."

"Wonderful. You'll never have fresher crab than this. Hauled it in today." He dropped to his knees with only his head showing occasionally, and she could see him working at something. Finally, he stood up with a handful of large crab legs. "There we are. Dinner."

"The water's too cold to swim out and get them," she teased.

"And it's too cold to swim in with them, too. But"—he pointed at the rubber raft that was tied upside down on the top of the pilot house—"where there's a will, there's a way."

"You're going to row them in."

"I wish I could," he answered with a grin. "Some fisherman I am. I left the oars on the pier today. So I'll have to use my hands to paddle them in." He knit his brows in thought for a moment. "Or better yet, so I don't look too dumb, why don't I just tie a line to the boat and push it in to you. You see, delivered fresh to your front door without either of us getting wet."

Jimmy untied the raft and lifted it off the top of the pilot house, easing it into the water off the stern. After wrapping the crab legs in newspaper, he placed the package in the little boat and pushed it away from the *Dream Girl* toward the shore, holding tightly to the bow line. It drifted within a few feet of the shoreline before catching against a rock just beneath the surface.

"Sorry," Jimmy said. "Unidentified underwater object. Let me try again."

"No, that's OK. Don't bother," she said hastily, bending over to slip off her sneakers. "I wade when necessary, especially when someone offers me a dinner on the house." She stepped into the cold water gingerly. "It's refreshing. You can't imagine how much I have to do this when I'm wading through marshes to look for nests. See, I'm smiling."

"That's not what we call a happy smile," he said as she lurched into an unseen hole and stepped on a shell.

"Damn shell. They're sharp," she muttered.

"Do you swim, too?"

"Not often in this water. Tried it once and gave it up as a bad habit." She retrieved the newspaper-wrapped crab legs and gave the skiff a shove toward the boat. "This makes me think I worked a little bit for my dinner. I hate to think I'm on the dole and . . ."

"You're not from around here, are you?" he interrupted.

Corinne recognized genuine curiosity in his eyes. "Why, what do you mean?" she asked as she sat back down on the rock to brush the wet sand off her feet.

"Your accent for one thing. You sound almost like one of us, but not quite. It's almost a Canadian accent I'm hearing, but maybe there's something more there, too. Of course, there's that term you just used—'on the dole'—that's not something you hear around here."

"You're a very sharp listener," Corinne answered. "But I think I must have picked that up from someone. I don't use it myself. I guess I said it without thinking, probably after stepping on that damn shell." She frowned inwardly. She knew she'd never picked up the Canadian accent. She'd made a conscious effort, an attempt to sound different when she was entertaining, and enough of the men said so to convince her she was successful. But that colloquialism was the kind of slip that a sharp agent might latch on to and follow up. If someone later on was tracing her and learned that she was on this island, it might just be possible to come up with Jimmy Cook, and on, and on . . .

"A shot in the dark," he agreed, shrugging. "So, now that you have your evening meal and your sneakers are just about back on your feet, I suppose you're going to disappear on me."

"Shortly, yes. But not without thanking you and the *Dream Girl* for providing me with a wonderful dinner." This chance meeting had been perfectly wonderful and she found Jimmy Cook a pleasant diversion from the crisis that seemed to be developing to the south. *How can such unpleasantness be taking place so close yet two absolute strangers can find a few nice moments with each other?* "So thank you for the crab legs, Mr. Cook. Thank you very, very much." Better to ease out politely and forget there were still people like Jimmy in the world.

"You're surely welcome, Miss . . . you know, if you're going to get formal on me, I don't even know your last name."

"McCarthy," she lied.

"Miss McCarthy. A pretty scientist is certainly a sight for a lone fisherman's eyes. If the *Dream Girl* drops anchor here again tomorrow, will you be back?"

That could be a mistake. She hesitated. "I . . . I'm not sure . . ." *Don't do it, Corinne. You're asking for trouble. They'd take Jimmy out just as sure as you're sitting here right now, and without a second thought.*

131

"Well, the *Dream Girl* and her intrepid captain will be back here again tomorrow if the weather's at all cooperative. Would some fresh abalone entice you back?"

Again she was hesitant. "I can't say . . ." *Don't give in.*

Jimmy was already on his feet and moving forward to the open pilot house without waiting for her to finish. He pushed a button and *Dream Girl*'s engine rumbled to life. He eased the boat forward about ten feet, then scrambled forward on the bow to haul in the anchor. Just as rapidly, he was back at the wheel, and holding the bow toward the open water.

"When you're a one-man band," he called over his shoulder, "you can't take it easy. Don't want the *Dream* on the rocks now, do we? See you tomorrow." He turned and waved, his grin widening into a full smile. Then the water swirled around the stern and *Dream Girl* moved away from the shore.

Corinne waved back. There weren't enough Jimmy Cooks in the world. Hardly any when she considered it. She shouldn't come back to Cook's Bay, couldn't—but . . . she might.

That evening, as she sipped wine with her crab legs, she knew she'd be back at Cook's Bay the following afternoon. But she was puzzled. She couldn't understand why. Even while she was drying the last of the dishes, the answer evaded her.

There were no shadow games that night. Instead, Corinne attempted to lose herself in some magazines. When they failed to hold her interest, she tried a romantic novel whose distance from reality left her wondering at the stupidity of heroines.

Nicholas Koniev's guard was down. He was visibly concerned. He chewed unconsciously on his lower lip, stared down as if an answer would miraculously appear from the crystal ball-like spit shine on his shoes, and he paced. He stopped for a moment and stared at the dials on *Gorki*'s control panel without really seeing them. His arms had been folded ceremoniously until he began pulling unconsciously

his left ear. Finally, he turned and strode across the
trol room to the chart table.

"I didn't expect this, at least not so soon," he remarked to
nskoi. Those were the exact words he'd used no more
an a minute before when he studied the mark on the chart.
was just off the eastern shore of the Hood Canal near the
llage of Vinland. The mark indicated the approximate
cation of the green flare Donskoi had seen. It was of more
mediate concern than the report of the dolphin attack.

Donskoi was slumped against the chart table. He glanced
p at his captain through tired eyes. "I'm absolutely sure."

Koniev wrinkled his nose and stepped back from the
chart. Donskoi smelled. While his mini subs were state of
the art, sanitary facilities were limited and men's odors
never changed. Naval designers would claim that such
nas were a design failure of the human body.

nskoi noticed his captain's reaction and was secretly
While he respected the man for his genius, he found
e in the confines of a submarine especially
rlook. Maybe it was the danger he'd been
ast two days. Perhaps it was just exhaustion.
Whatever, he hadn't the slightest intention of moving.

As offensive as Donskoi's odor had become, there was no
questioning his navigation. Men in confined spaces, especially exhausted ones, tended to magnify their problems.
That flare indicated the Americans had found something,
more than likely a mine. "In that case, I have a slight change
of plans," Koniev said as much to himself as to Donskoi.
Then, sympathetically, "You look tired."

"Exhausted."

"You'll get your sleep—eventually. But there's no time
now. We have one more mission." Men were expendable.
Missions were not.

"I will work with you to the best of my ability." Donskoi
made an effort to sound enthusiastic. After all, completing a
mission with the famous Nicholas Koniev would certainly
enhance his career. "I really don't know if I can handle the
submarine efficiently, Captain, for a lengthy period of time
anyway. If I made a mistake, we might lose . . ."

"That you don't have to worry about, Viktor," he sa
using the other man's first name with a trace of superior
"I'm joining you this time. To begin with, I'll be handli
the controls. You can relax then. But I need your he
because I plan to do some swimming of my own. At th
point, you will be required to resume the controls."

Donskoi had been leaning on his elbows on the cha
table. Now he rose wearily to his full height, which wa
shorter than Koniev. "Of course, Captain." Was he bein
relieved? He could feel anger building within that he knev
must be controlled. "Can you explain our mission so that
might prepare for anything new? Or are you assuming
complete command of my submarine?" What had he done
wrong? He looked away before he said anything he might
regret.

"I am not taking away your command. I'm assumi
control only for this mission. The responsibility wi
yours while I'm away from the submarine." He
briefly of elaborating on his intentions, then
wasn't the place. "You have purposely not bee
this mission because it is mine and mine ale
nothing you need to do before we launch."

No man, especially one whose command is being assumed by another, likes to be kept unaware of the purpose of
a mission. No matter what Koniev said, his position was
being usurped. "Would you prefer me to shower beforehand?" Donskoi spoke in a weary voice that might have
hinted of sarcasm.

"If you please." If Koniev noticed the tone, he appeared
unaware of it as he bent over the chart.

Before the miniature submarine was launched, Koniev
gathered his officers in the control room so that the entire
crew would know of his direct orders. "Captain Vaskiiy," he
said calmly to his executive officer, "it is likely that enemy
submarines will attempt to locate *Gorki* in my absence. I
leave everything to your discretion. You are authorized to
attempt escape or to attack. Your decisions will be based
entirely on the safety of the ship. You *will not* concern
yourself with the fate of the miniature submarines in your

decisions about this ship, and you *will not* concern yourself with my welfare. That remains my concern alone." His eyes roamed the control room each time he emphasized another *will not* to Vaskiiy. *"Gorki will not* be captured and if by some chance she is in danger of sinking, you *will* activate all destruct mechanisms. Do you understand exactly what I expect?" Again, his eyes skipped to each face that stared back at him, daring them to argue with his orders.

"I understand, Captain," Vaskiiy answered hoarsely, aware that his captain had no intention of revealing his mission to anyone. Koniev's well-known theory of sacrifice still held true. The mini subs were expendable, the crew was expendable, even *Gorki* was expendable. And to Vaskiiy's surprise, it appeared that Nicholas Koniev was expendable if it came to that.

But this mysterious mission was not.

"This has to be it, Bernie." Harry Coffin hung up the phone. "A P-3 from one of the reserve squadrons at Whidbey Island has repeatedly had an on again/off again magnetic contact off Dungeness Spit. Not a hell of a lot of movement to it, but there is some."

"How close to the *Seahorse* wreckage?"

"Just about due south, right close to land." Coffin pointed out New Dungeness on his wall chart. "Must be in this vicinity."

"Not too far from the Hood Canal. Could be a miniature submarine or it might even be the mother." Ryng measured the distance with a thumb and index finger, eyeballing the distance on the mileage chart. "Or both."

"I'm sending *Honolulu* to investigate. She was on the nearest barrier patrol."

"Who's commanding?"

"Dan Ward. He picked her up last summer."

"Good man. I've locked out on one of his boats before. Aggressive. Does he know . . ."

"He's been informed about *Seahorse*. I doubt the same thing can happen to him."

"There's an old saying about history having a way of

repeating itself. I think we might be able to avoid that if you'll give me an extra couple of hours." Noticing Coffin's hesitation, he added, "It might mean a lot to Dan and *Honolulu.*"

"I'm listening."

"Let me send Len Todd up there with Chester. I can have them in the boat in fifteen minutes—they'll be in the water up there in less than an hour."

"An hour's a long time," Coffin began, "and there's no guarantee . . ."

"No, none at all," Ryng interrupted. "But you've seen my dolphins operate. They're faster than any human being and if there's another submarine other than *Honolulu* up there, Chester can find it. All Dan Ward has to do is poke an antenna up and Lenny will be able to con him within strike range. The rest is up to Dan."

"Two hours . . . no more than one hundred twenty minutes. That's max, Bernie. Then I have to send *Honolulu* in blind."

"Fair enough." Ryng pulled a flashlight from his back pocket and stepped over to the window looking out toward the piers and blinked it a couple of times. "They're on their way."

Coffin came over to look out the window. "Anticipating?" he asked with a slight grin for Ryng's benefit.

"I was pretty sure you'd like the idea."

"I do. I just wish I could say it was my own."

"One thing, Admiral. Even if we get this unknown submarine, that doesn't mean there aren't others around. Miniatures more than likely. And I don't think we'd be wise to set your Tridents loose just yet, at least not until our sweep is complete. If there's one mine we've found, that means to me there must be more."

The explosive ordnance people had begun to take apart piece by piece the mine Danny West had located. It was normally a time-consuming effort at best to analyze a foreign explosive and continue to live. In this case, there'd been no time and the analysis was begun in a remote, wooded area. Fortunately, one of the first items they'd analyzed was a fairly new mechanism of Soviet origin used to detonate the weapon. It involved both an activating signal and then a time delay. Obviously it was intended to sink Trident submarines, but apparently only when an aggressive decision had to be made. Harry Coffin had been amazed. For some inexplicable reason, the Russians had included a "fail-safe" mechanism which seemed to broadcast a message that they really didn't want to activate it—unless they ran out of options. Yet . . . *Seahorse* . . .

"That was the hardest story to make the Pentagon and the politicians believe," Coffin said. "They're raising hell with the Russians through their Washington embassy, threatening all sorts of things that I don't think Moscow believes for a minute. But they've gone along with one of my suggestions. We still have attack submarines off the straits making like they're protecting Tridents on their way out to sea. As long as the Kremlin thinks there's a possibility that we're still free to come and go as we please, we may have a leg up on the diplomatic level."

It often proved difficult for the senior officers directly involved on the scene to convey their thoughts to a group of politicians in Washington who dealt with theory. In this case, the navy was dealing with a crisis involving direct contact with an unknown quantity. Until *Seahorse*, no one had fired a shot and there was no apparent reason she should have been sunk. The theorists were entirely involved in why the events were taking place during a period of military reduction and what they would lead to. It was a case of well-meaning individuals operating on separate planes with entirely different goals. Washington's objective was to present a threat to the threat, even though they were unaware or unsure whether it could be carried out. Harry Coffin and Bernie Ryng were attempting to satisfy needs on both ends of the spectrum.

Ryng nodded. "With the additional backup team that arrived earlier this evening, my boys ought to complete their sector search of the bottom of the Canal in the next twelve hours but that's still time for something else to happen." He found that he was already uncomfortable with what he'd just said. "I can't believe they'd just leave a series of mines and call it a day."

The phone rang on Coffin's desk and he had the receiver in his hand before it was silent. While he listened, he was nodding in Ryng's direction and it was his turn to point an index finger at Ryng's chest. As he replaced the phone, he said, "You have amazing prescience. Security forces around Bremerton believe they heard something on their hydrophones near the channel entrance, almost as if something was scraping the bottom. They're prosecuting it now."

Nine

For someone outside the Spetznaz brotherhood to comprehend Andrei Tarantsev's reaction to what he considered his final orders, it would be necessary to understand a most complex individual. He marked his life in two stages—before he was Spetznaz, and after. He cared nothing about what happened before.

Tarantsev was an introspective man, a likely explanation of why so many of his fellow Spetznaz thought he was moody and withdrawn. With his dark hair and black eyes and, more often than not, unsmiling features, his outward appearance was one of ferocity and many considered him dangerous. Even his instructors were somewhat intimidated when he went through Spetznaz training, to the extent that almost all of them saw little reason to treat him as roughly as his peers. The more perceptive members in his class felt Tarantsev frightened the instructors as much as he did his fellow trainees and that was why his treatment was more lenient. That was fine with him because human social contact offered little satisfaction as far as he was concerned.

Not only was he considered the toughest recruit in his group, he was forced to prove it twice. The first time was when he caught another trainee stealing a few rubles from his locker. Tarantsev turned the man's face into a red mush before breaking both of his arms, first above the wrists and then above the elbows. That solution appealed to his instructors who credited him with leadership potential as a result.

The second occurred during *sambo* training, which literally means "self-defense without weapons" and is generally intended to teach survival to a man who must survive on wit and strength. The training was brutal, the injuries often severe. The instructor, intent on showing that any available item could be employed to defend oneself, made the mistake of using Tarantsev to display the utility of the infantryman's spade. His error was to slam Tarantsev in the side with it, then on the head as the young recruit doubled over. The enraged student recovered instantly and broke the instructor's neck with a single blow, leaving him paralyzed. His leadership was now unquestioned.

He also displayed a superb intellect as a trainee and was given his choice of assignment. Naval Spetznaz appealed to him, and he was fascinated by the miniature submarines once he was apprised of their existence. As always, through each segment of his training, he was considered bright, highly capable—and moody. No one ever bothered to fathom the real individual because of his ferocious reputation.

Andrei Tarantsev was even brighter than he was given credit for. His silence was actually the result of his introspective nature. He was curious about his surroundings and about people although few of the latter gained his respect. He considered their fear of him nothing more than a display of ignorance. His silence was anything but moodiness. It was his way of being left alone to analyze his own abilities and study his reactions to each new challenge he encountered.

The situation at Bremerton presented a situation he'd often spent time considering—*when death presented itself as a probability, would he experience fear? And would he handle himself well?* As they approached Bremerton after a harrowing transit through Rich's passage, he could sense the fear that Tupolev and Osipenko were experiencing, and he was surprised to realize that he actually felt sympathy for them. They didn't want to die either but their Spetznaz training consistently presented death as a likelihood during their career.

Tarantsev was not afraid. As they maneuvered through the cluttered waters, frequently peering through the periscope for any sort of marker that would confirm their location, he found he enjoyed this final challenge. His only negative feeling was that this was to be his final mission. But there was no fear of death.

Instead, he sensed an increasing anger. He was angry because he was being asked to sacrifice himself for something he wasn't able to understand. It wasn't the concept of sacrifice. That was something that had been ingrained in all of them from the first day of Spetznaz training. It was simply that he lacked a reason for dying.

Nicholas Koniev was one of the few men Tarantsev had learned to respect, as much for his brilliance and cruelty as for his absolute disdain for officers who led only from shore, and Koniev was a leader willing to place himself before the enemy. *Then why would he ask as loyal a man as Andrei Tarantsev, one who was deeply honored to serve under him, to literally commit suicide without explaining the purpose of his sacrifice?* The more Tarantsev mulled this over in the self-induced silence of the miniature submarine, the angrier he became.

Fear was something for common men who would foul their pants in this situation. Tupolev and Osipenko were better than that, so he granted them the fear that others would experience in this situation. When Osipenko spotted the running lights and sweeping spotlights of the security craft operating outside the shipyard, he had a right to be frightened. Yet Tarantsev also knew the two crewmen would perform superbly because they were survivors—of Spetznaz training. Their fear would retreat.

But he came to understand that his anger would not disappear as they continued their harrowing transit.

Tarantsev had always anticipated an equivalent response to his devotion. He was surprised to realize his resentment was expanding in the final few hours of his life into a hatred of the man who sent him on this final, apparently fruitless mission. Tarantsev's passion for always understanding everything he encountered was now transmuted to a hatred of the one man he respected as his craft made the perilous journey toward the Bremerton basin. His only satisfaction would be to take it out on those whose job it was to defend themselves.

Tarantsev moved to the periscope and poked it up no more than two feet as they rounded Point White and set course for their goal less than three miles distant. It was so shallow that their small conning tower was barely below the surface. He twisted slowly on his knees and was shocked to see that his presence was no surprise. Bottom-based hydrophones must have picked them up. "They're using everything but kayaks," he muttered. The reflection of searchlights blinded him momentarily and he dropped the periscope to water level. "Whaleboats, tugs, mike boats. *A secret mission,*" he growled. "A sturgeon couldn't get any closer than we are with the defense they have. Depth?" he called out.

"Ten meters beneath the keel. It varies," Osipenko responded. "If this chart is accurate, we'd just about be aground at low tide."

"Stop engines," Tarantsev said softly, offering an encouraging grin to the other two. They were still a good distance from their goal. It was so unlike him. "Stand by to deploy mines. This appears as good a place as any other."

"Who will set the warheads?" Tupolev inquired, knowing he was assigned to do so as the external equipment operator. All three of them were trained to do the job, but he was the obvious choice when the officer in charge and the engineer were so vital in this situation.

Tarantsev didn't answer. He was intent on surveying the scene through the periscope. Once he'd accepted the impossibility of approaching any closer, he ordered them to settle on the bottom on their skids.

"I don't mind," Osipenko offered hesitantly.

"I'll do it," Tupolev conceded. "It's my job now."

Tarantsev let the periscope slip back into the well and grinned again at both of them. The past few minutes were the first time either one had seen him display any feelings before he spoke. "A fine fix we've got ourselves in, isn't it?"

Both men were baffled by his expression. It was as if someone had just struck an ancient vase causing cracks to appear all over its surface. Yet, even though by all rights it should have crumbled, it refused to break. The cracks were deep and marred the surface but it somehow held together.

"Do either of you have suggestions about how we're going to get ourselves out of here after we've left our packages?" Tarantsev actually smiled broadly as their faces registered surprise. "I'm more than willing to share the final decisions with you since we all know our odds are about zero." They would be lucky to survive another half hour.

"It'll be difficult to set the warheads at this depth," Tupolev said. That was supposed to be done in deeper water. "It's so shallow here, they could detonate while they're being set." He spread his hands. "We're in this together but I don't understand the purpose. We were supposed to . . ." His voice drifted off.

"We were," Tarantsev agreed. "And we might have except for that American destroyer that happened on us, and who knows what else. So, it didn't work out." He shrugged. "Those things happen. But, there's no reason we can't get even."

"Get even?" Osipenko asked. "With who?"

"With the Americans, of course. They intend to destroy us . . . and they will eventually. So we'll give them something for their troubles."

Tupolev smiled. "I think I agree with you. Why not? We want to give them a good reason to kill us, make all of this worthwhile for them and us." It was inconceivable that a Spetznaz would allow himself to be taken prisoner.

"Do you have a better idea?"

"How do you want to go about this?" Osipenko asked. His enthusiasm was less than Tupolev's.

"Obviously we can't place the mines, set the warheads properly, and escape. So we make this little ship one big bomb." He indicated Tupolev with a nod. "You know more about these mines than I do. They're designed to chase after a submarine once they hear it, and then the proximity fuse detonates the explosive within a killing range. Can you bypass the enabling run and just set the warhead?"

"I suppose anything's possible if we can somehow close the firing circuit whenever we want to. But I'm not sure if we can set the warhead to go off exactly when we want it to. We're talking about doing something the weapon wasn't designed for."

"But is it possible?" Tarantsev urged. The smile had returned to his face, which seemed a reflection of that precious cracked vase.

"It's worth a try."

"Good. We're going to be like those old Japanese suicide pilots, the ones who crashed their planes into the aircraft carriers. Except we're going to do the same thing with a submarine. Captain Koniev wants us to accomplish something. We'll give everyone something to think about." What Tarantsev really meant to say was that they were about to justify their Spetznaz training whether or not that was Koniev's intent. "We'll stay right here until we're ready. They haven't found us yet. If we're lucky, they won't find us for a while."

The discussion that followed turned on such a bizarre idea that their fears were forgotten. They planned exactly how to turn their craft and themselves into a high speed mine. Tupolev broke out the circuit diagrams of the warheads and decided on a method he thought might work.

In the end, there was no assurance that they could time the detonations properly. Whichever mine went off first would certainly set off the other. The idea was hopefully to withhold the explosion until the critical second. That would be difficult. They argued about the best way to make their approach. Finally, Osipenko suggested that it would be best to make their final run with just the conning tower on the surface. It was easier to pilot and they could approach at maximum speed. The lower they remained in the water the less of a target they presented. Their final decision was that Osipenko should become the pilot because Tarantsev simply couldn't conceive of his final mission without using a weapon, even if it was going to kill him and deprive him of the pleasure of seeing how well they accomplished their plan.

It was both refreshing and encouraging for Tupolev and Osipenko to see their commander, one of the most feared Spetznaz, actually smiling as they made final preparations. Tarantsev chattered away good-naturedly about how much he'd enjoyed serving in mini subs, how much he had gained personally from working with the other two, and how much it meant to all three of them to be Spetznaz.

As first Tupolev, then Tarantsev, locked out of their vessel for the final time, each of them enjoyed a spirit of camaraderie that had been missing previously. The swimmers plugged their external communications devices into the conning tower to communicate with Osipenko. The cold, machinelike attitude of the professional Spetznaz had been replaced by a premature feeling of accomplishment.

They'd found the warheads could not be set at that depth without blowing themselves up before they were ready. But Tupolev had figured out how they should be able to detonate them by hand at the right moment. Since the swimmers were blind beneath the surface, Osipenko became their eyes. After retracting the skids and rising to the surface, he relayed details of what was taking place outside the conning tower. They would depend on his timing.

"About three thousand meters from the main pier, maybe less," he announced. "We have a little more water under the keel now. Must be the main channel. Speed about five knots. I'm going to increase it slowly so we have a chance once we're spotted." He was perched in the conning tower, his head no more than a few feet above the surface.

"Very slowly," came Tarantsev's voice. "I can feel the drag already. I don't want to get washed off beforehand."

"The same here," Tupolev concurred. They were about ten feet beneath the surface clinging to the weapons.

A clanging sound against the conning tower caught Osipenko's attention. "We've been seen. They're shooting at us now. Just rifle shots, I guess. Can't see anything really. There are lights all around me. Sounds kind of like hail on a car roof, doesn't it?" He relayed the details of his impending death as if narrating a fashion show. "Wait a minute. I . . . see more of them coming this way . . . or more lights. They're shooting, too. We need to move faster."

"Not yet," Tarantsev shouted. "Distance?"

"Maybe twenty-five hundred meters now. There're more of them closing us, too many." The anxiety in his voice was evident. "I don't think I have any choice but to add more speed."

"Go ahead then," Tarantsev agreed. "We'll hold on somehow."

There was an explosion against the conning tower that could be heard by the swimmers. "They're using explosives now," Osipenko reported. "They're so close, I'm going to have to maneuver if we're going to have a chance to . . ."

"Do what you have to."

Osipenko jerked the wheel to the right to avoid a whaleboat that looked as if it were going to ram him. Bullets rattled off the tiny conning tower.

"I'm having trouble holding on," Tupolev called out.

"I am also," Tarantsev responded. "Keep doing what you have to, Osipenko. I'm preparing my detonator now. We may not be able to do exactly what we intend, but we'll give them a hell of . . ." His voice disappeared as the craft lurched sharply to the left at the same moment a surface explosion shattered their ears.

"They've pierced the conning tower," Osipenko cried out, shocked at the blood that was running into his eyes. He wiped at his face with a sleeve. "I'm wounded. Hard to see," he gasped. "I think it's still a little less than two thousand meters to go." He wasn't really sure. The lights were now a blur. His body seemed numb. "They're trying to ram . . ." His voice was drowned out by another explosion as he threw the wheel in the opposite direction to avoid a boat bearing down on him.

"I'm slipping," Tupolev called out. "I can't finish the detonator."

"Mine's almost done," Tarantsev responded frantically. "Keep on . . ."

He never finished the sentence. The men in the boats on the surface saw the water burst upward in front of them from a tremendous explosion. The nearest small craft were hurled into the air then backward by the pressure of the water thrown in their direction. Flying metal from the mines and the submarine shredded men and boats as the night was illuminated by a brilliant flash.

There was no damage to the ships and nearby piers from the disintegrating miniature submarine. It had been too far away to succeed. There was little divers could find the following day. Only one body was recovered in what was left of the submarine's hull and that was unidentifiable. But Tarantsev and his men had indeed attracted attention to themselves, just as Nicholas Koniev had planned.

Corinne was prepared. Anticipating that this night would justify the investment made in placing her on the island, she ate Jimmy's crab legs early that evening. They were a treat, especially with the wine she'd been so wise to insist on. After dinner, she stretched out on the couch under a gas lamp to read herself to sleep with a magazine. Her intent was to nap until midnight.

An hour passed, then another, until she realized that this would not be a time for sleep. She went out to the kitchen and fingered the various bottles before pouring herself a single malt scotch over ice. *Might as well do it right.* Back on the couch, she found herself unable to concentrate on a book. Even with the drink, it was no different than staring at the magazine. Instead, she found herself inundated by a rush of memories, old and new, some hazy and too many frighteningly clear. Just as soon as an image of Ken insinuated itself, there was a vivid scene of the accident and Cory's face flashing before her. But that was her first life!

No, that was the end of her first life.

Then came a flood of snapshots of the men she'd met—

her second life—especially since she'd come to Vancouver. Not one of them was clear enough to retain for more than an instant before another face swam to the forefront. They couldn't have been in order yet she had no idea of their progression.

Her handlers followed, first those in England who had recruited her and undertaken her training, then botched whatever it was they were supposed to do. Only the one called David, the one who asked for iced martinis and talked like an American, offered a pleasant memory. She smiled when she recalled the expression on his face as she told him all about himself. They were followed by those in Vancouver who'd managed to turn her into a polished creation. They were naturally more comfortable hovering in the background for it was these men who taught her there was a purpose and a goal. Her use of her natural assets, they assured her, was no different than one of them using a weapon. *The methods employed for intelligence gathering are blind,* she remembered one of them assuring her. They watched her, they were patient, they sometimes frowned, but never did they present themselves as an intricate part of her private life. They were shadows. She had selected a trade—or had it chosen her?—and they respected her ability to carry it off so well.

Eventually, and perhaps that was no more than a few moments in this review of her second life, Jimmy Cook appeared and he was smiling as much with those friendly gray eyes as with his handsome mouth. *Dream Girl* was there and everything he did with her was so smooth and confident, turning her into the wind, securing her anchor so quickly, scampering about his boat like a monkey, perching on the stern with one foot dangling just above the water, talking about himself as if he were narrating his life story. She liked him. There was no emotion she felt toward him, but he was refreshing. Perhaps . . . sometime . . . one like him . . .

But she'd only met him once! A friend maybe—not a lover.

And then, unmercifully, it all repeated, both the good and the bad. The scenes were repetitive, more disturbing this time than before.

No . . . no, there was no way she was going to sleep before midnight, not with her mind flashing one snapshot of life after another on her brain. She had to get up. She had to cleanse her mind.

Corinne stepped outside and sat on the steps. The last light in the western sky had quickly faded. The air was cooling rapidly but the fog was holding off. Her eyes fixed on the sky as tens of thousands of stars winked on in the gathering darkness, each cluster leaping into view in these untainted skies so much faster than she had ever imagined. She remained there, feeling the evening chill, until she was sure that each star had reported for its night's duty. Only when she began shivering did she move back inside.

When the Russian came on her radio well before midnight, there was none of the urgency or planning she had anticipated. In fact, after listening to his initial sentences, she was sure this must be another individual. He was equally precise in his method of conversing, absolute in his planning, and he indicated no further need for the type of communications she was expecting to provide. He told her that there was a distinct possibility they might not need further assistance. However, she was expected to guard the frequency on a twenty-four-hour basis until further notice. He never mentioned that he was on a mini sub entering the Hood Canal.

She found that report odd after everything she had been told to expect. Her original instructions had been so specific and now the critical party was deviating from them. It would be a long six hours until she could explain this at dawn to the men on shore, unless they again violated their own rules.

Corinne was able to sleep this time, but it was a fitful sleep full of the troubles that are compounded by a mind caught between rest and reality.

* * *

Ink! That's what it reminded him of. Ink.

Len Todd remembered what real ink was, or had been. He attended an ancient grade school that had existed in his section of the city well before his father moved there. Everything was old, the classrooms, the desks, the hard wooden chairs, even the teachers. But this brought back the memory of a teacher's explanation of why there were holes in the upper corners of the desks—for inkwells! She explained how students, now grown into adults, dipped metal-tipped pens into liquid ink kept in little glass jars that fit into those holes. Then they wrote their lessons. And, of course, his best friend imagined after school was over what it would be like to have a pool full of ink and get pushed into it and have to swim. Todd had never forgotten.

That's exactly how he felt now, except that the chilly waters of the Strait of Juan de Fuca added to the novelty. It was black and cold and he was forced to call up every aspect of his early training to accommodate his senses in such a hostile environment.

Chester displayed no concern whatsoever. The dolphin relied primarily on his sound system to see. It made little difference to him whether it was day or night when they played the barbell game. When his partner displayed the metal object hanging from the rope loop in the faint underwater glow of the light, the dolphin knew immediately there was fun to be had. Something was nearby, perhaps near the surface, maybe on the bottom. Sometimes he even found the object in between. Wherever, it was of little concern to Chester. It was a fun game and there would be a reward at the end as long as he found the object and left the smaller one attached to it.

Chester snatched the object, holding its rope loop in his mouth, and raced off into the night without a sound. First he would listen intently, varying his depth to see if something might be moving out there. Only if the water was absolutely silent would he begin to employ his sonar.

He arched out of the water for a breath then dove almost straight down, his auditory senses cataloging every sound within his range but searching for that elusive one that could only be made by one of the man's machines.

Nothing.

Somersaulting gracefully near the bottom he headed toward the surface on an oblique angle and that was when he was able to detect the faintest sound of something other than sealife. It was quiet—either distant or very slow moving—but he immediately reoriented himself in its direction.

What was it?

Chester sent out a series of shrill whistles at a decibel level beyond the human ear and was greeted with an immediate return. The image that formed in his brain was of something very large and very hard. If it had been alive, he would have been able to detect air spaces and cavities within its body. This was one of the man's instruments—and it was the reason for this game!

Employing a series of whistles and clicks that could have been understood only by another dolphin, Chester isolated the position of his target and its motion before picking his own method of getting behind it. That's what the men had made a vital part of the reward in the game—come from behind the object and place your magnetic barbell very gently against it. Make a noise and there was no reward.

The manmade object was slow and it was simple to slip in behind it and then sidle up alongside. These objects were unintelligent, unable to even sense his motion as he touched it. There was no sound as he allowed the barbell to attach itself.

Then Chester was off in a flash to show that he had earned his reward.

Shortly afterward, Len Todd rose to the surface. The Strait of Juan de Fuca was choppy that evening and he found it difficult to keep himself and the radio above the waves while he bobbed like a cork. But the American submarine did have an antenna in the air and responded on his second call. Their periscope poked above the surface just long enough to detect Todd's green flare. Then they marked his position on their chart and lay out the bearing of the target submarine from his location.

"Contact on port bow remains unclassified." Even over the control room speaker, there was an odd mix of question and curiosity as the voice followed standard procedures. "We do have definite cavitation on that bearing and what appears to be machinery noises. None of it is familiar." But the sound was emanating from the bearing indicated by the SEAL who had contacted them by voice radio on the surface. It was clear and obvious even with the constant sound of surface traffic that spread across the target area.

Dan Ward, *Honolulu*'s captain, considered the report from sonar and agreed silently with his sonar officer. Neither of them was quite ready to commit himself to the obvious, that this was the unidentified submarine that had apparently sunk *Seahorse*, yet that was exactly what each one was thinking. Their reasoning was simple, supported by logic. They were searching for a killer. This contact was well outside the Puget Sound traffic lanes, there were no other American submarines in the immediate vicinity, and the sound signature was unlike anything they had previously experienced. Nor did it compare with anything in their computer's memory.

It had to be close by because it was moving very slowly, most likely bare steerageway, and the sound would not have come to them under those sonar conditions at any great distance. This was a target.

Ward had listened to his executive officer in the background coordinating preparation for their attack from the first moment sonar had picked up the contact. The tubes had already been flooded, the torpedos warmed for their run, the pressure equalized in the tubes. There would be one dead giveaway, the obvious sound of the muzzle doors opening, but that would be followed so quickly by the water slug as the first torpedo was fired that it meant little.

No, Ward was sure there was no need for further analysis. This was the target that had sunk *Seahorse* without any kind of warning as far as Ward was concerned, and there was no need to provide any indication of *Honolulu*'s presence. That would come when the muzzle doors were opened and by then it would be too late. His orders were to sink it instantly. There would be none of the opportunities *Seahorse* had allowed.

"Contact is increasing speed, definitely moving across our bow. The water's deeper out there."

The weapons officer had already reported that his torpedo was ready.

Ward gave the order and the ominous sound of the muzzle doors snapping open on the tubes echoed through the ship. Unless the other vessel was searching for them, it would likely be lost in the clamor of surface ships.

"The solution is ready," the executive officer said evenly, anticipating Ward's next words.

"Shoot on generated bearings."

"Left full rudder. Emergency flank speed." Vaskiiy's reaction was automatic. "Depth under the keel?" he called to the man on the fathometer.

"Two zero meters."

"Muzzle doors opening on the bearing." A sonarman had been attempting to isolate the new sound when the unmistakable clang of the muzzle doors came to him.

How could they have gotten so close without being detected? Vaskiiy could feel the perspiration cooling on the back of his shirt and an empty sensation persisted in his stomach as *Gorki* reacted to his orders and heeled to port. *Muzzle doors!* They were about to shoot at him!

"Three zero meters under the keel."

They must get to deeper water. Vaskiiy had turned away instinctively from the intruder. His first concern wasn't depth as much as opening the distance between them, but intuitively he knew the water must become deeper. "Give me a course to the deepest water," he snapped at the quartermaster, "quickly. It doesn't have to be perfect."

"This . . ." the sailor faltered, "this is the deepest. It gets shallower to the north and west." The contact was east of them, land to the south.

"Torpedo on the bearing!"

Evade . . . evade . . . evade, Vaskiiy heard in the back of his mind. *Disappear! Hide! Get away!*

He couldn't go deeper. But he had to get away. He pointed at the diving officer. "Keep ten meters under your keel while we maneuver."

Gorki maneuvered like a scared rabbit darting through the brambles while sonar continued to report data on the incoming torpedo. To the men in the control room, the torpedo was an invisible threat, linked to them only by the faceless voice from sonar. But to the man reporting its progress, there was no doubt that the sound coming through his earphones was a menace, a terror increasing in intensity as it sought him out.

Vaskiiy placed a wall of noisemakers between them to draw off the torpedo's homing device. And when the water began to grow shallow, he reversed his course in a wide turn and fired his first torpedo and then a second as soon as the interlock closed the muzzle on the first tube. Neither one was well-programmed but it might put off their attacker if he could elude the torpedo that was bearing down on him. Once the homing device began range-gating on them, it would be relentless in its pursuit of *Gorki.*

"There's a shit storm of noisemakers out there, Captain, and he's running around like a chicken with his head cut off."

Dan Ward had no trouble picturing exactly what was taking place off their bow. He could see the Soviet submarine clearly in his mind and he was also able to place his first torpedo in perspective, boring in on its target. The noisemakers, placed out there to create a mass of confusion as the Russian maneuvered behind them, failed to concern him.

He knew the second torpedo was ready. Reports from the weapons officer and the executive officer had been repeated until he remembered to acknowledge those excited voices intruding from beyond his mental image of the Russian submarine and his torpedo.

"Bearing of contact has shifted from starboard bow to port."

The target had reversed course!

"My solution is ready, Captain," the XO repeated for the third time.

"Torpedo in the water on target's bearing."

They'd shot back at him. He would have done the same. Don't get mad, get even. No way the shot could have been a good one, though. Pure desperation. But get the hell out.

"Shoot on generated bearings," Ward ordered evenly.

The thud of the water slug hurling the torpedo from the port tube was felt throughout *Honolulu*.

As soon as the torpedo was reported running well, Ward gave the orders to evade and the submarine heeled sharply as she turned away and increased to flank speed. The water remained reasonably deep on this reverse course. *Honolulu* left a wall of noisemakers astern as she headed in the opposite direction at high speed.

Vaskiiy understood the meaning of honest fear as the reports from sonar became more frantic. The American torpedo was range-gating—homing on *Gorki*. Somehow it had gotten through the noisemakers that were supposed to have been so effective. That could only mean that there had been too much time for the American to close him without being detected and prepare a good firing solution. The torpedo had reacted to its instructions perfectly, bypassing the noisemakers and then activating its sonar to capture *Gorki*.

The hell with the depth. It was too shallow here to confuse the torpedo. Vaskiiy gave the orders for a sharp turn to keep the torpedo astern. If they could just move fast enough, hold the distance between them until the torpedo ran out of fuel . . .

"Constant range gate . . ."

The explosion from the starboard quarter seemed to lift *Gorki* and hurl her sideways as if she were completely out of the water instead of almost seventy meters deep. The control room was instantly black as equipment and bodies hurtled through the air and men screamed in fear and pain.

Vaskiiy lay in the far corner of the control room. Someone was on top of him. His entire body was numb and he didn't seem to have the strength to heave off the weight that held him down. *Gorki* had not righted herself and he could sense she was also down at the stern. "Emergency blow . . ." he began, but he was unable to hear if he'd actually completed his orders.

There was a deep rumbling sound from the engineering space. The angle of the stern increased so rapidly that *Gorki* seemed to be standing on end. Vaskiiy struggled against the body that pinned him against the bulkhead. But when he was finally able to look toward the control panel, there was no one there!

Then the second torpedo exploded directly outside the control room and Vaskiiy experienced a brief sensation of water all about him before he died.

Dan Ward had never imagined that he might relax in such a situation, but he found he was aware of everything taking place around him. The reports of the Soviet torpedo runs, the detonation of his first, then his second, the positive announcements that the target had been hit followed by the sounds of collapsing bulkheads, the assurances that the Soviet attack on *Honolulu* had failed—each of them became a part of his mental picture of the entire event.

That was the way they had all been trained to handle such an attack and it had worked. But what had they sunk? An enemy certainly, an enemy that was just as ready to sink them. At the same moment he savored his victory, he realized there was so much more to all of this and *Honolulu* was just a part of something he didn't fully understand.

He gave the orders to surface. The radioman already had the circuit ready to contact Admiral Coffin.

Ten

"STOP," KONIEV HISSED WITH AN EXAGGERATED WHISPER. They'd made the passage from the Strait into the Hood Canal quickly utilizing Donskoi's navigational notes on the chart.

"Engine is stopped," answered Tikhvin. Donskoi never required them to respond. But this one, he was a pain in the ass whether or not he was the father or the mother or whatever they wanted to call him. Now he had to worry about a buoyancy problem while they remained dead in the water. He was exhausted and his patience was crumbling as he struggled with the controls.

"Mark our position," Koniev ordered Donskoi, who had been forced to assume Kolarov's responsibilities on the miniature submarine. "Make sure set and drift are taken into account in case we can't take a visual fix."

"I can only estimate our dead reckoning position, Captain. There's a definite tide here." Certainly the man must know that.

"Do you intend to settle on the bottom . . . ?" Tikhvin began, irritated by the problems he was encountering trying to hold their trim with the engines stopped.

"Negative," Koniev snapped impatiently. "Donskoi is

157

correct. I need a visual on this. Take me to periscope depth."
He peered over Donskoi's shoulder at the chart on the tiny
table and placed his finger on the points he wanted. "I'll take
the tower between the piers, the Vinland Transit Station,
and try that flashing buoy at Hazel Point."

"Holding at periscope depth, Captain."

"Standby to mark," Koniev said as he eased the periscope
above the surface and made a cautious circle. There was
nothing moving near them. After a moment to confirm his
whereabouts, he picked out the locations he'd given
Donskoi and called out their bearings, sure that the one on
Hazel Point was too mushy to give him a perfect fix. On the
other hand, considering that he was about to undertake
an extremely dangerous mission ashore, he was secretly
pleased to be as calm as he was. He experienced a moment
of self-satisfaction in the knowledge that neither of the other
two could possibly imagine what he would be doing shortly.

"Good fix," Donskoi reported. "Perfect."

Koniev dropped the periscope back in the well. He
glanced with pleasure at the point where the three lines of
his fix came together to indicate the submarine's exact
position. Then he turned to Tikhvin. "We should have
about twenty fathoms here. I'll lock out in exactly thirty
minutes," he concluded, smiling casually.

As he prepared himself, Koniev explained exactly what he
expected of the other two men while he was gone. Their
current position was just off Brown's Point, almost directly
across from the triangular submarine pier where the huge
Tridents tied up when they were in port. It appeared to be
reasonably safe on that side of the canal since the area was
relatively undeveloped and there was nothing but a few
scattered houses and camps.

He said nothing about his mission, only that he anticipated being gone until just before first light. He intended to
allow himself five hours. If he wasn't back within that time,
Donskoi was to get underway and return to *Gorki*. His
orders to Vaskiiy had been to allow no more than twenty-
four hours after the mini sub's departure before withdraw-

ing through the Strait of Juan de Fuca and returning to Petropavlovsk.

No good-byes for Koniev. No words of encouragement. Nothing was expected. A lock out was the most dangerous part of the job and he expected a totally professional effort from the other two, just as he would have done for them.

A unique sensation always came over Koniev at a time like this. There was a special something about swimming alone in dark foreign waters, something that anointed one with a feeling of power. The release he experienced as he escaped the air lock was akin to the freedom of birth. The cord—in the form of the air lock—was the severing process, a release into another world which he knew was his. Here he was alone. It was here that he was also the master of his fate, and that was something Victor Koniev truly looked forward to.

Koniev learned that the truly successful in the navy achieved their success by working with others. He did so because he was ambitious. But he also saw in the Navy Spetznaz and then in the miniature submarine program the opportunity for achieving his goals on his own. Solitude was preferable to depending on other men not as competent as he. When he worked with others, he conveyed his sense of superiority over them in no uncertain terms. If they were involved with Nicholas Koniev, they learned that his way was the only one. Those who cooperated also found that they were well taken care of, though they did not make a friend in the process. He had no friends, through choice.

The evolution of *Gorki,* and the advent of the new mini sub program, required years of cooperating with others. Perhaps he realized partway through the development that he would be trapped forever working with others if he didn't forge a program that would allow him the freedom to accomplish his own goals—independently. Perhaps that was how the Koniev Abstract evolved a few years before. It was a theory that he knew deep inside would require only one man to achieve its end, eventually, and he knew he would be the one to see it through.

Now, here he was, a solitary soul finally free of self-imposed bonds, in the process of completing a mission only three other men were aware of. The sense of release was overwhelming. How long had he been pulled along by his silent swimmer propulsion unit on the initial course before he realized how cool the water was—five minutes? Even through his wet suit the chill reminded him of the Baltic waters he'd trained in. Cold water was preferable. It kept the mind alert and, unlike so many others, Koniev actually seemed to thrive on the cold. He experienced a sense of superiority whenever he knew his mind was still able to overwhelm the elements.

When he estimated the first five minutes had elapsed, he illuminated his watch. Perfect! Just ten seconds off. He knew the course he wanted instinctively, but checked his board purely out of self-discipline. He also checked his compass but he was already turned in the right direction and would remain on this course for another ten minutes.

A straight line would have been the quickest method, but it wasn't the wisest. Even men like Koniev could become disoriented. He had experimented on himself and found that he could be as mortal as the others when it came to maintaining a perfect course in absolute blackness. So, instead of admitting that he was no different from other men, he continually challenged himself on estimating time and distance against the instructions on his board. The results were consistently superior.

He remained alert for the slightest sensation of a foreign presence. Donskoi had run into a dolphin and his later sighting of the green flare logically suggested that American swimmers would likely be operating in the area. Even though the mines had been set to draw the swimmers north of the submarine pier, they were men like himself. And the creatures they swam with were both intelligent and dangerous. Better to anticipate them and be ready for a quick kill, then be thankful if they didn't appear.

There were no sandy beaches on the Bangor side. The shoreline was abrupt, often rocky, with underbrush down to the waterline in most places. He'd studied photographs for hours, taking pains to select the logical place to land, one certainly not obvious to the American marines who patrolled the area. But it couldn't be impossible for him to handle either.

Security at Bangor was superb. It had to be. This was the keystone of the American triad. But it wasn't perfect, not for someone like Nicholas Koniev who was willing to spend days analyzing the area until he was sure of exactly what he could accomplish in the time he'd allotted himself. He knew the base and the surrounding area by heart. When he was sure it had been committed to memory, he sat down at a chart table in a dark room and drew it until there were no mistakes. Then, under camouflage to discourage satellite snoopers, he had the engineers construct an exact model of Bangor on the Baltic coast. They had no idea what they were building, but it was correct according to photo intelligence blowups. Before *Gorki* departed from the shipyard, Koniev had come ashore on successive nights and completed a series of test runs on his model Trident base as similar to this one as possible. No one there knew what landing spot he intended to employ when he contemplated his final test landing. And no one knew he had accomplished that goal until his last effort. The security men he bound and gagged were released the following morning.

That had been fun. But this—*this was the ultimate.*

Koniev twisted his wrist slightly to glance at the luminous face of his watch. Thirty seconds before his final course correction. But first he should come to the surface for a visual check.

He eased himself upward, breaking the surface softly without a ripple on the still dark water. It was exactly what he'd anticipated as he looked through infrared goggles. The red lights on the Strategic Weapons Facility blinked directly in front of him, less than three hundred yards away. The building was outlined by the glow of light to the rear and appeared more like an aircraft hangar, which was the ID he had given to it after studying the satellite photos.

Perfect.

He submerged again, pleased. His compass check course

agreed with his visual on the spot he intended to go ashore. He'd anticipated no less.

The time it took to cover the next two hundred yards seemed endless. His heartbeat increased noticeably. *Almost there.*

He cut the speed of the SDU exactly on the second and poked his head above the surface. The hangar was now to his left, a pier facility on the right. He floated easily, allowing his eyes to adjust to the picture that came to him through the goggles. He was looking for movement of any kind, anything at all, the least indication of a marine patrol on the shoreline, a dog covering the thickest undergrowth. He could see the marine sentries to either side on the piers where nighttime satellite photos had indicated body heat. There were specific locations where he did expect guards and he was not disappointed in confirming each one.

But his gaze returned constantly to the underbrush directly ahead. His practiced eyes studied the terrain along the shore searching for anything different from the photos he'd studied. Nothing.

Koniev slipped beneath the surface again and allowed his SDU to pull him the last seventy-five yards before switching off the silent motor. The remaining distance was covered on the surface. At the same time, he scanned the bottom with a hand-held detector searching for any magnetic indication of listening devices. Ten yards out he let the SDU drift from a tether at his waist to the bottom.

There was still nothing along the shore as his feet touched the rocky bottom. He detached the line to the SDU and secured it to a rock beneath the surface. Then he removed each item of gear he would have no need for ashore and placed it in a bag which he ran out on the same tether so that the weight of the SDU would hold it beneath the surface.

Scanning just in front of himself with the detector, he once again searched for anything magnetic that might warn of his arrival. But with each step closer to the brush that hung over the high water mark, there was no indication of anything close by.

Very carefully, so as not to make a sound as his feet

touched the rocks beyond the water, Koniev eased into the undergrowth. Just as soon as he was safely out of sight, he sat down and inventoried everything he still possessed. Assured that it was all present and within easy reach, he removed his pistol from the watertight bag attached to his belt, fit the specially designed silencer over the barrel, checked the ammunition clip, then slipped it into the holster under his left arm. There was a small knife strapped to his left leg, a larger one on his left hip, and a garroting wire with handles at either end wrapped neatly and clipped on his right hip.

But his most dangerous weapons—his hands—required no such preparations. Victor Koniev had never before used a handgun close in and he would have to be looking the devil in the eye before he would. A few times, a knife had been necessary to shorten the distance between himself and an adversary. His preference had always been his hands, swift, lethal, and extremely quiet. And the sensation of actual physical contact with his victim was certainly preferable to utilizing a cold, insensitive weapon.

Koniev rose to a standing position. He had been absolutely silent during his preparation and had heard nothing around him. He scanned slowly in a 360 degree circle with his goggles and saw nothing. He was alone on American soil, on their Trident base, and he felt a strange sense of excitement, a more powerful jolt than adrenaline, surge through his body.

Victor Koniev glanced quickly at his compass though it wasn't really necessary. He knew exactly where he was going, exactly how many steps it would take to actually reach his goal.

Bernie Ryng tore his eyes away from the man with the headphones covering his ears and glanced over at Harry Coffin. The admiral was staring expectantly at the chief sonarman, who was concentrating so intently on the sounds coming through those headphones that his eyes were squeezed tightly shut. Ryng looked back at the chief, trying to imagine what the man was hearing.

Less than an hour ago, a helicopter had picked the tape up from the deck of *Honolulu* and flown it directly to the helipad near Coffin's headquarters. While the helo was still flying through the black night, the admiral's car was outside the chief sonarman's house in nearby Scandia where two marines were waiting impatiently while the chief dressed. They were too familiar with Admiral Coffin's temper at times like this and they weren't about to be the object of his anger if the helicopter arrived before the chief sonarman.

"Well . . ." Coffin offered softly, leaning toward the chief, ". . . any preliminary . . . ?" He halted when he noticed out of the corner of his eye that Ryng was shaking his head.

"He can't hear a thing you're saying." Ryng's lips cracked in a broad smile. "Look at him."

The crow's feet around the chief sonarman's eyes stood out in sharp relief as the man squinted in an effort to analyze absolutely everything coming through the headphones. He leaned forward slightly with his elbows on his knees, his thumbs placed under his cheekbones while his fingers drummed on his forehead. Occasionally, he reached out with one hand and pressed buttons on the tape machine to rewind and replay a section of the tape, but he never opened his eyes.

"But look. He's got something there," Coffin said, pointing at the chief as the man's fingers skipped from one button to another on the tape player.

Ryng was as anxious as the admiral, but he just smiled calmly and said, "You've got to give these guys some space, especially in this case. Look at him. He's sweating bullets trying to make up his mind."

The chief's head actually glistened as he concentrated on the sounds that he was attempting to identify. Coffin rocked back in his chair and waited, staring impatiently at the man who he hoped would have the answers he was looking for.

Eventually the chief opened his eyes and looked directly at Coffin, blinking against the sudden glare of the overhead light. "That's the big one, sir. Even with the sound of all those torpedo motors, I'm sure it was definitely something big, especially after it accelerated. Those little fellows the

Russians have been playing with for years have a much smaller engineering plant that's too silent to sound like that." He paused and stared at his fingers, which were now beating a pattern on his knees. "I've heard just about everything they've got in the water and there's enough there to confirm its Soviet origin. That one's definitely different. Must be a new class of boat or they've made some powerful engineering alterations to something that already exists."

"You're sure you haven't heard anything like that one?" Coffin asked.

"Nope. You can run that against our computer library but I'd know if I'd heard that one before."

"All that extraneous sound in the background doesn't make any difference?"

"Sure. Some. But that's nothing we have, and nothing they have that I've ever been exposed to before. And it's definitely full size."

Coffin looked over to Ryng. "Well, what do you think?"

"The cow. They got the cow."

"And we nailed the little fellow over at Bremerton," the admiral concluded forcefully.

Ryng nodded and pursed his lips. "There's still got to be one more." The limited data available had pointed toward a cow that could handle two mini subs.

"The one that laid the mines?"

"That's more than likely. I doubt they'd move the same one back and forth between Bremerton and here."

"Where?" Coffin's question was as much for himself as Ryng.

"Maybe out there, near the cow. Maybe right here in the canal."

"How do we find out?"

"When we get Len and Chester back here, I'll lay out another search plan. Chester and Bull are by far the most experienced, especially working with Len and Danny." He shook his head slowly and added, "They've all got to get some rest sometime, but we'll work that out after the first one collapses."

* * *

Donskoi hadn't been asleep but his mind was wandering when a scraping sound jarred his reverie. He checked the fathometer. *Shit!* Only a few feet of water under the keel. Then he looked at the dials before him. The mini sub was settling slowly because their speed had dropped perceptibly and her buoyancy was inadequate. They must have scraped something sticking out of the mud.

"Watch your speed," he snapped angrily.

There was no response.

"Damn it," Donskoi said, turning to look over his shoulder at Tikhvin, "we don't have enough way on . . ."

Tikhvin was sound asleep, his head across his arm. His hand was resting on the throttle handle that controlled their speed. There must have been just enough pressure on the handle to reduce their power.

"Wake up, damn it," Donskoi bellowed.

Tikhvin moved his head and mumbled but that was the extent of his response. He was completely exhausted.

Donskoi whipped the wheel about in an effort to point the craft toward deeper water. She responded sluggishly. This was the last thing Koniev would have wanted them to do but the alternative was grounding and taking the chance of damage, and that was unacceptable. Once they were steadied up, he locked the wheel, released his seat belt, and bounded across the tiny space. He was about to lean over Tikhvin and increase the speed himself when he remembered how delicate the adjustment must be. Sudden acceleration might be noted by sensitive hydrophones on the bottom. It could ruin everything Koniev had planned. Better that the engineer do it.

He drew his fist back in a fit of anger and was about to swing at a spot just above Tikhvin's ear when another scraping sound began, this time much louder and more prolonged. The mini sub heeled slightly to port before righting itself. The sound died away astern.

Donskoi dropped his hand to the other's shoulder. He had suddenly realized as the object outside affected their motion that he could not handle the craft alone. Whether or not

Tikhvin deserved to have his head broken, this was certainly not the time.

"Come on, asshole, wake up," he snarled, shaking the other man roughly. "You're looking at a court-martial . . ."

Tikhvin's head snapped up, his eyes widening as he stared about the tiny space. Then he looked up at Donskoi and understood where he was. His eyes fell to the speed indicator then darted to the throttle. "We're moving too slowly . . ." he began.

"You're goddamn right, you lazy son of a bitch. Bring her back up to speed. You almost just got us killed."

Tikhvin adjusted his throttle carefully, almost tenderly, before his eyes searched out the viewport in front of Donskoi's position. There was nothing to be seen. The blackness of the water outside left the window opaque. Then he glanced up at the course indicator, eyes again widening in fear as they turned to Donskoi.

"You see what you've done?" Donskoi growled.

"But . . . we're on the wrong course . . ." Tikhvin began hesitantly.

Donskoi was already back in his seat. "You stupid shit," he said, choosing his words slowly and pronouncing each one so that the other man winced as he heard them. "I didn't have any choice. You wouldn't wake up. I had to turn toward deeper water or take the chance of grounding permanently."

Tikhvin's head dropped. "I'm sorry." His voice was truly apologetic. "I didn't even know. I was dreaming . . ." He looked up. "We need three men, you know. At this point, it's just too much . . ."

"You don't have a choice." Donskoi didn't bother to look back as he brought the mini sub back on course again. Then he continued, "The next time I'll shoot you," and turned toward the other to make his point. "I will, you know. I should have then." He couldn't remember being on duty with another Spetznaz who had ever fallen asleep. Tikhvin had always been one of the hardiest of the lot. Was it just dumb luck that it had been Tikhvin rather than him?

He pulled back on the planes and felt the nose shift upward slightly. "Now we have to get back to where we were. Get over there and get me a position, then give me a course back to where the captain will meet us. We can't be too far away when he comes looking for us."

Tikhvin, ashamed of himself for the first time since he'd become a Spetznaz, began the process of locating their position on the navigational computer before he gave Donskoi a course. "You know, I am sorry. Of course, I take full responsibility for my actions if we get back and . . ."

"Believe me, I will shoot you next time."

"Next time, I'll deserve it." He meant what he said. He knew he should have been shot immediately. Hell, he would probably have shot Donskoi in the same situation.

Corinne surged upright in bed, staring into the darkness, not fully awake, instinctively putting her arms behind to keep from falling backward. Had she heard a voice? Or was it just a dream?

She listened intently, holding her breath until the thudding that was the beat of her heart seemed to echo through the room. But the only other sounds that came to her were carried on the wind—the water lapping on the rocky beach beyond the trees, and the soft, insistent rustling of dry aspen leaves. The rich, smoky taste of the single malt, now slightly acid, welled up in her throat.

What had she heard? Was it really a voice? Or maybe something from those dreams that had been balancing her on the edge between sleep and wakefulness. They kept coming back . . . and each time she had struggled to wake up, to escape the pain of the repetitive dreams that changed so little. They were the same. The person was the same. Only the face of the person . . . the man . . . no, there was no face. How could she tell if it was a man? That's what had hurt so much. She'd been straining to see the face, but it was always in the shadows . . . always.

No, she probably hadn't heard a voice outside. There was no one out there, and anyone who could possibly find their way through the dark to this place certainly wouldn't be calling out to announce their presence. No, that call was a cry from her soul, crying out to the man whose face she couldn't see . . . if it was indeed a man.

If there had been a voice, it was her own.

Corinne lay back down and pulled the covers up around her neck. The night was cool and her skin remained unnaturally warm from the extended time in the sun. Sure, she was turning brown all over but there was no one to appreciate her efforts, no one to whisper how beautiful and sensuous she looked. Instead, here she was shivering in a cabin all by herself out in the middle of nowhere, frightened by her own voice screaming inwardly to escape from a dream.

She closed her eyes and rolled onto her left side. No more than ten seconds passed before she reached tentatively up to her face with her right hand. Yes, her eyes were wide open. There was nothing to see but how the hell do you go to sleep when you're staring into space?

She rolled to her right side and pulled the covers up over her eyes. That would keep them blocked if nothing else. Her breathing became labored beneath the blankets and the air grew stuffy, not to mention that her breath smelled sour.

Corinne, there's no way, no way at all, you're going to sleep when your nerve endings are hanging outside your skin.

She threw back the covers and sat on the edge of the bed shivering, arms wrapped around herself in a feeble effort to stay warm. It was foolishness, pure foolishness, to sit there in the dark feeling sorry for herself. She slipped her feet into lined mocassins, pulled on her bathrobe and went out into the living room where she turned up one of the gas lights and flopped onto the couch.

A news magazine lay where she'd tossed it earlier in the evening. Looking more closely, she studied the cover picture of a Soviet military officer. Was that the one she'd dreamed about? No, it was an old man's face, probably a general or an admiral, certainly no one appealing to her. But she opened the magazine and flipped through the pages until she came to the cover article—and there he was! There was a photo of a Soviet officer with a submarine in the background. That's what she remembered from her dreams, that photo, the submarine, the man's uniform.

But his face wasn't the one she'd been straining to see in her dream. She was searching for someone else, someone who wore a uniform much like that—because that was distinct in her mind.

But that someone remained faceless.

The radio had been disturbingly silent. Why? That was irritating. She wanted to be a part of whatever was happening, to help this man who'd said she should now maintain a twenty-four-hour guard. Just what the hell did her handlers expect of her? What had they done this time? Had they abandoned this man when he was facing danger? This was more like the days in England with the well-meaning but useless ciphers who played at spy games. This . . . this was deadly serious. She understood that. It was serious because there was a man—men actually—in danger. She was supposed to be a relay, a method of communicating without creating suspicion, a buffer to minimize the possibilities of detection. Or that's what it seemed.

Had something happened to that man who'd called her, the mysterious submariner? Midnight had passed and . . . nothing, even though he'd asked her to maintain a twenty-four-hour guard on that circuit. Was he dead . . . alive . . . injured? Did he need her help? Was he trying to contact her and the equipment wasn't working properly?

She rushed to the radio set and studied it. But she knew nothing about radios. She turned the volume dial slightly higher and heard static increasing in intensity. No, there didn't appear to be anything wrong. It must be working properly. If there was something wrong, it would have to be with the other radio.

You're doing everything you're supposed to, Corinne. So relax. Relax.

Better said than done. *Not easy when you're fantasizing over a man you've never seen.*

She returned to the couch and slumped onto it with a sigh. Picking up the magazine again, she began leafing through it, stopping occasionally to glance over articles that offered little of interest to her. When she flipped the pages, she had no idea of what she'd read.

Nor did she have any idea when she fell asleep—on the couch, with the gas lamp still bright. Very little time had actually passed since her final radio contact with Koniev. Instead, the intruding dreams had been stretching her conscious sense of time into an eternity.

Koniev halted abruptly, lowering his foot ever so slowly until it touched the ground soundlessly. He remained in position, stock still, listening. His nose had given the warning. There was a faint odor of feces in the air. He hadn't stepped in it, but it was nearby.

Most likely a dog. He sniffed tentatively, moving his head from side to side. No, not fresh, at least not in the past few hours. The air, maybe insects and ground creatures too, had already begun their work on it.

But this was a place where dogs patrolled and dogs were by far the better hunter of man, much superior to man himself.

He was pleased he'd noted the aroma, more pleased that all his senses remained acute. If Bangor's security forces were as good as anticipated, they wouldn't expect intruders because they would have established a system to give them confidence that no one would be fool enough to attempt to breach it.

That made it more of a challenge.

He stepped off again in the direction of his goal, remembering the exact number of steps he'd taken so far, aware of how many more before he would halt to confirm his position visually. The spruce here were older, mostly bare of branches on their lower extremities, and they provided little cover. He kept close track of available underbrush in the event he heard something that required him to seek some sort of cover. But the shadows were as good as anything if one used them properly.

Ahead, he saw the glow from the first pier, punctuated by the red lights topping the crane and the much higher communications tower. There was a road to his left running along the shoreline and as he came to the point opposite the pier the trees became thicker. He knew there were marine sentries out there on that pier—and dogs. But the breeze was from the southwest, off the water, and those animals would have to be very, very close to smell him.

Another forty-five careful steps more and he saw the glow of the Delta Refit Pier sharpen into a clear image ahead of him. A Trident submarine was brilliantly illuminated in the drydock and a blinking red light indicated one of the cranes was working alongside it that night. All of that would produce noise, which was exactly what he'd been hoping for.

But now the most dangerous moment was approaching—crossing the road to get up the hill to the communications security building. He stopped briefly and checked his compass, then mentally reviewed the number of steps he'd taken. This should be the place; he turned almost ninety degrees to his left and eased up a short rise until he could see the break in the undergrowth.

Yes, there was the road. He could hear nothing moving on it, nor did any other sounds come to him except the round-the-clock work in the drydock. He crept up to the edge, staying in the darkness until he was able to confirm what he'd assumed from the satellite photographs. This section of the road was completely in shadow.

He crouched at the edge of the brush and slowly studied his surroundings for a second time. Good men had died because they relied completely on their initial assumptions. But there was nothing . . .

From a squatting position, he rose into a crouch, bent at the waist, and scurried across the road like a large, frightened night animal. He sprang lightly into the underbrush on the opposite side and instantly went silent again. Nothing . . .

Now it was a matter of getting up the hill without being detected. The night satellite shots had revealed infrared figures in the woods—dogs, he'd assumed. That had frightened him even when he was looking at the photos. Two-legged creatures were relatively simple to neutralize. Dogs were too fast. They were much harder to kill with your hands and wiggled too much. Dogs also were more dangerous in their death throes when you killed them with a knife.

When Nicholas Koniev heard the sound—a snort . . . animal . . . not human—just fifty yards from his objective, he was absolutely sure his heart stopped beating.

Eleven

SECURITY—NOT COMPLACENCY—SECURITY.

It was wonderful!

It was an inner sense, a certain special comfort in night operations that Bernie Ryng had always enjoyed. Although at this depth it would have been fairly dark for all practical purposes even in the middle of the day, there was a sense of security within this blackness that he'd enjoyed since his early days of training. It wrapped you in a cloak of invisibility. If you were good enough to be a SEAL, the fact that you couldn't see your enemy was of minimal concern. You were that damn good, that confident.

The water that night in the Hood Canal enveloped Ryng in a comforting cloak of security as he let the SPU pull him toward the opposite shore.

Less than an hour ago, one look at Len Todd after his return from the operation against the Soviet mother ship convinced Ryng that now it was his turn.

On the other hand, dolphins handled their natural environment much more successfully. Chester was fine, as ready as he'd been hours before when they transported him out to work with Len. Dolphins did sleep but they were also capable of functioning at high efficiency for extended periods of time. If a dolphin's performance could be compared to a human's, they almost seemed to enjoy themselves with a heightened hyperactivity as long as they were needed.

There were three SEALs in the water now—Danny West and Tim Sullivan were reasonably rested—and two dolphins. The fresher team was working toward the head of the Hood Canal. The humans were covering a search pattern hastily designed before they'd left the pier, the dolphins expanding that coverage by a multiple of ten. Their mission had become deadly serious when one of the hydrophones resting on the bottom in the channel northwest of the Bangor piers had detected an odd, scraping sound. Assuming the noise was manmade, and well aware from radar that there were no fishing boats operating nearby, Ryng had to believe it was the miniature submarine he'd anticipated.

Even though the SEALs used the SPUs, moving themselves across the canal more rapidly, the dolphins still darted curiously ahead of the men. West and Sullivan were in charge of the animals, repeatedly calling them back with their crickets. When they were two-thirds of the way across, each dolphin received one of the barbell-shaped tracking devices they would attach to anything they found.

The explosives were in a flotation bag tethered to Ryng's waist. He followed slightly to the rear, surfacing every few minutes to radio back to the piers to determine if any more sounds had been detected on the hydrophones. An accurate bearing would mean so much to their search.

They began a concentrated pattern five hundred yards off the western side at a point slightly below and opposite the base.

Nothing.

They reoriented north, brought the dolphins back, then directed them ahead for two minutes before calling them in.

Nothing.

Bringing men and dolphins together, Ryng gave hand signals to broaden the sweep.

Less than two minutes later Chester returned without his barbell.

* * *

"What the hell . . . !" Tikhvin exclaimed, reacting to the audible clunk against the hull. It wasn't that loud, certainly nothing they would readily have noticed under normal operations. But in their current state, any external sound had the effect of an electric shock.

Donskoi's eyes were instantly riveted on his gauges. But there was a good forty feet under the hull, and their depth was exactly what he'd expected. He checked the dead reckoning tracer that accurately displayed their track since Koniev had left them. No clue. They'd passed through this exact position at almost the same depth and . . . nothing.

He whirled about to stare at Tikhvin. "We can't afford any more stupid mistakes," he snapped, his voice low and threatening. "Your speed must . . ."

The other looked back at him and spread his arms in a gesture of confusion. "I didn't do anything, not a thing. It came . . . I think . . ." he added hesitantly, ". . . from aft . . ." He turned to stare blankly at the bulkhead behind him as if that might explain everything.

Donskoi stared uncertainly in the same direction, knowing he would see nothing yet unaware of how to react. There was nothing within reach that Tikhvin could unconsciously have made such a sound with. Yet how else could it have taken place? There was no doubt in his mind now that it had come from outside—he should have realized that immediately—because there was nothing around them that could have caused it.

"Koniev?" he suggested, knowing as soon as he mentioned it that his commander had explained very explicitly that he would be away from the vessel much longer.

Tikhvin was still staring astern but he had heard the suggestion and shook his head. "No," he answered softly. "That's not the signal. But there is someone . . . something . . . outside that made that noise."

Donskoi watched the other's head drop slowly to his chest as he spoke and understood exactly what he was implying. Something was out there, outside the submarine. But there was no other sound, no indication of further activity, nothing that would substantiate the deep fear that was growing in his gut.

Tikhvin turned now toward Donskoi, head only half-raised. His exhaustion was reflected in his eyes. "The Americans have been using dolphins. Remember? You were attacked by one and the captain assumed it must have been by one that was trained. But he didn't leave orders about what to do if we were found here, only if he failed to come back." His voice was dull and expressionless.

Donskoi considered this statement for a moment before acknowledging to himself that any solution to their predicament would have to come from him. Tikhvin was useless, but he was also probably correct. They couldn't leave the canal before Koniev's time was up. He may have been tired but his mind was still functioning on a higher level than Tikhvin's. They had to take some sort of evasive action.

He spun the wheel around and gradually the submarine began to respond. "Give me a couple of knots. Not too much—just enough to give me some added maneuvering speed."

Tikhvin responded automatically. "What are you going to do?"

"All of our operations have been to the north of the American base. So if they know anything about us, they're going to search in that direction. Why not head to the south where we haven't been before? Not too far . . . just to keep them from trapping us . . . if they've . . ." His voice trailed off realizing that most of their training had been based on the concept of remaining undetected.

The other man shrugged. He had nothing further to offer. He knew his thought patterns had been shorted out by exhaustion. It sounded as good as anything else they might have done. "Do we have enough way on?"

"Yes. Fine." Donskoi settled on a course that was exactly the opposite of the direction they'd been traveling.

It was also directly toward Bernie Ryng who was in the process of preparing the explosive devices that would be given to each dolphin.

* * *

The voice, when it came to Koniev's ears, seemed a piercing screech rather than the muted whisper that it was.

"What's the matter, boy? Something in the air? Something you don't like?"

Koniev was suddenly sure that he had to relieve himself although a second ago he was perfectly comfortable. All that had been taken care of in the water. It was second nature. He'd always been well attuned to his body, aware whenever there were any minor changes. He had pride in his perfect mental and physical control. Now he was absolutely sure the urine might flow uncontrollably down his leg.

And that, the aroma itself, would give him away to a dog, if nothing else. He experienced a brief moment of self-loathing.

"Here." The voice was soft but they were so close there was no problem in hearing each word. "I'll let you go and you can chase after whatever it is." Then, with more forcefulness, "Damn, Paco, hold still so I can unhook you there."

There was a sentry out there, obviously close, less than fifty yards away, and he was in the process of releasing the dog that had picked up a new scent. What kind of reaction had the dog exhibited for the man to let him loose? There was no growling or snarling. Had it simply been straining at the leash? Or was there another less obvious signal between man and animal? Was it evident to the dog's handler that there was an intruder or would that have brought a different reaction from the animal?

"There you go, boy, but leave it alone if it's a skunk."

No, there would have been less communication, more likely absolute silence if the animal had reacted differently. The sentry must have assumed there was another animal and with nothing more to do that night decided to let his dog chase whatever had excited him.

How remarkable it was his bladder didn't feel nearly as tight as just seconds before.

Koniev reached for his pistol, unconsciously checking the silencer to ensure himself that it was secure. There was absolutely no way he could handle a dog with his knife at this point. Just one wrong move on his part, less than an inch off the mark if he misjudged the dog's lunge in the dark, and the animal could injure him seriously. And if the dog made any sound, even a howl of agony as the knife searched for its heart, then that sentry would be on his radio. *And that would be the end of the mission.*

The pistol was one of the new Glock 19s, a rugged, virtually indestructible handgun that had been tested again and again under absolutely impossible conditions and continued to function up to the most exacting standards. The Glock was manufactured by an Austrian firm that had developed a proprietary plastic polymer proven stronger and more wear resistant than steel. Fully loaded with a fifteen-round magazine, it still weighed less than two pounds, and the silencer that had been designed by KGB specialists added only a few more ounces. The pistol had been adopted by a number of special forces around the world, and the naval Spetznaz selected the Glock 19 when it had operated well beyond specifications after a week on the bottom of the Baltic. Koniev, no matter how much he preferred to utilize his hands, knew the silenced Glock could be his best friend.

It would have to be a perfect shot. He must shatter the animal's brain before it was aware. The dog would have to be dead before it hit the ground or there would be noise and that, too, would negate his mission.

His eyes strained in the shadows to locate the dog. Nothing. No motion of any kind. He knew the dog would be silent but he'd expected the sentry to be more obvious.

Nothing.

Koniev held his breath and listened. There was a rustling just to his right. Very slowly he turned his head, just enough to search out of the corner of his eyes. He assumed the dog had no idea who or what was out here but any unnecessary movement on his part would be all the animal required.

The rustling stopped but was replaced by the sound of what Koniev was sure was a man moving from farther away. The dog had stopped! His handler was following.

Had it seen him?

He squeezed the pistol tightly. His chest was too tight. He needed to draw a breath or his hand, actually his entire body, would begin shaking. Knowing his accuracy would have to be absolute in the next few seconds, he released his breath slowly, then forced himself to inhale at the same pace.

There it was—another sound, something rustling the dry leaves on the ground—close to where his eyes were straining against the darkness. He stared intently where he was sure the dog must be, waiting for the least movement.

Then . . . there! There was the dog, hurtling through the air, almost at face level.

Koniev's arm was moving up at the first sign, his finger tightening on the trigger as his eyes and hand swept back and forth, no more than a few inches . . . but enough to satisfy him when he could see the . . .

Instinctively his finger squeezed the trigger because there . . . almost at the end of his hand . . . was the head. Perhaps the eyes had caught a flash of light for just an instant, making his aim perfect.

Whatever, he felt the bullet explode from the gun at what he was sure was the same moment he felt hot breath . . . or was it simply the heat from the shot . . . ? He heard the soft pop from the silencer and was sure it sounded like an explosion.

There was no other noise, not a sound. The dog was knocked to one side by the impact and fell to the ground with the soft thud any hundred-pound body would make.

The handler reacted to the new sound. "What've you got, boy? Find something?"

The voice was a bit anxious, and closer than anticipated. Koniev felt his heart beating more rapidly but that was also a good sign. His senses were at a peak now. He'd disposed of his most pressing problem.

"Come, Paco." That was followed by a short, sharp whistle.

Now the sentry's hand would be on his weapon because his dog had failed to respond to the command, nor was there any sound from him. With the exception of bringing his arm up and firing, Koniev's body had remained perfectly motionless. Now, with his arm extended, he leveled the gun in the direction of the voice approximately where he expected to see a head. It would either be a white face presenting a perfect target or there would be an identifiable piece of uniform that would tell him where to aim.

It was a white face.

Another whistle. "Paco, come on, boy." More anxiety in the voice.

Pop.

There was a grunt as the sentry's body lurched backward. Koniev leaped forward and was beside it before the knees buckled completely. The second popping sound was muffled against the side of the man's head.

As the body fell, Koniev's weapon was already up and ready to respond to anyone following closely. He knew what happened to even good men who let their guard fall for no more than a few seconds.

He counted to thirty, his breath shallow, alert for the slightest hint of another dog or sentry. But there was nothing near, nothing but the night sounds which he was already accustomed to. He felt around the sentry's waist and found his radio. After careful examination by a guarded beam from his tiny flashlight, Koniev concluded that it had never been touched.

Another twenty yards brought him to the edge of the clearing—and there was his objective. There wouldn't be anyone in the building at this time of night. It was only occupied during the day and was considered secure when empty. After all, no one had ever attempted to break into such a place on a military base on American soil. Compromises had been attempted, some even pulled off, at foreign bases or on ships. But nothing like this.

He knew where the security devices were because intelligence specialists had spent weeks analyzing satellite photos until they understood the habits and procedures of the people who worked there. At the same time his intelligence people were constructing a full-size model of the building and the area around it, local agents in the nation's capital were able to acquire copies of the design sketches of the security devices. Those not already in Soviet possession were acquired by other means. Time and again, Soviet intelligence remarked on how similar the security system was to so many others they'd compromised in the past. Often they commented on why the systems weren't modified or changed to discourage the possibility of this type of break in.

Now was the easy part for Koniev. This is what he had rehearsed for so long. Getting successfully to this point was something you could never anticipate. It had been temporarily inconvenient with the sentry, but from here on he was confident he could perform the mission with his eyes closed.

Proceeding mechanically through the steps he had memorized the previous month, he pondered the possibility that some security-conscious individual responsible for such things might not have just altered the system that day. After the months of planning, he could imagine how ridiculous he would appear—to himself especially—if he were suddenly surrounded by a squad of marines with automatic weapons. What would he do?

Pull his gun and be cut into pieces by a hail of bullets?

Quickly raise his hands above his head and surrender with hopes of being exchanged for one of their people?

No, not a chance with the second option, not when they learned who he was. Better to accept his fate.

Koniev was at the exact spot he'd proposed in the Abstract. He'd arrived utilizing the methods he'd stated were necessary. The masterpiece of deception seemed effective. To the United States, it would appear yet another Soviet intelligence blunder—losing a mini sub at Bremerton, planting time-delayed mines in an apparently blatant effort to neutralize the Trident submarines. It was unfortunate that such fine, loyal men had to be sacrificed but that had been part of his original plan. Certainly it was realistic. American intelligence would declare his mission an abject failure; their Trident missile would still be the ultimate weapon to confront the Kremlin. But of even greater importance, only he and three others would really be aware that the Trident was indeed under Soviet control. Regardless of how many moles existed, how many double agents, how many defectors, this secret would never get back to American intelligence. It was a daring mission, expensive in research, hardware, and human life, but it was well spent if the US no longer threatened the Kremlin with the Trident.

But there was no need to ponder the what-ifs of failure for too long. Neutralizing the security devices required intense concentration. He followed each step exactly as he'd memorized it back at his Baltic model. The systems were effective —he was better. He was relieved when he found that the digital registration code to be punched into the device to one side of the outer door hadn't been altered. Nor had the combination lock set into the heavy inner door been changed.

Once inside, he pulled the doors almost closed, leaving them slightly ajar in the event that he needed to make a quick departure. He knew from months of recent satellite pictures that no one had a habit of checking them in the middle of the night. To do so would have involved first disarming the security devices outside the building—and there was no purpose in going to all that trouble, not when nothing had ever happened before.

He was now so close to what he wanted—*the coded emergency message system to contravene a Trident launch order*. This system was nothing more than a combination of letters that were revised each month, no different from many other top secret directives, short and explicit, no time wasted. But if Washington ever sent that other combination of letters—the one that would order a Trident missile launch—the system for grouping letters to negate that order that Koniev was about to steal would buy precious time. It would allow Moscow enough time to issue their own launch orders, hopefully enough time to complete the first strike that had been originally ordered against them. If nothing ever happened, if Washington never had reason to attempt a first strike, then they would never be the wiser. Nor would anyone in the Soviet Union, other than Nicholas Koniev, his three superiors, and eventually their successors understand the enormity of his mission.

It was the final step in ensuring the Soviet Union's safety. They could already neutralize the other segments of the triad and Washington knew that as well as Moscow did.

That was the basis of the Koniev Abstract, the brilliant theory that had never been published because then it could never have been attempted. The three other men who were aware of Victor Koniev's proposal had faithfully maintained this secret because someone else would attempt this same mission if Koniev failed.

But he was about to achieve what had once been considered theoretically impossible. He moved to the safe which contained the system he was after and began to dial the combination. That had been acquired the month before from a sailor who had been so drunk that he never knew he'd been drugged; under any other conditions, he would have chosen death. Koniev held his breath as he studied the tiny numbers revealed by the pencil beam of his light. If he had been in charge—or if he ever was in the future—combinations would be changed once a week.

Oh, please . . . please . . . He was hearing a tiny inner voice murmuring that same word repeatedly. It was a voice that was strangely beyond his control.

But the combination hadn't been changed. The handle turned in his fingers and he was peering inside.

Koniev knew exactly what he was looking for. In a matter of minutes he'd taken double photographs of each page using a second roll of film for the additional shot of each.

Now it was time to depart—but oh so carefully. Everything was replaced exactly as it had been before he entered, right down to the position of the dials on the combination locks. And as he exited the communications security building, he reactivated each of the security devices that had been neutralized.

When he stood at the edge of the clearing, his eyes tightly shut, Victor Koniev reviewed every move he'd made in the last twenty minutes. That was how long he'd estimated it would take when he was practicing back home more than a month ago, and that was exactly how it had worked. It was vital to ensure that nothing he had done would raise any suspicion around the building.

The sentry's body in the woods was unfortunate, and his discovery would trigger an investigation, but sailors had been shot on this base before for other than security reasons, two of them just a few years before. No organization was perfect, not even the Trident program, and incidents such as this happened even among the best of people. There was no proof that a Russian intruder had ever been on the base.

Koniev had covered his tracks well.

He turned away to retrace his steps back to the canal and the safety of Donskoi's boat.

Tikhvin knew Donskoi's eyes were on him as much as they were the dials and gauges at the pilot's position, and it made him increasingly uncomfortable. He had lost the other's trust.

It was so stupid! He was incensed with himself . . . drifting off like that. And it was the first time, too, the first time ever. It was inconceivable that it could happen, and now of all times. Never in his career had he allowed himself to give in like that, and he'd been in a lot more complex situations, often life or death. Yet he'd survived while other men died. What was there about this miniature submarine, the most important step in his career, that had so exhausted him?

How many hours had he been awake now? Fifty? Sixty? Seventy? Maybe it was more than that. It was shameful that he'd been overcome like that but, then again, the other times he remembered he was always in the field and involved in a mission where death could come at any minute. The physical demands kept you going. The possibility of death at any moment by any number of methods was almost exhilarating.

Here it was different. Nothing had been happening. They were waiting, almost drifting to be honest, for Koniev to return and it had been mind-numbing, almost like he'd been hypnotized. One moment he was struggling to keep awake, the next Donskoi was shouting at him. He knew he would have been shot—and should have been—if it hadn't required two men to operate the submarine.

Would they shoot him when Koniev returned?

"I . . . I'm sorry," he began, feeling Donkoi's eyes once again burrowing into the back of his head. "It was inexcusable and I shall place myself on report when we return to *Gorki."* He desperately wanted to hear that he was forgiven so they could get on with it. Perhaps if Donskoi understood that it would never happen again, he'd say nothing to Koniev. Tikhvin really didn't want to turn himself in. It would be the end of his career. But of more importance was maintaining Koniev's respect through the duration of the mission. That was a matter of pride.

"Don't bother me with that shit now," Donskoi snapped. "That will all come later." He wasn't about to let Tikhvin off the hook, not when his laziness might have killed them both, not when the success of Koniev's mission—whatever it was—might have been jeopardized. "Mind your responsibilities." He turned back to his own position.

They were heading south. Donskoi intended to go beyond the rendezvous position into waters they'd never navigated before, and planned to return thirty minutes before Koniev's appointed time to meet up with them.

Tikhvin wasn't satisfied. Exhaustion toyed with his mind until his perception of the situation fully occupied his thoughts. He'd made an effort and been rebuffed, unfairly he thought. It wasn't as if he were some new recruit, or some snotnose drone who was kept around to chip paint and scrub urinals. His reputation had been enviable until this one mistake and his service around the world was exemplary. As tired as he was, he kept growing more defensive as he considered the disciplinary measures that could be taken against him.

"I don't think I want to wait to discuss things," he said with newfound confidence. "I'm quite able to handle whatever you . . ."

Donskoi was busy selecting his track on the chart overlay and interrupted irritably, "Listen, we don't have time to argue now. Get on the listening gear. I'm just not comfortable here."

Tikhvin picked up the headphones but hung them around his neck instead of placing them over his ears. "Just what do you plan to say to the captain when he returns?"

"That's my business. Now . . ."

"No. That's not enough. I'm not someone you can just . . ."

"Shit! With luck and if you do what I tell you, we might be able to stay away from anyone who may be looking for us. Just put those headphones on and . . ."

"There's no one out there to . . ."

And those were the last words Tikhvin ever spoke. There was a brilliant flash followed by a burst of shrapnel that tore through the tiny compartment. The water arcing through the small hole began almost immediately to short out electronic equipment. White smoke filled the space. But neither Donskoi nor Tikhvin were aware of the instant chaos in their tiny submarine. Both men had been shredded by a hail of metal shards in the instant after the white hot liquid metal in the warhead had burned through the hull.

Koniev, slightly back from the water's edge, waited silently almost as if he were in a trance. His glance moved from the red lights on the communications tower beside the explosives hangar to the one on the second pier to the Delta pier drydock, then back again. He studied the activities under the lights, the work at the drydock, the positions of the marine sentries, and then he would close his eyes and form a mental picture of what he had seen the first time. He could think of nothing that had changed. While his eyes remained shut, his ears seemed more attuned to the sounds around the facility. Nothing had changed.

Once satisfied, he inventoried each piece of equipment he'd come ashore with. Then he waded into the cool water and retrieved the gear he'd tethered further out. He operated so silently, yet so quickly, that a marine sentry would have had to stand on the shore and stare exactly at Koniev to notice him.

Ready, he submerged, and recovered his SPU. Then he headed directly out on exactly a reciprocal of the course he'd come in on. Once his watch indicated he was well beyond the piers, he surfaced and looked back, once again studying the entire area for any indication of unusual activity.

Nothing had changed.

Koniev managed to sublimate the tremendous urge to celebrate that had been welling up from deep in his body since he'd arrived back by the water. *He'd done it!* He'd actually accomplished what had been an impossible theoretical solution until a little more than an hour ago. He alone possessed the key to neutralizing the American Trident missiles should the United States ever make the decision for a first launch. This, and this alone, would allow the Kremlin to retaliate against the land-based missiles and bombers which made up the other parts of the American triad.

Stopping to check his compass in order to make the necessary course corrections was almost an effort, yet it was exactly such discipline that had made him a survivor. Celebration could come later. He had accomplished ninety percent of his mission, certainly the most difficult by far, but it was all worthless if he failed to return.

Koniev was more than halfway across the Hood Canal when he heard the explosion. It was unlike any underwater blast he'd ever heard. It was a sharp sound followed almost instantly by a muffled explosion. Other explosions he'd experienced in the water were more powerful and . . . he wasn't sure how to define it other than . . . just different . . . too different . . .

Quite suddenly he experienced a sensation of fear. Was it instinct that warned him rather than the explosion? Whatever, he increased his depth considerably and altered his course to come out to the north of the rendezvous point.

It was before he reached his destination that he heard the boat engines, distant at first, then steadily increasing in intensity. They were coming in his direction—from the

Trident piers! Instinct, which had never failed him before, abruptly became overwhelming. Something was very wrong.

Instead of heading for the pickup location, Koniev turned directly toward the shoreline and increased the speed of his SPU. What little noise might escape into the water would be easily drowned out by the larger diesels getting steadily closer.

When he sensed the bottom coming up rapidly, he rose slowly to the surface, poking only his head above the still water. The two high speed craft approaching from the opposite side, both with searchlights playing across the water, had crossed the canal in an extremely short time, too short to be a drill at this hour of the night. He left the SPU on the bottom attached to the tether at his waist and swam the last ten yards to shore, moving behind a large spruce that had fallen into the water.

The boats seemed unsure of their destination, slowing and playing their lights across the water, until one of them held its spotlight in position. Koniev could see nothing until both craft moved to a spot a few hundred yards to their south and stopped. The deep rumble of their engines came to him across the water as the bright lights settled on something in the water. As he watched, three figures, each with breathing apparatus on their backs, climbed up the ladder at the stern of one of the boats.

SEALs!

Now he understood. That was the source of the underwater explosion. And it was too close to the rendezvous point to be a coincidence. How the hell . . . ? His mind raced. How could he have gotten away with what he just did and yet they'd somehow gotten the mini sub? Donskoi and Tikhvin had to be dead. The SEALs wouldn't return to their boats until they were sure. Once again, Victor Koniev was grateful for his instincts.

He could wait until they were gone and then slip out to the rendezvous point, but Koniev was now sure without a doubt that the strange underwater blast that he'd heard had been the end of Donskoi and Tikhvin. In that case, he would have to be out of the water and on his way before first light. They would be back to investigate what they'd sunk and they would also be searching for anyone else, especially after that sentry was found.

Nicholas Koniev was surprised, even a bit pleased with himself, at how he had just accepted his situation. He might have expected fear, trapped alone in a strange country, yet he almost felt relieved that he would no longer have to depend on someone else for his survival. It was simply a matter of heading north as quickly as possible and getting close enough to the Strait so his radio would be able to reach *Gorki*.

Should he try to move farther north with the aid of the SPU? It would be quicker . . . but no, even if he remained quiet, they'd be listening for any odd sound . . . and the possibility of dolphins . . .

He slipped back into deeper water and retreived the SPU. He tightly secured to the unit anything that he considered unnecessary, then set the timer to open vents before sending it on its way. The water would be deep enough by the time the SPU filled and sank to the bottom.

Unless someone was extremely fortunate, there would be no trace of Nicholas Koniev, at least not until he was well away from this spot.

Back ashore, he checked his location on the map before determining his first objective. There were enough summer camps, and some occasional homes, in this area that would provide a solution to solve his first problem.

He actually smiled as he considered his fate. Surprise had been his initial reaction. Now, self-satisfaction took command.

What an opportunity!

Twelve

THE DENSE GROWTH OF TALL SPRUCE DENIED EVEN A GLIMPSE OF the faint lightening of the eastern sky. The heavily forested site around the corpses of the sentry and the dog would remain in enforced darkness for another two hours. The onlookers shifted nervously from one leg to another or sometimes stamped their feet as if they were becoming cold in the presence of death. Occasionally, one of the beams from the larger flashlights would rise from one of the bodies and cut through the underbrush to cast eerie shadows that shifted and danced with the motion of a nervous hand. They magnified the combination of emotion and apprehension that crept through this place of sudden death. The trepidation that each individual was experiencing was expanded by the scene as they gradually understood the last seconds of the young sentry's life.

"No sign of a struggle, Bernie." Admiral Coffin's light moved across the body, then settled on the dog. "Not even with the pup."

"And his gun was never used?" Ryng was still slightly out of breath from his rapid climb up the hill with a marine captain.

191

"He might have thought about it. We found it under the body. He may have taken it out of the holster and then fallen on top of it, but it was never fired. Someone would have heard it anyway, if he did."

"Radio?"

"Still hanging on his belt. Never touched. Never even hit the emergency switch, which they're trained to do if they run into trouble."

Ryng moved over by the dog's body and held his light down near the remains of the animal's large head. "Heavy caliber. Obviously a silencer since no one heard any sound. Perfect shot. Picked up the cartridge casing, too. But I can't understand why your man wasn't ready when he heard the dog attack. At least I assume it must have."

The marine captain in charge of security answered. "They're trained to track silently—mostly to avoid what happened here. The idea is for these dogs to be at your throat before you know they're there."

"I'll bet your man said something to the dog and that gave them both away. Nothing's perfect," he added softly, "not when you're dealing with someone as efficient as this."

"Efficient?" the marine echoed.

"When was the last time you heard from your man?" Ryng asked.

"Two hours ago."

"Efficient. Dead dog. Dead sentry. No gun shots heard. Silent killing. No time to even touch the switch on his radio. Look at the dog, the way it landed. It was in the air, attacking, when it was hit. And it never made a sound or your sentry would have reacted faster. Perfect shot. And look at your man. One bullet in the chest that should have knocked him back ten feet. But I don't think he ever had time to fall before the attacker grabbed him and put another slug in the side of his head to make sure." Ryng's light waved around the body. "Look around the corpse. That body didn't crash down there like they normally do. It was dropped there. That's why his weapon was underneath him. Wouldn't you call all of that efficient?"

Ryng could see in the glow of the flashlights that the

marine's jaw had already dropped. The marine looked first at Admiral Coffin, then back at Ryng before murmuring so softly that he could barely be heard, "Yes, sir."

"You were wondering if this was like some of the troubles you had a couple of years back, Admiral," Ryng said softly. "No way. Those were amateur jobs, what the police call fits of passion and lawyers call temporary insanity. There are very few people who do it this well."

"Captain," Coffin said to the marine, "I want the base secured. No one leaves. Only critical civilian personnel are allowed aboard today, and I want the names of each one. Anyone of them who leaves their normal workplace gets an escort from one of your men. Anyone who asks, tell them it's a security exercise."

"Yes, sir." The marine left after a sideways glance at the body of his sentry.

"You're thinking that mini sub, aren't you, Bernie?"

"Ummm."

"Think he went down with it?"

"That's probably where he came from. But there's no way he could have gotten back in time. My money says they were waiting for him."

"We'll have a better idea when we raise it."

"No time." Ryng glanced around. Nothing was visible beyond the thick, shadowy shapes of spruce trunks. "Where are we . . . I mean what are we near? What would he have been after around here?"

"Hard to say. Most of the admin offices are on the Delta Pier or down below us. There's a mess hall over there, and the barracks. Communications Security Building is just through there," he added, pointing to one side. "It all depends on what he was after."

"Communications security—what's in there?"

"All highly classified, I'm afraid. I couldn't even tell you in front of the others around us right now. But not a chance anyone got in there. There's no way they could even get to the door without lighting off the security system, all bells and whistles, and I . . ."

"Admiral, he wasn't supposed to get right where we're

standing either. Maybe he didn't get anything because he ran into this sentry, but we've got to believe that he may now have something that was valuable enough to go through everything that's happened around here so far. Bells and whistles are no problem for someone who's really good. Don't bet he wasn't in there. This corpse says different. It's too near to a high priority target. And don't bet nothing's missing either. The best ones don't leave a clue. But odds are he has what he came for, and what he came for is something you'd better believe is absolutely critical to the security of the Trident system."

"You tell me what you want me to do for you, and you've got it."

"I don't think he'd stay in the water, not now. But we should put all the patrol boats out right away. My boys will show them how to set up a random search pattern, something a swimmer or another mini sub couldn't figure out. And we want to cover the bridge so a salmon wouldn't have a chance of getting through. If there's any more of them, we can't afford letting them get into open water. And I need a helo to drop me up around the Strait, probably near Dungeness. Assuming he's loose, he's going to try to get to the mother ship."

"You can have as many marines as you want. That captain who was just here isn't anywhere near as confused as he acted. He was just upset about what happened to his man."

"Thanks, Admiral." Ryng shook his head. "But when you're after someone like this one, you have to play their game—one on one. I'll do better on my own."

When she opened her eyes, Corinne knew in an instant it was the soft hiss of the gas lamp that had awakened her. She had no idea of how many hours she'd slept, but the muscles in her neck were whispering that it had been long enough. She rose to her feet and swiveled her shoulders. Hunching her back and stretching slowly was always a glorious sensation and she bent from the waist until she almost touched her toes. Her watch read close to six, but it still seemed so dark that she stepped outside.

The air was damp and she hugged herself against the morning chill. There was a faint paling of the eastern sky beyond the trees and the birds had no doubt that it was time to start a new day. The first soft breezes rustled the aspens and brought the distant cry of a fog horn.

She briefly considered a quick wakeup swim but remembered how difficult that last one had been—and so cold. It wasn't worth it, not this early in the morning. She'd just wash up instead. Maybe later in the day, if the sun was warm again, she might go for a walk and see if she could find some place with a little sand, or at least fewer rocks.

Back inside, she stared ruefully at the radio set on the corner table. It had remained strangely silent throughout the night. *Don't call us, we'll call you,* she thought. Perhaps they were so hardened that they cared nothing for a man—men —in distress, maybe even dead or dying. They must have sensed trouble and were covering themselves by their very silence.

But she did! She cared!

Of course, they'd provided instructions for such a situation. Read books. Sit tight. Knit. Paint. No, she'd told them she didn't do either. But they were adamant that she remain there, waiting, listening, until someone came for her. But Corinne hadn't expected it to be like this. The radio had become an accusing mute, reproaching her in its silence.

She was learning something new about herself—no, not new, but certainly unwanted—something that she'd managed to bury for so many years, something she hoped had died the day Ken and Cory had been lost to her forever. On that day, Corinne had promised herself that she would never care about another human being again, not in the way she'd cared for those two. Physical pain was acceptable—but the anguish that had bored into her very soul was too much. She had survived it by extinguishing the inner fire of caring for others.

Now she knew there must have been a spark beyond her reach because she was silently cheering for a man she'd never met. And she was concerned for him because she apparently was sure he was just like her—alone and willing to stand by himself. But he was apparently in need and she wanted to give him the chance to continue. And . . . and she'd created a fantasy for herself, like a teenage girl, an adolescent sexual fantasy for a man she'd never seen, and one she would surely be willing to consummate if the opportunity presented itself.

Is that caring, Corinne?

It was. Regardless of how one defined it, she cared. And strangely enough she wasn't concerned with the sensation. She was comfortable with herself. She knew she was willing to do whatever was necessary to help this man, whoever he was.

Koniev was halfway up the hill that rose straight out of the water before the day became bright enough to force him to continue on under cover of the treeline. The strong smell of wood smoke had been his guide as he climbed. He had no idea of its source but it was close and smoke meant that someone was keeping themselves warm, and that in turn meant clothes and food would likely be present. It would be suicide to continue in the light foreign outfit he'd worn under his wetsuit.

The smoke grew almost overpowering at the same moment he was able to see it floating downward through the trees ahead of him. There was hardly a breath of air and the smoke curled slowly down the hill under the weight of the morning dampness. Coming to a clearing beyond the trees, he paused to study a small cabin. There was a single wire coming from a rough pole above one corner of the building which he hoped was electricity rather than a phone.

Circling above the cabin, he found an old car with balding tires and badly in need of paint. It was obvious the owner made little use of it. There was no other apparent source of smoke nearby but out of habit he followed the dirt road for a few hundred yards up to see if there were other structures. All he found was a shack that had pretty much crumbled away to a pile of gray boards. No tire tracks or footprints were evident in the dirt to indicate anyone had approached the cabin recently. Koniev smiled inwardly. The occupant appeared to be a loner like him.

He worked his way back down to a concealed spot where he knelt to watch the windows. A single individual, an older man with a beard, moved about inside. There was no indication that he was talking with anyone else.

Koniev worked his way down to one side, away from the windows, until he was able to creep up beside the building. There he settled down on his haunches to listen. There was no conversation. That didn't necessarily mean the man was alone, and Koniev would have to make sure as soon as he entered, but it was enough to go ahead with his plan. There was no point in knocking as if he were stopping in for a friendly cup of tea, not dressed the way he was.

When he burst through the only door with the Glock drawn, the older man took a step backward but said nothing. His eyes moved from Koniev's face to the pistol, then back again.

"Sit." Koniev indicated an old torn couch by waving the gun.

The man sat down.

There was another room to one side with only a curtain hanging over the doorway. Koniev moved sideways, keeping his eye on the man, until he could sweep back the curtain. There was nothing but a bed covered with crumpled blankets. "You're alone?" he asked.

"Doesn't it look like it?" Angry eyes followed Koniev's every move.

Koniev let the curtain fall back into place. "Telephone?"

The man simply shook his head.

Bacon was crackling in a pan on top of an electric stove. The smell of coffee filled the cabin and reminded Koniev of the last time he'd eaten. He waved the gun toward the stove. "Cook."

The man leaned forward as if to get up, then sank back, his eyes fixed on the weapon. "I don't cook for someone who's going to shoot me in the back."

Koniev slid the Glock into the rubber belt at his waist. "Is that better? I won't hurt you if you follow directions." They were the first full sentences he'd spoken and he was aware how obvious his accent must be. "But I am very quick if you try to make a move."

The man rose to his feet and shook his head. "I'm too old for those things now." He moved to the stove and turned down the heat under the bacon. "There's enough food. Can I put on enough for myself? It was supposed to be for me in the first place." The eyes were hard and held Koniev's until he received an answer.

"Of course." The room was warm and Koniev could feel the heat loosening his tired muscles. It would have been tempting to rest here but he knew there was no time for such pleasures. "I need clothes."

The man looked over his shoulder and nodded gravely. "You certainly do."

"We'll both be better off if you can forget what I look like."

"To stay alive, I can forget almost anything. There're some clean clothes there that ought to fit fair enough," he said; pointing at a stack on a chair by one of the windows.

Though the man was a bit taller than Koniev and a little heavier, the clothes were comfortable. There was bacon and eggs and some muffins filled with some kind of berry that Koniev was unfamiliar with, and he ate with gusto. The man picked at his plate, occasionally fixing Koniev with a hard glare.

Finally, Koniev said, "Eat. I won't hurt you if you help me. I mean that." Yet he was unsure why he actually wanted to let the man live. Perhaps it was those brave, defiant eyes.

"I'm not used to people with guns breaking in here. My stomach's a little nervous."

"Whatever. I'm not going to feed you myself."

The man nodded and began to eat.

"Does the car work?" Koniev asked after they cleaned their plates in silence.

The man nodded again. "Doesn't have much gas."

"How far can I get?"

"Five gallons. Probably seventy-five miles."

"How far is that in kilometers?"

The man shrugged. "I don't know what they are. Where are you going?"

"It doesn't matter." Koniev stood up. "I need a jacket."

"Over there, on the hook. There's a couple. Probably fit as well as the clothes."

Koniev selected an old wool plaid jacket along with a baseball cap with MARINERS across the front. "Keys?"

"On the hook by the door."

Koniev slipped the keys into his pocket.

The man's eyes followed his every move.

"I have to tie you to that chair so that you can't get hold of anyone too soon." He'd already found some cord on a shelf. "You'll be able to get yourself loose in good time, but no one will be able to find me by then."

The man turned slightly in the chair, draping his arm over the back. "Why are you doing this?"

"You mean letting you live?"

"I guess so. I was sure you were going to kill me," he added calmly.

"But you've given me food and clothes and your car, and you won't be able to warn anyone too soon. You're lucky." *You don't realize how lucky.* "I'm going to put out your fire. It might draw someone here too quickly." *Are you taking too much of a chance? Would they stop at this out-of-the-way shack first?*

With that, Koniev hurriedly secured the man's arms behind the back of the chair and his legs to the chair legs. Then another thought struck him. "I need money."

"I'm no good to you. Got a couple of bucks and that's all." *What the hell were bucks?* "What will that do for me?"

"Not a hell of a lot. Hey, they're yours if you want. I'm not going to argue with you."

"Forget it," Koniev said, his mind already elsewhere. Time was more than precious. He muttered a few words about the food, and was out the door, still curious about his decision. Was he leaving a trail by allowing the man to live?

The car started the first time but stalled as soon as he put it in gear. He gave it a few moments to warm up, continuing

CHARLES D. TAYLOR

to wonder what it was that had kept him from shooting the old man. Killing had never concerned him before and he knew that wasn't the reason. Was it because he saw himself in that lone individual surviving in the woods by himself? It would be foolishness to make a mistake that put them on his trail. He was sure that he wasn't getting soft. It was just that the man had shown no fear and spoke directly rather than pleading for his life. And he actually liked those bold eyes that held his own. *You will not be a survivor if you continue to be too kind,* he decided as he eased the car into gear and turned up the hill.

Before ever departing the shipyard, he'd been given a Texaco road map that showed a paved secondary road not too far away. When he got to it, he stopped at the edge and studied the route up to Dungeness. Then he saw the tiny numbers along the way that he assumed indicated the distance between points on the map. Adding them up in his mind, he decided it was less than fifty miles. *How many kilometers? Maybe ninety.* He could make it.

But first he had to contact *Gorki* somehow. The batteries in his small radio were low and he wanted to save them. Most likely they didn't have enough power to reach out to the submarine antenna well to the north. Either he would have to discover another means of communication or find some fresh batteries. But he had no money to buy them with even if he did find them, and frankly Koniev had no idea of where he would go to purchase them. And with the Soviet labels on them, it would be foolhardy to show the old ones to anyone.

The paved road was narrow with sharp curves that wound up and down steeply graded hills. Occasional dirt roads ran off into heavily wooded areas with little sign of habitation. At one point, he came to a cleared area and looked up the hillside toward some houses that seemed to be built with the explicit purpose of looking out toward the Hood Canal. But he never passed another car and saw only an old man bent over his garden who never glanced up.

Then, toward the top of the ridge to his left, he saw a house with a large radio antenna on the roof. He had no idea

200

what it might be but, coming to a narrow road on his left, he decided to turn uphill.

The pavement extended only up the first rise before changing abruptly to dirt with a high crown in the middle. Rains had washed out either side and the old car bumped along occasionally scraping bottom until he was forced to slow down. There were a series of switchback curves before he came into a level clearing containing at the other end the house he'd seen. An old pickup truck was parked under the only tree. The antenna actually was not on top of the house but set on a cement base in the backyard. There was a hand-lettered sign attached to it with a series of letters and numbers which meant nothing to him. But it did indicate that there could be a transmitter of some kind here.

Koniev got out of the car warily and turned slowly around in a complete circle. There were no other houses within sight. He possessed no sense of fear but was surprised by an inner hesitancy that he'd never previously experienced. In other operations in remote parts of the world, Spetznaz had always been aggressive because they were confident. But this time his only choice was caution. It was a different matter here because he was a lone stranger attempting to escape with a prize that any American would be more than happy to kill him for.

His gun was tucked in his belt under the plaid jacket as he walked toward the house, curious if someone was watching him and wondering if they were armed. He'd read that many Americans owned guns. Could there be one aimed at him now?

The house and yard were both in need of care. The lawn hadn't been cut for some time and the weeds in the gardens were choking out the few sorry flowers struggling to share the sun. Small weeds had taken hold in the moss that covered the wooden shingles on the roof. The wooden siding was badly in need of paint.

Koniev reached for the handle of the outer door and noticed that it was swinging loose. The ripped screen hung halfway down. He was sure he must have been seen—why, that old car made so much noise coming up the hill. He was about to knock when he caught sight of movement inside. His hand slipped under the jacket.

But no one came toward the door. He shaded his eyes and peered through the glass on the upper half. Inside, he saw a man in his underwear seated in a wooden chair with his back to the door. Then Koniev understood why his car hadn't been heard. The man had earphones over his head and was intent on the equipment on the table before him. It was a radio set of some kind.

Pulling the gun from his belt, he turned the door handle slowly and felt the door open inward. There was still no indication he'd been heard. He watched the man curiously for a moment before stepping inside.

Then he was startled when he heard the man talking. "That's right, Bluebell. The weather for the next twenty-four hours is supposed to remain clear. There's a front to the northwest that may reach us by the end of the day tomorrow, but you ought to be OK until then."

A voice immediately responded. "Roger, Sandy, I thank you. I plan to be in before dark and I'll bring you something fresh for dinner. You take care of yourself until then. OK? Over."

"I do look forward to seeing you, Bluebell. Out." The man reached up and flipped a switch and sat back in the chair with a sigh.

In an instant, Koniev was behind him, the muzzle of his gun in the base of the man's neck. "Don't make a move. Calm now," he continued as he felt the man's body jerk and the shoulders hunch. "I'll tell you when you can turn around. Did you break your communication with the person you were talking to completely?"

The man shuddered. "Yes," came the answer in a falsetto voice.

"Turn around."

Very slowly, the man turned in his chair. He was overweight and his whole body was shaking when he looked up. A couple of days' growth of beard covered his face and his breath stunk of alcohol. His undershirt was filthy and an unwashed aroma assaulted Koniev's nostrils. There was nothing to fear with this one. He was already probably pissing his pants.

Koniev stepped back, the gun still leveled on the man's head and glanced around the room. Dirty dishes littered a table across the room and the sink was full of more. There was a picture on one wall of this man and a woman smiling at the photographer.

"The woman, where is she?" Koniev snapped.

"She . . . she died six months ago," he squeaked. His chin trembled in fear.

Next to that picture were those of a young man and woman. "And the younger ones?"

"They've moved to . . ." he hesitated as Koniev looked down at him and waved the gun irritably. ". . . to Seattle."

"You're alone then."

The man nodded and ran a shaking index finger under his nose, then wiped it on his shorts.

"Get up."

The man stood, pathetic in his underwear, his entire body shaking in fear.

"We're going to look through each room and make sure you're alone."

"I swear . . ."

"We'll do it anyway."

They moved slowly from room to room, the man sniffling quietly as his nose dribbled. His shoulders became more rounded and hunched each time Koniev prodded him with the gun barrel. There was no one else in the house.

"Is there anything underneath, a storeroom?" Koniev pointed at the floor.

The man nodded, unable to speak now.

"Show me."

There was a door just beyond the kitchen where the man halted and pointed.

"Open it." Then, "Turn on the light." Then, "Now go down ahead of me."

The floor of the basement was dirt, the earthen smell musty and stale. An odor of rotting apples was evident in the background as they reached the bottom of the stairs.

"Go over there in the corner and turn around."

The man's legs began to give out. He stumbled against the wall, putting out a hand to steady himself. Tears ran down his cheeks as he turned around clasping his hands to his chest. Then he lost control of his bowels and the sudden stench assaulted Koniev's nose.

Koniev raised his gun and shot him twice in the head, turned around, and walked quietly up the stairs, snapping off the light before he closed the door. He hated people who were so afraid to die.

He sat down at the radio and snapped on the switch he'd seen the man turn off at the end of his transmission. There was a familiar hum. The equipment was ancient but also rather simplistic as Koniev studied it. There was a dial that could be turned by hand which he assumed was to change frequency. There was a mike on a stand and he had seen the man push the button to talk.

Koniev would never have transmitted on the assigned frequencies at this time of day on such equipment but now there was no choice. Somehow, he had to get back to *Gorki*.

Turning the dial to the frequency the submarine was supposed to guard, he called again and again without success. He looked at his watch. The time was right. They had agreed to poke the antenna above the surface for five minutes on either side of the hour after sunup on this day if he, Donskoi, and the others hadn't returned to *Gorki* by now. But there was no response.

He pulled his portable radio from the pocket of the jacket and checked the frequency on that. It was digital and the correct frequency came up by punching one of the memory buttons. The numbers that showed were the same he'd used on the dial on the large set. This equipment had to work. The man had just been talking to a fishing boat somewhere.

Koniev pushed the button on the mike again and called for the next two minutes until he was sure he was past the time. He slammed his fist on the table in frustration before taking a deep breath. *You must remain calm and rational.* He got up from the chair, folded his arms, and walked over to look out the window toward the submarine base on the opposite side. He would try it again the next hour. If there was no answer, then he would have to call the alternate, that woman, whoever she was.

When he stepped outside to study his surroundings, he was able to look down on the canal where little patrol boats raced back and forth along the shoreline. Down to his right, near where Donskoi should have met him, there was a barge and another craft with a crane. There was no doubt in his mind that they were preparing to raise the miniature submarine.

He watched for a while before heading back inside where he found some oil and clean, soft cloths to clean the Glock. He counted each second of each minute until he could once again call *Gorki*.

Corinne started, almost dropping a plate when she heard the voice on the radio. She'd been rinsing her breakfast dishes. Quickly drying the water from her hands, she moved to the radio. She could tell the voice was one of her handlers. What in the world were they calling her for at this time of day? Had they completely abandoned the discipline they'd emphasized before she ever came out to the island?

The explanation was short and to the point. No details. There was evidence that the mission had been interrupted and could not proceed as planned. This would be their last radio contact with her. They knew no more at this stage about the mission. Possibly she could help but they doubted it. She was to guard the submarine frequency completely. As soon as they received permission, someone would pick her up at the island. Due to security requirements, she was to avoid initiating any contact with them.

And then, as she stood there staring at the radio, she was aware of how ominous the silence had become.

She followed her orders mechanically, leaving the radio on the submarine frequency. Then she backed slowly away from the radio as if it might threaten her, and went back to her dishes. So that was it. Something had gone desperately wrong. It was all so casual. Did "going wrong" mean that a lot of people had died? Had the Russian submariner that her handler had casually mentioned—the one she'd been unable to exorcise from her dreams—been killed, too? Did they even care? At least they wanted her to listen for him, just in case . . .

Corinne stared for a moment at the dish in her hand. It seemed as fragile as a dream, so easy to smash without a second thought . . . like a dream. Was that how they treated people? She hurled it against the wall in a fit of anger. The dish was plastic and ricocheted back in her direction before bouncing on the floor, still in one piece. Her submariner should be so fortunate. *Her* submariner? Yes, *her* submariner now.

Her orderly mind forced her to pick up the dish, wipe it again, then place it neatly back in the cupboard. Very carefully, in an effort to gain full control of her temper, she wiped off the linoleum countertop and spread the cloth out to dry.

She desperately wanted to go back home to Vancouver at that moment. There she could return to a simple life, sleep late, enjoy good food in fine restaurants, dress in fancy clothes, and spend time in the company of gentlemen who appreciated her. She would have no need to think about other people—and there would certainly be no . . . like hell there wouldn't be. There was one individual she wouldn't be able to get out of her mind.

Outside, the sun had burned off the last tendrils of early morning mist hiding in the tall spruce and the air was warming quickly. Should she go off in search of that little beach she'd thought about when she first awakened? It would be pleasant to feel sand beneath her feet, anything but the cold, slippery rocks she'd discovered that first day.

Forget it, Corinne. Remember what your handlers said about that other frequency. Maybe . . . just maybe . . .

She went over to the radio set and turned up the volume on the speaker. The dull background hum increased in resonance until she was positive she would hear anything out front if someone called. Then she moved the outside chaise into the middle of the yard and went back for her book. But before she even sat down, it was obvious the air was still too cool. She looked up at the treetops. The mist had indeed disappeared but tiny water droplets continued to sparkle where the sun filtered through the tops. It would be another hour.

She went back inside for a sweater and stopped to stare at the radio set. Nothing was any different. It remained on the table, squat, dark, ugly, its dials staring back bright but unseeing. Its hum was steady—but lifeless. A machine. Another depressing instrument of modern man.

Back outside, propped up on the chaise, the pages of her book remained lifeless also. The sentences ran together in a language that appeared foreign to her. There were no words. It was just black against white and it seemed to move whenever she attempted to separate the words from each other.

It was no use. She couldn't concentrate on a thing. The air was full of sound and she tried to separate each noise. Seagulls fought over scraps beyond the shoreline, screaming with success, screaming with anger, screaming just to be heard. The breeze brought the sound of various engines across the water, the low rumble of a ferryboat, the higher pitch of fishermen's diesels, the steady pitch of tugs moving garbage barges from island to island, sometimes the sharp whine of an outboard. The sounds had traveled a long distance on the winds and they disappeared just as quickly. Eventually, she was able to shut them out and concentrate on the birds and the soft rattle of the aspen behind the cabin.

She had no idea how long she lay there listening, nor could she remember any of the thoughts that had passed through her mind, but she literally jumped into the air when a loud crackling of static came from the radio speaker inside. The chaise tumbled over as she leaped to her feet.

Before she got through the door, a slightly accented voice bellowed through the room, "Vancouver station, this is Dragger. Do you read? Over." The volume had been turned so high that the words were barely understandable. They filled the room with a torrent of sound that she was sure carried all the way to Friday Harbor.

Corinne's heart felt as if it would break through her chest

as she lunged to turn it down. The thumping sound filled her ears until the voice came back again. "Vancouver station, Vancouver station, this is . . ."

She snatched up the mike, breaking in on the call. "This is Vancouver station," she shouted breathlessly.

There was no response. What had gone wrong? Had he . . . ? Then she realized that she'd cut in on his transmission. There was no way he could have heard her. She waited, ashamed of how stupid she'd been, afraid that she may have destroyed his one last chance.

"Vancouver station. Are you trying to call me? Over."

He was back again!

"Dragger, this is Vancouver station. Please relay your message. Over," she said evenly.

"Vancouver station, I have a full load and I'm unable to locate my mother ship. Do you have a message for me? Over."

He was alive . . . and he was in need of help. This was the reason for her existence on this lonely island. Her mind was racing. What did he need? What could she do for him? "Dragger, all I know is you cannot proceed as planned. Your mother ship may have problems and will be unavailable. The owners contacted me and I was told to offer you help. Over."

This was met with silence. Perhaps he hadn't heard her. Corinne hesitated. Had she said something she shouldn't have? Would he be frightened away?

"Vancouver station, where are you? Over."

Corinne hesitated. *Remember,* she'd been ordered, *don't give away your location to anyone.* But this was different. Dragger was lost, alone. Her handlers had forsaken him. They'd left him to her. "Dragger, the San Juan Islands." She knew she couldn't say more. "Over."

There was another long pause. Corinne desperately wanted to say more. If he understood how badly she wanted to help him he'd come to her. He was more in need of a friend than she was at this point. And she would be sure to . . .

"I think I should meet with you, Vancouver station, but I

have to decide which is the best way to get to your location. I will call you back in six hours. I should be closer to you by then. Over."

"Six hours, Dragger. I'll be waiting for your call." Before Corinne could think of anything else to say, she could tell that he had gone. *But he intends to come to me. He needs to.*

She looked at her watch. Ten after ten. He would be back to her at four this afternoon. What were his plans? Where was he and how would he get to her? The questions raced through her mind and there were no answers. But he must have a map of some kind and he would somehow figure out how to locate her. It must be that he wanted to get closer before he called again.

What was she going to do for the next six hours? *You've got to think, Corinne. You've got to determine ahead of time what he may want to know and be ready. This is the most important thing you've ever done in your life.*

Koniev switched off the equipment and sat back in the chair, arms folded, chin on his chest. He wasn't so much despondent as saddened. *Gorki* must be gone, too. His entire miniature submarine program was in shambles. He had no idea how the Americans had known, although it could have been as much his own people's stupidity as US brilliance. Either way, that part of the mission was over. But the most critical element of the operation, the real basis for the entire mission, was still alive—Victor Koniev.

His mouth was dry and metallic-tasting. He went over to the sink and turned on the water. Every glass in sight was filthy. He went from one cupboard to another until he found a clean one and, just as he was about to push the door shut, he saw what he'd been dreaming of only moments before—batteries. He couldn't tell from the printing on them, but they looked to be the same size. He pulled the radio out of his pocket, slipped off the back, and removed one of the tiny batteries. Yes, they were the same size. He replaced his own with the others and dropped the spares in his pocket.

Now he had to study the map to determine how he would get close to that Vancouver station.

Thirteen

A NOON SUN AND A LIGHT BREEZE SET THE HOOD CANAL to sparkling as Bernie Ryng gazed across at the Trident base. He wondered briefly if the dead ham radio operator ever realized the magnitude of what was across the water. If he had, Ryng surmised, he might have had a better understanding in his final seconds of why he was about to die. Actually, considering the position of the body and the two bullet holes in the head, it was more an execution. Ryng could imagine the uncontrollable fear that must have overwhelmed the poor man as he was marched down to his basement, and then the agonizing realization as he turned to see the gun barrel level with his face.

I understand you, Ryng murmured silently to himself. This Russian was a man with a mission and he knew without a doubt that it would be insane to leave a trail for someone like Ryng. *I have studied the computer printouts, the personality profiles, the psychological assessments, and even the wonder in the faces of the innocents who prepare such things. It is probably of no concern to you but they don't understand what makes you tick. They're unable to comprehend how or why you think the way you do. It seems incongruous to them that you can function as a normal*

*human being in everyday society and be as callous as you are
on a mission. They understand society's miscreants because
they end up in prisons or mental institutions. But they can't
comprehend how you can be lionized and promoted to vital
positions of responsibility after you have committed such
acts. The reward system for violence, justifiable or not, is
totally foreign to them—as are you.*

"But I understand you completely," Ryng said out loud.
"As unfortunate as it may be, I suppose we are brothers
under the skin." That was why, as he crossed the Hood
Canal from the Trident base, he had intuitively ordered his
helicopter down the minute he spotted the ham radio
antenna from the air. If he'd been on the run like this
Russian—and he had been—the first thing he would have
done was attempt radio contact with whoever was waiting
for him. It would have been instinctive for Ryng; it should
have been for the Russian. Neither the body in the basement
nor the fact that the radio dial was set on a frequency used
by the local fishermen surprised him. He knew the radio had
been used and he appreciated the fact that the tracks were
well-covered.

As he was about to turn back to the house, another
helicopter similar to the old Huey he'd ridden into the
backyard rose over the hillside to his right. It circled once to
check the wind before landing dangerously close to the
other. Harry Coffin pushed open the door and climbed out
before the rotors had stopped, then turned back to help an
older, bearded man step down.

"Bernie," the admiral shouted over the whine of the dying
engine, "this is Mr. Warner, and he's full of good stuff on our
man."

"He's seen him?" Ryng asked with surprise. So this
Russian had made a mistake, perhaps an indication that he
could also make a fatal error. He'd left a witness.

"Better than that. Had breakfast with him."

"You are indeed fortunate to be alive, Mr. Warner. The
gentleman who lived here wasn't as lucky as you." Why
would the Russian kill one and not the other? A mistake.
Perhaps he was more exhausted than Ryng assumed. That

also meant there was a flaw there, an unanticipated weakness in his personality. If this Russian allowed himself to make such a foolish error, why not one more?

Warner's face softened. "You mean Lewis here, the old radio nut . . ." He stumbled over his words as he realized what Ryng was saying.

"That's right," Ryng answered. "You must be an exceptional cook, Mr. Warner. Perhaps that's why he didn't kill you." He turned to Coffin. "How'd you locate him?"

"Your man, Danny West, noticed his cabin from the barge where they're trying to raise that mini sub. He figured that if your man swam across the canal to meet that submarine, he might come out of the water somewhere below that cabin so he suggested by radio that we check it out. Mr. Warner here was trussed up pretty good, and he was happy to see us."

"Mr. Warner," Ryng said with a pleasant smile, "I hope you won't mind going back across the canal with me for a while so I can take down all the information you have. You see," he continued, looking to Admiral Coffin, "the fellow we're after belongs to us and I'm sure with all these helicopters buzzing around that the sheriff's department is going to turn up here pretty soon, and I'd hate for them to interfere with us or pick up something that might be misinterpreted by the newspapers. I'm sure you understand."

Warner had been watching Ryng's face as he spoke and those eyes told him this man was much like his earlier visitor. "What you mean is that I don't have any more choice than I did this morning. Isn't that it?"

"I can guarantee you we'll take much better care of you than the sheriff's department, Mr. Warner," Coffin responded.

Warner checked the admiral's insignia on Coffin's uniform before nodding and saying, "I used to be in the navy myself, Admiral. Never got higher than a seaman in the deck force. But I guess if I can't trust you, I can't trust anyone." His eyes darted to Ryng, then back to the admiral. "If you tell me that this fella's okay . . ."

"You have my personal guarantee that Mr. Ryng will

make sure you're well taken care of. I'll be back with you both shortly." Then he added, "After the sheriff's department comes by, I suppose."

"Admiral," Ryng said, "I'd like to suggest you explain to them that we were investigating some odd radio transmissions we picked up last night. Tell them it looked like it came from here and we were just checking it out."

"And the corpse?" Coffin asked.

"I'm sure you'll think of something, sir. Just because we intercepted something odd on the radio, that doesn't mean it was our man. We just happened to discover the body after noticing the antenna and checking out the victim's radio." Ryng escorted Warner gently toward one of the helicopters as if he were afraid the old man might bolt in the other direction.

In less than an hour, Ryng possessed everything he needed—an accurate description of his man and of the clothes he'd taken, the license number of the old car, and after some more detailed questions an added insight into the man's psychological profile. When it was all faxed to Washington, the response wasn't long in coming.

Ryng read everything the intelligence people had on Koniev, appreciating how little they really knew about the man. Learning his background was the easy part. Like every Russian military man, he did attend special schools. He did have operational assignments that progressively enhanced his talent and increased his responsibilities. And like most men, he eventually married and fathered a family. But active data also disappeared from Washington's files about six years before, almost as if he'd ceased existing. But he hadn't done that at all. It was simply a way of the Kremlin's allowing only what they wanted known about an individual to appear once he became a challenge to their enemies.

The oddest twist was what Warner had to say about Koniev. His impressions were punctuated by the fact that he'd had breakfast with this individual and talked pleasantly with him. Yet less than an hour later, the next individual he encountered was murdered in cold blood. Warner could no more understand this than the people who prepared the profiles. But Ryng understood. His target was totally unpredictable, preferring to make decisions on the spot. It would be almost impossible for Ryng to narrow his own assumptions about what the man was likely to do from one hour to the next.

But Bernie Ryng already understood Victor Koniev.

Corinne decided there was only one thing she could do if she was to maintain her sanity through the hours before four that afternoon. The sponge bath had done nothing at all for her. That swim she'd been promising herself, the refreshing jolt of icy water, was exactly what she needed.

The sun was as high as it would climb that day and the air had warmed to a comfortable sixtyish temperature. Grabbing one of the large towels, she put together a light lunch of bread and cheese and a juice container of cold white wine, and slipped it all into a small duffel along with her book and a few magazines.

This time she wandered down an old, unfamiliar path that was slightly farther inland. Since Jimmy Cook's little bay the day before had as rocky a bottom as the one near her cabin, she decided to explore the area toward the western tip of the island.

The trail was barely visible even in the middle of the day. Deadfall from the trees had crisscrossed it over the years until it appeared that either no one ever used this path, or they simply had no more urge to move these impediments than she did.

The woods were alive at that time of day. Squirrels leaped from tree to tree chattering at everything that moved. Twice she saw rabbits perched on their hind legs watching her with unblinking, black marble eyes. But when she stopped to stare back, they'd turn tail and scamper off. She was never that far from the water because she could still hear the screaming of seagulls fighting over scraps. And the other birds, mergansers, herons, scaup, cormorants, all could occasionally be seen in the air in their never-ending quest for food.

When she thought she'd gone far enough, Corinne turned

down what she was sure was more an animal path than anything human beings had tramped. But she'd covered no more than fifty yards when she emerged in an open area that had obviously been cleared by someone long ago. The tumbled remains of a rock foundation indicated that a cabin had been there. Now the clearing was deep in wild grass. A movement to one side caught her eye and she turned her head to see two deer on the far side, a doe and a young spike horn buck, staring back at her.

Neither human nor animal moved, each as surprised and curious as the other. Corinne stood very still for what seemed like minutes until the deer turned and wandered out of the clearing, their white rumps reflecting the sun's rays streaming through the treetops.

Nature was both a profound and foreign experience for Corinne. Beyond occasional weekends in the country, she was a city girl. It had been a humbling experience to find that she was suddenly an integral part of nature, so much so that those beautiful animals had actually accepted her presence without bolting. She squeezed her eyes tightly shut. What was she doing in this clearing among such innocent creatures? The answer came to her much too quickly and was so overpowering when it struck her that for a moment she felt like falling to her knees right there and crying.

For just a moment, she had enjoyed a moving experience that now escaped her mind as quickly as it had come. But it was one she would never forget. What was there about this island that was affecting her in this manner? She had come here for a specific purpose—essentially she'd been ordered to do so—and the emotional experiences, much of her own making, of the past few days were unlike anything she'd encountered since Ken and Cory.

That's it, Corinne! That's it! You were finished with that. Get it out of your mind.

With that, she crossed the clearing toward the water. Beyond some madrona stretching longingly for the sun, she stepped down a slight incline cut out by the waves onto a sandy beach. It was no more than twenty yards from one end to the other. The land projected straight out on either side another thirty or forty yards to shelter the tiny bay. A few dozen tiny scaup bobbed on the wavelets like so many wooden decoys. It was perfect.

Corinne slipped out of her sandals, rolled up her slacks and waded into the water. It was surprisingly warm. Moving out farther, she found the bottom to be very gently sloping and shallow enough for the sun to warm the water to a comfortable temperature—or at least better than any she'd experienced so far.

Pleased, she went back to the edge of the beach, lay her clothes neatly in the grass, and waded back out again. A soft breeze formed tiny, ticklish goose bumps on her skin and made her feel deliciously sensuous as the water reached gradually over her knees to her thighs. The sand was soft and the bottom gave way gently, allowing her to wade for about thirty feet before it suddenly sloped off. She splashed some water on her chest and the breeze instantly made the air feel cooler than the water. An involuntary shiver brought a smile to her face. The sensation was wonderful.

Taking a deep breath, she dove straight out, then let her body sink slowly. The water temperature dropped rapidly beneath the surface, but when she came up for air, it was still comfortable on the top. She dunked her head again, then smoothed her hair down her neck before swimming out to where the little bay opened into the main passage between the islands. It was much colder out there but so refreshing, too, that once again she forced herself to get used to the change. But just as she got out far enough to turn around for a better perspective on her tiny island, she caught sight of a fishing boat coming from the direction of her cabin.

Wouldn't you know it, she said out loud to herself with an amused smile, *and here you are as naked as the day you were born, Corinne.* She turned back toward the little bay and set out with an easy side stroke.

Toot . . . toot. A puff of diesel smoke escaped from the stack as she heard the boat pick up speed.

Now it's not as funny as you thought, lady. She began to swim faster. *Now you've probably got some kink to worry about.*

Toot . . . toot, again. As the boat drew closer, the man at the wheel waved and turned the boat in a tight circle so she could see the name on the stern—*Dream Girl.*

"Hey, Corinne McCarthy, it's me, Captain Cook. I'm not going to run over you," he shouted across the water. He cut back his speed and stopped the boat expertly within ten yards of her.

"I didn't think you were going to," she answered defensively. "It's just that I don't have a bathing suit."

Jimmy Cook grinned down at her. "So I see. I guess you must be the first mermaid I've found in these waters. Must say it's quite a change from my everyday catch."

She was facing him while treading water. "If you were a gentleman, you'd pull away and let me go in to get my clothes." She was damned if he was going to intimidate her.

"Well, I am a gentleman. But I really don't want to go away now that I've found you. Don't you remember you said you were going to meet me in Cook's Bay? I've been cruising back and forth looking for you. If you hadn't been bobbing around the water like some sort of albino cormorant, I might have decided you were throwing me over and that you'd gone away forever." He smiled and his white teeth set off his weathered copper skin. "Then you wouldn't have had any abalone."

"That's right. I forgot."

He was perched comfortably on the gunwale and continued to grin. "Your lucky day."

"I still don't see what's so funny about this. I'm getting cold."

"You can come aboard. I have a towel."

"No, thank you, Captain Cook. My clothes are in there." She pointed toward the beach.

"Tell you what. I really am a gentleman and I also really sympathize with anyone swimming in this water. So, as much as I'm enjoying this, why don't you go back in and get your clothes on before you sink to the bottom." He reached down and came up with a towel. "Need this?"

"No, thank you again," she said, turning toward shore. "I brought one of my own."

"Great. You just dry yourself off then and put your clothes back on while I drop the hook right out here. Cook's Inlet is too shallow for the *Dream Girl*."

Corinne paused and began treading water again. "You mean to tell me that every little body of water is named after you?"

"It is now. Got a nice sound to it, doesn't it? Go on now. You really have to be getting cold. I don't want to have to take you ashore to a hospital. I've got a skiff with me today and I'll be in with your dinner in just a moment, about the time you're more presentable." And with that, he scampered up on the bow to drop his anchor.

When Jimmy Cook climbed out of the skiff and hauled it up on the sand, Corinne was dressed and drying her hair. "I'm sorry. I forgot you said you'd come back with some abalone. It just slipped my mind . . . and I guess I thought you'd forget. But I really do appreciate the idea."

"You must be a pretty lonely lady if you think I'm going to forget someone like you." Once again he was wearing a chamois shirt but this one was a bright red that emphasized his handsome, weathered features and blondish hair. "As a matter of fact, I was looking forward to seeing you so much, I prepared these before I headed over to Cook's Bay." He unfolded the newspaper package he carried and showed her the delicate, white abalone that had already been pounded flat.

"Umm . . . it does look good," she said, wrapping the towel into a turban on her head. "Makes me hungry just thinking about them."

"Me, too. I should have remembered to bring lunch." He shrugged good-naturedly and tapped his head with a finger. "I forget it almost every day though."

"Well, Captain Cook, today you're in luck. That duffel has our lunch in it. It's just some bread and cheese and white wine, that is if you don't mind driving the *Dream Girl* after drinking."

It occurred to Corinne that her conversation with Jimmy Cook made no sense at all compared to how she'd felt over

218

the last twelve hours. Her emotions were like a bouncing ball. Just twenty minutes before, she'd almost been overcome by her sudden sense of the helplessness of the animal life around her. An hour or so before, she was still experiencing the depression that had affected her earlier in the morning. Now she felt like a schoolgirl with this handsome stranger who was smiling broadly at her. It was a feeling she didn't think had been a part of her since before Ken had come into her life.

"First, I accept your kind invitation to share your lunch. Now do you mind if I ask you a question?"

Corinne wasn't sure whether the expression on his face was simply quizzical or if he was about to tease her again. She simply nodded—"Go ahead"—not knowing why she was opening herself up like this.

"Is this another research trip? I mean you told me yesterday you were doing research for a paper. But I haven't seen a notebook or anything like that. And all the researchers I've ever seen pictures of are a lot older and kind of dowdy-looking . . . you know, thick glasses, a man's haircut, always serious . . . and I must admit you didn't look anything like a researcher bobbing around out there." He waved his hand toward the water. "Nothing personal, of course. Honest. Just curious."

Corinne could feel her face warming as the color rushed to her cheeks. One thing she'd never been was shy, or embarrassed, about being seen without clothes. And she hadn't been embarrassed when he stopped the *Dream Girl* near her. But now when he spoke about her being naked out there— with that slight grin that never seemed to disappear—she felt wholly different. This wasn't a prospect to be cultivated, not even one of those whom she felt a part of when they were off for a weekend or even longer. This was a charming man who would have been strangely appealing to her if . . . if . . . no, there was no "if" because Jimmy Cook was a pleasant interlude, nothing more.

"I prepare my notes . . . when I get back to the cabin," she stammered. "I keep everything up here during the day."

She tapped the turban with an index finger. "Don't you . . . ah, think a researcher can relax once in a while?"

"I apologize if I've offended you." His response was quick and the grin disappeared momentarily. "I don't want to let these moments get away, if you understand what I mean. Fishing is a lonely business. I'll tell you what," he concluded hastily, "I brought that extra towel in and we'll use it as a tablecloth for lunch and you can tell me all about research and I'll listen intently. Friends?" he added.

Jimmy moved an old log so they could sit on it, and spread the towel between them. They tore chunks off a loaf of slightly stale french bread that had come out to the island with her and cut off pieces of a sharp cheddar cheese to wash down with the wine. Corinne carefully steered the talk to Jimmy in an effort to avoid explaining her research in detail. Most of the men she spent any amount of time with were successful, often wealthy, and mostly talked about how well they had done. She found Jimmy as uninhibited as any man she'd ever met. Jimmy Cook was open about both his successes and failures and found humor in everything that had happened to him.

"What time is it?" she interrupted suddenly, jumping up to search her pocket for the watch she'd removed before she went swimming.

Jimmy's eyes never left her own except to glance at his watch. "Almost two-thirty." Then, just as if he were continuing the conversation, he asked, "Is there a problem?"

"No, of course not." She was still fumbling for the watch.

"You're sure, absolutely sure there's nothing I can do to help you." His face was serious for the first time that day.

"Of course I'm sure. Why do you ask?"

He shrugged. "It just sort of struck me that someone watching birds and doing research as casually as you seem to be wouldn't be so concerned about the time. After all, you're by yourself. No appointments. No phone. No planes to catch. That's one of the advantages of life out here. Time doesn't matter, never has." He touched her hand. "Sure?"

"Yes, very much so." But she was unable to look him in the eye. "It's just that there's an eagle's nest back near my cabin and he wasn't there this morning . . . and I expected he'd be back . . ."

"Never saw an eagle with a watch before."

"Neither have I," Corinne laughed. "Don't you think that I may want to study their habits at different times of the day?"

"OK, maybe that makes sense." He took his hand away but his tone of voice said that he wasn't satisfied.

"Would you like a boat ride back to your place? I'd love to have you see how the *Dream Girl* handles."

"No, I think maybe I ought to walk." Then, changing her mind, "Oh, why not? I'd like that."

"Me, too." He patted her hand, then squeezed it and added self-consciously, "Maybe if you enjoy a short ride, I can interest you in a longer trip next time."

She studied his face, then looked away quickly, realizing that he was serious, even more surprised to learn that she would have liked to take that ride, if . . . "Yes, maybe we can do that sometime." In another time, another world, she would have enjoyed it.

As Jimmy pulled on the oars and glanced over his shoulder toward *Dream Girl,* a thousand thoughts coursed through her mind. *I don't want to be late in case he calls early. Now shape up, Corinne. Don't do anything to encourage Jimmy too much. He's too nice . . .* and then they were beside his boat.

It was a short trip back to the cabin by water. Jimmy kept *Dream Girl* offshore because of the rocks and explained that she would have to row the skiff in with a line attached to it, and he would pull it back.

While Corinne balanced on a rock and watched as he hauled in his skiff, he called out, "What would you like for dinner tomorrow?"

"You've been kind enough already, Jimmy. Thanks just the same." *Another time, Jimmy, and you might have been just what I needed.*

"How about some salmon?"

"You're too kind. Really. It isn't in season now anyway, is it?"

"Jumps right out of my freezer. Almost as fresh as the day I caught it, and perfectly filleted, too. I might even return the favor and bring some bread for lunch, fresh from the bakery this time."

Oh, no. Don't encourage him. Maybe . . .

"I'm sorry. I'm not going to be here tomorrow. I'll be doing some field work on the other side of the island."

"What better way to find you than with the *Dream Girl?* I'll bring along some wine."

"No . . . really . . . please . . ." she said haltingly. "I've really enjoyed this but I don't want to . . . I won't be on the island many more days."

Jimmy's broad smile seemed to fill his handsome face. Nothing appeared to bother him, not even an honest effort to discourage his obvious interest in her. "Well, I'll check back just in case. Never can tell, Corinne. We might just discover a new little bay and we'll have to christen it Corinne McCarthy Bay . . . in your honor." *Dream Girl* was already backing down.

"I'm sure you won't see me," she shouted back.

"Never can tell." He waved as *Dream Girl*'s engine growled and her stern dug into the water.

She thought she might have convinced him until she heard his final words floating back in her direction. ". . . salmon . . . a fresh loaf from the bakery . . . and I won't forget the wine."

And then the boat disappeared around the bend.

God damn you, Corinne! You're actually charmed by the guy. And how long ago was it you were fantasizing about a Russian submariner who desperately needs your help? Christ, for a minute there you could even imagine him climbing on top of you. How long before you need your own personal shrink?

She couldn't remember the last time she'd felt as upset with herself and confused by her actions as she stepped through the door and stared at the radio set in the far corner.

It was times like this she almost felt like she could honestly cry again. *Another time . . . another world . . .*

But she knew if she did cry, it still wouldn't be an honest cry.

Standing resolutely in the black sand that lined Dungeness Bay, Nicholas Koniev had come to terms with the fact he had anticipated earlier that day when his efforts to contact *Gorki* had failed—she was gone, somehow detected and sunk by the Americans. It was painful to a degree even though casualties were a fact of life in his world. There was no war and it was likely there never would be, at least not one that would destroy Russian cities, not if his theory became a reality. But casualties were a result of maintaining one's own concept of peace and they were acceptable.

Out beyond the stark whiteness of New Dungeness Light were the telltale naval vessels that told of a sea tragedy—a victory for them, a tragedy for Nicholas Koniev. His dreams surely lay beneath more than four hundred feet of the Strait of Juan de Fuca. He was briefly left with an empty feeling, not from the fact that he had failed for he still carried what he'd come so far to possess, but more a sense of loss. It was like losing a woman, the body was gone but the memories were still his.

He'd driven the old car to Dungeness after studying the map. Perhaps it was unnecessary but his deep sense of responsibility for the ship he'd given birth to wouldn't allow him to do otherwise. Now it was time to get rid of the car. He looked over his shoulder at the snow-covered Olympic mountains, then his eyes dropped to the sign identifying the Three Crabs Restaurant. There was no one about at the moment, in fact there didn't seem to be a human being within hearing. Yet he must assume it was the type of place where there would soon have to be people. It would be no problem to acquire another vehicle.

There was also no doubt in his mind that the SEALs, after destroying Donskoi's craft, would have covered the western shore of the canal at first light inch by inch. And in their thoroughness they would eventually find the old man and start the search for his car. They would find the house with the radio, too . . .

Wandering down toward the main highway after driving the car under a thick grove of trees at the end of an overgrown dirt road, he determined there was only one safe way to get to the woman on the radio. A boat. It would be too hazardous to remain on the highways for any period of time with the road blocks that would probably be set up. Nor would public transportation be safe once they had a description of him. He reflected on his first mistake. *It was foolish not to have killed that bearded old fool!* Never before could he remember doing anything so stupid, so utterly contrary to everything he'd learned during his career. Exhaustion, however, was a poor excuse for failing to cover his tracks properly. Carelessness, pure and simple. Perhaps this was the first indication that he should retire if he managed to get home. *Stupidity!*

The next vehicle that came along stopped when he stuck out his thumb. He saw the crab traps in the back end and knew he would be able to get the information he would need from this fisherman. It turned out that a lot of private and commercial boats, many of them large enough to cruise the sometimes rough waters of the Strait, often tied up at the John Wayne Marina in Sequim Bay which was less than half an hour away. The driver wasn't going that far—"just home for lunch"—but he was willing to show his passenger how to get there.

Koniev kept his pistol under cover until he saw a dirt road ahead that turned off into a grove of trees well back from the highway. He left the body in a dry creek bed beyond the trees covered with brush. There would be more than enough time for his purposes before anyone noticed something amiss. More likely it would be a local dog in a day or so that would attract attention to the unfortunate owner of the pickup.

He was as familiar with the name of John Wayne as any other Russian and it was not difficult to recognize it on the signs. The driver had pointed out the John Wayne Marina on his map. The huge billboard identifying the turnoff to the marina left no doubt where he was. He drove down the entry road and left the truck beside some other cars in a huge parking lot that was only half-full that time of year.

The marina was absolutely perfect, enough fishermen, pleasure boaters and leftover tourists to make him inconspicuous as he meandered down to the piers, his hands stuffed casually in his pockets. There was a store with food and supplies for boats, launch ramps, picnic facilities, even a pier where a couple of people were fishing—a peaceful place.

Koniev walked up each of the piers casually examining the boats, keeping a running inventory in his mind of those that appeared to have only one person working around them. Those few that were being filled with fuel as he watched were of special interest for he wanted one that was obviously preparing to leave with a full tank.

Eventually he selected one, *Sea Chase*, at the end of the second pier when he saw that the single individual aboard had spread out a chart and was making detailed marks on it. The engine had already been started and made a pleasant low grumble as the exhaust bubbled into the water.

Koniev squatted and cleared his throat. "Nice day to be out on the water."

The man looked up with a half-smile. "You got it. My old lady's gone into Port Townsend to spend my money and this is my chance to drink a little beer and chase some fish until the sun goes down."

"Where are you headed?"

"Just out today." He went back to his chart. "Maybe to this hole right here," he added, tapping a spot on the paper with a finger, "that a friend of mine told me about. Big halibut, he claims." He turned away.

"How big is that?" Koniev inquired, trying to keep the conversation going.

The man looked at him curiously. "You're not a fisherman, I guess."

"No . . . I'm not."

"Well, they're real big, maybe a hundred pounds or more sometimes." He looked at Koniev curiously. "Look, I'd be happy to talk with you some other time, but I got to get out of here. Have a nice day now, OK."

The man reached up and undid the stern line and was about to climb up to get the bow line when Koniev said, "Don't bother, I'll get that for you."

"No need to."

"Please, allow me to assist," Koniev answered. He couldn't let this one get away. Glancing over his shoulder to make sure there was no one watching, Koniev lifted the line from the cleat on the pier. Then he stepped down on the bow with the line.

"Ah . . . no need to do that, mister. I'll get that . . ." But before he could finish his sentence, Koniev had dropped the line and moved like a cat down the railing and dropped onto the deck beside him.

"Please, don't do anything that would cause a problem." The gun in Koniev's hand was allowed to glisten in the sun for just a second, long enough for the man to appreciate it, before it disappeared back in his pocket. "My finger is on the trigger and I would be happy to use it once more again today. The last person misunderstood my intentions. Do you understand?"

The man nodded dumbly. His face sagged with fear.

"Good. Please take us out then. But don't look so frightened or it could get you killed. All I want is a ride, and I won't hurt you if you drop me off at my destination. If you see anyone you know, you may wave or say hello or whatever you do to be polite. But I can promise you that if you don't, or if you cause someone to ask you if there is a problem, then your friends will die just like you. Again, I want to be sure that you understand."

Another nod.

"Good. But you are still staring at me like an idiot and your boat is free of the pier. You could also die from a stupid accident." He moved the gun in his pocket so that the barrel stood out. "So, please, let's go fishing."

They moved away from the pier and maneuvered past the end of the breakwater into Sequim Bay, then on out past the protecting sand spits into open water without a soul noting their passage. Soon the boat was riding comfortably on a course directly away from Sequim Bay.

Koniev kept the man alive long enough to learn the essentials of running the boat. He studied the chart and even asked a few questions about the San Juan Islands. Once they were beyond the few other boats fishing the area, he killed the man with one bullet in the forehead, quickly lashed the anchor rope around the corpse's feet a couple of turns, and dumped the body over the side weighted with the anchor.

Fourteen

CORINNE REMEMBERED SIMILAR SITUATIONS WHEN SHE WAS younger, often because others were just as pleasant and innocent and naive as Jimmy Cook. The details were a little foggy but as she had watched Jimmy haul the skiff back aboard *Dream Girl,* those memories came back to her. Each time, she'd known her actions wouldn't receive the approval of those who managed her life, whether they involved her parents or her friends. And each time, she went ahead and did what she wanted to do.

Stubborn, Corinne. Bull-headed. Too independent for your own good. But that had been the story of her life.

Corinne had few friends growing up because her parents had no desire to become involved with other people. They found reasons to discourage any friendships she ever attempted. They had no enemies nor did they have any friends.

The first time Corinne encountered a situation where she wanted to reach out to someone, it involved another girl her age who had just moved into her Coventry neighborhood. She was a Pakistani and most of the locals weren't about to welcome such a different family. They were dark, spoke with heavy accents, and they wore old, out-of-date clothes. The Pakistani girl was just as lonely as Corinne and had gone out of her way in school to be friendly to her. Perhaps she saw a reflection of herself when Corinne smiled shyly at her. Even though Corinne feared going against her parents' wishes, she also felt sorry for the little girl because she could imagine herself in an equally difficult situation if she moved to a strange place. Thinking back on it now, Corinne remembered that she had been just as lonely in that Coventry neighborhood even though she'd been born there.

Corinne decided to help the Pakistani girl adjust at school. She even did homework with her. In return, her new friend did what people from her own culture did when they were befriended—she gave Corinne little gifts, mostly trinkets that appealed to her curiosity. Corinne loved the tiny earrings even though she couldn't wear them.

Eventually, her parents learned what was taking place. Her father whipped her with a switch; her mother went to the school and told the teacher Corinne would be withdrawn if she associated with the Pakistani girl. Then they spread rumors about the family until the neighbors made a point of totally ostracizing these different people. Many of the local merchants refused to do business with them.

Eventually, the Pakistani family was forced to move to a bigger city. When they left, Corinne's father told her it was her fault that her little friend had to leave. He said that if she had obeyed her parents and left the other little girl alone, nothing like that ever would have happened. It was her fault the family had to find a new home.

For years, Corinne felt guilty about what she had done. But she had liked the other girl, and besides, the trinkets she'd received in exchange for her friendship seemed to draw her back each time even though she knew her parents would be mad. It was also one of the events in her life that turned her against her family. Perhaps, in retrospect, that was also the reason she had made the effort to seek out the undesirables when she went away to the university.

That was why now, as she stretched out on the couch in

the little cabin and stared at the silent radio, she once again pondered the meaning of that earlier experience. It wasn't the same with Jimmy Cook. True, he seemed to be a loner but he certainly wouldn't be unattractive to anyone anywhere, not with that thick blond-brown hair and his handsome face that seemed all coppery in the sunlight. Would he, or his family if there was one, suffer because she was willing to give her friendship?

It was just . . . just that someone else—her handlers—had told her explicitly that she was to avoid any outside contact. The consequences for Jimmy, for both of them actually, could be extreme if someone else got wind of the attention he was paying her. But they hadn't threatened her really. They wouldn't do that because she was much too valuable to them. What had been lurking in the back of her mind was that the one named Roberts had indicated that the man she was responsible for, the submariner, could be the one to suffer if anyone else ever became aware of what was taking place on this little island.

And here she was encouraging Jimmy . . . no, not encouraging, just not discouraging him. Like the Pakistani girl, he brought trinkets, but they were crab legs, and abalone, and innocent conversation. She didn't need the wonderful fish he brought for her, but it was a treat and in just two days she found herself looking forward to seeing him appear in *Dream Girl. You're taking a chance because you're greedy, Corinne. This time, instead of trinkets, he's plying you with fish . . . if you can believe that.* She laughed silently to herself. *No, it's not the fish, honey, it's the fisherman that amuses you. Don't let them hurt him.*

And that made her sit bolt upright as she realized exactly what had been troubling her. She was falling in love just like a schoolgirl, not with someone she knew, not Jimmy Cook, but with the image of a powerful man she had never seen, with an illusion she had created. And handsome Jimmy Cook was filling that image because she was so lonely.

This, Corinne, from a woman who swore she would never again love anyone. You're allowing yourself to be charmed by

*a man whom you've met twice and you're having wet dreams
over a man you've never met. All this even though you're not
supposed to be seeing anyone. Just like the Pakistani girl,
because there was this void in your life . . .*

"Vancouver station, this is Dragger. Over."

To Corinne, the voice seemed to rock the room like a
thunderclap. It was so unexpected that she caught herself in
the act of screaming, barely stopping before her shriek
escaped.

Her eyes automatically swept the room for an intruder
even though her mind had already acknowledged that the
voice had come from the radio speaker. Then she was on her
feet and darting across the room to the radio.

"This is Vancouver station. Over."

The response was sharp. "Our transmissions must remain
short. Forget call signs. No unnecessary words. Now switching to another transmitter. Out."

Koniev turned off the boat radio. It was too powerful, too
long-range, too easy to be overheard even though that
frequency had been selected because it wasn't normally
covered by the boats in this area. He picked up his small
portable and keyed it. "Do you copy me now?"

"Weak but I copy."

Good for her. She did exactly as she was told. Nothing
unnecessary.

"I have a boat. Do you have a chart?"

"One moment." A pause. "Yes, right here."

"I will come to you. My position is ten kilometers south
of Lopez Island. I can see Iceberg Point. Provide me only
with instructions to cover the next hour. Then I will call
back."

There was little hesitation. "Proceed north through Middle Channel to Turn Rock."

"One hour. Out."

Koniev switched off the tiny portable radio, pleased that
he was close enough to his goal to maintain contact and that
he wasn't broadcasting to the entire world.

Middle Channel passed between San Juan and Lopez, the two southernmost of the San Juan Islands. It appeared to be about twelve kilometers to Turn Rock. That would probably be where he'd contact Vancouver station again. But he also noted how close it was to a town on San Juan Island called Friday Harbor. His next radio contact would have to be extremely limited. Too much chance—luck was what it would be—for someone to happen on to that frequency. But luck was also what killed people.

The channel between the lower end of the islands was narrow. As he moved through, a passing boat slowed and the man at the wheel waved. "Any luck today?"

"No, just out for a little pleasure," Koniev called back.

"On a day like this? Hell, I thought all you did was fish." *You've been recognized . . . no, it's the boat . . .*

Koniev's hand slipped over the cool metal in his jacket pocket, hoping the other man didn't know the owner of the boat. "It was so nice that I decided just to cruise a bit. The old lady went shopping in Port . . ." *What the hell was the name of that place?* He glanced frantically at the chart and saw—Port Angeles.

"Strange place to go shopping," the other called back as the distance began to open between them. He seemed to stare at the stern of Koniev's boat as he waved. "Well, hope you kill 'em the next time out."

"Thanks." Koniev looked back at the chart. He must have picked the wrong town. He ran along the coast of the Olympic Peninsula with his finger until he saw what he should have remembered. *Port Townsend, that's what the man had said to you back at the pier! And that's the type of stupid mistake that can put you in an early grave.*

He would have to get rid of this boat soon.

It was later that afternoon when the nondescript vehicle, intentionally inconspicuous with a sailor in civilian clothes at the wheel, pulled up beside the sheriff's car in the parking lot at John Wayne Marina. Bernie Ryng, also in civilian dress on the passenger's side, climbed out. He noticed that an older woman sitting in the back seat of the other car, loose gray hair cascading over her face, was sobbing audibly.

A uniformed officer, his elbows resting on the hood of an adjacent pickup truck, glanced down at the government license plates. "You the navy fella I was told to wait for?"

Ryng nodded. He looked again at the woman. "Is that the wife of the one who owns the pickup?"

"Sure is. She's the one who called me. Apparently she'd spoken with her husband, Charlie, just before he left Dungeness. He was on his way home. When he didn't show, she got scared. So I put out on the radio to my boys to keep a lookout for Charlie's vehicle, you know just in case he'd stopped at a bar on the way home."

"He's a fisherman," Ryng said, pointing at the crab traps in the back end. "Why wouldn't he come here to the marina?" Bernie Ryng was no detective but when Harry Coffin heard about the missing fisherman in the same area the pickup had been dumped, they recognized an instant correlation.

"Might have, but his boat's next door in Discovery Bay. Charlie was sort of semiretired and a little bit slow, too. That's why when he said he was on his way home, his wife expected him. Charlie never did anything out of the ordinary. Very dependable like some of those type are."

"You've already talked to people here?"

The sheriff nodded. "No one's seen him. And some of the old-timers would have noticed him because everybody liked Charlie. He always stopped to talk with anyone he knew."

"Do you know if he ever picked up hitchhikers?"

"Yeah. Up here a lot of people do. No harm in that. I'm sure Charlie did, too. He liked everybody."

Ryng looked again at the old lady in the back seat of the sheriff's car and shook his head sadly. "I'd suggest you get your people out searching around any turnoffs on the main highway between Dungeness and here, sheriff. That's probably where you'll find him."

"Dead?"

"Right."

The sheriff looked Ryng up and down. "I know you're military, mister, 'cause I got a call from my boss telling me to help you out, but I don't know who you are or who you're after. It sure would help us a lot if we knew more of what was going on."

"My name's Winslow," Ryng lied politely. "Military Police. We'd appreciate it if you kept our end of it quiet for a while. This is nothing big, but the guy we're after is obviously dangerous and it's embarrassing as hell that he got away from our people. The less he's aware of how close we are to him, the better, and we don't want to scare civilians if we don't have to."

"The idea's great, but if something bad's happened to Charlie, we aren't going to be able to keep it quiet for long."

"If you don't want a lot more Charlies around here," Ryng answered roughly, "you'd do well to keep it quiet as long as possible. What I need to know is whose boats are out now."

"You figure your man would grab a boat?"

"He'd grab your car if you went in to take a leak. Look, sheriff," Ryng said impatiently, "if you can get the information I need, I'd really appreciate it. There's a time element here." Then he reached into his own car and pulled out a portable transmitter. "Ryng Two, this is Ryng One. Over."

A clear voice, Len Todd's, came from the radio. "This is Ryng Two. Are you at the John Wayne Marina yet? Over."

"Roger, Two. I'm sure we'll have another corpse on our hands soon. I need the admiral to call Whidby Island and ask them to establish an air search off this position. And you need every patrol boat out there you can find. Anything they see floating that looks the least bit like a body should be identified. I also need a visual on every small craft in this vicinity until it's too dark to identify their names. The sheriff here should be able to give us an assist in narrowing that list down shortly. Over."

"Ah, Bernie, this is Coffin. Are you free to talk? Over."

"Reasonably. Go ahead. Over."

"We'll be off John Wayne in approximately thirty minutes. We'll refuel one of our Seafoxes there and then it's yours if you want. Over."

"The offer's appreciated, but I think I'll be better off with a civilian craft. Our man would never show if he ever saw your Seafox." The Seafox was a high speed patrol craft whose engines could be heard for miles but it could also do thirty-two knots. "I've got a sheriff here who's agreed to cooperate." Ryng smiled and nodded at the sheriff who was taking in the entire conversation. "I think if you talk with him when you get here, Admiral, we won't have any problems. Can you please arrange for a helo from the base to fly in some weapons for me? Over?"

"Do you have a laundry list? Over."

"All I have is a handgun and my K-bar. I'll need an automatic rifle, frag and stun grenades, and another knife would help. Better yet, Len Todd can lend me his K-bar. That'll do for traveling light." He stopped for a moment and pointed toward the piers. "Sheriff," he said irritably, "could you get that information I asked for? About the time you're finished, I think my party here will want to talk with you."

For some reason unknown to him, the sheriff answered, "Yes, sir," and was gone.

"Admiral, I'm sure our man's grabbed a boat. I don't know where he's headed but it's got to be some place where he knows there's help and it has to be nearby. My boys will coordinate for me, but I've got to go after him alone. Believe me, it's the only way we have a chance. Too many people and he'll dodge us all."

When he called again, the sun had already slipped behind the trees leaving the cabin dark enough to turn on the gas lamps. Corinne had gone back over the chart so many times that she'd memorized the points of land he would pass when he took the courses to get to the cabin. Yet when the radio suddenly came alive with his voice, its sharpness coupled with the terse efficiency of his few words to make it an unnerving experience.

There was no call, just—"I am at the correct position."

She could tell by the choice of words as much as his accent that he was foreign. "Too much traffic here. What is my next course?"

"You will turn to your right and pass between two islands." There was something about his method that made her realize she shouldn't mention the names of the islands. "Your course should be about . . ." How the hell did you use the right terms? Would he understand? ". . . ten degrees magnetic . . . for about eight kilometers . . . until you open into a wider channel beyond those islands and . . ."

"Enough for now. I will call in no less than forty-five minutes."

That was all. No nonsense. It was apparent that he knew exactly where he was and, if there were no mistakes, she now had no doubt she would finally meet him that evening. How long had it been since his first call? No more than seven or eight hours?

Corinne had no idea where he had started from after that initial contact this morning, but she could hardly believe that a foreigner, a Russian submariner, could handle himself so well in an unknown country. There was something both entrancing and frightening about a man like that. She had created a superman in her dreams the past few days, but he was more a woman's idea of a superman—attractive in a rugged sort of way, reasonably well-built though not overly muscled like those ugly weightlifters, an aggressive but not brutal lover, and a certain grace that most women looked for in a man and rarely encountered. Yet now that she was about to come face to face with this man, his abilities bordered on the terrifying. Her superman had become too powerful, more frightening than awe-inspiring, his personality already too overwhelming.

Oh, he had been handsome in her dreams, when she eventually coaxed him out of the shadows. Her submariner had been tall and rather dark with flashing black eyes and a dark mustache over a confident, somewhat cocky, white-toothed smile. Hadn't she seen a movie with a submarine captain who looked like that? But the *voice* over the radio was that of a different man. She couldn't tell about his size but there were elements of vanity and cruelty in his method. She couldn't imagine a smile from such a man.

Corinne shuddered and moved out the door to sit on the front steps. The last gulls of the day were cruising in the twilight foraging for any scraps missed after the day's businesslike search. A faint aroma of decay hung in the almost still air, a combination of mosses, moldering mushrooms, spruce needles, and fallen branches. When the sun dried it during the day, it was a pleasant, spicy smell. But at night, it seemed to carry the aroma of something better left unknown.

Tell me, honey, what's made you such an incurable romantic the past few days? She picked up a twig to detour the last ant of the day on its way home. The creature was dutifully struggling to haul a tiny treasure back to the nest. No matter how Corinne blocked its path, the ant managed to avoid the stick, then resume the same direction as before. Eventually, she took pity on the creature and tossed away the twig. *And tell me more, how come you're getting cold feet now that you're about to meet the man of your dreams?*

It was just before six that evening that a Whidby Island helicopter vectored a patrol boat to a suspicious object near Hein Bank, a bit more than twenty miles northeast of Sequim Bay. The object proved to be the corpse of an older man. A shark had been frightened off by the helicopter, but not before one arm and both legs had been torn away. The remnant of a length of rope appeared to have been wrapped around the legs. Whatever had been attached to the rope had come loose, but the petty officer on the boat assumed it had been an anchor or something equally heavy intended to drag the body to the bottom. But the main point of his report concerned the obvious bullet hole in the victim's forehead that had blown off the back of his skull. He had to assume this was the object of the search.

There was still some light when Bernie Ryng arrived on the scene aboard the *Voyager*. She was a new, sleek private fishing boat designed by the wealthy owner for speed and seaworthiness. Her electronics for both fishing and communications were state of the art. It had taken Admiral Coffin just moments to convince the owner of the patriotism of his decision to loan the boat to Ryng.

Since the body had been in the water for only a few hours, facial features were still identifiable enough to allow a comparison to the composite descriptions of boat owners who had left the John Wayne Marina that afternoon. Within minutes, Ryng had narrowed the number of boats he was looking for down to two—*Morning Sun* and *Sea Chase*. Considering how far north of Sequim Bay the body had been found, the odds indicated his man would most likely be heading for the San Juan Islands with the stolen boat.

"We've got some additional data for you on this Koniev," Coffin told Ryng before *Voyager* had gotten underway from the marina. "There's not a hell of a lot on him, a mysterious sort of guy, but this is what intelligence pieced together for us." He handed over a copy of the information that had been faxed to him in Bangor. "He's apparently been camera shy so there's still no photo and he seems to have had a way of avoiding the media, almost as if he planned it that way."

Ryng flipped through the pages for a moment. "Most of this covers his early days. It's almost like he died."

"Not on your life. Check out the last paragraph. He's a senior officer and it appears he was heavily into the miniature submarine program, but we can't get more of a handle on it than that. I think he's their kingpin but I can't imagine why they'd send their top guy into the lion's den."

Ryng tapped the last paragraph with his index finger. "It also says he's Spetznaz," he murmured. "That explains a lot."

"I know you mentioned that before. But still, why a guy on Koniev's level?"

"If you're going to do it right the first time, your only choice is the best," Ryng said as much to himself as to Coffin. "I thought it looked like a Spetznaz operation before, but this sort of wraps it up." He looked at Coffin. "I'm familiar with Koniev, Admiral. I don't mean personally, but there's very few like him. He's got to be one of a kind, one of

the meanest sons of bitches in the world. That's why his trail
is going to be all corpses."

"You're sure about taking off alone on this . . ."

"Only way. More than one of us, and he'd be on to us in
an instant."

On the east end of Corinne's island, Sister Mary Catherine methodically locked up each of the cabinets and then the
front door of the little general store that served the local
fishermen, summer residents, and solitude lovers. Although
there had again been no customers, the store would be open
every day but Sunday. Then she took her habitual side trip
to the pier before heading home. It was a gorgeous sunset
with the colors in the western sky dappling the twilight
waters with an invisible paintbrush. Since she knew there
wouldn't be many more days like this one, Sister Mary
Catherine decided a few moments of relaxation in the little
grape arbor overlooking the strait between the islands
wouldn't be an inconvenience to the others. The sisters had
cleared a comfortable space and set out deck chairs for
whoever desired a few moments of solace against their long
days of loneliness on the island.

Sister Mary Catherine collapsed in a comfortable chair
with a sigh. The sounds drifting across the water were as
pleasant as the cool evening air. She lifted the binoculars
that hung from a long, solid nail and sat back with a
comfortable sigh to watch her favorite birds. Even the
scavengers, trailing returning fishing boats for the leavings
of the day's catch, were appreciated. They had a significant
job in this complex world and performed it with gusto.

Before she realized it, the binoculars gradually came to
rest in her lap and she was dozing comfortably in the
security of the tiny arbor that had come to represent their
only luxury.

When *Sea Chase* cruised beyond the long shadow of the
island to his left, Koniev was surprised by how bright the
open water remained in the early evening. Perhaps he would

be able to find this woman who would be his savior before dark. *What better way to meet a strange woman than in the dark of night on an island halfway around the world?* It was not the first time he had thought about the woman in that manner but now she was so close that it caused him to shiver with delight. *It has been . . . how long since your last one . . . yes, Petropavlovsk . . . Alix, wasn't it?* Galya, his wife back in Leningrad, had escaped his mind completely. And back in Severodvinsk, that double-crossing, traitorous bitch, Anna, was dead. He wished he'd had the time to make her suffer more. But those women were half a world away . . . and his destiny was in the hands of another woman.

"I am now at the next location."

Her voice was firm. "You should turn left to about two sixty and pass between . . ."

"Don't use the names," he snapped harshly.

The circuit was silent momentarily before she responded just as sharply, "I had no intention. You should pass between"—and here her intonation was obvious—*"two islands* for approximately ten kilometers . . ."

"That's enough."

Again, her impatience was obvious. "No. Now listen. Otherwise you will pass me. Night falls quickly here. There will be a lantern on shore to your left. Then call me again."

"Agreed."

Koniev, noticing some hesitancy in the woman's voice during their earlier conversations, assumed she was just one more female operative recruited as a backup only to find that she was in over her head. But this one could assert herself. *Would you act the same way if you knew who you were talking to? If you knew what I have accomplished?* It would be fascinating to find out. He was exhausted and food and sleep were a vital necessity before he made his next move. *But man cannot survive by bread alone. How wise our people in Vancouver have been, even brilliant to anticipate each one of my needs. If only they understood how cooperative they are.*

As *Sea Chase* moved west between the two islands, a

large, mountainous one that rose straight out of the water on his right, and a smaller, relatively flat one to his left, he marveled at their beauty in the final, long green shadows of the evening. His binoculars revealed beautiful little retreats, like the dachas at home, snuggled along the shore behind stands of trees. But the darkness came quickly, just as the woman had said, and those shadows merged and began to turn the islands into floating black hulks. He had expected to see lights wink on everywhere, but there were very few on his right, hardly a one on his left where the fading sun created elongated shadows. Many of the cottages and houses he had noticed were apparently unoccupied this time of year.

As he swung the glasses to his left, he noticed a large wooden pier, much like the one a ferry was beside on the other side of the channel, and a woman who seemed to be staring back at him. Her dress was so strange to him until he realized that the shadows had camouflaged the black and white nun's outfit.

Koniev slowed *Sea Chase,* realizing as he watched for other lights ashore that his own running lights should be on, but he hadn't taken the time to look for them earlier. Where were they? A series of toggle switches to the right of the wheel looked possible and he flipped one of them. The interior lights came on, too bright, so dangerous! Like a spotlight on his face! He turned his binoculars back toward the pier and there she was again—staring directly back at him. He fumbled at the switches, finally snapping off the offending light, before looking back in her direction. But she was gone. Was there something about him that had frightened her? *Could she have known . . . ?*

He finally located the proper switches by trial and error after lowering his speed in the unfamiliar waters. He was almost to safety and it would be ludicrous to sink himself now. But he continued to worry about how long his lights should have been on. Nothing had happened but the chance remained that someone else might inadvertently notice his error—and remember that he had passed in the night. It could even be the immense ferry boat that now appeared like a floating palace as it pulled away from a dock to his right.

The curious nun was forgotten as he speculated on the female voice on the radio. *What does she look like? She must be older to feel free to treat me so abruptly . . . but then you do prefer slightly older women.* Her body—could it be as lush as he was now imagining?

He had already forgotten the nun with the binoculars.

Sister Mary Catherine had no idea what awakened her. She sat upright in her chair and might have leapt to her feet if she hadn't felt the binoculars begin to slip from her lap. It could have been a sudden sound of some kind, or maybe it was just that the air was cooling so quickly. She did feel a chill. Her sweater had dropped beside the chair and she slipped it over her shoulders.

Then she noticed the sleek, private fishing boat passing offshore. It must have had a powerful engine for the deep growl of the exhaust was unlike most of the boats in the area. She'd never seen it before and that made her even more curious. After all, she was so sure she now knew every boat in these waters. For that matter, just about everyone with a boat gave her a toot on their horn or a wave as they went by. Even when they didn't see her, most of the locals now acknowledged the sisters who operated the little general store and handled the ferry landing whenever a passenger asked to get off there. Eventually, she was sure, the friendliness of the locals would rub off on the other sisters and they would be just as outgoing as she was. Somehow, it made their withdrawal from the world a bit easier.

But there'd been no acknowledgment from this one. She studied the odd boat through her binoculars. It was difficult to pick out distinguishing characteristics in the faint light that remained now and . . . and that was it. That's what bothered her most. No one with a brain traveled this narrow channel without running lights.

Sister Mary Catherine was very curious now and she left the arbor and moved out on the end of the pier where the occasional ferries landed. It was so odd that anyone who knew anything about boats would try to make their way up a restricted waterway without lights at this time of night.

She concentrated on the stern, trying to make out the name, and had just about given up when a swell lifted the boat high enough for her to catch it—*Sea Chase,* Sequim Bay—and then it settled back down again. At that moment, the interior lights snapped on in the cabin. She saw a single man by the wheel looking directly back toward the pier. His binoculars seemed fixed on her like a magnet. That was frightening, to think that someone in a strange boat like that might be looking for her, and she stepped back in the shadow of a piling.

When she felt brave enough to peer back toward the boat again, the interior lights were out and the running lights were on. That had been too much for Sister Mary Catherine. Now she wouldn't be able to see if he was still looking back at her—but he might see her!

She tiptoed down the pier very quietly, as if her silence would make her invisible, and disappeared down the narrow road beyond the general store.

Corinne could compare her nervousness only to her very early days in Vancouver. And those hadn't lasted, not when she realized there was no reason to worry about the reaction the men might have to her. After the first few times, she realized that she was in control, not the men. They were the nervous ones.

Yet now she was apprehensive. After the last radio contact, she'd turned up the gas on the water heater and taken a quick shower. If there'd been time to dry her hair, she would have washed it, too. Luckily, it was shoulder length and straight and she was able to brush it well and tie it back with a pretty scarf. She'd even opened a perfume bottle and had it tipped against her index finger when she realized the absurdity of the whole effort. She wasn't entertaining a customer in an exquisite Vancouver club. This was a Russian submariner, a desperate man who'd apparently escaped certain death and was on the run. He would be dirty, hungry and tired and have no interest in a woman. She was certain she'd already noted that in his voice. He wouldn't care if she were a trained monkey.

But when she closed her eyes and imagined what he might look like, he was beautiful, just like that captain in the movies.

Fifteen

APPROXIMATELY TEN KILOMETERS . . .

In that distance, the horizon had dissolved completely into blackness leaving the stars to twinkle in a distant, cold, moonless sky. What breeze there was before Koniev turned onto the last leg had drifted into stillness. It was deathly quiet in the channel except for the ferry disappearing astern and the low rumble of *Sea Chase's* exhaust.

Ten kilometers and there should be a lantern to my left . . .

The shoreline was black. Once he had seen a light well back in the trees but that had been discounted. The woman had been correct so far and there was no reason to assume otherwise now. Nothing, he was sure, absolutely nothing could have happened to the woman in that amount of time. There wasn't a soul to interfere with her as far as he could be certain. The shoreline of her island seemed deserted.

There it is—a light!

"I see a light," he barked into the mike.

"Stop right there. The channel is very narrow. Give me thirty seconds after this transmission, then turn your lights off. In ten seconds, turn them on again. I will wave the lamp to confirm."

"Then what?" He interrupted before she could continue.

"Then wait," she snapped angrily. "I said the channel is narrow. It's very dangerous. If I am able to identify you, then I will give instructions. I'm leaving the radio now."

His first reaction was an indictment of—*any bitch who would talk to me that way!* Then he nodded with satisfaction. She was thinking. There was no one visible on the water, but as remote a possibility as it seemed . . . there might just be someone who could stumble on them by mistake. She was indeed an interesting woman. Koniev wished at that moment that he had a chance to shower and shave and put on a fresh change of clothes. He knew from years of experience how important that first impression was, no matter what the situation.

Thirty seconds. He snapped off his running lights.

Ten seconds. He turned them on.

The lantern ashore appeared to be lifted down from its position. It was swung back and forth, then replaced.

Less than half a minute later—"I am looking forward to meeting you."

Koniev smiled broadly. *Damn.* "I am anxious also. Will you now tell me how to get there?"

She enjoyed the oddness of his phrases as much as the accent. He was intriguing. "Do you have a tender?"

"I don't understand."

"A pram. A skiff. A rubber boat. Something small that you can get ashore with. There's no pier here. The bottom is rocky. You'd damage your boat. You need something you can paddle in."

"I can't use this boat anymore. They'll be looking for it. I'm going to sink it. I have a rubber raft though."

"What do you want me to do for you?"

"Just leave the lantern where it is. I'll be there."

"There are rocks coming into this cove. They could tip you over."

"Do you have a flashlight?"

"Yes."

"Go down by the water. When I'm on my way in, I'll flash mine. You can guide me in."

"There's no one around here at all. It's completely deserted. We can talk to each other when you're close enough. That'll make it much easier for you, too."

"Fine." Koniev switched off the radio. They'd talked too long as it was. Too much opportunity for someone to overhear them.

The rubber raft was tied on the roof over the pilot house. He undid the lines and lifted it down to the stern, placing one paddle loose inside and tying a backup securely to a line attached to the raft. He also tossed in a small duffel he'd packed with a clean change of clothes found in the cabin.

Then he studied the chart carefully before easing *Sea Chase* ahead. It was so slow that he had bare steerageway, but that was fine for his purposes. He wasn't sure how far away the rocks were. It seemed much longer than he'd anticipated before he felt the boat grind to a stop. He immediately put her in neutral and peered quickly over each side with his flashlight.

Perfect. Absolutely perfect. The rocks on both sides jutted sharply upward, perfect for his purposes. He looked back over the stern to make sure of the angle of the green flashing buoy to his line of sight. Then he eased *Sea Chase* into reverse and backed far enough off the rocks until he was certain he would have enough speed.

Lying flat on the deck would have been preferable from a safety aspect but he decided against that. Instead, he perched on the seat in front of the wheel and braced his feet against the dashboard. That would be sufficient.

Then, glancing over his shoulder at the flashing buoy one last time, Koniev jammed the throttle forward to the speed he would need. He gripped the wheel tightly in both hands for additional support. She surged forward with a growl from the powerful engine. The stern dug deeply into the water. The bow lifted in a perfect presentation of *Sea Chase*'s bottom.

She wasn't at full speed when she piled into the rocks because that might have driven her too far forward. It was just about as he'd anticipated. When she hit, he could hear and feel the bottom being torn out. His hands and feet absorbed the impact adequately, but it was still a tremendous jolt.

He yanked back on the throttle and threw her into reverse to counter *Sea Chase*'s forward motion. She hung there momentarily, the engine roaring as the propellors reversed and dug deeply. Then she began to cant to one side. He was afraid for just a second that her speed might have been too much and she would be marooned there. Then, thankfully, he could feel her sliding backward, very slowly at first, until she finally began to right herself.

The grinding sound continued until she was free of the rocks. While she was backing down, he could hear the water rushing in, and his body sensed the bow falling off until she was definitely canted forward. He continued in reverse until he was sure he was in deep enough water to cut the engine.

All was suddenly silent, except for the gulping sound of water pouring into the hull. He stepped down into the cabin and undid the traps on the deck to allow the water to flow into the cabin. Then, using a hatchet he'd found in a tool box, he chopped holes wherever he anticipated air pockets until he was sure she would sink.

The bow was already beneath the surface when he put the rubber raft over the side and climbed in. He paddled just far enough away from *Sea Chase* to avoid any damage to his raft. He had to be sure.

It seemed so noisy, the gurgling, the bubbles, the pop of air pockets, the sound of equipment sliding forward. He thanked his good fortune that the area was deserted for certainly someone would have heard and understood the cry of a dying vessel. As the weight of the water overcame *Sea Chase*'s natural buoyancy, she began to slide under even faster. Even when the stern finally disappeared, bubbles still roiled to the surface with loud gushing sounds as the last pockets of air were forced out.

Koniev spun the raft around expertly and began to paddle. He'd lost sight of the lantern but the flashing green buoy was a perfect marker until the glare of light came through the trees. When he was perpendicular to the lantern, he turned and paddled directly toward it until he was about fifty meters offshore.

He lay the paddle carefully in the bottom of the boat and pulled the flashlight from his pocket. *Well, my friend, you have put in a very long day but you are alive and in good health and an angel of mercy is waiting ashore. If you are indeed fortunate, she will provide you with everything you need and maybe even everything you desire. And if she doesn't, maybe you will take it anyway.*

He snapped on the light and pointed it toward the lantern.

Corinne was settled on a log to one side of the lantern. She aimed her flashlight to one side to avoid blinding him. It was obvious that he was probably balancing his light on his lap since the beam seemed to sway rhythmically with what she assumed were his paddle strokes.

She'd been frightened by the grinding crash of his vessel on the rocks. He'd said he was going to sink it but it never occurred to her that he'd ram it into the rocks. It had been a loud, grinding sound and Corinne imagined that he might have been hurt. She could picture him lying unconscious on the deck as the boat sank. But if he'd planned the entire thing, she decided he couldn't possibly hurt himself there after all he'd been through.

Now, honey, you are inextricably involved with a very strange, very powerful man. He's no more than fifty feet from you. There's no backing out now.

She was pleased at how remarkably calm she felt as the raft drew closer. Then it seemed as if her heart skipped a beat, or had she been holding her breath? Something deep within her had just sent a message and as much as she was surprised she also understood immediately what it was. This was almost a physical sensation of release after the anticipation that had grown the past twenty-four hours. From the moment her handlers had extricated themselves from what surely must have been a broken operation plan, she had been concentrating on the fate of this man with her whole being.

Now he was here.

"There should be a rock jutting out of the water to your left," she called, focusing her beam in that direction.

Both of their lights found it at the same time, even closer than she had expected. He was near enough now for her to hear the splash of the paddle and she could see him change his direction.

"Are there any others?" he called out.

"No. You're clear now."

His voice was so much different. It was hard to determine a personality over the radio. Of course, you could pick up intonation, anger, impatience, that sort of thing. But now that he had spoken directly, his voice was so much stronger . . . almost as she'd expected nothing other than that from such a man.

She rose from the log and took the few steps to the landing spot she had selected. There were no rocks and the raft could come right up into the mud. "Come right toward me. It's soft here. And you won't get your feet wet."

"Now I have the chance to thank you in person. I have been looking forward to that opportunity."

His voice was masculine and well-modulated. How could anyone sound so calm after the experiences he'd been through?

"Then we both have," Corinne responded firmly. "I'm pleased that I was selected to help you." Somehow that sounded neither decisive nor romantic, certainly a neutral approach at this point.

As the raft ground into the mud, they illuminated each other's faces with their flashlights at the same time. *Why, he's as curious as I am,* Corinne thought, blinking at the sudden brightness.

Realizing what they had both done, they lowered their lights, each half-blinded.

"I'm sorry . . ." she offered. ". . . I was just . . ."

"I was also," he interrupted politely. He rose to his feet. "Oh," he groaned, "my knees are cramped from this tiny boat. Give me your hand."

"Of course . . . I didn't think . . ." She reached out. His

grip was firm but he did not use her strength to help himself onto the beach. Nor did he let go of her hand immediately.

"My name is Nicholas Koniev and I thank you again." He gave her hand a squeeze before he let go.

Corinne smiled to herself. *I suppose some men would do that to a woman just to see if there was a reaction no matter what they'd been through.* "And my name is Corinne . . . Corinne Foxe," she responded evenly. "Come on, follow me." She pointed her flashlight down. "After you step up onto the dry ground, there's a path. The cabin's close. I have food waiting for you."

"Would you have a shower? And I have to change clothes."

She laughed pleasantly. "I don't believe this meeting between us was in the plans, at least not your coming here. I can turn up the gas on the water heater for you." They came into the glow of light from the cabin and she looked closely at him for the first time before laughing lightly. "But I'm sure none of my clothes would come close to fitting you. I'm sorry," she added hastily, "I'm not laughing at you."

He was returning her stare with a slight smile on his face. "No, I don't think they would fit, and I'm very happy about that." He indicated the small duffel. "I have a change of clothes here, some I borrowed. The style isn't to my taste, but they are clean."

It was dark out when Bernie Ryng decided to tie up alongside a pier at Friday Harbor on San Juan Island. He wanted to keep going. But his body also told him he had to sleep for a few hours or he would lose that fine edge he'd always depended on. It was senseless to search unknown waters on a night with no moon . . . foolish . . . no matter how badly he wanted his man. At that very moment, it would have been easier to locate that needle in a haystack. And he knew Koniev would have to stop, too. But, where? He looked at his watch and remembered Admiral Coffin was waiting to hear from him.

"All I need is a couple hours' nap and I'll be fresh as a new baby," Ryng said over the phone. "There's no point in tiptoeing around in the dark when I don't have the vaguest idea where the hell I should be looking."

Coffin had established a command center at his Bangor headquarters that was serving as Ryng's eyes and ears. The boat he was after was definitely *Sea Chase,* formerly owned by the late Mr. Lawler who had fortunately bobbed to the surface with the compliments of a hungry shark so he could be identified. The data compiled through every US agency with anything on Nicholas Koniev had been combined to construct an intimate picture of the man. His educational records as a youth and in the Soviet Navy were superb, generally in the top one or two percent in the country. He appeared to have had his selection of naval assignments. His ability to write research papers of strategic value may have been the major reason he had become a mystery man. Most available data on Koniev's life existed before that unique talent was revealed.

Apparently, he'd volunteered for Spetznaz training even though it could have been avoided. That was where early indications of a latent brutality began to surface. While that wasn't unusual in Spetznaz training, it wasn't expected of more senior officers. There were also reports of injuries and death in what little could be learned of his miniature submarine program—but again, Spetznaz volunteers were involved in that.

What attracted the most attention among the military psychologists participating in developing Koniev's profile were the incidents in his private life. While much of his background had also been suppressed, it was more difficult to hide those items that ended up on police or hospital reports.

The psychologists described it as aberrant behavior. It seemed that Koniev, at times, was unable to fully control himself with women. He was married. He did have children. He also had a problem. In every duty station, there were reports of either beatings of women he was with or injury to men also involved with them. Officers who had served with him explained that almost every female he came in contact with seemed to offer him a challenge. It wasn't necessary that they be beautiful—just that they were there. His attention included other men's wives and lovers. He was apparently able to get away with his actions because of his brilliance and the knowledge that he had killed or injured others from the time he undertook Spetznaz training.

His profile delineated the ideal Spetznaz leader.

"I've tangled with others like him," Ryng explained. "Believe me, Admiral, that's one more reason why this has to be done one on one. Whatever he's got, I think he's convinced it's worth as many lives as necessary to escape with it. If just for an instant he feels that there are others close to him, he'll go underground so fast I'd never find him. What I need is to learn what the jungle tom-tom is around here. There must be people in these islands who know everything that happens, people who see every boat that goes by."

"We'll dig, Bernie. What time are you planning to get underway?"

"Before first light. I've got a full tank and the harbormaster here said he'd leave a door unlocked so I can use his shower. So I'll be off about four-thirty. Believe me, Admiral, the sky's getting a little gray by then."

"I'll get back to you before you leave, Bernie."

Though she tried, Corinne found herself unable to hold back a smile when Koniev reappeared in the kitchen. Whoever the change of clothes belonged to had been much heavier, and obviously much older.

His eyes left hers, looked down at himself, then back again and he nodded with understanding.

"I think I could select something more your style if we shopped together." Then she felt her cheeks redden slightly. How could she say that to someone she hardly knew?

"I hope we'll have that opportunity. I'd enjoy doing the same for you." He looked pointedly at her slacks. "I think I would like to see you in a dress." He leaned against a cabinet next to her while she worked at the gas stove. "I already like the perfume you're wearing."

As soon as Koniev had gone into the bathroom to enjoy a quick shower, Corinne had slipped into her bedroom and dabbed perfume behind each ear. As soon as she'd done it, she stared at herself in the mirror and was sure she heard herself whisper—*now why did you just do that?*—but it was only that inner voice again. It was something she'd made a decision against earlier that evening and now she'd changed her mind. *But why?* The answer was something she was having trouble admitting to herself.

After she'd come back in the kitchen, she almost wished she hadn't. Now he'd complimented her and she was pleased, but all she could say was, "Thank you."

"You had a razor in there. I used it."

She looked up at him. "You don't look quite so desperate now."

"But no cologne. At home, I have a number of different aromas. I enjoy them," he said. "Do you enjoy male scents?"

Corinne smiled but said nothing. *If anybody has ever been preparing to make a pass at you, it's this one, honey. So far, he hasn't said a word about what happened to him, but he's probably lost his submarine, his only ticket out of here, and he's desperate. Yet here he is making like you're the last woman in the world. You're up against an odd one. Stay on your toes, lady.*

"What are you cooking?"

"Abalone."

"I am ignorant. What is abalone?"

She looked at him with raised eyebrows and cocked her head to one side. "I apologize. I forgot. You're Russian, aren't you? There's no reason you should know what it is."

He tilted his head to one side to imitate her. "My first trip," he said with a grin.

"An abalone is a large shellfish, like an oyster only much bigger . . . much bigger," she said, gesturing with her hands. "The fishermen open them up and cut out the muscle that holds the shell tight. It's very tough and chewy so they pound it until it's soft. They taste wonderful."

"And you did all this yourself?"

"No. They were given to me by a local fisherman today. He even flattened them out before he gave them to me."

Koniev's relaxed expression altered radically. His hand shot out and gripped her arm tightly. "You mean someone else comes here?" The easy smile on his face had narrowed to a straight line drawn tightly over his teeth.

Watch yourself, Corinne. "He's a young fisherman who found me. I didn't find him. He thinks I'm a biologist doing research on birds. He's just being nice because he's lonely. And he only shows up in the middle of the day." She looked down at his hand. "If you please," she said firmly.

He let go of her arm. "I'm sorry. I guess it's just that I'm very tired. How often has he come?"

"Twice. Just the last two days."

"Do you expect him again tomorrow?"

"He said he was coming back."

"What is his boat like?"

"A fishing boat. Very nondescript. It's a good size though. Why?"

"Just a thought. We need a boat to get out of here."

She noted the word—*we*—but said nothing, pleased in a way that he would consider her in his plans. It was also disconcerting. Traveling with this man hadn't been part of what she was sent here for.

Corinne looked at him again quickly, then back at her cooking, trying to remember how she had envisioned him. Yes, he was about as tall, and he did have dark hair. But she thought she'd imagined a mustache and he was clean-shaven. He was also a bit older, graying at the temples. The high cheekbones and green eyes presented a striking appearance—but not handsome as she'd dreamed. What was the difference? Handsome or striking? She'd known both. Each one had its own special appeal.

But what the hell is so fascinating here? You're acting just like you're in heat, lady.

"One of the amenities I insisted on before I agreed to come out here was wine," she said, slipping the abalone onto the plates. "I've learned to enjoy it with dinner. Would you care to . . ."

He took the plates from her. "Let me take these. You pour the wine. You know, you make me feel very special when I should just be thankful that I'm alive. You are my angel of mercy, my benefactor, my . . ." He set the plates on the table and turned around as she placed the jug of wine between them. He put his hand on hers. "You're very special. I hope you understand that."

Give him more time, lady. Overlook it.

It was necessary to keep reminding herself that she'd experienced men like this before. *You know how to handle them.* Her instinct was to lift his hand. Yet her own reaction, doing nothing, was comfortable . . . strangely enough. She looked down at him sitting quietly and staring up at her with a serious smile on his face. "I think that's very nice of you. But you'll never get any wine this way, and you must be very hungry."

He removed his hand. "Please pour. But there must be a toast, Corinne, and that will be mine." When she was seated, he lifted his glass. "To my lovely angel of mercy, the woman who saved my life . . ."

"No, I didn't do that."

"Yes, you did. To the woman who saved my life. If you hadn't been here, waiting to hear from me, I don't know what would have happened. And if you remain as lucky for me, we will soon be able to escape."

We . . .

They touched glasses.

But I don't have to escape from anything, Corinne told herself as she raised the glass to her lips. Koniev's eyes, almost hypnotic in their intensity, had never left hers. *Do I?*

Sister Mary Catherine moaned in her sleep and her body writhed in an effort to escape. The man on the boat, the one gazing back at her with his binoculars, was reaching for her and she couldn't escape. They were out on the pier beside the channel. It was still almost dark, just the barest twilight. He was still in the shadows . . . faceless . . . but this time he had been so close she didn't see him until it was too late. Now he had her in his grasp . . .

"Sister . . . please wake up."

The nun opened her eyes to a face, no longer in shadow, just above her own. She sucked in her breath to scream.

"Sister, please," Sister Mary Margaret repeated in a soft, soothing voice. "Don't be frightened, please. You're having a bad dream."

She sat up in bed and looked about the room. It was her bedroom, no different than it had been when she went to bed. There was her simple, wooden dresser with the pictures of her family, the straight-backed wooden chair where her bathrobe lay, the carved wooden cross on the wall that her mother had given her. She wasn't out on the pier. She was safe.

"I was so afraid," she said to Mary Margaret. "It was a bad dream. Did I wake you?"

"No, not at all. I was sleeping, too, and then I heard the phone in the commons ringing." The commons was the central room in their converted barn where they ate their meals, talked, read, and said their evening prayers. The phone, similar to a car phone, had been given to them by their order for safety purposes.

"Who would be calling at this hour?"

"It's the sheriff's office on the mainland . . . Anacortes. Apparently there's someone who may be around the islands that they're after. They know we—you, I guess—know almost every boat. It reminded me of the one you mentioned you'd seen without lights last night. They asked if they could talk with you."

"You mean they think . . ."

"They're waiting to talk to you," Sister Mary Margaret answered.

Sister Mary Catherine hurriedly put on her bathrobe and went out to the commons where she explained to the sheriff what she had seen that evening—the boat without lights when it was growing so dark, seeing the name *Sea Chase* through her binoculars at the same time she saw this man looking back at her. She was sure he was looking for something on the island, or someone. When she inquired about whom they were looking for, she was told that even they weren't sure. It was just some assistance they were providing the navy.

Sister Mary Catherine went back to bed, but she didn't sleep again that night.

Nicholas Koniev thrived on exhaustion the way some people savored sleep. For reasons unknown to him, his mind grew more alert. Fatigue became a rush, similar to an athlete's second wind when he overcomes the sensation that he is about to collapse and dredges up newfound energy.

Perhaps this latent vigor resulted from the need to answer all his questions before he slept, for he knew he would have to be on the move the following day. They would be after him. No doubt about that. Another individual like him— almost as good—would be sniffing for his trail. Of course, there should have been little enough trail. Letting that old man live may have been his greatest mistake. Koniev still could not come to terms with himself for allowing that. Otherwise, he'd moved fast enough. Both the vehicles and the bodies had been properly taken care of. Of course, if they were looking for him, they would find that trail but he'd bought himself enough time. Instead, what he feared most was someone like himself, someone with similar instincts.

As he'd navigated through the islands that day, he'd concluded that the most logical means of escape was to get into one of the larger Canadian cities, Vancouver most likely, where he could contact the Soviet consulate. All that was necessary was a phone call. There were certain code words that automatically warned any consulate that a critical individual or situation had just dropped in their lap, and then the wheels would start turning. Once one of the three in Moscow was aware that he was safe, everything would fall into place.

Now here he was, on an out-of-the-way island in America aware that he was the object of a manhunt. Most men would have been paralyzed with fear in this situation. But instead, he was sipping wine over a most pleasant dinner, and quietly acknowledging his good fortune to have found this charming woman who was certainly the answer to his dreams. She possessed a maturity he was sure he would appreciate even more in the coming days.

As they talked over dinner—he asking questions about her background since coming to Vancouver to understand how much she knew about his mission, she asking questions to learn as much as she could about him—he made a silent promise to himself that he would not take physical advantage of this woman, not tonight, not even tomorrow or the next day, if she refused, for she was the key to his survival at this stage. But he could not imagine her refusing for that long. They complemented each other so perfectly.

"When I came up the channel from the eastern tip of the island, I saw a woman out on a pier looking at me through binoculars. Are there many people on this island?"

"Not this time of year, certainly not around this part of the island. How far away from here?" Corinne asked.

"Four or five kilometers. It looked like a landing of some kind. I could see the pilings, big ones out in the water, and it looked like something could be lowered to a boat coming in."

"That's the ferry landing. I was told it wasn't used that much this time of year. It's run by the nuns . . ."

"That's why she looked strange to me . . . the black robes . . . white collar. It was dark there and I could just barely make her out. But she was looking at me through binoculars. Are there many of them . . . the nuns, I mean?"

"I don't know." Corinne couldn't imagine why he was concerned about a few nuns.

"Do they have a phone, or some way to communicate with shore?"

"Honestly, I really don't know anything about them. I was told only that they existed out here and I think they're very secluded. Are you worried about a single nun?" she asked incredulously.

Koniev smiled. "There is a great deal about me you would like to know. I can tell by your questions that you're very curious, but you're also hesitant because you're afraid you'll upset me. Don't be. I am so grateful that I don't think there's anything you can ask that will make me mad." He shrugged.

"If I don't want to tell you something, I won't. But I won't get mad either. And to answer your question—yes, I worry about a single nun. I worry about everybody because if I leave a trail, there will be someone following it very closely. Does that satisfy you?"

Corinne had been leaning forward as he spoke and it was almost an unconscious reaction when her hand covered his for a moment. Then, realizing what she was doing, she reached awkwardly for her wineglass. *What is it with hands, lady? Second childhood?* "Am I prying? I don't mean to."

"I don't know prying. Does that have something to do with my hand?" he asked with a mischievous grin.

"No, it means am I being too curious? And now I'm embarrassed." *How in the world could your hands do something like that, completely on their own?*

"Embarrassed I understand. Please don't be, Corinne." It was the second time he'd used her name with familiarity. "I'm so thankful that you're here that I don't know how to thank you." He patted her hand, then squeezed it, perfectly at ease with himself. "This is all I can do now, I guess, but I want to make sure you receive a strong message about how grateful I am."

You're in deeper than you've ever been before, lady. Remember, this was never going to happen to you. You're the woman who's capable of controlling every situation.

Koniev offered to help clean up after dinner. It wasn't something he ever would have done at home for his wife, Galya, nor would he have been willing to do so in most situations. As he hoped, she refused on the basis that he was exhausted and needed rest.

"Yes, I would like to sleep. But first I must explain what I intend to do. I'll need your help." His eyes seemed to implore her. "I don't think I can survive without it. Will you come with me?"

She'd known it was coming. There had never been anything like this mentioned when her handlers arranged this for her. They told her so little and, of course, they showed their inventiveness by backing out when Koniev needed them most. Did she have anything to lose? "What do you expect me to do for you?"

"My English is poor. I need you to help me there."

"Your English is excellent."

"There are words, as you have already noted, that I do not find. Also, my accent stands out heavily."

"It stands out among Americans. You'd be surprised how many people speak with various accents in Vancouver."

"All the same, they are looking for someone with an accent. I cannot allow that to create suspicions. I also don't know this area well. I need you to tell me whether we could get from one place to another safely."

Corinne dried her hands with a towel and hung it over the edge of the sink. Yes, she wanted to go with him. It would be the most exciting thing that would ever happen in her life. It would also be the most dangerous. "I know next to nothing about navigating a boat around here."

"You knew enough to tell me how to get here." That same knowing grin that so disconcerted her reappeared. "You are my angel of mercy."

"See—you're embarrassing me again." She sat on the other end of the couch. "Where do you think you must go?"

"Vancouver. We have a consulate there. But it's a long trip from here according to the chart and if I were the hunter I would anticipate that. We should get into Canada another place."

"Does it matter where?"

"That is exactly why I want you with me. I don't want to spend unnecessary time anywhere. If I knew where I was, it would be a circular route . . ." he shrugged, ". . . but not through the United States."

"Maybe Victoria. Then we could go north up the island all the way to Nanaimo. No one would expect us to do that. You could call your consulate from there. Then we could cross from there to Vancouver by boat." *We . . . us . . . why am I using those words? He knows he's got me.*

"Then you'll go with me."

"I didn't say that," she answered defensively.

That grin again. "Your eyes say so."

She turned away. *And I suppose he thinks that grin will make me take my clothes off, too?* "I . . . I'd like to help you . . ."

"Now that my angel of mercy has agreed to save my life, I am going to be able to sleep soundly." He rose to his feet. "Does this couch fold out?"

"I don't know. I never checked." She stood up and lifted one of the pillows. "Why, yes, it does."

"Then I will help you make it up. But I will sleep here tonight. It would make me feel most badly to take your bed."

"But . . ." She'd never offered her own bed, never broached the subject.

"No. That I insist on. I need you well-rested if you are to continue to save my life."

There was no arguing with him. At least she wasn't being forced into making a decision whether she would sleep with him. *You want to, lady. You want to desperately. But if you do, he will have total control of . . . no, not will . . . he does. Look in the mirror if you don't believe it.*

Sixteen

BERNIE RYNG AWAKENED EASILY, BUT BEFORE HE BOTHERED TO open his eyes his nose provided an accurate report of weather conditions. There had been a temperature inversion during the night. The result was a damp fog. It magnified the stink of old bait scraps on the crabbers, the pungent creosote aroma on pilings, and the diesel-soaked decking in old fishing boats parked four deep at the piers. The sun would be forced to take an extra hour bringing the day to Friday Harbor. Everything would move that much slower when he needed the advantage of speed more than ever.

Thankfully the shower in the harbormaster's shack was steaming hot, a perfect place to sort everything out. He was about to contact Admiral Coffin when he found a note urging him to enjoy the fresh donuts and coffee that had been left in the office. The harbormaster in Friday Harbor understood the care and feeding of SEALs—leave them on their own. By four-fifteen, Ryng was wide awake and anxious to get on with it.

"This *Sea Chase* you're looking for," Coffin told him, "goes about twenty-six feet and has one hell of a power plant for a fisherman. She can cruise comfortably at eighteen

263

knots, and I'm told she'll do over twenty in flat seas. There's a flying bridge with full controls on top that ought to give her away if that blue stripe I told you about earlier isn't obvious. But the best part, Bernie, is that she was sighted last night."

Coffin explained Sister Mary Catherine's response to Anacortes' call a few hours before. There was no doubt about the ID because this nun was an expert on everything that floated around the San Juans. She'd seen the name across the stern when the boat rose on a swell and it wasn't familiar. But the woman was frightened. The man on the boat had been watching her with binoculars. As soon as the fog lifted enough, the Coast Guard had reassured the nun that they'd run over to talk with her.

Ryng studied the chart on the wall. "If the Coast Guard is approaching from the east, I'll turn north after I get out of Friday Harbor and come up on the west side of the island."

"Are you figuring that's where he might be now?"

"I don't know, Admiral. I'm still sure we're not dealing with anyone who's going to do what you expect. How about somebody helping him? Some of my most brilliant thinking goes on in the shower and that's when I decided he just might have a contact somewhere around here. Why would he be headed north from Sequim Bay and then turn down that narrow channel toward the west, especially when it's almost dark and you wouldn't expect anyone to see you? My guess is that he's probably trying to get to Vancouver. That's the location of the Russian consulate. So we want to put the Coast Guard between the San Juans and there. I'll tell you what." He'd changed his mind. "Tell the Coast Guard to make a pass through that channel north of the island if they want but I think they'd do better heading north of Orcas Island right away. I'm going to stop and talk to that nun myself."

"The weather the same up there as down here?"

"Yeah. If it doesn't lift, it's going to give our man an even better advantage and he's already got a running start on us."

"According to Whidby Island meteorology, it won't last once the sun gets high enough to burn it off. As soon as they can see, they'll put some helicopters out. Bernie, I can't imagine anything can get through the type of sweep we've got set up."

"Never say that, Admiral. *I* could. If I could, so can he."

The sun and the wind combined to chase off enough of the fog so that Ryng was at the western tip of the island by seven in the morning. He turned into the channel on its north side and cut back his speed to bare steerageway while he studied the shoreline with his binoculars. There was an occasional cottage in sight near the water, but he assumed most people probably built their cabins back far enough to keep their privacy. No sooner did he put down his binoculars then the huge ferry *Nisqually* came into sight; what better reason to build your place behind the trees than a vessel that size passing fifty yards offshore?

Ryng experienced a sense of futility. Unless he came upon a blue striped boat with a flying bridge and *Sea Chase* on the stern, which he doubted, he put his chances of seeing anything of value at close to zero.

It was barely light yet she felt wide awake. Corinne peered at her watch, then surged upright in bed shocked at the time. How could she have slept so late?

When she slipped between the sheets eight hours before, she was uncertain how she wanted the night to turn out. This was a matter of choice, not a matter of business. Even though a deep, unexpected yearning struggled to surface, she refused to go out to the other room and crawl into bed with Nicholas Koniev. She knew he was in control of his destiny, and probably hers also, but she wasn't about to acknowledge that to him.

The last thought she remembered before falling asleep was the alternative. What if he came into her room? *Submit?*—which admittedly fascinated her. In the past, it had always been the men who'd submitted to her. What would it be like to physically yield to a man like Nicholas Koniev? *Or will you put him off just to show that you can exert some power of your own?*—important for her ego but disastrous physically considering how much she wanted to have him.

But she had slept through the night, she was rested, and she was now sure there was a moral victory of some kind there. On the other hand, he had succeeded, too. Somehow Corinne was sure he understood that.

She slipped on her bathrobe and stepped out into the living room. But he wasn't there! The covers were thrown back and the clothes he'd left neatly on the chair were gone. She caught her breath. Had he left without her?

Corinne went out on the porch. Her eyes followed his path scuffed in the morning dew across toward the shoreline. She saw him outlined against the trees, his arms raised, binoculars to his face.

When she was still a good twenty feet away from him, certain she'd made no sound, Koniev whirled and jumped to one side in a single motion. When he landed in a half-crouch, a gun in his right hand was pointed directly at her middle. Her hands flew to her face.

"Shh . . ." Koniev's index finger was instantly at his lips, recognition flickering in his eyes. The gun was slipped back in his belt. His face softened into a half-smile and he beckoned her toward him.

Corinne knew she would never forget the look in his eyes. He had not been afraid when she surprised him. His expression had been as hard and unforgiving as a cat. It was almost as if he looked forward to the kill, for there appeared to be a moment of disappointment before that smile appeared. His expression wasn't guilty. It wasn't forgiving. It suggested to her that she should forever thank her lucky stars that she would live another day.

Halfway across to where he stood, her entire body began to shake. She knew it was a reaction to the nearness of death. Yet as she drew closer she also knew she wanted to throw herself into his arms—for protection, for forgiveness, for the beauty of life. It had been less than twelve hours since they met and he already exerted a strange control over her. As she approached, his eyes never left hers. His gaze seemed almost hypnotic. His smile broadened and she reached for the hand he extended to her.

"You frightened me," he was first to say. "I could

have . . . I could have hurt you . . . killed you." Now it seemed that his entire being radiated deep regret. His expression could change instantly—hot and cold, wet and dry, black and white. "I don't know what I would have done." Now his head was hanging. "I am not a wonderful person, I guess, but I have never before hurt anyone I cared for."

Lady, he's almost hinting. You may even see tears. But don't fall for that one. Corinne was shocked that one part of her could reject his act while another still urged her to run to his arms. The desire that had been a fantasy when she knew only his voice was in grave danger of becoming uncontrollably physical.

Her instinctive shaking had begun to abate as quickly as it had come. "Why didn't you shoot?"

"I've never shot anyone like that before. Only when I've had no option . . . an enemy . . ." His voice projected his despair at what might have happened.

A superb actor, she knew. *He cares,* her alter ego responded. "I didn't mean to . . ." she faltered, ". . . surprise you. Really. You were looking at something."

He relaxed. "Yes. Come." He gestured for her to follow him to the edge of the trees and handed her the binoculars. "Look at that boat out there. Have you seen it before?"

Her hands were still shaking badly enough that nothing would register. She was about to hand the binoculars back to him when she felt an arm go around her waist. Her body was pulled gently against his. She could feel his breath on her neck.

"I can't think of the words in your language to say how sorry I am for frightening you like this." Then his hand was stroking her neck, his fingertips kneading tight muscles. "There, I can feel you relaxing. Try to look again, right out there," and he pointed toward a fancy private fishing boat that had already passed by about seventy-five yards offshore.

His touch seemed to be all that was necessary. Her shivering disappeared. She breathed deeply and brought the glasses back to her face to see a streamlined white boat barely moving eastward. There was a man braced against the pilot house support searching the coastline with a set of binoculars. *"Voyager,"* she whispered.

"What is that?"

"The name on the stern—*Voyager.*"

"Can he see your cabin from there?"

"No, I'm sure he can't. I couldn't tell there's even a clearing behind the trees when I was looking for it. The fisherman I told you about was amazed to learn there was a cabin here and he knows the island as well as anybody."

"Good. Good." His fingers continued to work the muscles in her neck. "You know, I was shaking almost as much a moment ago when I saw that it was you."

Now, his hand had slipped down and he was rubbing her back gently. "There, now if you feel better," and his voice was so soft and apologetic that she desperately wanted to turn around and be held tightly, "let me take a look again before he gets around that bend."

Corinne turned and held out the glasses.

He leaned forward and kissed her gently on the cheek. "I am so sorry." He placed his fingers under her chin and lifted it slightly. His lips brushed hers. "So sorry." Then he stepped forward and the binoculars were back to his eyes. "When we have breakfast," he said softly as he studied the boat, "I will explain what happened. It never should have. But after the past few days, I am having difficulty controlling my nerves. Why don't you go back inside and get dressed if you like. I must watch until I am sure that boat has gone."

"Do you think . . . ?"

"I think we are very lucky," he interrupted, "and, believe me, I think I am the luckiest man in the world to have you with me. Now go ahead, I'll be in shortly."

Corinne looked at her watch. She had come out of the door no more than three minutes ago. Those three minutes had been both the most terrifying and surprising in her life. What shocked her most was her reaction to Nicholas Koniev. She'd never met a man like him. There were books about such men, but here was one who actually possessed the cunning and genius of storybook characters, and he reacted like a jungle cat.

Fascination—that was the only word that came to her mind. He was casting a spell over her. His eyes, his words, his hands barely touching her . . . fascination! And then there was the rational voice deep inside that insisted— *you're a masochist, lady.*

Bernie Ryng turned his boat toward the ferry slip on the big island to port. The sun had popped above the distant fog bank and illuminated the fresh white hull of *Nisqually* snuggled into the slip. The ferry captains had to know every boat that crossed their paths.

The captain was out on the bridge wing when Ryng cut *Voyager's* engine. He returned Ryng's wave as the smaller boat drifted to a stop four decks below.

"Good morning," Ryng called out. "The fog was pretty heavy this morning."

"Sure was," came the response. "But there's not much that stops us."

"I didn't think so. I was curious to know if you'd seen a fishing boat called *Sea Chase* in your travels. White hull with a blue stripe down the side, good lines, flying bridge. She can go like hell when she wants to, I'm told."

"So you're looking for her, too. Coast Guard mentioned her to me before I got underway this morning."

"You haven't seen her then."

"Nope. But I'll put it on the radio if I do."

"We'd appreciate that, Captain. Maybe you can tell me how I can find the nun who runs some ferry slip across the way."

"My stern's pointed almost toward the landing. Just about a straight shot across. You must be looking for Sister Mary Catherine."

"She's the one."

"Good soul. Takes good care of us. If you don't find her at the general store right beside the slip, one of the others ought to be there. They take shifts. While one's handling things across the way, another will be working their garden. They keep pretty busy."

When Ryng climbed up on the pier from *Voyager,* he was

greeted by a terrified Sister Mary Catherine. The call from the sheriff's office in Anacortes, combined with her dreams, had so upset her that she hadn't slept again. She had become a member of the order to escape the realities of the outside world and now she was convinced that they were going to appear on her island.

There was little she could tell Ryng that Admiral Coffin hadn't already explained. Sister Mary Catherine was comfortable with observing that other world through her binoculars, but she had been so shaken by someone peering back into hers that she could relate little about the man she'd seen. It was twilight, darkness was falling rapidly, and he was in shadows.

Before he returned to *Voyager,* Ryng reassured the frightened woman that she had nothing to fear. Now he would head back to the west. He couldn't imagine Koniev retracing his steps after seeing someone studying him and *Sea Chase.*

Koniev heard the next helicopter coming from the east when it was still miles away. The unmistakable sound of the rotors beating through the damp morning air told him that it was flying low, probably coming up the channel between the islands. Corinne had assured him after he'd heard the first one that morning that no others had come up the channel since she arrived on the island. This one had to be military, just as the other had been.

He rechecked the area outside the cabin to make sure nothing had been left astray for prying eyes, then went inside. "Here comes another one."

"Another what?" she asked.

"Helicopter. They're searching for us . . . or for me actually. We can't stay much longer." He was visibly nervous.

Corinne knew he wanted her to say something. "What do you want to do?"

"Where's that fisherman friend of yours?" he asked irritably.

"It's usually after noontime before he comes around, although he did say he was going to come back with some salmon and wine for lunch."

"How charming," Koniev remarked acidly. "What reason is that?"

Corinne couldn't help being amused that he appeared a bit jealous but nothing in her face or answer revealed that. "I went for a walk yesterday to the western end of the island. He happened upon this little bay where I was swimming and eventually I asked him to share my lunch. It was completely his idea to come back today with his own lunch. I did tell him not to and I also said I was going to be off for the day. But I don't think he'll stay away."

"I'm thankful for that. We need his boat quickly."

"What will you do with him?" Corinne asked anxiously. Although she was looking away from him, he could sense the fear in her voice. "Remember, I can only kill an enemy."

Corinne turned around when she felt a hand on her shoulder.

"I don't want to frighten you again." He pulled her against him and kissed her on the forehead like a child. "I promise I will leave your friend very much alive. But," he added as he pulled back to look at her, "you will understand if I have to tie him up, won't you? We can't have him running off to tell everyone about us."

Corinne had remained purposefully subservient up to now because she was unsure of her feelings. But she wasn't one to encourage a sisterly relationship, nor would she hide her emotions for long. She pulled him close, resting her head on his shoulder. "Of course I understand. I agree with you completely. It was just that he's been so nice to me and he's so damn innocent anyway. All I want to really be sure of is that Nicholas Koniev is able to get home. What do you think of that?" She looked up at him expectantly with a wide smile, pleased because she was finally able to express herself.

He understood how she anticipated being kissed then. It would be a perfect response on his part, a perfect calculation on hers. He knew he could make love to her at that moment. She'd also made it clear that she understood both of them. But it still wasn't the right time. What she failed to understand was that when that time came, she would be completely under his control. It would take time for her to comprehend that but he was absolutely sure it would happen. It always had in the past.

"This is absolutely the first time I have ever wanted to take anyone home with me." He kissed her lightly on the lips and stepped back, holding her hands. "And what do you think of that?"

"You mean you don't have a wife?"

"Never, because I never before met anyone like you."

Corinne was about to pull him close, to express herself with a meaningful kiss when she noticed him cock his head to one side. She listened but the only sound she could hear was the helicopter disappearing to the west. "What is it?"

"A boat."

"Perhaps it's . . . *Voyager*—the one we saw earlier."

"No, this is a different engine."

His change in expression astonished her. One moment he was gentle and understanding, almost mesmerizing. Now his teeth were clenched tight, his lips slightly parted. With his head still cocked slightly to one side, he was barely breathing.

"Hear that?" he whispered.

She nodded.

"It's not in any hurry," Koniev said. "Come on." He went out the door with the binoculars in hand.

Together they stood at the edge of the trees while he focused the glasses on the boat. "Fishing boat. One man. Just like that last one. I don't like it. Here. Take a look."

Corinne steadied the binoculars and *Dream Girl* swam into focus with Jimmy Cook at the wheel. "That's him— Jimmy, the one I told you about."

Koniev's jaw relaxed and he drew a deep breath. "I couldn't have asked for more. Quick, let's go back inside. We can't let him see me."

"What do you want me to . . ." Corinne began.

"Nothing. We'll wait. Let your friend come to us."

The wait seemed interminable as the sound of *Dream Girl*'s engine came closer. Then it increased slightly as she backed down.

"He's stopped just offshore," he said.

Dream Girl's whistle tooted twice.

Then Jimmy Cook's voice boomed out, "Yo, ashore. Your caterer has arrived."

"Caterer?" Koniev's forehead wrinkled. "What does he mean?"

"Don't be concerned. He means he's brought the food he promised. He's just being sweet."

"Corinne McCarthy," Jimmy bellowed after two more toots, "am I too late to deliver my bread and wine?"

"What should I say? How do you want . . . ?"

"Go out there. Talk with him. Whatever you do, make sure he comes ashore. Get him in this house and I'll take over."

"You promised," she said softly. She studied his face for any reaction at all.

Koniev's face remained expressionless. "He won't be injured as long as he cooperates."

"Corinne . . . are you still in residence?" Jimmy shouted.

"Yes, right here," she answered as she went out the door. "I didn't hear you at first." She stepped through the trees and out onto the rock-strewn beach. "So the caterer has arrived."

Jimmy held up a jug of wine. "Your wine steward, too. I was hoping I'd catch you before you went off like you said. I really wanted to see you today. Would you like to come aboard and I can take you wherever you want to go?"

"I changed my mind, Jimmy. I decided to stay home today and work on my notes. Why don't you come ashore and we'll have our lunch right in front of my cabin out in the sun?"

Jimmy looked at his watch. "I'd like that, but it is a bit early for me. It's not even ten in the morning. I'll tell you what—why don't I go out and check some crab pots I'm running near here, and then I'll come back around noon."

That could be too late! "Well, at least bring the wine in to chill in my refrigerator . . . and you do have that salmon you mentioned, don't you? That should be cooled, too."

"I love your ideas. But Jimmy Cook is no dummy, ma'am. Got it all here on ice. So I think I'll just be on my way for awhile and then . . ."

You've run out of options, lady. Now you turn into the bitch you've probably always been. "Mr. Cook, I hardly slept a wink last night thinking about you. And the reason I decided to stay here for the day instead of going out in the field is that you insisted on coming back today." She could see that she had his attention. "Most gentlemen cooperate when a lady throws herself at them, and you better believe I've thought a lot about this since I last saw you yesterday. Do I have to strip naked to make my point?"

"Well . . . I . . ." he stammered, ". . . I didn't realize the old Cook charm was so effective . . ."

"Well, it is. Now I'm going to be the most frustrated woman in the world if you don't get that little boat off the top of the pilot house and come on in here."

"Yes, ma'am." The grin on his face stretched from ear to ear. He undid the lines to the pram and lifted it down to the water. Then he very carefully placed a cooler with the jug of wine visible into the bottom of the boat and said, "I really did want to have lunch with you."

They pulled the pram up onto the rocks together. Then Corinne scampered through the trees, stopping in front of the cabin to call out, "What are you waiting for, Jimmy Cook? Catch me if you can."

Jimmy picked up the cooler from the bottom of the pram and called out, "I think I'll save my strength if it's all the same to you."

As he skipped through the front door, a happy man with a mission, Jimmy Cook came face to face with reality. The smile on his face melted into disbelief. Nicholas Koniev was standing in the middle of the room with a gun leveled on his stomach. Corinne was behind him.

"I'm sorry you chose to save your strength, Mr. Cook. You were misled, mostly for your own good. However, Corinne remains concerned about your safety and I have assured her you won't be hurt—that is, as long as you obey."

Jimmy looked from Koniev to Corinne, then back to Koniev. He was speechless. The man who stared back at him remained expressionless as if he had just asked the time. But Jimmy had seen desperate men before and he sensed that this man wouldn't hesitate to kill him.

"You would be most wise," Koniev said, "if you place your hands on your head for a moment."

Jimmy's hands moved to his head.

"Corinne, would you please check his pockets?"

She came up with a wallet, some loose change, a comb, a handkerchief, a penknife, and a nail clipper.

"You may place everything from his pockets on the table, except for that knife," he said, indicating Jimmy's small pocket knife. "I wouldn't want to leave him with anything that would hasten his escape after we depart."

Koniev ordered the young man to sit in a wooden chair that he placed in the center of the room. He then had Corinne follow his detailed instructions in tying Jimmy's hands behind the chair, checked the knots himself, had his feet tied to the chair legs, checked again, then pocketed the gun and added more cord.

As soon as he was satisfied, he sat down by Jimmy and reassured him in a soft, soothing voice that no harm would come if he answered a series of questions. He learned that *Dream Girl*'s tanks had been topped off that morning, the engine and power drive had been overhauled at the beginning of the season, there were no glitches in the electrical system, her cruising range was more than adequate for Koniev's needs, clean clothes were stored in the cabin, and there was a hunting rifle and full box of ammunition under the bunk in the tiny cabin.

"I'm sure, young man, that you will eventually be able to release yourself before you starve to death," Koniev said before he and Corinne went out the door carrying food she'd packed. The radio had been destroyed. Everything personal that Corinne had brought with her was carried away with them. It would take experts a good deal of time to determine who had occupied the cabin.

Koniev spent ten minutes going over *Dream Girl* before he started her engines. "She's perfect, Corinne. She'll serve our purposes well. If anyone stops us, we're just a couple who decided to take a day off from fishing and go on a holiday. We have identification and . . ." He paused and began to rifle through the drawers in the chart table. "But I don't have the registration certificate for this boat. That could be a fatal mistake," he said shaking his head sagely. "I'm going to have to take the little boat back in and go through his wallet. I didn't check thoroughly but I'm sure it must be there. You just sit out on the deck like a tourist and wave at anyone going by."

Of course, the registration had been in the chart drawer and Koniev had pocketed it. Back in the cabin, he went directly to the kitchen and removed a sharp knife from the drawer. "Don't worry, Jimmy," he said as the fisherman's eyes widened.

"But Corinne said . . ." Jimmy began, his voice growing high with fear. Koniev's face told him that something wasn't right.

"Corinne convinced me that you'd never be able to escape the way I've got you bound here, and she does have a way of convincing a man as you're aware. I promised her I'd take care of those ropes. So, I'm going to make it a little easier for you to escape." He moved around behind the chair and with one rapid movement yanked Jimmy's head back by the hair and cut his throat. It was done so quickly and so expertly that his hands were clear before the blood began spraying from severed arteries. Koniev knew that Corinne would never have been able to understand. But he'd promised himself after leaving the old man alive in that cabin never again to leave anyone behind who could talk. Sympathy had no place in the real world, not the real world of Nicholas Koniev.

Koniev was in a fine humor as he pulled the pram out of the water and secured it to the pilot house roof. "You have fine taste in men," he told Corinne. "He saved me some time by telling me this was in his wallet." He waved the boat's registration. "And I decided that some of those ropes were too tight, so I loosened them. He won't ever like us but at least he'll be free soon."

Corinne, perched on the stern with her face turned to the sun, smiled her thanks. Jimmy had been one of the few men she'd ever identified with. In his innocence, she recognized a trace of human decency that touched her. It was an emotion she'd particularly enjoyed because she never felt anything about the men she normally entertained; there were simply some who were nicer than others, but all were objects to be used.

As she pondered these ideas, she was amazed how much she had wondered about Nicholas Koniev. Considering how she had turned him into a superman in just a few short days, she felt relieved in his basic expression of humanity toward Jimmy Cook. Yes, there were elements of pity and human understanding in every individual, even in this strange and wonderful man she was now committed to. Her fantasy lover had become a reality.

But as *Dream Girl* moved up the channel at a leisurely pace, a tiny spark of fear struggled deep inside her. She understood how men like Koniev killed. They disposed of anyone who became a threat to them. She remembered the look in his eyes when he whirled and aimed the pistol at her. *Killing is second nature to that man.* She considered asking for reassurance about Jimmy, then rejected the idea. Corinne didn't want to know the truth. And when she asked herself what was wrong with the truth, she discovered that she no longer understood what it meant because she had now committed herself to whatever Nicholas Koniev was.

They were heading east since the direction of the helicopters indicated that the search was oriented to the west. Koniev was explaining that since he was sure the name on his last boat, *Sea Chase,* might have been recognized by the nun, that was the major reason he had sunk her. Therefore, it wouldn't be wise to keep *Dream Girl* for that long either. Somehow, someone would develop a clue that would make her a target.

His plan was to head east, pass down the Rosa Rio Strait, then turn west across the Strait of Juan de Fuca to Victoria. It was quite possible they would have to change boats more than once.

Sister Mary Catherine had set this day aside to inventory the meager supply of goods in the general store. She enjoyed detail and the other nuns were happy to let her play amateur accountant. It allowed them more personal time and the order left their tiny group alone because they were so pleased with her accurate records.

But she could not concentrate on her work today. Each count of canned goods resulted in a different figure. The candy bars left over from the summer visitors became a blur as she tried to separate them. In the confines of the tiny store, fear of the man with the binoculars grew into an overwhelming claustrophobia until she knew she would scream if she didn't escape to the sunlight.

There was always a solution on such a sunny day. Sister Mary Catherine removed her heavy nun's habit. It was all right in the cool store but it was warm outside. It was for times like this that she wore a pair of slacks and a sweater underneath her habit. You could get away with such informality out on the island. Then she took down her favorite Mariners baseball cap to shade her pale face, and went out to the arbor with her binoculars to watch the passing boats.

Sure enough, the beautiful white wedding cake that was the ferry *Illahee* was just passing. She stood up and waved to the grand old friend, a sure sign that everything was in its correct place that day. The captain stepped out of the pilot house onto the bridge wing and waved back, then shouted into the pilot house. She saw the familiar cloud of white steam from the stack before she heard the friendly howl of the whistle. The day was improving.

The number of familiar pleasure craft were decreasing each day. Autumn was slipping rapidly across the San Juans and now the fishermen didn't use the channel as much because they were crabbing in other waters. But enough people went by who hoped she would be there in her arbor so they could wave a greeting. Three boats passed in the next hour.

Then she recognized the solid lines of Jimmy Cook's *Dream Girl* coming down the far side of the channel from the west and wondered why he was around. He should have been crabbing, too. She could see extra crab pots stacked in the stern. Then she saw that Jimmy had someone with him, a woman who sat to one side of the crab pots with her face to the sun.

Sister Mary Catherine liked Jimmy and she hoped he would get married some day soon. He was such a nice boy. From time to time, he'd stop to leave some crab or salmon for the sisters because he knew they didn't go to the mainland and survived mostly on what they grew on their land. If she had a favorite among the locals who worried about their well-being, it was certainly Jimmy.

She walked out to the pier with her binoculars to get a better look at the woman. The other sisters would want to know what she looked like and if it was someone they might know. As *Dream Girl* came closer, Sister Mary Catherine saw that she was very attractive but didn't recognize her. Then she decided maybe Jimmy would come over and introduce the lady if she waved.

At first, there was no acknowledgment from *Dream Girl*, so Sister Mary Catherine waved again. Then she knew Jimmy saw her waving but for some strange reason he didn't wave back. Instead, he said something to the woman who disappeared down into the boat's cabin. When he looked back at the pier, she waved again. Then, even though he'd forgotten to wave, Jimmy turned toward the pier.

Dream Girl was less than two hundred yards away when Sister Mary Catherine realized that Jimmy Cook wasn't at the wheel. This was another man, a complete stranger, who was staring back at her. It seemed almost as if . . . as if this was the one she'd seen last night . . .

Then Sister Mary Catherine felt her chest tighten as last night's fear returned, washing over her with a chill that slashed at her heart. She turned away from the pier and ran, the binoculars crashing against her chest as her feet slipped on the damp planks. She crossed the paved landing and was scrambling up the incline in front of the arbor when she felt something slam into her left shoulder. The impact spun her completely around before hurling her to the ground. The unbelievable pain in her left side forced her to move. She rose to her hands and knees and was desperately clawing her way up the embankment when something hit her again, driving her facedown.

In her last seconds, knowing death was quickly overtaking her, Sister Mary Catherine repeated her prayers at the same time she scrawled an agonized "DREAM" in the dirt with a fingernail. She desperately wanted someone to know who had invaded her peaceful world—but the word GIRL would not transmit to a finger which she no longer controlled.

"You can come out now. It's safe," Koniev called down into the cabin.

Corinne appeared at the hatch, her face a map of both fear and concern. "Are you all right?" she asked tentatively, her voice a whisper.

"Yes, I'm fine." The rifle had already been stowed beneath the deck boards. "He did have a gun," Koniev claimed, shaking his head gravely, "and he did shoot at us. But his only shot went wide. There's no chance he'll be able to send anyone else after us now." Then he reached down with his hand extended to Corinne. "You do understand why I had to do that, don't you?" he asked, squeezing her hand tightly.

She came up the three steps from the cabin and was delighted when he slipped his arm around her shoulders. "It's not something I could do . . . but I understand. He didn't give you any chance." Actually, she was surprised how little it did concern her. The objective was to escape and if any man could survive it would be this one. And he had become her man. *We will survive together.*

Koniev pushed the throttle forward and brought *Dream Girl* up to full speed. It was obvious to him when the nun waved that she knew Jimmy Cook and his *Dream Girl*—he couldn't allow her to tell someone what she'd seen. Now it was important to distance themselves from the island for he was sure the nun would be missed shortly.

Bernie Ryng heard the helicopter report over his radio when he was returning from the southeast end of the island. At his request, one of them had been overflying the island, checking each building near the shoreline, each clearing, any place there might be an unexpected sign of life for that time of year. Ryng had come back in the channel, once again studying each tiny inlet for anything he might have missed the first time.

"We're over a pier," the voice from the helicopter said. "Looks like a ferry slip. There's someone lying facedown in the dirt. No movement. There's not enough room to land to investigate."

"This is Ryng. I'm probably the closest in a boat coming up the channel toward you. I'll be there in about fifteen minutes."

He knew who it was before he rolled the body over. Sister Mary Catherine's tiny corpse was pathetic, her face mirroring her fear and agony in those last seconds. He was sure from the position of the body and the tracks in the dirt that she had been running away from the pier when the shots came from the water. He also had no doubt who had killed her.

Then he saw the word—DREAM—near the blood that was already coagulating in the dirt. She had scratched it in desperation with a broken nail that now hung from her finger. In the end, Sister Mary Catherine had made a valiant attempt to tell that frightening outside world who had invaded her peaceful one.

Seventeen

Between the harbormasters in the area and the Coast Guard, Admiral Coffin had obtained a list of boats with the word DREAM in their name early that afternoon. More than thirty vessels qualified. The various sheriffs' departments began the process of tracking down the owners of each one with a promise to have answers before five o'clock.

An hour after Ryng identified Sister Mary Catherine's body, one of the helicopters making a last sweep of the channel caught sight of what appeared to be a sunken boat just beneath the surface near the western end. Len Todd was in the water within another hour and confirmed the wreck of *Sea Chase*, the boat Koniev had stolen the day before.

"He must understand that we've got the Strait closed all the way to the ocean now, so there's no way any submarine's getting in to pick him up. I still think his best chance is to get to Vancouver, Admiral," Ryng said over the radio. "That's the only Russian consulate near here that could help him. He must have been headed east from where he sank *Sea Chase* when he killed that nun. If he turned south and went inside Lopez Island, he might have run into me and he'll never get past Danny West. Danny's covering the passage between Lopez and San Juan."

"Why would he go south?" Coffin asked. "It doesn't make sense. If you still think Vancouver's a possibility, it's a hell of a long haul to the north."

"Since he was heading east, his only northern option would be to take Rosario Strait and head north. The other passages are pretty narrow and we've got them blocked. The Coast Guard promised you that if he does go north up Rosario they already have an effective roadblock around Lummi Rocks. That means nothing's going to get through there. So, either he's in the process of testing that approach or he decides to do whatever isn't obvious." As he explained it to the admiral, Ryng was sure more than ever that he was right. "This guy's too smart to do what you'd expect. If it was me, I'd start out by heading south," he concluded.

Coffin was studying the same chart down in Bangor that Ryng had aboard *Voyager*. "So you're absolutely sure of yourself, Bernie?"

Ryng had a mental image of the admiral shaking his head in doubt. "Well, nothing's absolute, but there's open water. That's what I'd head for. You can disappear there. You've heard how the Sixth Fleet figured out how to lose an aircraft carrier in the Mediterranean. Think about how many exercises they managed that. Remember how those carriers always turned up where they were least expected and launched a perfect strike on their targets."

"Submarines found them," Coffin responded, "eventually."

"After they'd launched, sure. Koniev is probably running around in a boat no more than thirty-five feet long and he's got hundreds of square miles of water to play with. You've got a good profile on him now and everything your people have turned up on him guarantees that he's a survivor, cagey as hell. For all we know, he may have someone with him by now who knows their way around. And he has a high-powered rifle if anyone he doesn't like gets too close."

"How about you, Bernie, you have one of those—just in case?"

"What I'd really like is one of those Soviet AK-74s. A little automatic firepower might do me."

"We'll have one lowered to you within the next hour, along with a bag of clips. Where are you going to be?"

"Give me a little more time and I'll be at the Belle Rock beacon in the lower end of Rosario Strait."

"Why are we stopping here?" Corinne asked.

"The Americans are looking for someone who's running away from them. Now that we're out in the open, there's no need to make ourselves obvious." *Dream Girl* had come through Thatcher's Pass an hour and a half before and they were now at the base of Rosario Strait a few miles off the southeast tip of Lopez Island. It was open water and the boat rolled easily in the long swells. Koniev had changed into Jimmy Cook's clean clothes. "So, to show we're not worried about anything, we're going to fish until sunset."

"And then?"

"We're going to make the crossing and get into Victoria, just like you suggested."

"I hate fishing," Corinne said.

"I don't fish either, but I think the military, especially their Coast Guard, are still looking for one man and will leave us alone if they think we're just another couple out on a holiday."

Corinne giggled. "They might think so as long as they don't talk to you." She enjoyed the way he chose words and put phrases together. His speech patterns were effective but he would stand out in any crowd.

"I don't mean to tease, but between your accent and the words you use, they'll know you're foreign." It was the only time she'd seen disappointment on his face. She'd met other men who had an equally perfect image of themselves and none of them accepted defects well.

"I thought my speech was perfect," he said haltingly. He folded his arms across his chest feigning seriousness, but his eyes twinkled with a humor Corinne hadn't anticipated. "Alright then, you will do all the talking if it's necessary. Now we will not discuss this matter any further." Then he grinned and winked at her.

"Well, at least you're easy to convince." She enjoyed the

gentle teasing. "Why don't we put the fishing rods in the holders like we were fishing and we can put the lines out. Luckily we don't have any bait," she added with a grin. "I'm sure no one will notice. Then we can just relax and . . ."

His face lit up and he interrupted her. "See, you're finally relaxing. I'm happy about that. You seemed so afraid when I had to use the rifle and I was worried you wouldn't understand."

"I was terrified because I thought that man you saw through your binoculars might shoot you . . . but I know it was something that had to be done." Then her expression became serious. "You know . . ." she began, ". . . it's not easy to ask you . . . and I know I shouldn't . . . but whatever you've done here . . . can you tell me . . ."

"No!" His voice and his eyes seemed to change instantly with his emotions. They softened visibly when she drew back from him. "I am sorry to talk to you like that. Please accept that it's better you know nothing more. If something happened to me, the Americans would try to torture it out of you. So it is better for my mission." He shrugged helplessly like a little boy excusing a mistake. "After all, that is the reason we are together."

"I'll change the subject. Are you hungry?"

He remembered the wine Jimmy Cook had brought. "And thirsty also."

"There's a small stove down below in the cabin. Do you want me to try to cook that salmon?"

"Not now. We still might have to move very fast at any time. But I am hungry. Why don't you get some of the cold food you brought from your cabin and we can have an outdoor party on the back end of the boat."

"You mean a picnic," Corinne exclaimed.

"If you say."

Koniev set up the fishing rods on the stern while Corinne spread a blanket and two pillows from the cabin on the deck. She brought out the jug of wine, two plastic cups, and some cold cuts and the fresh loaf of bread Jimmy had brought.

"Everything but the ants," Corinne said as she curled up on the blanket with her legs tucked under her.

Koniev stared back at her curiously,

"Just a Canadian joke," she answered, smiling. "Nothing to worry about out here." She was sure she was as happy as she'd been in years as she pulled the bread apart with her hands.

For the next hour, they ate and drank wine and talked about anything that came to their minds. Corinne found that he was willing to talk about places he'd lived and the countryside he enjoyed, but he offered nothing about himself. He preferred to switch the conversation back to her whenever she asked a question that involved his background. But she decided it didn't really matter. She was fascinated more by the myth she'd created for this man than something that might disappoint her. When she noticed that half the jug of wine was gone, Corinne realized why in the last few minutes she had promised herself they would make love before the day had ended. She was wondering how she would accomplish this when . . .

"Helicopter." Koniev had been stretched out on the blanket on his stomach, supported on his elbows. Instantly he was on his feet scrambling for the binoculars.

Corinne strained to hear what had caught his attention. There was almost nothing out there on a relatively flat sea. An occasional boat had passed that afternoon, other fishermen who waved but continued on their way. *Dream Girl* was just outside the shipping lanes and saw freighters and tankers passing to the east, but they were just as silent. The light wind, which might have carried the sound, was from the south, but Koniev was looking directly to the east. She could neither hear nor see anything.

"There it is. Military, just as my ears told me."

"We saw a lot of them earlier today. Why do you . . ."

"That was in the channel, around the islands, where they were looking for us. Something's wrong now. We haven't seen the military flying out here today, not on the open water."

"You think they're looking for us?"

"I don't know. It should just be me. That's why I'm watching to see what they do."

286

He was silent for awhile, perched on his knees with the binoculars balanced on the railing. Corinne lay back on the blanket, a pillow under her head. She watched the seagulls outlined against the blue sky as they approached *Dream Girl,* hovered to see if there was garbage or bait in the water, then swooped away to investigate the next boat.

"What do they know?" Koniev hissed.

Corinne rose on her elbow. "What do you mean?"

"That helicopter is coming down almost to water level to study other boats. They're circling and . . . I can't be sure what they're doing. I just don't like it."

"Do you want to start up?"

"No. They've probably already got us marked on their radar. If we move, they'll wonder why."

"Are they checking every boat?"

"I can't be sure."

"What should we do?"

"I don't know. If they come toward us, we'll . . . I don't know."

"May I look?"

"No. I don't want to take the chance of missing something," he said roughly.

Corinne poured another glass of wine. Never had she witnessed moods switch so quickly. One moment he seemed sensitive and interested only in her, the next he was treating her more like a disobedient sailor. An enigma—and an extremely dangerous one! *You've certainly got yourself into a wild situation this time, lady. Here you are with the man you fantasized about—you actually started an all-over tan just to tantalize him. Yet you haven't even made love to him. Or, if you want to be honest with yourself, he hasn't shown much interest other than a sisterly kiss and that tan is just going to disappear without any man ever getting excited about it.*

"Here they come," Koniev shouted. He turned and looked at her with an evil smile. "Take off your clothes." It was an order.

"Why?" She decided her response was a romantic reaction to his romantic approach. *So much for story-book love!*

"Don't question." He was unbuttoning his shirt. "Take off your clothes. We are going to make love."

Love? Could it be more preposterous? Then Corinne began to giggle. There was no doubt he was serious because he was removing his own clothes. His shirt was already off. So she pulled her sweat shirt over her head. "You really mean it, don't you?"

"Yes."

"Do you approach all women in this manner?"

He raised his eyebrows without answering.

"What I mean is—are you always so romantic?"

He was untying his sneakers but paused to look up at her with a broad grin. "No, I am generally less aggressive. But usually there is no one about to watch me make love who would kill me if they knew who I was."

His eyes were fixed on her as she arched her back and unsnapped her bra, distinctly pleased he was continuing to watch. *It's got to be the tan, lady. You just didn't plan it quite this way.* "While we are doing this very romantic striptease, can you explain what . . ."

Dimples appeared at the corners of his lips. "You have used the sun very artistically."

Corinne inclined her head slightly, but said nothing.

"Seconds ago, I was thinking that we would make-believe we were making love, just so that helicopter would go away. But now," he nodded in her direction, "I know you will not allow me to make-believe."

He tossed his sneakers and socks to one side and stood up to take off his pants. As he stepped out of them, Corinne burst into hysterical laughter.

"What . . . ?" He pivoted as if something funny had miraculously appeared behind him. Then he turned back to Corinne, his face actually reddening. "Are you laughing at me?" he asked incredulously.

She was sitting on the blanket, her knees drawn up with her slacks around her ankles unable to control her laughter. Her shoulders slouched forward as she squeezed her arms around her middle. Then, after kicking off her slacks, she pointed at his crotch.

"They're wonderful . . . wonderful . . . I've never seen any like that . . ." Her laughter grew louder.

Koniev looked down at himself, confused. He stood there in Jimmy Cook's shorts and stared in confusion. No woman had ever laughed at him before. Then he understood—it was the shorts—and began to laugh himself.

"You see what I mean," Corinne roared as she rose to her feet. "They're gorgeous." She hooked her thumbs in her panties and slid them down until they fell to her ankles, then stepped out of them. "They must be birds of paradise. Absolutely perfect," she added as she stood there naked, still laughing.

The shorts Koniev had found in Jimmy's cabin were black and decorated with pastel-colored birds of paradise. "Yes," he said awkwardly. "I had forgotten them until you . . ."

"Well, take them off," Corinne said with a lewd grin. "If your friends in that helicopter see those, they'll shoot you for sure."

Koniev removed the shorts, then looked across at her quizzically. He saw that he was not in complete control of this situation and he was uncertain. She had made it all so easy for herself, laughing at him as if he were a clown. None of the others had ever treated him that way.

"Come here, Nicholas," she said. "You want them to see us making love, not standing here leering at each other. You're almost ready." And when he didn't move, she stepped across the blanket and pulled his face down so that she could kiss him. "There, it won't be so difficult, will it?"

"I never thought it would be." He took both her hands and together they lay down on the blanket.

The helicopter came in low on their beam and hovered off their stern. Corinne opened her eyes once and turned her head back to look up at the helicopter. She could see the two men in the front pointing at them.

"What are they doing?" Koniev whispered in her ear.

"Taking notes on your style. Don't look up. You're doing so well and you don't want them to go off thinking they've ruined our day."

You've done it, lady. You just may have regained some

control again. And to think you got it by doing what you do best.

"Completely negative, commander. Zippo." The senior helicopter pilot back at the Whidby Island Naval Air Station was on the radio with Bernie Ryng. "We set up a grid from south of Belle Rock down to Smith Island, just like you ordered, and split it between us. Nothing got away because everything large enough to paint on radar was tracked. So I'm absolutely sure we checked everything out there that would attract a hungry seagull. We learned more than you care to know. I can guarantee you the crabbing's only fair and the fishing was lousy today. Hell, there was one couple out there with lines over the back just banging their ears off—never even waved at us."

Oh, shit, just made believe a helicopter the size of a ranch house wasn't there! "How close were you to their boat?" Ryng's eyes were shut tight. *That had to be Koniev. Anyone else would have been embarrassed, even frightened. If they'd gone below to their cabin, then it wouldn't have been suspicious. The son of a bitch was brilliant. He'd do anything to get away.* Just fifteen minutes before the pilot had called him, Ryng had been talking with Len Todd. There was a cabin back in the woods not too far from where the wreck of *Sea Chase* had been located. Len had found a body, throat sliced expertly from ear to ear, probably dead no more than six hours. No ID. But Ryng was sure that when they had a name, it would be the owner of a boat with *Dream* in its name.

The one thing that Len mentioned that had caught his attention was an empty tube of lipstick in a wastebasket. Ryng asked for an inventory of the remaining contents. There was a grocery slip from a Vancouver supermarket, the normal trash, some empty cans, one of them apparently opened just the day before because the inside was still damp. Len said the lipstick was on the top of the trash. Koniev had been there! A woman had been there with him!

"We weren't close enough to give any pointers, command-

er, but close enough to read the name on the back end—
Dream Girl."

Dream Girl—that was it! They'd been tracking down
owners and the word about that name—*Dream*—hadn't
been passed on to this helo crew.

"Hell, we never had a chance to see if she really was a
dream the way they were going at it. I didn't want to get so
near my downdraft could blow the guy right off her. The
CO's always told us—civilians sue the government over
things like that." He was laughing at his own good humor.

Dream Girl. *That would have to be it.* "You're sure you
can't give me a rough idea of what either of them looked
like."

"You serious, Commander?"

"Serious enough to want the grid locator on that *Dream
Girl* and one of your birds back there super fast."

"It'll be dark soon, Commander. Hard to pick out someone unless we spotlight them, and that pisses off most
civilians."

"You just get your ass out there and piss off everybody
you see," Ryng answered. "I've got my boat, call sign
Voyager, at full throttle right now and I'm going to head for
that grid locator as soon as you tell me where it's at."

Ryng was sure, absolutely, unequivocally, that no matter
which one of them arrived in the area first, there would be
no Nicholas Koniev even if they found *Dream Girl* again.

Well, lady, what did you expect—sweet nothings?

In the past, the gentlemen who had enjoyed her company
had in almost every instance been just that—gentlemen.
When you are entertaining the rich and powerful and you
are a lady, and each of you realizes and appreciates the
other's abilities, there is an element of mutual respect. No
one ever expressed love for that simply wasn't the situation.
But when they enjoyed an evening or a weekend together,
there was that sense of respect engendered by mutual
pleasure and fulfillment. It didn't necessarily require
afterplay or words of endearment, but it was decidedly a

relaxing period of time. The men were especially apprecia-
tive. In every situation, they'd never met a woman quite like
Corinne Foxe.

Nicholas Koniev bore no resemblance to those men.
When he lay back on the blanket in the stern of *Dream Girl*
and Corinne threw an arm across his chest, the moment of
bliss lasted no more than twenty seconds. Then he was on
his hands and knees, shading his eyes against the late
afternoon sun, peering cautiously over the railing in the
direction the helicopter had disappeared.

That was irritating . . . rude. "It seemed to me that you
were enjoying yourself," Corinne said acidly.

"Most certainly," he answered, seemingly oblivious to her
as he rose to his feet to look across the bow. Then he put an
index finger to his lips for quiet and kept it there as he
turned still naked in an almost complete circle. "Gone," he
concluded looking down at her. "It was successful."

"Terrific idea . . . I mean banging away like that,"
Corinne said bluntly.

"I don't understand." He wasn't apologetic. He didn't
understand.

"I'm attracted to you. I like you. I enjoyed that. I guess I
thought it would have been pleasant to lie back and enjoy
each other for a few minutes after we were finished. That
was sort of like the third out and everyone runs off the
field."

Koniev looked at her curiously. "Yes, I think I said before
that it would not be make-believe . . . that it would be real.
I, too, enjoyed it. Is that what you want me to say?" There
was no doubt from his expression that he really wasn't sure
what she meant.

"OK. You win." She sat up and pulled her knees up tight
against her chest. "I hope that the next time we have a little
more time to play . . . both before and after. Do you know
what I mean?"

"Yes," he answered absently. He was again scanning the
horizon.

"It's not getting any warmer out here, is it? Aren't you

chilly?" The breeze was drying her perspiration and she could feel the goose bumps rising.

"We should put our clothes back on," Koniev noted. "We have to get another boat, quickly—but first, please, stand up."

She rose to her feet, still hugging herself against the cold.

"No, please, drop your hands to your side . . . just for a second."

She did so.

"You are very beautiful," he said, speaking as softly as he had since they'd met though his voice still carried that neutral tone as if he'd rehearsed each sentence. "I mean that."

Corinne smiled but said nothing. She'd learned long ago that there was little point to speaking when a man was admiring her like that. She wanted to believe that his mannerisms and tone were the result of speaking an unfamiliar language. Yet he spoke English so well. He was opaque. She couldn't understand him, nor could she remember any man so difficult to comprehend.

"Now," he said, "we really should put our clothes on because there is much to be done."

"You said something about another boat."

"I'm sure the helicopter recorded the name on the stern. They'll report every boat they checked out here. If there is any chance that someone may be aware this boat is missing, they'll be back." He was about to pull his pants on but stopped and looked at her with a grin. "You're not going to laugh at me again when I take off my pants?"

Corinne was dressing quickly against the late afternoon chill. "Oh, I don't know. I might. It depends on the situation. You've got to admit it was very funny at the time." *He's an enigma, hot and cold, black and white—one minute he's all logic, the next he's joking.*

"I will have to look for more clothes then. I don't like to be laughed at." There was still the trace of a smile on his face but it was disappearing rapidly. "I never have."

"I'll remember that." She stepped over beside him and

rose on her tiptoes to kiss his cheek, then his lips when he looked down at her. "But please also remember that it wasn't really you I laughed at. It was what was all happening so fast."

Koniev changed the subject again. "We are going to find another boat if we are to get to Victoria tonight, and I'll need you to understand that it will not be pleasant. We can't have anyone identify us."

Corinne squeezed her eyes tightly shut, nodding her head ever so slightly before she said, "I understand. Alive is much better than dead." Her words were barely audible. And at that moment, Corinne acknowledged what she'd understood since she agreed to join Nicholas Koniev, that she had crossed another invisible barrier forever. She would never be able to go back to Vancouver. In less than a day, that had become part of her past. If Nicholas Koniev survived, she would also but she would have to start a new life whether it was with him or on her own.

Her fantasy, surely harmless a few nights before, had become a reality that had changed her life forever. It was as powerful an influence as the day Ken and Cory had died. She considered the major events in her life: Coventry to Oxford—Ken Foxe and radicalism to a mother—the violent death of her family to a chosen life of isolation—Vancouver to Nicholas Koniev. Her choice this time was irretrievable for she would have to live with violence . . . as long as she remained alive. Fantasy had become reality.

Koniev scanned the horizon through the binoculars before he noticed a private fisherman that would cross his bow at high speed no more than a kilometer away. It looked as much like *Dream Girl* as any he'd seen that day. When he saw someone seated in the stern of the other craft, he allowed *Dream Girl* to go dead in the water. He and Corinne immediately began waving frantically and he sounded his horn until the other turned in their direction.

"Do you need some help?" an attractive young woman called out as they came parallel to *Dream Girl*.

"Our engine isn't getting any fuel," Corinne answered pleasantly. "My husband thinks there's something in the gas line. And now we find that someone seems to have stolen our tools. Do you have any we could borrow?"

"We've run out of beer," the young man at the wheel shouted back. "How about a fair exchange?"

"Come alongside," Corinne said. "We've got plenty. I'll put some fenders over the side for you."

As the other boat turned, the name on her stern, *Remember,* stood out in large red letters. When they were tied up beside *Dream Girl,* Koniev spoke for the first time. "Where are you going tonight?" he inquired pleasantly.

"Back through Deception Pass to La Conner."

"What I was thinking—I may have a gas leak and might need some gas to get home. Do you have enough if I pay you for it?"

"Sure," the man answered good-naturedly. "If you have something to siphon it, I guess we could spare some. We topped off this morning and we have a two-hundred-fifty-gallon tank. We probably still have a couple hundred in the tank."

"Then I would like you to come over here and join us." Koniev's gun was pointed directly at the man. His voice was no longer pleasant. "You first. Come on," he snapped when the other hesitated. "Faster or you are a very dead person."

"What do you want , . ." the man began, pausing with one leg across *Dream Girl*'s railing.

"Faster." Koniev turned slightly and leveled his gun at the woman. "She will be dead if you aren't in my boat by the time I count three. One . . ."

"Please . . ." the man began as he hurriedly heaved the other leg over and stepped across to *Dream Girl.* "Don't hurt her . . . don't . . ."

"Sit on the deck. Hands on your head." Koniev looked over to the woman. "Now you. Hurry." When she was sitting beside the man, silent tears running down her cheeks, hands on her head, Koniev told Corinne, "Get whatever we may want and move it over to that boat."

"Please, take our boat," the man whimpered. "Take everything. Just don't hurt us. Please . . ."

"Be quiet," Koniev snarled, "or you die right there."

At that, the woman's crying increased in intensity until her entire body convulsed. Her hands had fallen from her head.

"May I . . . please . . . may I help her?" the man pleaded, reaching for her.

Koniev's gun leveled on his head.

"No, don't," Corinne called out anxiously as she was climbing back aboard from *Remember*. "Let him help," she chided. "He's not dangerous to us."

Before she'd finished those last words, she was sorry for speaking out. Never before had she seen anyone's personality alter so radically through the expression in their eyes as Nicholas Koniev's. She knew he'd been about to pull the trigger and she was afraid she would actually see them killed in front of her. In just seconds, she'd witnessed a paradoxical transformation to pure viciousness in Koniev's eyes as they narrowed, almost as if he'd already grown to hate these people and was about to gain revenge for some unknown crime. Was there also pleasure, anticipation perhaps, in his expression? Corinne shuddered, wishing she could take back those words. "Just a second and we'll have everything over there," she mumbled half-heartedly.

"Don't waste time." His voice was a lethal whisper.

Corinne was sure she'd never moved as fast before and in less than a minute she said she was ready.

"The two of you," Koniev said in that deadly soft voice, "down in the cabin." He gestured with the pistol. "I promise you won't be harmed if you cooperate." Yet a few seconds later, when the man had trouble getting the woman to her feet, he said, "If you can't lift her, drag her or I'll kill her right there."

Corinne watched as the man finally placed his hands under the woman's arms and dragged her down the few steps to the cabin. Then she turned away to the railing and closed her eyes, dreading what would come next.

She knew the first shot hit the man because the woman started screaming hysterically. Her cries rose in volume until the next two shots silenced her. There was one more and that was followed by an ominous silence. Corinne, her eyes still tightly shut, vomited over the side, wretching until she sank to her knees. *How many more do I have to endure before we can be by ourselves?* None of it had been part of the fantasy she'd constructed around this man.

Koniev reappeared on deck, his face and eyes completely normal again, and he called over to her, "Undo all the lines but one. I'll be there in a moment. Time to head for Victoria." His voice was jovial.

Corinne heaved once more without responding.

"What's wrong with you?" He had a can of gasoline which he splashed liberally around the boat surfaces, making sure to cover the back of the boat before he poured it down into the cabin. Then he put down the can and turned to stare at her back, waiting, his face still hard. Finally, he spoke. "There, that will make sure no one knows the name of the boat. It may also give someone the idea that we died here."

There was still no response from her.

"You must understand, Corinne, that in this business you can never leave someone who can identify you." He spoke as if he were lecturing a child. "If we were in the same situation as those people, an American would never have left us to draw a picture of him."

There was still no response.

He moved over beside her and lifted her slowly to her feet, saying more pleasantly, "We want to get away fast. Do you know how to start the engine?"

"I think so . . . yes, of course I can." She sat down at the wheel. "There's a key. It's in neutral."

"Go ahead."

The engine rumbled into life.

"Good. Undo the last line, then sit down on the deck because we're going to get away as fast as that boat will go."

Koniev balanced himself on *Dream Girl'*s gunwale, lit a match, then the entire pack, and tossed it toward the cabin. Before the pack landed, he had already leaped aboard *Remember,* bolted to the wheel, jammed the boat into gear, and pushed the throttle all the way forward.

There was a flash and the heat from the flaming gasoline washed over Corinne even before the sound of ignition came to her. It wasn't really an explosion because the gasoline wasn't contained. But there was a frightful roar as the fuel combined with oxygen and the entire boat exploded in flame.

Remember's stern dug deeply into the Strait of Juan de Fuca as she raced away from the burning vessel into gathering patches of fog. *Dream Girl* was so involved in flames that no one could have identified her.

Ryng had seen the dying flames on the horizon, acknowledging instinctively what had happened. The helicopter on the scene reported no survivors evident. The boat was burned to the waterline, still too hot to lower a man to investigate.

Ryng circled the hulk slowly. It was much like the description of *Dream Girl*, but it would be impossible to identify because the stern plate was completely charred—even though it was beneath the surface.

"She's lower in the water than when we arrived, Commander. I wouldn't be surprised if she's going down soon," the helicopter pilot said.

"Did you get a chance to see the name on the stern before you arrived on scene?" Ryng asked.

"Not a chance. She was completely involved, stem to stern. Must have been a hell of an explosion."

"I'm going aboard," Ryng said.

"I wouldn't advise that, sir," the pilot countered. "She's in danger of sinking."

Ryng cut his engine to an idle as *Voyager* scraped alongside. "You haven't seen anyone in the water or in a raft, have you?"

"Negative again, Commander. Like I said before, they were probably trapped by the explosion."

Ryng secured a strong line to a cleat on *Voyager* and tied the other end around his waist. "So that's why I'm going aboard now. See if there're any corpses that might tell us something. Stay close."

He stepped gingerly down from the railing and felt his feet

crunch on the still-hot, charred deck. The acrid stink that came to his nostrils was overpowering as he took his first step. His foot broke through the decking. He reached out for the railing to balance himself. The crisscross supports underneath held. Then he recognized the sound of gurgling water. She was filling! He knew he wasn't going a hell of a lot farther.

A couple more steps brought him just close enough to shine the beam of his flashlight down into the cabin. It was almost impossible to identify anything in the mess. The heat had been intense. Then the boat lurched and he heard the anxious pilot's voice across on *Voyager*'s radio. "Get the hell off there, sir. She's going down."

Ryng carefully retreated, placing his feet exactly where they'd been before as the boat shifted even more. He had seen what he wanted although they were unrecognizable as male and female. They were shriveled up like mummys, but he'd seen corpses before after a napalm attack. At least two people had died in the boat. It was even possible that Koniev had died in the flames, perhaps with that woman, whomever she was.

Just what Koniev would want us to see! Take time out to ID them. Delay us. I don't believe for a second either of those is Koniev.

As he moved back across the burnt deck, Ryng hauled himself in like a climber on the line attached to *Voyager*. He leaped across to his own boat just as the other heaved further over. Then there was the sound of cracking hull and the rush of water. In less than a minute, only the bow peeked above the water.

Ryng called up to the helicopter, "Ask your radar operator exactly how many other boats were in the vicinity while you were approaching."

"Nothing close, sir. It was getting dark enough and the fog was getting patchy, so they were hard to identify. Some of the boats had seen the flames and were coming to help. We chased them away just like you said. Told them it was a military test."

"Anyone going away at the time?"

There was a pause. "Radar operator said there was one or two. The only one he tried to keep a track on was heading west, but she was small enough so she disappeared in the sea return a while back."

West.

Ryng turned *Voyager* to the west and studied his chart.

Eighteen

KONIEV ESTIMATED THE DISTANCE TO THE ENTRANCE TO VICTO-
ria Harbor at approximately sixty kilometers. There was
more than enough time. He had no intention of arriving
before midnight. *Remember* was under American registration. They would be entering Canada, a foreign country, and
he had no interest in tangling with their customs and
immigration department. That would be a mistake even if
he could bluff his way through.

He'd considered coming into one of the smaller ports but
discarded that idea because the two of them would be too
obvious—was there any small town anywhere in the world
where everyone didn't remember strangers? The idea of
beaching the boat on a deserted coast lost its appeal when
Koniev imagined a satellite looking down on Vancouver
Island and sending a perfect image back to the Americans.
There was no better choice than to disappear into the crowd.

Corinne was seated at the wheel, her face outlined by the
dim light from the chart lamp. They'd talked for a while as
the darkness settled around their new vessel. He'd softened
as soon as he became confident they were definitely on their
own. His words were full of understanding, sincerely con-

cerned that others must die in order for them to survive, promising some day when they were safe that she would be told of his mission and realize that so much death was justified by the good that would come as a result. Needing to accept everything he said, she stretched her imagination to believe each word.

She couldn't help but smile at the paint on Koniev's arms and hands. He appeared so innocent in the faint light. While rummaging around in the cabin he'd found an old can of white paint and decided to paint out *Remember* on the stern. He claimed it would be twice as hard to remember a boat without a name, especially so late at night. It had been funny to watch him hanging over the stern as the boat bobbed up and down in the chop, once almost dumping him in the water.

"When do you want to arrive?" Corinne asked as he bent over the chart.

"Late. After midnight. Maybe even later. The less people around, the better." He glanced up at her. "Have you ever been in Victoria?"

"A few times. It's nice."

"When were you last there?"

She thought about the weather on her last visit. It had been a weekend visit with an American gentleman, one who had access to technology that appealed to her handlers. They'd spent occasional nights together before and enjoyed each other's company. Victoria had been his idea—*because there are so few Americans there this time of year and we can surely have the run of the city without anyone recognizing me.* He enjoyed good food and fine wines and loved to take a bottle of very old Remy Martin to bed. It had been a wonderful weekend.

"I think it was last February," Corinne answered. "It's not a high season then. Very few tourists. It was cool and rainy." She smiled to herself as she remembered their stay. It could have been pouring mud and it wouldn't have mattered.

"I'm not interested in a weather report," he said, impa-

tient again. "How busy is it? I'm trying to determine when it
will be quiet enough to arrive without worry."

"It's a very quiet city all the time, very British. After
midnight, I would think the only people who would be
awake in midweek would be the street sweepers. I was
always in bed before then and I don't remember anyone on
the streets. It really is a delightful place."

Koniev straightened up with a sigh. "I'm sure it was a
pleasant visit for you. Now can you tell me about the
harbor. Were you down there at all?"

"Oh, yes, we stayed at the Empress. It's a grand old
hotel—still serves high tea by the way." Even in the
reflection from the light above the chart, Corinne recognized the change in those telltale eyes. He was becoming
impatient. "It looks right out on the harbor. We walked all
around. I could draw you an outline of the harbor, if you
like."

"Then why don't you do just that. I'll take the wheel and
you fold the chart over and outline it for me."

Corinne was very precise. Victoria was the only city on
the north shore of the Strait of Juan de Fuca, situated at the
east end. Sailing into the harbor, the city was on the right
side. There were mostly homes and bed and breakfasts
looking out on the Strait to the east of the city. But as soon
as the channel began, there were some cruise ship piers, then
the buildings became more commercial, apartment houses
and hotels with some private moorings on the water. The
inner harbor turned to the right into the heart of the city.
There were some piers there with bigger boats, some of them
with cranes on deck, and a number of buoys out of the
water.

"That's the Coast Guard, I guess," she added. "I think
there was a big fence around those piers."

"What else?"

"Then there was Fisherman's Wharf. We wandered down
there both days because there was a wonderful little fish and
chips place with oyster burgers. That's fried oysters in a roll.
There must have been half a dozen piers for the fishing fleet.

There were all sizes of boats all lined up next to each other, sometimes six deep. You could almost walk across them from one pier to the other. And there was one pier, this one," she indicated tapping her drawing with the pencil, "lined with houseboats, some of them quite large. They're so cute, some of them like gingerbread, some with window boxes and flowers. I guess the people live in them all year round."

She explained that there was an old cruise ship farther on that was permanently tied up there, then the ferry terminal where she'd seen the official signs of the customs offices. There was a wide walkway that went around the entire inner harbor that she was sure was lovely on a pleasant day.

Corinne went on explaining the beauty around the harbor but Koniev paid little attention. He already knew where they were going. They were going to get lost in Victoria's Fisherman's Wharf.

Remember was rolling more in the trough as the wind increased and the distance between the swells shortened. The sky had begun to cloud over shortly after sunset and the wind was gradually increasing from the southwest to blow away the ground fog. They had more than enough time before arriving off Victoria, so Koniev was able to slow the boat to ease their ride.

"We've got a forecast for cloud cover the next twenty-four hours, Bernie. According to meteorology, you can expect heavy rains after midnight," Admiral Coffin reported. "The satellites are useless. If he goes ashore anywhere out there, he can probably sneak in free as far as taking pictures of him are concerned. You've got to assume he'll head for a population center to lose himself."

"He's not going to the States. That's for sure. With all the helos sweeping the water today, I'll go along with you. He's got to want to get ashore. The only choice in this direction is Victoria. There isn't another Canadian city on the chart if he's going to lose himself. He could go anywhere else and shake us, but all there is is small towns and he's got the problem of being recognized as a stranger. And a guy like

Koniev knows damn well we'll have every village checked automatically. I've got to take the gamble there. What's Victoria like?"

"Flowers, Bernie, lots of flowers. Very British. My wife found out they had high tea in the afternoon and dragged me along. No beer during high tea. It was all very proper."

"A good place to hide," Ryng said. "How can a guy in an American boat sneak in there without messing with customs?"

"Believe it or not, they close up shop at midnight. There's a little note here on my data sheet that gives a number to call if you show up later than that. What do you think of that for security?"

"Not likely Koniev will show up before then. Can you talk them into staying up a little later tonight? Tell them there's a homicidal sex maniac armed to the teeth who's trying to sneak into their city in the middle of the night. I don't want anyone on the piers—no one in a uniform or carrying a weapon that he can see—or we'll lose him. He'll keep going or turn around and breeze it. But if they can get some armed men back from the piers so that he may think twice about going ashore, it may give me some time before he figures out how to outsmart them. I don't think he'd try to move inland in the middle of the night without getting some rest and getting a feel for the place in the daylight. These guys don't do anything without thinking first."

"How about attempting to contact someone in Vancouver?" Coffin asked.

"Probably. But there's no way we'd ever be able to trace him. It'll be a perfectly innocent call prefaced with some code words that'll alert their consular staff. Let's not worry about that. If he's there, I'd just like to see if we can keep him around the piers until I have an even chance. If he's not, I don't know where to turn next."

"We'll do everything we can," the admiral said. "I've got one of their flag officers up there who owes me a favor because he got a ride on one of my boats. He ought to be able to get some troops where you want them without causing too much fuss."

"Anything but a parade. Very subtle. It's got to be something Koniev can discover for himself, if he actually gets there, something that'll slow him down for a while, make him think. He'll figure out how to circumvent them but that'll give me time."

"What I'd suggest now, Bernie, is getting your butt as close to Victoria as you can before this weather builds up. You've never seen a good southwest storm up here. I'll fax everything on Koniev to my contact. Now when you get to the mouth of Victoria Harbor, give me a call. I'll be able to tell you how to contact my man then."

The storm began as intermittent showers. The first drops were light but the wind lashed them against the boat's windows as if a monsoon raged outside. The swells grew closer together until they became a confused chop that tossed *Remember* about no matter the course or speed.

Corinne had never been comfortable on the water and now she reacted to the constant motion by hanging desperately to the railing with her head over the side three separate times. Koniev locked the wheel during her last trip and circled his arms around her waist, concerned that she might fall overboard. He'd never experienced the problem but he understood how others suffered from seasickness. As he held tight and felt her entire body shudder with each heave, he remembered his earlier years as a junior officer helping others in heavy weather, especially on the round-hulled submarines rolling helplessly on the surface.

"Anything but romantic, isn't it?" Corinne gurgled.

He leaned forward and whispered in her ear, "When I was a young officer, we used to make awful noises in the ears of men who were heaving, like . . . ahhhhhhhhhh." He made a retching sound in her ear. "Then they used to get even sicker, and they didn't have the strength to fight back."

"That's not funny." Corinne heaved again. "I don't think I have anything left inside me and I don't think I have the strength to slap your silly face for doing that."

He laughed out loud and kissed the back of her neck. "I'm so used to someone feeling like this, I could sing." He moved his hands up and caressed her breasts. "There is nothing I can imagine that bothers me. I could even make love to you right now."

"Ohhhhh," she groaned. "That's the farthest thing from my mind. Take your hands off." She pushed feebly at his arms. "Go away."

"Just trying to make you feel better," he said with another laugh. Then he stood up, uncertain of himself. This one was so very different from any of the others. "I was just teasing you. I know how you feel. But I can assure you that half an hour from now when we've turned into the harbor and the boat is steady you will be surprised how fast you'll feel better. I tell you—there are some crackers below in the cabin. If you go down there and get them and then come back in the fresh air to eat some, your stomach will be better. It's an empty stomach that gives you those heaves."

"I don't know if . . ."

"Go ahead now. Do what I say and you will feel better." He waved a hand at her. "Go on. Go on."

The crackers did help some. They didn't come back up. They expanded in her stomach and replaced the empty feeling that contributed to the heaves. And when Koniev turned north toward the harbor, the combination of shallower water and the sheltering peninsulas to the southwest calmed the seas. Then she was able to wash the remaining crackers down with a cold ginger ale and was amazed how quickly she regained her strength. The churning stomach, the cold sweats, and the recurring dizzying sensation were a thing of the past.

Koniev put the boat in neutral. "You feel better, don't you?" His smile was actually soft and understanding and he swept back some loose strands of hair from her forehead. "I hope you don't hate me for the teasing."

"I did when you were doing it."

"But not now."

"I wouldn't have done that to you," she said defensively.

He held her face in his hands and kissed her forehead, her nose, and finally her lips. "I apologize then. It was just a tradition of the sea and I was making you a part of that." As soon as he had said that, he realized that he'd actually rehearsed those words. For a short time, he'd forgotten he was running. Instead, he was enjoying the stolen time in this small boat with such a strange and beautiful woman.

Corinne smiled. "And now that we're close to a landing, you're thinking about sex again and you don't want me mad at you. See, you're just like other men."

He patted her rear affectionately and moved back to the wheel. "That, too, would be nice. Yes, maybe later. But I am not like any other men." He inclined his head and looked from the tops of his eyes as if he were a teacher contemplating a student. "Not like any other," he concluded.

Corinne saw that he meant exactly that. *Lady, he just said a mouthful.* "I think we're sort of committed to each other for the duration. Wouldn't you say?"

He looked questioningly at her.

"I mean we're a team for the time being. We have no choice but to stick with each other at this point. There's no one else who's going to help us. You knew you'd be on your own if the submarine was lost."

"You are correct," Koniev answered, nodding. "I was the one who specified that originally." He waved that fact away with a careless flick of his wrist. "Now, it is time to go into the harbor, time to start the next life. And I need you to help me."

Remember moved in slowly. Koniev wished they could have made themselves invisible, but the black, rainy night protected them as much as he could have hoped. Few people would venture out on a night like this. They moved past the cruise ship piers, then the smaller, protected wharves for pleasure boats, finally beginning a wide turn to the right. It was much too dark for Koniev to identify the ships that he suspected were Coast Guard, but he was sure that anyone awake on those vessels would pay little attention to him.

"Fisherman's Wharf should be next," Corinne said. Her hand rested on his shoulder and she was whispering as if someone might be in the boat with them.

"I'm going to move in closer. I want to check each of the

piers before we decide." He, too, was whispering even though the engine would have drowned out their voices. "Keep an eye for anyone wandering about. We can't afford to be seen."

There were dim lights at the heads of the piers but with the rain almost nothing could have been distinguished in the long, wet shadows. A heavy aroma of diesel fuel and ripe bait underscored the sharper smell of fresh paint, water-soaked wood, and drying nets. There were shrimpers and crabbers and draggers of all sizes, their masts or outriggers or outhauls presenting a seemingly impenetrable forest. The boats nested side by side literally connected the piers in some places so that the inboard boats at the front of the pier would have to wait for thirty others to depart before they could get underway. For Koniev, it seemed a perfect place to hide . . . to disappear.

"Right in there." He pointed at an opening between boats that would allow him to move up about three layers before tying up, like burrowing in a haystack. There it would be almost impossible to recognize *Remember* from the water and he hoped that if the foul weather held, there would be no one to notice a strange vessel in the nest—at least not until they were far away.

He eased the boat around, backing down slowly until she was aimed directly for the hole between the outboard craft, and then moved ahead gently. They passed between the first nests without touching the boats on either side. There was a scraping sound between the next ones but *Remember* slipped through easily. The third set was much tighter and he had to push the throttle forward somewhat until she began to move through, pushing the other two aside with a loud grinding.

"What the hell do you think you're doing?" It was a voice from the dragger to starboard, a bulky boat with nets hanging over an outhaul on the stern. "You can't go through here." The man who spoke had a loud vibrant voice and from the way he was slurring his words he was obviously drunk.

Koniev stopped his engine. "Stay here and take the wheel, just in case," he said to Corinne. "Don't let anyone see you. Let me handle this."

"So who do you think you are?" the drunken voice challenged as Koniev appeared on the stern of *Remember*. "We don't allow no sport fishermen in here. Getcher ass outa here."

"What seems to be the trouble?" He watched the man pass from shadow through a wide ray of wet light that fell across his boat, then back to shadow as he came closer. Koniev had noticed the heavy metal balls, lead probably, lined up in chutes along the railing and assumed they were most likely weights for the nets. The man carried one in his hand as he approached.

"This is all commercial docking area. Who the hell do you think you are trying to cram that piece of shit in where it's not wanted . . . scraping working men's boats like that . . ." He brandished the ball like a weapon. "Go on, getcher ass out of here before I crack your worthless skull."

"Please," Koniev said as calmly and politely as possible, "I'm just looking for a place to get out of the storm. I'll leave in the morning." As he spoke, he drew closer to *Remember's* railing.

"Screw off. I'm not gonna warn you again." He lifted his arm and slowly drew it back, taking tiny steps to keep his balance.

"Can't we talk about this?" Koniev's foot was now up on the railing.

"I warned you." The drunk cocked his arm, but before he could heave the heavy ball, the intruder was vaulting through the air. Then he threw it wildly.

Koniev was on top of him, twisting, using his weight to flip the man to the deck. The drunk landed heavily with a grunt. Before he could scramble back to his feet, Koniev's fist caught him on the cheek, banging his head on the deck. Another grunt. Koniev grabbed one of the metal balls from the tray and swung around, smashing the man full force just above the ear. He could feel the skull give way instantly. That was followed by total silence. Koniev lowered his face close to the man's. No breath. Quickly, he got to his feet and hauled the body back to the stern, slipping it into the water without a splash. He picked up a long pole lying on the deck and gave the corpse a push toward the harbor.

Back on *Remember,* Corinne was at the wheel, exactly as he had asked her.

"I had no choice . . ." he began, concerned she might be affected by another killing.

"I know. He would have caused us too much trouble. He forced you. It's just something I don't think I could do, not by hand."

Once again, he was amazed by this strange woman. "Don't be concerned," he answered pleasantly. "When I'm forced—when I have no choice—I do it well, and quickly. That's why I'm here instead of someone else . . . on this mission . . ." he added, ". . . which you are helping me with. If you just remain with me, Corinne, I believe we'll be a good team, just like you said." He squeezed her hand, hoping she'd understand that he really meant it. "Together —we'll make it together."

"What we'll remember, after this is all over, is ourselves," she answered. *Hopefully.*

He eased the throttle forward and *Remember* ground and scraped between the boats into the space Koniev had chosen. He secured her to the boat to port with nylon line before sitting down on the rail with a heavy sigh. "I am tired," he said in his correct English.

"We should sleep."

"Not here. Someone may come looking for that drunk. We can't have anyone see us here."

"What do you intend to do?" she asked wearily.

"We're going to find one of those houseboats you told me about until I can scout the area. It's still possible someone else may have seen us. I want to be sure before we move out."

"The houseboats are over at the farthest pier, that way." She gestured toward her left. "Do you want me to go with you?"

"Not yet. Get everything together while I'm gone. It'll be

easier to avoid being seen if I'm alone. If I'm not back in an hour, then disappear. No one knows you're with me. No one will ever know." He shrugged. "No one."

"Don't say such things." She sat on the railing beside him and kneaded the muscles in his neck. It seemed as if they'd been together for months. Yet it had only been . . . how long? Not more than thirty hours. "After the past day, I couldn't stand being alone." And she realized that was exactly how she felt. After all the years alone, the past thirty hours meant more to her than anything else since Ken and Cory died. She was needed once again.

Koniev paused as he was climbing over the railing onto the next boat. She was correct. It hadn't been much more than a day. He was probably alive because of her. And if he survived to get back home, he was sure that he would remember every minute with her. He rolled the same words over in his mind again—*a strange and beautiful woman.* "You know, I thought that also. I've enjoyed being with you." Then he disappeared into the shadows.

Bernie Ryng raised Admiral Coffin by radio as *Voyager* approached the entrance of the harbor. "You couldn't have been more right about the weather. Hard to believe this could come up so quickly after such a nice day."

Exhaustion was evident in the admiral's voice. "Other than that, Bernie, other than all those bodies, how's tricks?" Even his attempt at humor ended in a soft background snort to simulate laughter.

"I'm a little damp and a little cold and I'd be a lot happier if I could climb into a warm bed and say the hell with it all."

"On a brighter note, Bernie, it pays to have friends. Canadian Forces Command has been more than cooperative. If Koniev is in those piers around Victoria's inner harbor, he won't move out far from there without knowing something's up. It'll all be very subtle. My man promised it's the type of thing the average citizen shouldn't pay much attention to, probably won't even notice, but Koniev ought to. He won't go wandering off during the day anyway and disappear in the city."

Sheets of rain pelted *Voyager* as Ryng passed the cruise ship wharves and headed for the turn at the Coast Guard pier. "Were you able to get any ID on that boat that was torched or those bodies?"

"The Coast Guard traced the registration number from a sticker on the bow. It belonged to that young fellow back on the island—the one whose throat was cut. *Dream Girl* was the name of his boat."

"That's what Sister Mary Catherine was trying to tell us."

"A Coast Guard diver recovered what was left of those corpses and the Seattle coroner's office is giving us an assist on them. So far, all they'll say is they're definitely one male and one female. They'll probably have to try to locate dental records, and there's obviously none we have on Koniev. For that matter, they don't know where the woman might have come from. So it's not going to be easy to come up with names anyway. Our only chance is if someone reports a male and female missing on a similar boat. Then we compare. If we can't do that, then it could be Koniev and the girl."

"By the time they come up with anything then, a live Koniev will be long gone."

"You know, Bernie, I'm beginning to feel like we're running a sheriff's office here with all these corpses. You can't believe the questions that have been directed our way by the civilian authorities. And I can assure you they aren't smiling when they're told that everything's hush hush and that there's a guy chasing down an unknown alien and he won't let anyone else work with him. They don't see this as a military operation when it looks like we're chasing Billy the Kid."

"Have you put them in touch with any of our spooks, someone who might explain this is more than a bank robbery?"

"No, I didn't bother. The law and order types don't care for that sort of thing. I explained it myself to three of them that we had heloed in here this evening. I gave them the old pep talk about how they couldn't imagine what they were doing for their country if they just gave you another twenty-four hours."

"Yeah, I guess in the next twenty-four hours, it'll either be me or Koniev, or else he'll be on his way home with our jewels by then. If you have to, you can tell them there'd be a lot of dead sheriffs if they tried to do this themselves. No, don't do that. They wouldn't be able to understand Spetznaz."

"For that matter, Bernie, how about SEALs? They aren't too excited about your methods either."

"Next question." Ryng had passed the Coast Guard boats and was coming up on Fisherman's Wharf.

"What do you do if you can't find him in Victoria?"

"Head for Vancouver I guess. What else is there? I've been following hunches so far. The odds say I'm due to run out of luck."

"What else can I do for you now? Coordinating's nowhere near as much fun as being there."

"Nothing, Admiral. I'm going to get familiar with this harbor to see if there's any other logical place for Koniev to go, then I'm going to work Fisherman's Wharf. One other thing. Don't forget to fax my picture to the Canadian Forces so they don't try to nail me."

Shadows were lovely. Nicholas Koniev had always been very attached to them, but now he respected them more than ever. There was something about their darkness, their impenetrability, that appealed to his inner self. They were like an invisible cloak that shielded you from the outside world. You appeared only to those you wanted to see you—and the rest of the world be damned.

Corinne squinted into the darkness to see where he was going but he moved from one boat to the next and finally to the pier so stealthily that she never saw him. The wind blew the rain into the boat from every direction. No matter which way she turned, no matter what she huddled against for protection, rain splattered into her eyes and ran down her neck. It was cold and raw and miserable and she finally decided to go down into the cabin where it was dry. Less than a minute after she sat down, she was asleep.

Koniev was like a cat. He stopped in selected shadows where he easily blended in with his surroundings. His eyes searched in every direction. His ears picked up each sound. Once he reassured himself that he was absolutely alone, he would pick his next destination and move rapidly to that point where he would repeat exactly what he'd done before. Like a cat, he was patient. And like a cat, he remained invisible.

He arrived at the head of the pier wishing instead he was in a large warm bed with Corinne, perhaps a bottle of champagne on the bedside table. It was a habit acquired early in his career. He'd always found that the best way to combat discomfort was to imagine exactly the opposite. That way he could forget the cold, wind-driven rain that had soaked him completely. He imagined fluffy pillows, an overstuffed mattress, soft, warm sheets—soft, warm Corinne . . .

He turned left at the head of the pier and crept among the shadows until he was past the lighted sign that identified "Barb's Place—Fish and Chips," the food stand Corinne had mentioned. A lighted phone booth looked bleak as the rain and wind rattled the folding door and soaked the inside as much as the outside. The next thing to do was to make that call to the consulate after they had a safer place to hide for the night. A call now would be fielded by a night duty clerk who'd then have to call the senior intelligence officer. That would take too much time. Safety was paramount.

Outside of the well-spaced lights around the piers that did little more than prevent total darkness, the only other illumination was around the parking lot above the wharf area. Koniev had yet to see a soul out in this foul weather and fully doubted he would at this time of night.

The houseboats were as bizarre as Corinne had explained. Most were built on one level, covering most of the surface of whatever they floated on. Some seemed to be no more than oversized rafts supported by empty, sealed barrels which rattled against their supports as the wind rocked them. Others, much larger, seemed to have been built on small barges that provided a much heavier, firmer base. There was no motion or noise from these and some of them had a second level which likely served as sleeping quarters.

Koniev, ever conscious of the shadows, worked his way up the pier, fascinated with what he saw. One of the houseboats was no more than a house trailer on a float. A few were apparently motorized and presumably could travel to other locations at the whim of the owner. There were window boxes with flowers, some planters with tomatoes still on the vines, and one with a green artificial outdoor carpet which he was sure simulated grass for the occupants. He could tell a couple of them were freshly painted because the reflection of lights showed the rain running off them. There were obvious signs of workmanship among others with blinds around each window, and one displayed intricate ginger-bread woodwork. And there were a couple no different from any neighborhood he'd ever seen back home—dilapidated.

What were the chances of picking one that was unoccupied? But there was no point in considering that. They desperately needed a place tonight. He automatically dismissed the fancier ones because it seemed obvious they were used full-time, probably by younger people who did work like that. He decided they were also too inviting to visitors. Slovenly was also crossed off his list. He was going to sleep in a comfortable bed with Corinne this night and he knew they must both sleep and eat before the final effort to get to Vancouver.

He settled on a single level houseboat that needed work but still looked neat. There was a BEWARE OF THE DOG sign nailed to the gangway from the pier. *I hate dogs!* Koniev thought back to the one that had attacked him on the submarine base. *Was that only two nights ago . . . one night?* So much had happened since then. That dog had come so close . . . so close. Right then, he knew if he ever returned home that he could never own a dog. He hated them. If one of his children ever had one, the animal would probably attack him. *Hateful animals.* Their only value seemed to be protecting people and he didn't require that kind of protection.

He decided that the sign, which was as worn as the houseboat, was as much an indication that the occupant didn't care for visitors as the fact that a vicious dog might actually live there. The best approach was to go aboard and examine the place. If a dog barked, then he'd just have to dispose of the animal before he took care of the owner. For some reason, he was sure this one was more right than any of the others. He slipped the silencer over the barrel of his gun.

This houseboat was like a single-tier cake situated in a slightly larger, flat pan so one could walk the three foot wide deck all the way around it. Just off the gangway was a window that revealed in the glare of the dim light from down the pier, a tidy little kitchen and dining area. No animal there. Koniev moved along the narrow passageway on the pier side, prevented from peering in windows by closed curtains. There was a door on the other end that opened onto a deck containing lawn chairs and an outdoor grill. He could vaguely see inside what might have been a living area. Apparently, sleeping arrangements were in the middle.

Moving next down the outboard side, his foot kicked a can that rattled as it bounced along the deck. He stopped instantly. If that didn't awake the occupants, it would certainly excite any dog inside. Nothing. It was either old and deaf or the sign was a sham. But that was fine with him if it would give the two of them twelve hours of rest.

Now he had completed the circle around the living quarters. Probably no dog or at least the sign didn't live up to the threat. The best place to enter was the door on the back deck. He tried the handle. It was locked. He went down on his knees and examined the lock—as simple as could be! His knife slipped through the crack between the door and the frame and within seconds the simple bolt slid back and the door opened.

The warmth washed over him in a cloud. Whoever lived there liked the heat. But it was dry and comfortable inside and he could identify the aroma of garlic in the air, which instantly reminded him of how hungry and tired he was. And if he felt this way, he could imagine how Corinne must feel.

He remained in one place until his eyes became accustomed to the interior, which was outlined only by the same faint light from the head of the pier. There was a soft-looking couch against the back wall with a coffee table just in front of it covered with magazines. Three soft chairs were on the pier side of the room facing a television set on the water side. The furniture was old and covered with a colorful mixture of materials. Older people lived like this.

There was a closed door leading to the next room. It was the only access to the forward area where the kitchen was located. Gun in hand, Koniev turned the handle to the door. He pushed it open a crack. The sound of deep breathing floated out to him. Soundlessly, he pushed it open all the way. The only light was a faint beam from the pier that fell on a wall switch. He listened, his eyes now shut, considering how many were in the bedroom. There were two steady, deep breaths—two people—and there was also a raspy, uneven sound he was unable to identify. He could barely make out the dull white of sheets and pillows as he tiptoed across to the switch, gun barrel centered on the bed.

The sudden brilliance of the overhead light startled the two people in the bed more than the old dog stretched out near the foot between them. Koniev's eyes were slits against the brightness as he leveled the gun barrel on the old lady whose mouth was slowly opening in a soundless scream. Before she could find her voice, he said, "If either of you makes a sound, the woman will die instantly."

The dog, a small terrier blend with a curly beard and fur arched over its eyes like an old man's eyebrows, had risen painfully into a sitting position on arthritic limbs. It studied him through friendly, sleepy eyes, tail wagging lazily.

"Hold the dog," Koniev ordered. He didn't want to shoot it there and make a mess in the same room he intended to sleep.

The man obediently hooked his fingers in the animal's collar. "He won't do anything. Please, he's deaf and almost blind. He's all we've got." The dog stood up and stretched unsteadily.

"Hold him," Koniev snarled. His eyes grew wider as he became used to the light. "You," he nodded his head at the woman. "Get out of bed." He looked at the old man. "Don't move a muscle."

"Don't . . ." the woman had found her voice, ". . . oh, please, God, don't hurt us . . . oh, please . . ." Her words came in a rush as she sat up on the edge of the bed, both fists clenched beneath her mouth. She was tiny, bird thin, her white hair pinned tight to her head in curls. "Oh, please don't . . ."

Her hands were shaking so badly that Koniev knew she was helpless, but her mumbling irritated him. "Be quiet," he snarled.

"My . . . my bathrobe . . ." she whispered. "I'm cold." She pointed at a worn, quilted bathrobe over a chair.

"Put it on and sit there." He turned to the man. "Now you." He gestured with the gun. "Don't let go of that dog."

"He can hardly walk either. I have to lift him off the bed. You don't have to worry about him. He really is harmless."

Koniev's mind was working rapidly as he watched the old man pull on an old flannel bathrobe. This was the right houseboat. It was pure luck but he had picked the easiest one. Now he also had to determine how he and Corinne could spend an uninterrupted period of time without neighbors becoming curious.

"How long have you lived here?" he asked.

"About a year."

"Do you have a family here?"

"Not in Victoria." The old man's shoulders were stooped and he talked in short phrases, gasping each time he spoke. "What do you want?"

"A place to stay for a day."

The woman spoke up with the tears running down her face. "You can stay here. We won't say anything. Just don't . . ."

"Be quiet," Koniev barked. "You have family elsewhere?"

"In the States. Seattle. Our son works at Boeing." He gasped for breath. "But my wife's right. Honest she is. We won't do anything."

"Who lives in the other boats? How well do you know them?"

"Mostly youngsters. I think they all work. Someone says there's a young punk up at the end who's selling drugs. We don't see much of anybody. We're too old for them." His eyes implored Koniev as he said, "Please, don't hurt us. We can't do anybody any harm."

"You don't have anything to worry about. I won't hurt you as long as you do what I say." He looked down at the dog which was again stretched out in its original position. The animal might just be a disguise for Corinne if he needed to send her after something. "Do you walk this dog?"

"Twice a day. We take it up to the park across from the parking lot above the wharf."

"Good. Now, tell me, do you have a storage place aboard here, someplace where you put all your junk?"

"Up forward, the other side of the kitchen. It's outside on the water side."

"What will the dog do when we leave this room?"

"Nothing much. Scruffy pretty much sleeps most of the time."

"Can I pat him? Will he bite me?"

"He doesn't bite. He can hardly chew anymore."

Koniev reached down gingerly and touched the dog's rump. There was no reaction. He ran his hand across the dog's head and scratched its ears. The tail flopped a couple of times but the animal did nothing more than open its eyes and let out a deep, raspy sigh of contentment.

"Let's go forward. Show me this storage area." He indicated the woman with his gun. "Both of you. I've got to be able to see both of you at all times. Come along now and I won't hurt anyone."

They passed through the door on the other side of the bedroom into the kitchen area where the old man pointed through the front window. "It's right out there. See, where that boxlike structure is on the deck. It goes down below in the hull."

"Let's go see it."

"Mister, it's raining up a storm. We're both in bad health. It's cold out there. We'll catch our death . . ."

"You'll catch your death if you don't do what I say. That's where the two of you are going to stay until I leave here."

"Oh . . ." The woman's hand went to her mouth. "You can't put him out there with lungs like his. It's so cold and damp down there. Why he'll never make it through the night. Please," she said when she saw the menacing look on Koniev's face, "at least let us put on something warm. Don't make us . . ."

"She's been awful sick, mister. She can't survive out there."

Koniev was growing impatient with this charade. It was taking too long. He didn't care to mess up the inside of the houseboat if he and Corinne were going to stay there, but he was getting so tired. He didn't expect them to survive but he didn't want to have to use the pistol if he could avoid it—the mess it would make, and the nuisance of bodies. He saw some coats draped over a chair in the dining area. "Put those on."

"But . . ." the old man began. Tears were forming at the corners of his eyes now.

"She is going to die right in front of you if you don't shut your mouth and put on those coats."

Very quietly, the old couple helped each other with the coats. She picked up a scarf and wrapped it around her husband's neck, then turned resignedly to Koniev. "I don't know if we can make it through the night out there."

"I'll let you out before I leave," Koniev promised with a growl. "Go."

They went outside into the driving wind and rain, the old couple's shoulders hunched against the storm, Koniev to one side with his gun pointed at them. The old man opened a low door at the front of the structure and hesitated, looking up at Koniev.

"Is there a light?"

The man reached down into the dark and turned on a switch. A single bulb at the bottom of a short stairway illuminated what passed for a basement on the house-boat.

"You first, down the stairs," Koniev said to him.

The old man looked over his shoulder and knew by the expression he saw that there was no choice. He put his hands out on the walls for balance as he took one step at a time. As his foot touched the sixth step, he stumbled and fell head first, hitting his head with a hollow thud on the wall at the bottom. He rolled over slowly, dazed, blood flowing down his face.

The woman stumbled down the stairs and knelt beside her husband, then turned, hugging herself, to look back up at Koniev, her eyes imploring. "Please, he'll die here," she whimpered.

Koniev raised the gun slowly until it was leveled on her forehead.

She closed her eyes, anticipating the bullet.

"Open your eyes," Koniev snarled.

Very slowly, eyelids fluttering, she opened them. She was still hugging herself and her jaw trembled.

"I'm going to turn out the light and lock the door. If I hear so much as a sound from here, I'll come down and kill you both. If you're quiet, someone will let you out after we're gone. I'll leave a note. It's your only chance. Do you understand?"

The woman inclined her head slightly as tears rolled down her cheeks. Then she reached down and cradled the old man's head to her chest.

Nicholas Koniev was satisfied as he turned out the light and latched the door to the storage area. The howl of the wind would carry away any sound as long as the storm lasted. He went to the gangway leading ashore and looked up and down the pier. Nothing moved. Not a soul.

He went back into the kitchen and turned out the light there. As he was passing back through the bedroom, he bent

over and scratched the dog's ears before he turned out that
light. Then he exited through the back door, off to fetch
Corinne.

Oh, my, how warm and soft she would be. She would like
the cozy little houseboat, too. It was absolutely perfect for
their needs.

Nineteen

No MATTER HOW MUCH LOWER BERNIE RYNG YANKED THE BILL of his baseball cap down over his eyes, it didn't help. He'd grown wetter and colder with each hour before *Voyager* came into Victoria Harbor, but at least there was some protection beneath the pilot house roof on the small craft. Now, as he walked down the pier at Fisherman's Wharf, there was no windshield. The wind came from every direction, sweeping the cold rain into his eyes no matter which way he turned his head. It couldn't have been a more miserable night.

The only light for the piers came from the head of the wharf and there was little he could make out other than the endless nests of fishing boats. There was no way he was going to locate a strange vessel until daylight came, but he was almost sure after circling the inner harbor that this was the most logical place for Koniev to disappear.

There wasn't another human being on the piers that night nor was there any reason there should have been. Ryng turned down the wharf toward a lighted sign that identified a fish and chips place. It reminded him that he'd had nothing to eat except for some stale sandwiches the pilot of a helicopter had tossed down to him earlier that day.

It wasn't easy to just say the hell with it for another four or five hours. In that time, Koniev could have arranged his escape. He might have made a call to his consulate and coordinated some sort of assistance, a pickup right here in Victoria maybe, or perhaps something out on the Strait. Hell, if they had one submarine out there, they could have half a dozen. Or who knew how many contacts were right here in the city, people who could spirit him underground until arrangements could be made to smuggle him back home with whatever he had obtained at the Trident base?

Ryng was paying little attention when his eye caught something moving ahead. He stopped and ducked back into the shadows, sure that he saw a figure dart up one of the piers. He waited silently, straining to see through the wind-driven rain. It came into his face in blinding sheets with each gust, shimmering in the dim light, almost creating its own shadow—was that it? Had he imagined a person moving when actually it was wind-blown rain playing tricks on tired eyes? He gave it more time. When nothing moved, he crept forward, keeping himself invisible, waiting for someone to give themselves away.

But there was nothing. It was just his imagination. Or could it have been an extra large wharf rat? He moved on down the pier.

Nicholas Koniev had just then decided that breathing was inherently dangerous, a habit that would make him a dead man. He was so tired, so happy to be going back to pick up Corinne, looking forward so much to climbing in that big double bed with her. No more hard deck on a fishing boat with an audience for them. No, this would be the real thing . . .

Then—there he was! Someone coming down the wharf directly toward him.

Up until that moment, Koniev had been extremely careful to conceal himself—*but this was just plain careless*. Here he was with the object of his mission in a sealed plastic bag on his person, and he wasn't paying attention to the possibility that someone else might be on the pier on a night like this. *Carelessness!*

He hurled himself into the darkness of the pier to his right. Landing on all fours, he crept away, careful to keep the boat at the head of the pier between him and that other person. But if he'd been seen, he must stop and hide. Someone looking for him would be alert to movement, even in the dark. If they were really good, all that would be necessary to identify his position would be a single motion.

There were some empty barrels of diesel fuel by one of the boats and Koniev slid behind them and held his breath. He continued to hold his breath. His chest ached and his heart was pounding furiously, but he was afraid that he might make too much noise if he exhaled and gasped for breath again. So, true to his Spetznaz training, knowing that he could do what he had never done before, he held his breath even longer and peered around the barrels.

There was movement down there . . . on the wharf! Someone was in the shadows looking toward him, curious, but far enough away for Koniev to breathe. He concentrated on letting his breath out in short gasps until he was sure there would be no noise. It didn't matter that the wind would carry the sound away as long as he thought it might possibly attract attention. It would be insane to be caught after everything he'd gone through. Then he sucked in the much-needed oxygen.

He looked out again and saw the person move on down the wharf. If he'd been seen, Koniev was sure that the other person decided it was only his imagination. No one would be crazy enough to be out on a night like this. But he would stay away from the head of the pier.

He began crawling across the nests of fishing boats toward Corinne. When they went back to the houseboat, this was the way they would have to do it. It would take more time but there was no sense in giving it all up just to climb into that bed a few moments sooner.

And he wouldn't be so careless again—*no, not careless, just plain stupid!*

* * *

Ryng knew he'd have to get some sleep after he talked with Harry Coffin again. He should have been more alert when he caught that movement in the shadows. Had he been dreaming when that rat took off up the pier? Or was it Koniev? Could he have turned himself into a wharf rat. He seemed able to accomplish whatever he wanted. Sleep—that's what he needed. A few hours, that would be sufficient.

There was a pay phone outside Barb's Place, the fish and chips stand, and that reminded him exactly of what he should have asked Coffin earlier. If Bernie Ryng could pick up that phone now and place a call to Coffin at the Trident base, why couldn't Koniev call anyone he wanted? There had to be someone who would help him if he just dialed their number. Hell, the man could call information for almost any number.

"Admiral, I know a lot of people are going to hate you for waking them up at this time of night, but we need a tracer on all public phones anywhere near Fisherman's Wharf. If Koniev hasn't already dialed his way out of here, he just may try it soon. We need to know every call from this area and which phone it's made from." Why the hell hadn't he thought about this sooner?

Admiral Coffin had already received permission from Canadian Forces for the remaining SEALs to arrive after first light to set up a barrier patrol with the Canadian Coast Guard just outside the harbor. Every human being on every departing boat would be identified. If Koniev was supposed to meet another submarine out there, he'd have to run a gauntlet to get there.

Ryng went back to *Voyager* to sleep for three hours. He'd be up before dawn again.

Koniev's first sensation as he awoke was that someone had hold of his right arm. The grip was so tight that the limb was numb. *The man in the shadows!*

He rolled instinctively to his left wondering if a bullet would find its mark in his back. The grip on his arm released as he grabbed for the gun on the side table, all in the same motion. Landing on the floor with his back against the wall,

327

he grasped the Glock in both hands and aimed into the dim light.

"No . . . don't!" Corinne shrilled. "It's me . . . me . . ."

Koniev shut his eyes and let the gun sag in his hands. "It's alright. It's alright," he repeated softly. "I . . . I . . ." He remembered now. They'd dozed off with her head resting on his arm.

Corinne snapped on the light on her side and came up on her hands and knees to stare at him curiously, her eyes wide, as he sat on the floor. "You thought I was going to kill you," she exclaimed.

He looked down at the pistol, then back up at her. She was naked, just as she'd been since they'd taken an extra few minutes to make the bed with fresh sheets they'd found in the bureau on the other side of the bedroom. Her hair was rumpled now and there were sheet creases on one side of her face, but she looked absolutely lovely—and he might have killed her right then! "I don't know what to say. It's not enough to say I'm sorry, is it?" This was the second time he'd been about to squeeze the trigger on her.

She straightened up, sitting back on her feet, and pointed at him with a giggle. "Do you know how funny you look? Really. Look. Look where that gun's pointed."

He was as naked as Corinne, sitting on the floor with his back against the wall, knees drawn up. His arms rested on his knees and the gun dangled limply from his right hand. The barrel, elongated by the silencer, was pointed directly at his crotch. He looked up to her smiling face and grinned back.

"Don't shoot," she murmured. "We're not finished yet, at least I hope not." She reached out her hand. "Come on. No, wait a minute. I'll fix the bed." She hopped out and pulled back the blankets, smoothing the sheets before she fluffed the pillows. "There we are, all ready to make a wonderful mess again."

Koniev climbed back in bed and kissed her gently before pulling the covers halfway down. He stared at her for a short time before saying, "I am sorry. I really am." He had no idea why he was speaking in this manner. It was just something he wanted to say. "I'll try not to do that again. Leave the light on and I'll show you how I want to apologize." Even before he'd finished the sentence, he knew that he wanted her to understand the real Nicholas Koniev —if he could find the real one himself.

When he awoke again, it was to the roar of an aircraft engine that sounded as if it were directly outside the bedroom. His eyes snapped open and moved about the room while his body remained rigid. Were his senses betraying him? They were supposed to be in a houseboat in Victoria Harbor, but where were they? That plane?

He turned his head. Corinne's long, brown hair was spread across the pillow. She was here. But . . .

The engine revved even louder as if it would come right into the room. He remembered the previous night, the wind, the rain. No aircraft would be flying. But this was getting closer . . . or was it just louder?

He climbed out of bed and went over to the single window, gun in hand. Very cautiously, he pulled back the curtain. It was still raining out, but not as heavily, and the wind had apparently died because the water was smooth enough to see the raindrops. The day had become light enough to show that the clouds were also higher. The end of the storm. But what time?

Koniev noticed a clock on the bureau. Almost six-thirty already! He was sure he would have been awake before six, but then he remembered Corinne and how much they'd made love. *And you thought you were exhausted before then, old man. They certainly don't make them like her in the Soviet Union.* He briefly wished he could take her back with him, but that wasn't part of his mission. Complete that before you start worrying about the woman, he told himself. But, perhaps . . .

Then the aircraft engine noise increased to a howl. What the hell? He pushed open the bedroom door cautiously and stepped into the kitchen where everything seemed to be shaking. Looking out the window, he saw no more than a couple hundred meters away, a seaplane—AIR B.C. was on the fuselage—kicking up a great cloud of spray as it picked up speed to take off. He watched until it disappeared from view then went back into the bedroom.

Corinne was up on one elbow, her eyes wide with surprise. "What the hell was that?"

"A wake-up call courtesy of the local airline—seaplane. I thought we were under attack. Looks like it frightened you, too."

"Especially when I reached across the bed and you were gone."

"That you don't have to worry about. I'm one person who can't go wandering off. You can be sure of that. From now on, you are going to be my eyes and ears, even my voice." He put the gun down on the bureau.

Corinne stretched like a cat and grinned when she saw him watching her appreciatively. "One more?"

He began a count on his fingers before smiling. "Not now. There's a shower in the toilet and I'm going to clean up and put on my last change of clothes. And," he said, heading for the bathroom, "you're not going to laugh at my shorts this time."

When they were putting fresh sheets on the bed hours before, Corinne had suddenly straightened up and asked, "Whose boat is this? Did you . . ."

"It belongs to an old couple. That's their dog," he answered, pointing at the animal stretched out in the corner. "I thought it would be a good disguise for us."

"What happened to them?" she asked, her eyes still on the dog.

"They're down below, locked up for safekeeping. But I assure you I gave them food and blankets and told them they'd be let out when we no longer needed their boat. Believe me, they're just fine—a little scared maybe, but just fine," he added.

Koniev didn't leave the bedroom until Corinne had pulled all the curtains in both the kitchen and the living area. There didn't appear to be anyone on the pier at that

hour, but he couldn't afford to have his face seen. With the
BEWARE OF THE DOG sign on the gangway for helpless old
Scruffy, he assumed the couple didn't have too many friends
and probably didn't want any. Still, Corinne would be the
only one he wanted people to see. If anyone asked, the old
folks had gone off to visit their son who worked at the
aircraft factory in Seattle because he'd had an accident.
She was a niece who was taking care of the houseboat and
walking Scruffy. That way, she could buy food and make the
necessary phone calls because there was no phone on the
boat.

After Corinne had showered, Koniev said, "There's a
phone out near the center of the wharf, near that food place.
That's why I kept the dog, so you'd have an excuse to go out
occasionally. I want you to call the Soviet Consulate in
Vancouver now, before we eat. When the phone is answered,
you say exactly—'I would like to speak to the Chief Political
Officer.' It is my understanding from past experience that
will bring the intelligence specialist who understands my
message to the phone. Then you will tell that person
exactly—'your man is ready to be transferred tomorrow.'
He should know who I am without question since he's
supposed to have limited information concerning me."

"I wasn't aware there were people other than my handlers
who knew about you."

Koniev nodded knowingly. "With something like this,
intelligence is limited as much as possible. So, when one
person is working on a particular element of a mission, he
may not necessarily know if another is also, nor does he
need to know. It's safer that way, for everyone involved. Of
course, your phone call should create some interesting
discussion in the consulate since your own people decided
things were too hot for them. I don't expect you'll need to
say anymore. It ought to be enough to activate an immediate
message to Moscow. They'll approve a plan to get me out of
this country. The person on the phone will tell you when to
call back. That's when we can tell them how long it will take
you to get me to Vancouver, or whatever place they can

arrange a turnover." He stopped for a moment and looked thoughtful. "You can also get me one of those oyster burgers you told me about."

"You don't forget anything, do you?" Corinne said with a grin. "I think I mentioned that place to you exactly once."

"But it sounded so good that I think I should have one before we—I—leave this country."

She looked back at him warily, the smile gone from her face. "That's right, isn't it? We may not even have one more night together." She moved over behind Koniev and kneaded his neck and shoulders softly. "I'm not looking forward to that."

He looked up at her. "Nor am I. I don't know what can be done about that in the future, maybe something." He didn't want to leave this one. She was special, nothing like the others, not even the admiral's woman. "But we can make up for it this morning after you make that call. Making love is as much fun in the morning as any other time." He slapped her on the rump. "Now, go do the call. The dog needs a walk before he shits on the floor. I'll find some things in the kitchen for breakfast."

Ryng woke up with a jolt to the crackle of Harry Coffin's voice on *Voyager*'s radio. Not wanting to get too comfortable, he'd simply wrapped himself in a blanket and stretched out on the bunk in the cabin. But he was more exhausted than he'd realized and it had been like a waterbed. It was full daylight out when he opened his eyes. He pulled back his sleeve and looked at his watch. *Almost seven-thirty!* Almost five hours, two more than he'd planned.

"God damn it all, Bernie, I know you're there. Wake up call. Wake up call. Get your ass in gear." Coffin's voice grated loudly over the speaker.

Ryng's mouth was dry and his voice sounded deep and furry when he answered. "Overslept. My fault. Go ahead."

"Bingo on your phone call, Bernie. Koniev is very much alive. It was made by a woman with a slight British accent about ten minutes ago. The Soviet Consulate in Vancouver.

Some sort of cryptic message." Coffin repeated the words handwritten on the sheet of paper in front of him.

"So he definitely has someone with him—a woman. Where was it made from?"

"Your backyard there, I think. A pay phone beside a restaurant of some kind named Barb's Place."

Ryng banged the heel of his hand against his forehead. "I'll bet it was him last night. Oh shit, oh shit, oh shit," he repeated to himself and over the radio.

"Koniev?" Coffin asked.

"Could have been. Maybe it was just a wharf rat. I'll probably never know. I was so beat to shit, I decided I was just imagining things." He sucked in a deep breath. "OK. Time to get on with it. The Canadian Forces are ashore and out of sight. My boys—they're off the harbor now?"

"Len Todd's on the surface with the Canadian Coast Guard. The others are taking turns down under with the dolphins. Harbor's sealed, Bernie. A maverick dolphin couldn't get through without giving name, rank and serial number."

"And all I've got to do is find Nicholas Koniev. His boat's got to be around these piers somewhere. And now we're sure there's two of them. Maybe if I'm lucky . . ." His voice drifted off.

"You can have as many of the Canadian troops as you need," Coffin said.

"Not yet. Maybe I can get him without anyone else getting killed." He told Coffin that he would carry a portable radio with him and gave the circuit the Canadians should monitor in case he got himself in trouble. Then he climbed out on *Voyager*'s stern and considered the sea of masts around the piers. There were hundreds of them. Where to start?

He located a sport fisherman two hours later nestled among commercial boats. He might have overlooked it if some of the locals hadn't been looking it over when he happened by. The name on the stern had been painted out. They were also wondering where one of the crew of another boat astern of it had gone to. He was a drunk who never left his boat. It was his home. Ryng searched the mystery boat and found exactly nothing that would indicate Koniev and a woman had arrived on it. The boat had been stripped of anything that might identify the owners. If it was Koniev, he was smart enough to have abandoned it. He never stayed with anything long enough to be caught. Just the fact that there wasn't a trace of the people stunk of Koniev.

But if it was, he also shouldn't have gone far this time—not if he was aware of the Canadian Forces ashore—and now Ryng knew he definitely had a woman helping him.

Koniev was resting easily on top of Corinne, smoothing mussed hair behind her ears.

"You know, most gentlemen roll off when they're finished," she teased.

"Perhaps I may not be finished," he mused. "And perhaps I am not a gentleman."

"Most men aren't like you either," she teased, anticipating him.

"I am like no man," he stated evenly, searching her eyes to be sure she understood. The others had always forgotten that too soon.

"I've come to appreciate that recently." She surprised him with a playful nip on the nose. "And I'd like this to go on, but since you're unlike any other man you also have to keep moving. I do have a responsibility to you even though nothing was planned this way. We are what I would call fortunate victims of fate. Besides, the people who were supposed to help you, the ones who sent me to the island, sort of threw you to the dogs. You've got nothing left but me."

He rolled onto his side. "You're correct," he agreed. "I have lost everything, my ship, my men"—he shrugged casually—"but they were all expendable anyway as long as the mission was successful. I still have what I came for. But I have to give up one thing I never anticipated," he sighed with finality, "and that is you. Would you come with me if you could?—I mean if they don't kill us first," he added casually.

"Of course—if they don't kill us first," Corinne answered softly.

"Then it's settled. If we die, we die together. If we survive, I will try to arrange it after I am home. Do you believe me—that I really will, I mean?"

"I want to."

"Then plan to. Somehow . . ." His voice drifted off as he considered her earlier comments when she'd returned from making the phone call. She had explained how Scruffy pulled hard enough on his leash after she left the phone booth that she let him take her to the street on the other side of the parking lot. The dog seemed to know where he wanted to go and she let him waddle along until he found a lawn to do his duty. While she waited, she noticed a car parked down the street with two men inside who appeared to be wearing identical clothes. So Scruffy had to follow Corinne as she walked him past the vehicle. One of the men inside was speaking into a small, hand-held radio. Their open-necked shirts and pants were identical, not military uniforms but definitely not normal Victorian wear. In the back seat, she noted two black berets and what she later assumed were military flak vests. It struck her so oddly that she continued on for a few more blocks and passed another vehicle, also apparently civilian, but with similarly dressed occupants. She hurried back to the houseboat as quickly as Scruffy would move.

"Why don't we look at the map," Corinne suggested as they lay on the bed. "We don't have to dress to do that."

"No," Koniev answered seriously, "we don't. But I think you are right and for once I may not be serious enough. I want to spend the entire day in bed with you, but I don't think well next to naked women. It would be better to stop now so there may be many more days in the future to do this."

After dressing, Koniev laid out the map on the coffee table in the living room. He was indeed concerned by the apparent military presence she'd seen. He'd survived over the years because he'd reacted instantly to the slightest indication of trouble. It was decided they should leave shortly after she completed the noon phone contact. He would remain in the houseboat until then.

Corinne would rent a car in Victoria. No one knew her. No one knew she was with him. When she brought it back to the parking lot, he would be ready. It was a matter of some rumpled clothes as a starter. He would use the old man's cane and hat and hobble down the pier with Scruffy on the leash. No one would ever suspect. Never make anything more complex than necessary. They would drive north on the island to the village of Departure Bay, no more than a hundred kilometers, and leave the car. The next ferry to Vancouver would bring them to safety.

"I've been noticing someone," Corinne said. "There's a crack there." She pointed at a window. "Where the curtain doesn't quite cover. He's been going to each of the houseboats near the head of the pier. I don't think anyone would be trying to sell something door to door around here. I wonder . . ."

Koniev was at the window in an instant. He watched the person Corinne had pointed out carefully. The man went to another houseboat, talked to someone for a moment, looked up the pier in their direction toward the remaining houseboats, then headed back to the main wharf to look up and down before he came back again. Koniev studied the way the man carried himself, the manner in which he walked, the careful way he studied his surroundings, the constantly moving eyes, and in moments he was sure this was no salesman. He was watching a dangerous man.

"Corinne, you go outside with the dog. Don't let that man come aboard. Talk to him out there if he wants to ask about here. Tell him the same thing you would tell the others—that you are taking care of the dog and the boat while these people are away. The Americans have no idea I am with you. They won't ever suspect."

Corinne forced Scruffy to waddle out onto the deck. There she checked lines, swept the remains of the night's rain away, and looked busy until the man appeared near the gangway. He had a clipboard in his hand.

"Good morning," he said cheerily. "I'm from the human

services office, taking a poll of the residents out here." He pointed at Scruffy. "Is that the dangerous dog?"

"Sure is," she responded, eyeing him curiously. Government employees in British Columbia normally wore ties. This one was dressed like anything but a bureaucrat. She never heard one speak before with an American accent either. And he was built like an athlete, thick neck, expressionless eyes like Koniev's usually were. She didn't like him.

"I have some questions the city needs to know about the residents on the houseboats. May I come aboard?"

She shook her head. "Scruffy's too dangerous." The dog flopped down on the deck with a thud and a whimper. "I'll come across to the pier."

Ryng nodded. "I take it you don't like visitors." As he spoke, his eyes roved over the houseboat's exterior. "Or does Scruffy kill on command?"

"It's not my boat. It's my uncle's. I don't think I can help you. I'm just here to take care of the dog and watch the place. He and my aunt went down to Seattle to see their son in the hospital."

"I see. Well, I guess you can answer some questions for them. Do you mind?" he asked as she stood at the end of the gangplank.

"I'll try." She stepped down onto the pier still blocking his way. Corinne had been with Koniev less than two full days, but she understood him because she understood men. She specialized in them. Her handlers used her to learn what they might never learn about other men, and they used her to sway men's minds. They were convinced there was no one better than Corinne and she had no doubt about it. She had never disappointed them.

There had been enough men that she knew instantly when they were lying, when other men would have trusted them implicitly. She could also pick out the few really dangerous ones like Nicholas Koniev, even when they assumed a gentle mien. This one was like Nicholas. It was in his face, in the manner he spoke, but mostly in those cold, blue eyes.

Ryng asked a few innocuous questions and her responses were equally harmless. He wandered the length of the houseboat as he talked and she followed him, her arms folded in boredom as she mumbled her answers.

"You're not Canadian," he said, turning toward her.

"I most certainly am."

"But your accent's British."

"I thought that was mostly gone." She placed her hands on her hips. "Listen, I'm a Canadian citizen now and I live in Vancouver. What does that have to do with your questions?"

"Nothing," he answered, smiling. He was willing to bet that if they had time, Coffin's recording of the woman with the British accent who called Vancouver would match this one. "I just like to pick up accents. Not part of my job, of course, but you can imagine how boring this gets—asking dumb questions I mean."

This was no government servant. He was probing, looking for something. "I was writing a letter before you came," she said. "I don't think there's anything I can help you with. Why don't you come back when my uncle's here?" She strode back to the gangplank and crossed over to the houseboat. Scruffy rose unsteadily and wobbled over to the door.

"Look out for the dog," Ryng called out. "Looks like he could go wild any minute now." He smiled broadly.

Corinne found it hard to smile back. The man's eyes had never been part of that smile for they were again going over every inch of the houseboat. She said nothing as she held the door long enough for Scruffy to make it inside.

Koniev was sitting on the edge of the bed when she came in. "I saw him. What did he say he was?"

"Government. Some phony story about human services."

He shook his head and stared back at Corinne, surprised at the hardness in her face.

"I hate to ruin our party but there's not going to be any phone call back to Vancouver at noon. No oyster burgers either. No car. It would be too late by then. There's something about him I could smell." Corinne bit her lower lip. *Lady, now that you've made your bed, you have to sleep in it. You have something here you'd be insane to give up.*

338

*This is your choice and you'd better take good care of him.
Now you've got to get him out of here because that asshole is
going to come back and spoil everything.* "He'll be back. It's
just a matter of how soon. We're leaving on one of those
fishing boats as soon as possible."

"You really are special, aren't you?" He stood up and
placed his hands on her shoulders. "You really are." Then
he pulled her close and stroked her long hair as she rested
her head on his shoulder.

Corinne finally pulled back, looked down at her feet, then
back up to his face. She remembered that it wasn't the face
she had imagined back on the island when she created her
fantasy man, her brave, dashing submariner. Instead she
saw the features of a very dangerous man who was now
smiling pleasantly at her and she liked it. Even his eyes were
smiling. "Maybe we're special," she murmured as she
reached up and put her arms around his neck.

"Yes," he whispered in her ear, "we're both special." He
squeezed her tightly. "And, yes, you are right. We'll leave on
one of those fishing boats." He pulled back and looked down
at her. "I promise I will do everything to make sure you stay
with me. Perhaps if we stay together, we'll survive."

Twenty

CORINNE SAUNTERED CASUALLY DOWN THE PIER AS IF SHE hadn't a care in the world. Scruffy followed painfully alongside. Corinne was the deceiver in Koniev's hurried plan. Since neither one of them had any doubt that the man with the cold blue eyes would be back, their intention was to create uncertainty, challenge his suspicions, cause enough confusion in his mind to purchase whatever extra time was possible.

"Deception is most often preferable to a gun at this stage," Koniev had told her. "When bullets start to fly, there are no further choices. You are either dead or alive when they stop. If you can deceive the other party, you have purchased time before guns become the final choice. Always attempt to avoid that finality. And when there is no alternative, you should have purchased the time to be in the best position, to have the first shot."

It was her responsibility to create confusion. Scruffy was her disguise. A tired, old dog out for a constitutional was anything but a sign of fear or concern. Scruffy's stamina allowed about twenty yards between sniffs. It could be a discarded container from Barb's place, an empty beer can, or an oily rag—whatever, it allowed Scruffy a moment of relaxation before Corinne pulled gently on the leash. It was a delightful temptation to surprise the dog with a good solid yank, but she constantly reminded herself that a caring niece would never treat the animal that way. Too many people on the pier were more than likely on a first name basis with Scruffy.

Barb's Place was entertaining a growing late morning coffee crowd as sun filtered through thinning clouds to warm the air and shrink the puddles. The phone booth was occupied. Corinne waited outside looking casually for the American who had asked all the questions while Scruffy rolled over on his back for a tummy scratch from passing friends. A few asked about the old couple and found no problem with their having gone down to Seattle. Almost all of them knew there was a son there, and they were happy to see Scruffy so well taken care of.

Corinne went up to the grassy areas around the parking lot, just as Koniev had asked, to see if there were any additional signs of the Canadian military. They remained inconspicuous, noticeable only by a trained eye. The dog was tiring again, sitting down every time she stopped. When she returned to the phone booth someone else was using it. Corinne wrapped the leash around a post and Scruffy promptly lay down, contented to be off his feet, while she paced.

Very gingerly, Koniev lowered himself near the rowboat tied to a ladder just ahead of the houseboat. The boat was full of rain water and in danger of sinking if he placed a foot in it. He held on to the ladder with one hand while reaching out with the other to paddle a floating tin can over in his direction. It also contained water and almost sank out of reach before he was able to grasp it. Everything he had done since Corinne talked to the American seemed to him to be in slow motion. Yet time wasn't slowing down—it just seemed as if he could do nothing rapidly.

He bailed as quickly as a one-armed man could, wishing the can were bigger, wishing there had been less rain the night before, knowing there was nothing that wishing would bring to him. There was a vague suspicion in the back of his mind that maybe he was wasting his time bailing. The oars had been left in the boat and people usually were careless like that when they were sure no one would steal it. Would it serve his purpose before it sank?

As soon as he felt he could safely row away, he climbed in, set the oars in the locks, and pulled toward the end of the pier. The American could come back at any time and there would be Nicholas Koniev sitting in a half-swamped row boat waiting to be shot like a duck. But the far end of the pier meant safety. If the houseboat was found empty, or even if just Corinne was there, the American would have nothing to go on. *Safety . . . sanity . . . call it what you will . . . just get your ass around the end of that pier!*

When he was finally able to give one last, hard pull on the left hand oar and their houseboat disappeared from sight, he felt he'd slipped behind a wall. Now he could relax, think, select his means of escape. He sensed his muscles loosening, then his nerves, his stomach, even his mind seemed lighter. He was reasoning again.

Some of the nests of boats were now almost empty. The ending of the storm allowed them to head out and once again earn a living. It was of no great concern to the fishermen what time they left because they would stay out until their holds were full anyway. But there were still enough tied up that Koniev was sure he would be able to find at least one almost ready to get underway with full tanks. His luck would hold—he would find a good one.

There was a dragger at the next pier, smaller than some of the others, and its engine was already running. The name *Sangria* was painted on the stern in wine-red letters. Koniev could see only two men aboard, one checking the equipment on the stern, the other taking in the lines securing it to the inboard boat. It was just about right. No more than two people needed to operate it.

"Good morning," he called out to the man in the stern. "Getting ready to fish?"

"Looks like it, doesn't it?" The man never looked up.

"I sure am bored these days since I lost my own boat,"

Koniev persisted. "Need an extra man?" He glanced about in every direction. Not a soul in sight on the closest boats.

"Two of us have been able to handle everything up to now." The fisherman looked down at him for the first time. "Don't recognize you either."

"I'll tell you what. I'll work for free if I can join you." Koniev's eyes again took in every boat in sight. No one was paying attention to them.

"The two of us share the profits, mister. There's not enough for three people in a boat this size." He finished what he was doing and came over to the stern rail. "I'm going to back down now so you better get that piece of shit you're paddling out of the way. I don't like to run people down."

"Place both hands on the railing where I can see them." The barrel of Koniev's gun was pointed directly at the man's chest. "That is a silencer you see on the end of this gun and your friend handling the lines won't even hear it if I kill you right now. Do you understand me?"

The man nodded, his mouth half-open, eyes wide with shock. His knuckles whitened perceptibly as he squeezed the railing with all his strength.

"If you move, you're dead. If you speak to your friend before I tell you to, you're dead."

Another nod.

"I'm coming aboard now. I will have to stick this in my belt for just a second, but I assure you I can grab it and kill you if you try to move. Now back away from the rail. Don't even turn your head."

With two quick thrusts on the oars, Koniev was beside the fishing boat's stern. He rose to his feet easily with one hand touching the hull for balance and reached up for the railing. Then, like a cat, he hauled himself up and was over the edge. His feet hit the deck at the same time his right hand covered the grip on the gun though he didn't remove it from his belt.

"Call your friend over here."

"Mario, come here." The fisherman's voice was barely a squeak. He cleared his throat and called again, "Mario," and waved his hand when the other man turned around.

Mario sauntered across the deck wiping his damp hands.

"What is your name?" Koniev snapped at the first fisherman.

"Paul."

"Mario," Koniev said as the other stopped suspiciously a few meters away, "Paul has agreed that I am going to join you today."

"What do you think . . . ?" Mario began, raising both hands in question.

"Mario. Please listen to me," Koniev said evenly. "Look in my hand."

Mario's eyes seemed to fill his face.

"That's right. I explained to Paul that this is a silencer and you will both be dead in an instant without anyone around hearing it if you don't do exactly what I say. Is that clear to both of you?"

They nodded.

"Now, Mario, I want you to take in that last line because we're leaving here. Who usually takes the boat out, Paul?"

"Either of us can."

"Paul, you will back out of here and go over to the pier where the houseboats are tied. We will pick up someone else."

"The water is very shallow there . . ."

"If you go aground, you will die. Do you understand?"

Paul nodded solemnly. "We shouldn't go past the end of the pier."

"Mario," Koniev ordered, "you will secure us with a line to the end of the pier until the other person comes. My gun will remain in my belt so that other people can't see it. But one word from either of you, one move that bothers me, and you will die. I am desperate enough that killing others means nothing to me. Now, do you want to live?"

Both men nodded again.

"Then do what I have told you."

The rattle of the phone booth door startled Corinne. She turned around and stepped toward the phone booth only to see someone step in. "Oh, please, I've been waiting to get in there for so long." She glanced at her watch. God, she'd told Koniev she'd be back by now. "It's very important. Please."

The man moved out of the booth, looked her up and down curiously, then stepped back with a wave of his hand.

"Thanks," she murmured, stepping inside.

Very carefully shielding the phone, she dialed the consulate number in Vancouver and deposited her change. As soon as the switchboard answered, she prefaced her request with the word "emergency," then followed the same process as before, meaning that this time she must talk instantly with the other party.

"Yes," came a voice just as urgent as her own.

"He cannot do what I told you earlier—the Americans. We are going to be on a boat. There is no choice."

"Wait."

She could hear muffled voices in the background.

"He must head west up Juan de Fuca . . ." The words seemed to come in gasps. ". . . as fast as he can . . . look for a helicopter . . . just maybe it's possible . . . just maybe . . ." the voice repeated more softly. Then, "Tell him we will try . . . there is a chance . . . tell him he'll know what he must do . . . do you understand?" The voice broke off.

"Yes." Corinne hung up and stepped out of the booth clenching her lower lip between her teeth.

"Well, hello there." Bernie Ryng was kneeling and scratching Scruffy's ears. "The dog attacked me." He was grinning up at her but his blue eyes appeared paler and more expressionless than before.

Corinne said nothing as she unwrapped the leash from the post.

"Calling your uncle?" Ryng asked, rising to his feet.

"A friend, for dinner. I told her how boring it was on that houseboat with just an old dog. She said she'd come over tonight." Corinne pulled on the leash. "Come on, Scruff."

The dog looked up at her mournfully and slowly rose to a sitting position. She yanked on the leash twice more before the dog stood up.

"I think Scruff's had too much exercise," Ryng said. That

accent of hers. It certainly wasn't cockney or anything that would ring a bell, but it was British enough to say she hadn't been in Canada forever.

"Then he can sleep all afternoon." She headed in the direction of the houseboat, pulling the reluctant dog.

Until she turned the corner and walked up the pier toward the houseboat, she was sure the American's eyes were on her. It was tempting, so very tempting, to look over her shoulder to see if she was correct, but that was stupid. No need to encourage him. He'd asked questions, she'd indicated she was alone and bored. Was he fooled? Not for long she was sure.

Scruffy was wearing down again, stopping at every possible item on the pier to sniff. Pulling on the leash did no good. She glanced at her watch again. Damn, she had to get back. Exasperated, she yanked hard on the leash. The dog fell over. Then she bent down and hauled the dog upright, setting it roughly back on its feet. The unsteady animal looked warily at her.

When she stood up, she noticed a fishing boat with its bow against the far end of the pier. It seemed so odd there . . . what was it doing? . . . until she saw a figure waving at her—*Nicholas!* He had a boat. She began to walk faster until she felt a sharp tug on the leash. Scruffy had fallen over his own feet.

Corinne leaned down and picked up the dog, heading down the pier as quickly as she could without running. There was no one about, but she didn't want to attract attention, and she couldn't let that American notice. She wanted to look back, hoped that the American wasn't still watching, but knew Nicholas would handle everything if it became necessary.

He waited for you, lady. Oh, God, he waited for you. He could have gone off and there would have been nothing you could have done about it. And if the American had questioned you afterward, there would have been nothing you could tell him about what Nicholas was going to do. But he came back . . . he came back for you!

Koniev watched her progress down the pier, sharing her frustration each time the dog stopped. He waved twice but each time she had turned to encourage the dog to move. She saw him the third time, and he actually laughed out loud when she picked the dog up in her arms.

Doesn't my Corinne look beautiful, even with that stupid dog. What is there about that woman that you waited for her? Minutes, even seconds, may be the difference between life and death. You've never let anyone slow you down before and now, when your ass is almost in the American's hands, you take extra time to come back for a woman, a woman who seems to have made you forget your mission.

Paul and Mario watched the woman climb over the railing. Even when the man with the gun had been waving to her, his eyes rarely left their own. There was never more than a second or two that they might have done something before they knew he was again watching them.

"Time to go. Back down and head out into the channel."

"Where are we going?" Mario asked.

"Quiet," Koniev ordered. He had Corinne's hand in his own. "Did your call go through?"

"The response was very strange," she answered, bending down to put the dog on the deck. "Go west up Juan de Fuca . . . toward the ocean, I guess. He said something about a helicopter. That was it, except that you'd know what to do."

"No, I don't know what they mean. I can't believe one of our own . . . no, not a chance . . ." Then his eyes brightened. "But maybe from a ship. Maybe we have a ship with a helicopter out there. No, that's crazy . . . they wouldn't . . . not in foreign territory . . . but maybe a freighter . . ."

"The man on the phone just said they'd try and you'd know what to do." She spread her hands. "That's all. But it's worth a try."

Sangria had backed away from the pier and was now heading out toward the channel. "I shouldn't be out here," Koniev said. "I'll tell you what we're going to do now," he said in a louder voice for Paul and Mario. "I'm going down

347

into the cabin so no one can see me, but the door will be left open. I'll be watching both of you. Mario, you do whatever you normally do when you're going out, but remember to stay in my sight at all times or I'll come out of that cabin and kill you the first time you disappear from view. Anything you do, you ask me. Understood?"

Both men nodded.

"The lady will stay out here with you, so she can call me if she's unhappy about anything. If today is the day I'm scheduled to die, I promise you will go before me. But if you do everything you're told, you'll both be able to laugh about this over a beer someday. Would that be better than being dead?"

Paul and Mario agreed that was a better choice.

Sangria moved into the channel, passed the Coast Guard piers, and turned out toward the Strait of Juan de Fuca. Paul held onto the wheel as if he would fall off a cliff if he let go. Mario acted like he was checking the nets even though his hands shook so much he was barely able to scratch his ear. Corinne sat in a chair that Koniev had handed out from the cabin and enjoyed the sun while Scruffy fell asleep in her lap. It was a scene of tranquillity.

Bernie Ryng sipped thoughtfully at a cup of coffee outside Barb's Place, his eyes roaming the piers. Everything about that woman was plausible, the uncle and aunt, the dog, her story, but that British accent . . .

The coffee was half-gone when he decided to go back to *Voyager*. Maybe when he was plunked down in the midst of those boats an answer would miraculously come to him. Yet once he was there, he was upset with himself. His earlier misgivings about the woman had diminished to a weak hunch, but now returned as a full-blown suspicion. She was good at what she'd done—putting him on the defensive. And it had worked. It might have continued to work under other circumstances. But this situation was different. Nicholas Koniev possessed something so vital to US interests that Ryng had decided to jump in feet first. If he was wrong about the woman, about the houseboat, then he and the US were going to owe someone a heavy apology, but he had to be sure.

He used the portable radio to explain to the Canadian Forces what he was going to do and asked for backup just off the pier. Time was too short to wait for Koniev to make a mistake. As each hour passed, their odds of finding him were decreasing. *Be aggressive!* If there was any shooting, he told them, they should move in.

As Ryng moved up the pier, the houseboat looked no different than before, perhaps a little neater than some of the others, but in need of a young handyman to really square it away. It appeared exactly like an older couple lived there. It made sense, but . . .

All the curtains were drawn, as they had been before. He stopped on the pier beside the houseboat and listened. Not a sound from inside. He stepped past the BEWARE OF THE DOG sign and crossed the gangway. "Anyone home?" he called out. He reached inside his jacket, his right hand resting on the gun.

No answer. Hell, she'd come out before he'd ever gotten to the houseboat the first time. "Ma'am, could I talk with you again for a minute?" Too quiet. She—they—would have heard him. He pulled the gun out. Now it was a matter of nerves.

He crept to the kitchen windows and peeked tentatively inside. Not a soul. He tried the door handle. The door was unlocked. He pushed it inside and stepped into the room. The deck squeaked ominously under his feet. He stopped and listened. There was absolute silence.

Ryng was unhappy. He preferred to be out in the open. This kind of thing was crazy, too dangerous in close quarters. But he stepped over to the next door, which was ajar, and pushed it sharply, taking a few quick steps back as he did. "This boat is completely surrounded by Canadian Forces. Any effort to resist will result in your deaths."

He held his breath. Still nothing. "I'm alone out here. Two men are at the back end. Let the woman come out alive anyway."

As he spoke, Ryng lifted a plate from the strainer by the

sink. Then he dropped to his knees and crept to the door, flinging the plate through the opening. It shattered on the deck with a resounding crash.

No reaction.

His 9mm Smith & Wesson eased around the door an instant before he hurled himself through and landed on his belly in an empty bedroom. He kept going, scrambling low as he dove through the open door on the other side into—*another empty room.*

The houseboat was empty. *Absolutely empty.* And if Koniev had been here, he'd escaped! Again . . .

As he raced down the pier, Ryng used the portable radio to explain that the suspects had disappeared. But how the hell did they do it? He'd been talking to that British woman no more than half an hour before. And now she'd disappeared into the air. Why the hell hadn't he followed his initial impulse? That arrogant, standoffish response—the dog, too—had been enough that he was dumb enough to question his hunches. He hadn't been put off for too long, but it was enough time for them to slip away once again. And if he was wrong, if that woman was clean and he was chasing a bad hunch, then Koniev had outsmarted him. The son of a bitch had . . . what had he done? Had he made contact again through the woman? Why hadn't he checked with Coffin after her phone call? Coffin would have the answer if there was one.

He slipped into the empty phone booth by Barb's Place. That was faster than going back to *Voyager.* Admiral Coffin was on the line in seconds.

"Bernie, I couldn't raise you on the radio. There was another call to Vancouver again, less than an hour ago. They said it was a disjointed confusing conversation, hard to piece together. Apparently she must have figured you out. There was something she said about a boat. She was told to go west in the Strait, and there was something about a helicopter. The only possibility we have is a Soviet destroyer that we've been tracking the past few days, even before all this started. She's stayed about fifty miles offshore. Intelligence figured it was out there to try to track any of our Tridents that came out."

"Does that one carry helicopters?"

"Yeah. Udaloy class. A new one. A couple of helicopters, I'm told. They're antisubmarine though."

"Admiral, I think they want Koniev back so bad they'd try anything. With everything that's happened the last few days, someone back in the Kremlin must have considered that destroyer as a desperate last-minute backup if everything else failed."

"How'd he get loose, Bernie?"

"All the fishermen are getting underway today. They must be on one of them. That's how I'd do it if I was told my last chance was at the mouth of the Strait. I'll be underway on *Voyager* in a few minutes, but I'm an hour behind. If they're headed for the Strait, you've got to get more Coast Guard in on this."

"Hell, Bernie, they're right across the strait in Port Angeles. They'll give us whatever you need."

"What is it?" Koniev demanded. "What . . . a problem?" He'd seen Paul pick up the binoculars and look through them directly off the bow.

"Coast Guard ahead."

Koniev leveled his gun so that it was aimed directly at Paul's head. "How far away?"

"Maybe a kilometer." Mario had come over beside Paul and took the binoculars.

"Give them to her," Koniev snapped. "What are they doing, Corinne?"

She steadied the binoculars and watched for a few moments before answering the impatient Koniev. "They've got the fishing boats bunched up for some reason, slowing them down before they go out. It looks like they're making some sort of check."

"Are they going aboard?"

"I don't think so, not all of them anyway. It would be impossible with just a couple of boats to do the job. They just seem to be going alongside to question each one, and I've only seen a couple they've boarded. There's an American flag there, too. One of their Coast Guard boats, I think, one of those white ones with the bright-colored ribbon across the bow." She watched intently before handing the binoculars back to Paul. "The only ones I saw boarded were a private yacht and a couple of fishing boats. They're letting most of the fishermen continue after they go alongside."

Koniev moved halfway out of the cabin and sat on the top step. Paul and Mario made every effort to avoid looking at him or the gun in his hand. "You probably have figured out they're looking for me and I'll bet you'd like to get rid of me, wouldn't you?"

Neither man responded. Mario studied the gulls floating on the wind above the boat.

"I think they have a chance of finding me, that is if you were willing to give me away. I'll tell you what—if you do that, they'll get me because there's probably too much firepower on their side. But there are two bullets here for both of you. Before they kill me, I'll be sure to kill you. Tell me, is that a fair exchange?"

Paul looked ahead and swallowed. Mario put his hands in his pockets and stared at the deck.

"Do you want to be dead? Or would you like to lie to them so that they let you by and soon enough you'll be rid of me anyway? Because if you lie to them, even if they find out later that you lied, they won't do anything to you because they'll know I was going to kill you if you said anything. What do you want to do? Do you want to lie or do you want me to kill you?"

Mario was shaking uncontrollably. Paul was like a statue, staring resolutely ahead.

"One of you has to answer. So, Paul, make the decision for both of you. Live or die? Tell me out loud."

Paul swallowed. "I promise we will say nothing. Just don't shoot us."

"I won't. I've always stuck by my word before," Koniev said seriously. "Now Corinne is coming down into the cabin with me because they may just want to see her, too. I want

Mario to sit on the railing right there where I can see him. He doesn't say a word unless someone speaks to him directly. If he moves for any reason, he dies before he takes more than one step. Paul, you can move around within a couple of feet of the wheel, just so they don't think you're a statue. But you must keep in mind that if you move out of my sight, you will die just as quickly as Mario because those people will know I'm here and I think they will shoot first without asking any questions. Understood?"

"Yes," Paul croaked.

"Remember, you have to speak up when they talk to you. If you make a sound like that, you'll make them suspicious. I want you and Mario to practice talking with each other right now, like the old friends you are. I want your voice strong and believable." Koniev noticed the dog stretched out on the deck. "Mario, the dog's name is Scruffy. You can pat him, even hold him in your lap. That ought to make you more natural. How far away is the Coast Guard now?"

"Maybe five hundred meters."

Koniev gestured with the gun. "Go ahead, Mario. Pick up the dog. I like that idea." Corinne was already sitting well forward in the cabin and Koniev had moved back down inside and propped the door half closed with an old boot. "Good. I can still see you clearly, Mario. You make a perfect target. Remember, Paul, follow instructions exactly and you will love life more than you ever did before."

They could feel the speed of the boat decrease as Paul eased back on the throttle. The sound of other boats came clearly into the cabin now. They could even hear the sound of a voice over a megaphone up ahead.

"On board the *Sunset Patriot,* where are you heading today and what are your intentions?"

"Off Race Rocks," an irritated voice from another boat answered. "What does it look like we're going to do, shoot geese with these nets?"

"Have you seen any strange boats today, anyone coming out of Victoria you don't know?"

"I know everyone in Victoria Harbor and you do, too," was the answer. "The only ones coming out are fishermen who were smart enough to have stayed in until the storm was over just like you did. What are you looking for?"

"Immigration just has us checking for illegal aliens, sir. Go ahead. Good luck."

"Did they board?" Koniev hissed.

"No," Paul answered. "The Coast Guard is right next to our piers. These guys know all of our boats and most of us by name, too. They're just coming close aboard to take a look inside each boat."

"Alright. I'm going to open this cabin door all the way so there's nothing to concern them. It's dark enough that they can't see much in here and we'll be well back out of the way. But I'll still be able to see you and Mario. Remember, in less than a second you could both be dead."

A voice over a megaphone boomed out, "On the *Sangria*, hold your course and cut your speed to steerageway while we come alongside."

Koniev could hear the deep rumble of another diesel engine as it came close to *Sangria*.

"Where are you fishing today, Paul?"

Paul seemed to choke for a second before he answered, "We're on our way out to Swiftsure Bank, maybe for a few days depending on how quick we fill the hold."

"You heard what we asked the vessel ahead of you. Have you noticed any strange boats or anything unusual with . . ."

The man with the Coast Guard was interrupted by a loud barking as Scruffy vaulted out of Mario's lap and fell flat with all four legs splayed. Mario reached forward for the dog, then haulted in mid-motion and stared toward the cabin, his eyes blinking rapidly before he fell backward against the railing again.

The dog picked himself up into a sitting position and barked half a dozen more times before settling into a mild growl. Then he lay down and rolled over onto his back. The laughter from the Coast Guard boat drifted down into *Sangria*'s cabin.

"That's some dog you have there, Mario," the megaphone

voice said. "Scared some of us half to death. I guess you can go ahead. Good luck."

When they were far enough away, Koniev poked his head out of the cabin. "That was very close, Mario. You did very well. I was frightened for a second, too. I think the only one who might have survived would have been the dog."

At full speed, it was a little more than an hour before *Sangria* passed Race Rocks and turned up the Strait of Juan de Fuca. Koniev ordered Paul to stay close to the Canadian coastline. If it became a no-win situation, they just might have a chance of getting ashore. With the Vancouver embassy aware where he was heading, anything was possible . . . even a helicopter . . .

Voyager's engine was sputtering badly as Bernie Ryng pulled her alongside the US Coast Guard patrol boat. He tossed a line over to Danny West. "Having an exciting day?" Ryng inquired facetiously.

"Nothing's getting by underneath us, I can tell you that. Not a sign in the world there're any surviving minisubs either. And, so far, this harbor patrol hasn't come up with anything but fishermen heading out to make a buck. The ones that appeared suspicious have all been clean so far." Danny had been working beneath the surface and was still in his wetsuit. "I've only been on top for a while, but all I've seen is pissed off fishermen who make it very clear they don't like to waste their time with dumb questions."

"Nothing odd? Nothing these guys can say was out of the ordinary?" Ryng persisted. He was unhappy with himself, unhappy with *Voyager's* engine, generally unhappy with Koniev's cunning and his own hesitation.

"You better ask the coasties, Bernie. I haven't been up long enough to hear anything. Our boys are providing backup just in case. The Canadians are doing all the talking in their own waters. We're the guests."

Ryng had the patrol boat's skipper, a young boatswain's mate, move him closer to the larger Canadian boat. The responses were no different than West's.

"I wish I had a little better idea of who, what, and why, but we've been around here long enough to know most of the fishermen. They don't like this any better than I do, but I think I got a good idea of whether they're lying. I searched a couple just to keep everyone honest." The Canadian officer went on with a hoarse laugh, "the only thing out of the ordinary was the boat carrying a vicious dog. It just about scared us all to death." The officer laughed along with the others.

"Vicious?"

"Not exactly. More a fat, little, old mutt who must have thought he was a Doberman. We were talking with the skipper and the dog all of a sudden decides we're horsemeat and jumps off his mate's lap and starts barking its fool head off. Of course, it was so old it fell flat on its face."

"Attack dog," Ryng murmured to himself. "No woman with it?"

"Just these two guys. I've seen them before. They've been together for years. The mate, whose lap the dog was in, started after it and then stopped when it fell flat on its face. He just shook his head." He laughed again.

"Did the dog have a name?"

The Canadian looked oddly at Ryng. "No one called it anything, and we haven't been asking names from man or animal, sir. Like I said, we see enough of these guys."

Ryng received a description of the dog from a thoroughly confused Coast Guard officer before he said sarcastically, "That dog was sending you a message. I want the name of that boat and where it was headed. Did you at least get that from them?"

"Name was *Sangria.*" The officer flipped through the pages on his clipboard. "She was heading for a few days fishing up on Swiftsure Bank. But I can tell you, sir, there were just two local fishermen aboard out to make a living."

Ryng turned angrily away from the officer and asked the skipper of the US boat, "How many knots can you get out of this boat?"

"They're designed for twenty-two but that was a long time

ago. I can get you where you're going a tad under twenty if the engine's nice to us today."

"What do you have aboard for small arms? Any rifles?"

"A couple of rifles, some forty-fives, some grenades. That's about it, sir."

"Well, our man has an hour on us, and my boat's useless. So you're going to give her everything you've got. Detail one of your men to get mine back in. You've just inherited two extra crewmen."

"Whidby Island has a patrol plane out beyond the Strait," Coffin said over the radio. "That Russian destroyer's been operating helicopters for the last couple of hours, doing some sort of exercises. They're still beyond the limit and there's nothing we can do to them in international waters except dog their helos. But I'm told there's more going on there than most Soviet ships do off our coast."

"I'm pretty sure Koniev's heading up the Strait in a commercial fishing boat called *Sangria*. What else do we have in the air?"

"Not a hell of a lot, Bernie. If you remember, you seemed to think you had Koniev isolated ashore. We've got some other stuff on standby, but it still takes time to get them airborne."

"Understood. Can your patrol aircraft swing back up the Strait and see if he can locate *Sangria?*"

"Sure, but that means the only data we maintain on the destroyer is radar, nothing visual until we can get another aircraft on station."

"Let's just confirm Koniev's position. Have them maintain radar contact on those helicopters. That destroyer's not about to come into our waters." Ryng knew he needed a helicopter. "How soon could you get some helos from Whidby?"

"It would take much longer, Bernie. Coast Guard has a closer one across from you at Port Angeles, same place that patrol boat you're riding came from."

"Ask them to send that helo out after *Sangria*. Once

they're on top of her, then the plane can go back after the destroyer."

The patrol boat was as close to her top speed as she'd been in years. The remnants of the storm were long, sharp swells on the Strait of Juan de Fuca. The little boat would race up one side and poke her bow out of the water before crashing back in with a flurry of spray rising above her pilot house. Ryng had matched their speed against *Sangria*'s on the chart and estimated they might overtake the fishermen about thirty miles before the mouth of the Strait.

But that distance was minimal to two Soviet helicopter pilots, especially if their mission was to pluck an individual vital to the security of the motherland off the deck of a fishing boat. Ryng could imagine the Russians being willing to gamble with those helicopters, even sending them over American or Canadian territorial waters to snatch someone like Koniev. It was worth everything as far as they were concerned to recover whatever Koniev had stolen at Bangor.

"We must go faster," Koniev snarled at Paul.

"We're going as fast as we can," the fisherman pleaded. He pushed the throttle as hard as he could. "See?"

Koniev looked skyward again with the binoculars. How had they found out? Had someone seen them at the piers? Did something pass between Paul and that Coast Guard officer? The dog maybe? The American patrol aircraft was circling ahead of them. He knew its radar was maintaining perfect contact with *Sangria* and reporting their position. How much more time did he have? It no longer mattered how they'd been spotted. What was important was somehow getting aboard the helicopter that was supposed to rescue them.

"What's happening?" Corinne asked, squeezing his shoulder as he peered up at the plane.

"That's an American plane and they're tracking us with radar and reporting our position to people who are chasing us." He let the binoculars fall to his chest and reached out to squeeze her hand. "It won't be long before an armed plane, or a helicopter, or a ship of some kind comes after us. And then . . . then it is most likely all over." He stepped over beside Paul. "Move as close as you can to the shoreline."

"What good will that do?" she asked.

"Maybe it will be harder to track us on radar. Perhaps they'll lose us on their screens because we are too close to land." He put an arm around her shoulders and gave her a hug. "We've tried everything else the past couple of days, haven't we?"

"Everything else worked for us."

"You're not afraid, are you?"

"No. I thought I would be. But I guess being with you is all I need now."

"I feel the same way," he said, and was surprised to realize that, although he failed to understand why, he really meant what he said. He turned and raised the binoculars to his face to look behind. "Yes . . . yes, there is someone behind us. I can see the white water from their bow. They're much faster. Eventually they will catch us."

Corinne noticed Mario staring over his shoulder and she looked up in the same direction. "Look," she called out urgently, pointing up off their beam.

Koniev followed her finger and saw a Coast Guard helicopter approaching low on the water. "You must have emergency flares," he said to Mario. "Where are they?"

"In the cabin."

"Tell her how to find them."

Corinne came back with a carton of flares and Koniev showed her how to set them off. "They're going to have two uses. If there really are any of our helicopters in the area, these will draw them to us. And if that American gets close enough, we're going to show him what it's like to dodge these."

"Bernie, there are two Soviet helos who've left international waters. They're heading up the Strait," Coffin had reported moments before. "They're down on the deck hugging the land. Patrol plane's having a hell of a time holding them visually or on radar." It was going to be close . . . so close!

Ryng put out a hand for balance as the boat rolled heavily to starboard. He could see the fishing boat ahead of them through the binoculars, still too distant to make out the name, but he had no doubt that it was *Sangria*. "Request your helicopter to make a pass on that boat ahead," he ordered the skipper. "I want to confirm the name and I need to know what he sees aboard."

Koniev watched the helicopter bank as it turned toward them. "Now, I want you to lead them, just like I explained. I don't think you can do any damage but they'll worry enough to give me some time. Don't be frightened when they look like they're going to land on us. There's not enough room. And the pilot knows what he's doing. But I want to have them right on top of us if that pilot is brave enough. I'll only have a few seconds at best." His voice was calm and even as he spoke to her. He had shown her how to set off the flares and hold them so that she wouldn't be burned.

Paul looked over his shoulder in surprise when he heard the sound of the helicopter. "And you," Koniev said, "I want you to hold the wheel tight. Don't look at him. Keep your course. If you do anything, you will be dead and your friend, Mario, will take the wheel."

The helicopter was low as it approached from *Sangria*'s port quarter. The pilot cut his airspeed to avoid overflying the fishing boat. As he drew closer, they could see the pilot and copilot clearly through the perspex canopy.

"Now," Koniev shouted above the roar of the engine and rotors.

Corinne set off the first flare. It arched out on an angle in front of the helicopter, but passed by too far ahead.

"Again. Make it perfect."

The second one was almost perfect, appearing to float back right into the craft. They could see the pilot jerk the controls with both hands to avoid the flare. The helicopter had almost begun to turn away when Koniev, who'd been lurking in a corner of the pilot house, opened fire. His back was braced against the side of the pilot house and he held the Glock in both hands at arm's length.

Corinne saw the spider web effect as the first bullet pierced the perspex. A miss! The helicopter was beginning to bank into a turn away from them. Then a second one blossomed right in front of the pilot and she saw the man's hands fly up in the air. The helicopter was still turning, the bottom of its fuselage now visible, the angle increasingly difficult. Koniev fired twice more. It appeared that he had missed as the copilot reached forward to take the controls almost in what seemed to be slow motion. But Koniev had let his arms drop. He knew what had happened. The slow motion of the copilot continued as he slumped forward over the controls.

The helicopter seemed to bank more sharply to the left before its belly began to show wider, then wider still. Then it was on its side, sliding down toward the water. Just before it hit, it turned completely over. The fuselage spun wildly for a moment as the rotors bit into the water. Then it cartwheeled, throwing chunks of metal in a wide circle before hitting with a tremendous burst of spray.

"If we ever get home, I will make sure you receive a medal for that," Koniev said with a burst of pride, patting Corinne's rump. "Now you must start firing the remaining flares in the air. If there are any of our own nearby, they will see them. Otherwise . . ." he looked back at the patrol boat that was closing them. ". . . I do not think we can sink a boat."

Ryng could see the navy patrol plane as the pilot's voice came over the radio. "Those Soviet helos are almost in the water. I'm having a hell of a time tracking them."

"How far are they from *Sangria?*" Ryng queried.

"Maybe ten miles. I keep losing them in the land. They'll be there before you are."

"Forget the tracking," Ryng said. "Go down on the deck yourself and make a run on those helos. Scare the shit out of them."

"Will do. But did you know we don't have any guns

aboard? We're a patrol plane. I've got torpedos. I can sink submarines. But no guns."

"Maybe the helos don't know that. Make a run on them anyway. We're desperate here. Coast Guard helicopter just went in. You have to slow them down for me."

"On our way."

Koniev saw the patrol plane well before he saw the helicopters. It was a strange sight watching the huge, bulky aircraft circle out wide over the Strait before it went into a long dive. For a moment, he thought it was going to crash until he saw that it was in full control. Then he followed its line of flight and caught sight of the helicopters. At first, they blended with the land but it was just moments before he identified the familiar boxy lines and dual rotors of the Soviet Helixes racing toward them.

"More flares," he shouted. "More flares."

The helicopters had also seen the patrol plane coming down at them. They dropped lower over the water and moved into the shoreline until Koniev lost sight of them again. All he could do was watch the lumbering plane on its approach and wait for it to fire on the helos.

Eventually, he thought, he should have seen the line of tracers as they zeroed in on the Helixes. But there was nothing. The big plane was down low over the water, almost skimming the surface, but no tracers. Then, as the three objects appeared as if they would merge, the larger one was forced to climb.

"No guns!" he bellowed with delight.

But Corinne was facing astern, her face a mirror of dismay. The high speed boat was closing rapidly. "They're picking up speed."

"No, we're just too slow. Time is all that will save us now." He knew their speeds hadn't changed, but at this range it appeared the other was increasing its speed. He raised the binoculars to his eyes and could see two men with rifles leveled on *Sangria*. Then he saw the barely visible puffs of white smoke as they fired.

"Corinne, get down to the cabin. It's much too dangerous up here."

The bullets raised little puffs of spray as they hit the water around them. Then there was a nasty splintering sound as one ripped through the woodwork in the pilot house. A second shattered the window in front of Paul. Two more ricocheted off the dragging equipment on the stern.

Koniev raised the pistol in his hand and stared at it helplessly. They were still too far away. "Zigzag," he shouted to Paul. "Move from side to side."

Paul stared back at him, a terror-stricken look on his face. His mouth was open but he seemed unable to speak. His jaw moved. He raised a hand in Koniev's direction, then he stumbled forward against the wheel as the boat slid down the other side of a swell. But he didn't straighten as *Sangria* came back on an even keel. Koniev watched as the man's knees began to buckle. A red stain was forming on Paul's sweat shirt as he slumped to one side.

Sangria swerved toward the rocks just off their starboard side. Koniev leaped for the wheel and yanked them back on course. "Mario, take the wheel!" he shouted over his shoulder.

Mario was on the port side, his legs braced against the motion of the boat, his fists drawn up against his chest like a child. His head moved in circles as if he might say something but his lips were tightly sealed.

"Mario, get your ass over here or you are a dead man." Koniev had watched the patrol plane make a turn in front of *Sangria* and head directly toward the Helixes, its fat belly almost skimming the waves. Bullets were slamming into the boat with regularity now.

Koniev slewed the wheel from one side to the other. "This is it, Mario. This is all I want you to do." The man hadn't moved a muscle. "I told you. All you have to do is take the wheel." Koniev pointed the gun at him.

Mario remained fixed, muscles rigid, unseeing.

"Mario," Koniev screamed wildly, desperate for the other to take the wheel.

There was absolutely no reaction, no recognition of the gun.

Koniev pulled the trigger twice. Mario, his fists still held tightly to his chest, stumbled backward, then pitched over the side.

Koniev continued to jerk the wheel back and forth, varying the length of *Sangria*'s direction shifts. The number of bullets hitting the boat lessened. No more than a couple of kilometers ahead, the patrol plane and the Soviet helicopters were on a collision course. Koniev was sure the plane intended to commit suicide to knock the Helixes out of the air.

And just when he was positive his last chance of survival was over, the helicopters slewed to either side of the huge plane's wing tips. They were both going to make it!

Then there was a puff of smoke as the helicopter closest to the land failed to pull back quickly enough and plowed into the rocky coastline. A sheet of flame erupted in its place before the sound of the explosion reached Koniev's ears.

Just one now!

"Corinne. I'm sorry. I need your help," he called. He must reload his pistol, prepare the last of the magazines, be ready if that remaining Helix came overhead . . .

"What . . . ?"

"Just take the wheel. Do what I'm doing. Keep swerving. If that helicopter makes it, pull back on the throttle when I tell you. I'll stay right behind you."

For the first time since he'd left Leningrad, Nicholas Koniev experienced a tinge of fear. It wasn't for his own destiny so much as for his mission. It had taken so many years—from initial concept to that moment when he completed photographing the manual that was the Kremlin's key to defending against the Trident—and now a man who must be much like himself had actually been able to track him and was now endangering the entire mission. Was it fear? Or was it anger? He had the world within his grasp, *and a woman like no other,* and someone was attempting to take both of those treasures away from him.

* * *

Danny West and Bernie Ryng altered their rifle fire to the Helix as it made its approach. The pilot was jinking his craft expertly as he came around *Sangria* and raced directly at the Coast Guard boat with machine guns blazing.

The skipper tanked his wheel one way, then the other as the flood of bullets crossed the water, touched the boat for an instant, then splashed into the water on the other side.

"He's going to make another pass," Ryng shouted, "then place his back to us while he tries to lift them off. Just keep going right at that boat. Don't stop for anything."

The Helix banked sharply and came in on the Coast Guard boat from astern, machine guns blasting a trail through the water right up onto the stern as the boat darted to the left. Splinters flew as the bullets chopped away at the boat. The skipper yanked the wheel frantically to the right as the helicopter passed and made for *Sangria*.

Danny West was on one knee. His left hand grasped the right side of his chest. Blood ran down his arm. Then he slumped forward.

Ryng saw the skipper wiping his face with a bloody cloth. "Can you still drive?" he shouted.

The person that turned to him was unfamiliar. Folds of scalp hung over one ear and his face was shredded and covered with blood, but the man was nodding. "Splinters from the windshield. I can't see very well, but we'll get there." He pointed ahead toward the helicopter, which was now lowering a cable as it neared *Sangria*.

Ryng slammed another clip into his rifle, switched it to automatic, and fired at the Helix. But when he realized he was just spraying bullets into the air at that distance, he used the next clip on the boat.

"Cut the throttle . . . pull back on the throttle!" Koniev shouted above the beat of the rotors overhead.

Corinne yanked back on the lever. *Sangria* seemed to pitch forward as her propellor stopped spinning.

"Get down now. Stay down until they're ready. Then you go first." *Corinne will go first?* But nothing was worthwhile if the mission failed, not life, nothing. He seemed to hear himself repeating the words—*your own life is meaningless without the mission . . .* —but he couldn't tell if he was saying them or if they were a product of his mind. He yanked the package from his pocket and shoved it roughly inside her blouse. *Your own life is meaningless . . .*

"What . . . ?" her lips mouthed words he couldn't hear.

Pointing at the harness that was swinging down toward the deck, he put his lips to her ear. "Don't worry, I'll help you into it." Then he was back on one knee aiming his pistol with both hands as the other boat raced toward them. *Sangria's* pilot house was splintering with the force of Ryng's automatic fire. Koniev rolled over on his back, looked up at the crewman in the open door of the Helix, and jerked his hand toward the closing patrol boat, then made a cutting motion across his throat.

Another man appeared in the door of the helicopter to fire an automatic weapon down toward the patrol boat.

"Now," Koniev shouted to Corinne. He crawled over the deck and grabbed the harness which was swinging just above their heads. "Put your arms up." *Now, Corinne, you are the mission.*

Corinne held her arms above her head.

Koniev pulled the harness down and around her, under her armpits. "Drop your arms." *Now you are the mission.* Automatic fire ripped at the pilot house.

She dropped her arms to her sides.

"Hold on." He gave the signal and she was jerked off the deck and found herself swinging wildly up toward the Helix.

Why did you do that? Koniev asked himself. *The whole reason for this madness—the film—is with her now. You're no longer needed in this world. And you just gave that woman a chance you probably won't live to see. Which is the greater treasure? The film? Corinne? Why . . . ?*

The rage he'd been struggling to keep under control bubbled to the surface as he stubbornly acknowledged he was in increasing danger of losing the one woman he ever really cared for. Corinne, if they could live, would make everything he had done since leaving home worthwhile.

There was no fear for himself now, never had been—for Corinne maybe, but not for himself—only deep hatred for this man who was about to take her away.

"Bastard . . . bastard . . ." Every word that could express the depth of his hatred spewed from his mouth as he saw the man's automatic fire rise toward Corinne. The bastard was going to kill her . . . take her away from him! Koniev emptied the magazine at the man with the rifle before he looked up. He was sure he saw Corinne's body jerk from the impact of each of those bullets. Then it was still. She could be dead! The words he screamed ran together unintelligibly.

Koniev shook with fury as the patrol boat bore directly down on him. It was close enough now, and he placed his final magazine between his teeth as he tried to center the Glock with both hands on the man who was taking away his Corinne. He glanced skyward once more and saw that her head hung limply. Red patches were visible on her body.

His eyes came back to the other boat and he began methodically to squeeze the trigger, aiming each shot at the man with the automatic weapon who stood totally exposed firing back at him.

Ryng attempted to shift his aim back to the swinging body as it rose toward the helicopter but the fire from the Helix forced him to stay too low. He was sure he'd hit the one almost in the helicopter a couple of times. Ryng's skipper was swinging the wheel from side to side with one hand, wiping the blood streaming into his eyes with the other.

Now the first one was in the door of the helicopter. *Koniev—he was getting away and he might still be alive!* Ryng remained in the open, firing wildly as he saw the cable drop back out. They were going to haul up the other! Then he realized, as the firing resumed from *Sangria,* that the first figure dangling at the end of the hoist must have been the woman.

He turned his attention back to the other boat just as a bullet slammed into his left shoulder, knocking him backward into the stern. Ryng rolled over and rose to his knees, surprised that there was no pain. They were so close now that he was able to recognize that it really was Koniev—still aboard, and still shooting at him. The cable from the helicopter was almost on deck again. Koniev was reaching up for the sling. He was going to make it!

Ryng struggled with the rifle. Only his right arm would function. Gasping with pain as the boat rolled and he slammed into the rail, he grasped the rifle with his good hand, struggling to raise the weapon to fire again. The boat was rolling too much. He sat down on the deck, bracing his back against the stern, and hoisted the rifle toward the helicopter with his one good arm.

"Crash it," he screamed.

The young skipper turned and shouted something unheard. His face remained unrecognizable through the blood, but he appeared to be smiling. He gave Ryng a thumbs-up signal and aimed his boat directly at *Sangria's* midships.

The man firing the automatic weapon pitched out of the Helix as the harness swung just above Koniev's head. The remaining crewman in the door was gesturing wildly as Koniev draped the loop of the harness around his body, then gave the sign to retract. *The mission . . . Corinne . . . the mission . . . Corinne, I love you . . . I'm coming up to you.*

Koniev brought the Glock back to bear on the closing boat. It was almost on top of him now. He could barely see the other man. He was down on the deck and only his head and shoulders were visible. Koniev pulled the trigger three times before he realized through his rage that the magazine was empty. He released the empty one just as the sling tightened and he was swept from his feet.

That is him. Koniev could clearly see the face of the man whose automatic rifle was swinging back and forth in time to his body. He reached to his mouth for the last magazine. *I can kill him now, kill him so that Corinne and I . . .*

The helicopter lurched, slamming Koniev hard against

the splintered roof of the pilot house. He felt his right arm snap with the impact. Then his body dropped slightly before the sling again tightened and he was yanked head first into a support beam. The magazine fell from his lips.

Now he was yanked straight up and the sling turned his body directly toward the closing boat. It was just yards away now. The other man's face was clearly visible, the automatic rifle tucked just beneath one arm, his lips pulled back in a death's head grimace. Koniev felt slugs tear into his body twice before the sling turned him around and he was dragged brutally across the torn roof of the deck house. Then he felt himself rising.

As he was hauled into the air, his body swung around to face the patrol boat. It covered his entire field of vision boring in on *Sangria* at full speed. Koniev's body was halfway up to the Helix, halfway to freedom, when he saw the impact.

Corinne, I'm coming up. Another bullet slammed into his belly as the two boats became one. Pain ripped through every cell of his body. *Will I die this time . . . die before the mission . . . before Corinne . . . ?*

Koniev stared down in horror as the two vessels seemed to lift into the air, a gout of flame erupting upward as they burst. Then the explosion was lifting him toward the helicopter, the flames licking up at him, searing heat overwhelming the pain of the bullets, agony suffusing his entire body. He seemed to be suspended in hell, a moth burning in the flames. The helicopter was no longer retracting. When he lifted his head to look up, his last vision was of the Helix beginning to roll onto one side. Then the rising flames engulfed him.

The Helix plummeted into the wreckage, its own tanks bursting and spreading fire across the water.

Silence followed, punctuated by the crackling flames.

"What do you have down there?" Coffin shouted over the radio to the patrol aircraft. "Can you see . . . is there anyone alive?"

"We're going in again. Nothing but flame on the first pass. That helicopter fell right into the mess. We couldn't see anything through the smoke."

"Do you have rescue gear to drop?" Harry Coffin asked frantically.

"We're on the deck now ... and there's another explosion ... can't see how anything could live through that. Wait one ... there's something moving in the water ..."

Admiral Coffin could hear the copilot's voice in the background marking the seconds to drop a life raft.

"Bull's-eye ... twenty yards away ... and we got movement from two forms in the water. Circling again. Wait one."

"Raft's in good shape," the copilot commented. "Still have two of something down there. Too much smoke to be sure. Stand by."

Coffin waited.

"Will you look at that," the pilot said in surprise. "I wouldn't have believed it. We have one man in the water ... a guy who's mostly bald ... or has white hair ... and he's waving to us ... and there's a dog by him. They're both headed for the raft."

"Don't lose that SEAL. Help him." Coffin's voice was urgent over the radio. "You do whatever you have to, but you make sure he comes home."

Ryng grasped the side of the raft with his one good hand and held on for a moment. Then he let go and gave the little dog a push from underneath. It seemed to pop out of the water as it rolled over into the raft. Ryng grasped the raft again, gasping for breath before he threw a leg up over the side. Then, very slowly, his strength drained, he hauled himself over the side, collapsing into the bottom. The dog, head cocked to one side, eyed him curiously and then, shivering furiously, curled up by his shoulder and licked his ear.

Ryng rolled over and stared up at the patrol plane as it made another pass. He was too weak now to wave. There really was no pain from the burns—instead his entire body was numb—but he could sense the telltale coolness spreading across his skin like a blanket, warning him that he was losing consciousness.

I never got to touch the man, never got my fingers around his neck, but I did see his eyes . . . that rage of a man who knows he's lost everything. And I know what you were like. Oh, I knew you well. You almost made it . . . no one else could have done what you did. But why the hell did you ever let that woman go up ahead of you? If you'd gone first . . . you just might have gotten away . . . the son of a bitch would have made it! Why did you . . . ?

Ryng could hear the patrol plane pass overhead again, but his eyes were too heavy . . . and then he passed out. The dog licked his ear again and huddled closer.

The pilot of the patrol plane described the scene over the radio to Admiral Coffin as a navy helicopter swept in low over the water to a position on the lee side of the raft. Before it had come to a complete hover, a long rope was tossed from the open side door. Tim Sullivan and Lenny Todd, the second only feet behind the first, were down the rope and into the icy waters. In just moments, the two SEALs had rolled into the raft.